seers

book 1 of the seers trilogy

seers

heather frost

sweetwater books
springville, utah

an imprint of cedar fort, inc.

This is for you, Mamsie.
"Have I told you lately that I love you?"
Good Charlotte, track 13—wait for it . . .

ISBN 13: 978-1-59955-792-2

Published by Sweetwater Books, an imprint of Cedar Fort, Inc.
2373 W. 700 S., Springville, UT 84663
Distributed by Cedar Fort, Inc., www.cedarfort.com

LIBRARY OF CONGRESS CATALOGING-IN-PUBLICATION DATA

Frost, Heather (Heather Marlene), 1989- , author.
  Seers / Heather Frost.
      p. cm.
  Summary: After being involved in a car accident, Kate Bennett sees
peoples' "mood auras" and is pulled into the world of the Guardians, where
immortals are at war with each other.
  ISBN 978-1-59955-792-2
  1. Clairvoyants--Fiction. 2. Immortality--Fiction. I. Title.
  PS3606.R646S44 2011
  813'.6--dc22
                                    2011001407

Cover design by Danie Romrell
Cover design © 2011 by Lyle Mortimer
Edited and typeset by Heidi Doxey

Printed in the United States of America

10 9 8 7 6 5 4 3 2 1

Printed on acid-free paper

prologue

June 4, 1798
Wexford County, Ireland

I was lying on the long grass, only distantly aware of my surroundings. I could feel the light breeze rushing across my still body, but other than that outward sensation, I felt nothing. I heard nothing. I saw nothing. I was nothing.

Deep in a remote corner of my mind, I knew that I was dying. But that knowledge was not frightening at the moment. For now, I could think of nothing but the last conversation I'd had with my father. If it could be called a conversation.

It had been weeks ago, but I could remember every detail. My mother's worried face, my brother's hunched shoulders, the pulsing vein in my father's forehead.

"My sons are cowards!" He shrieked, his Irish accent thick and forceful. "They tell me they know the truth, but they do not fight for it. They refuse to dedicate themselves to a cause greater than themselves!"

I sat in my chair at the kitchen table. I kept stealing glances at my younger brother, but his head was always ducked. I couldn't blame him. Ever since father had become involved with the United Irishmen, he'd been seized with passion. Quick to fits of anger and frustration.

• • • ❖ | ❖ • • •

I realized the strain he was under. He was a rebel, a member of one of the greatest uprisings Ireland had ever known. He was completely dedicated to resisting the British rule. He wanted freedom for his beloved country, and he was willing to sacrifice everything for it.

He hadn't always been like this. Once, he had been one of my greatest friends—my wise mentor, my confidant, the anchor to my beliefs. But last year everything had changed. He'd gone from calmly tending his parish to contending for the title of the most dedicated rebel Ireland had ever seen. The change had been from one day to the next, though his temper flared more hotly now than it had in the beginning.

I understood him and his desires—it was what I myself desired. I was hardly a man, just barely eighteen, but I understood several things about the world. With my countrymen I had first looked to America's revolt against the British Empire, and more recently, the French Revolution. It seemed that the time for freedom was now.

I understood all of this, but the thought of joining the United Irishmen had hardly occurred to me. I wanted to be a painter. I wanted to capture the beauty of life with just my hands and my paint. It had been my only great ambition in life. I didn't want to fight a war.

But then my father had joined the rebellion, and for weeks he had been subtly dropping hints that had become increasingly unsubtle. Tonight, everything had come to a head.

Sean, my sixteen-year-old brother, was now taking the brunt of my father's rage. "A younger son does not have to be more ignorant than his elder brother. He could stand tall and march bravely into the face of truth without the example of a brother. He does not have to turn his back on the right path, just because he is younger."

Sean seemed unmoved by my father's ravings. He didn't raise his head or visibly show any sign that he had heard the hot words.

But I knew he had, because I knew my brother. He was hurting. Just as I was hurting.

We did not wish to shame him. We wanted his praise and love as we had once had it. But now, there was only talk of the rebellion. Of death. Of justice. Of sacrifice. Of brave men and cowards.

"Patrick," my father barked roughly, at last demanding a response from me.

I raised my head slowly and took in the sight of my father. He was red in the face, like he'd drunk one too many pints at the town pub. He was staring at me so intensely, I worried that his heart might seize and stop.

His mouth was working rapidly, but no words emerged. He was too angry for words.

My mother suddenly stood, her arms wrapped tightly around her thin waist. "Patrick," she whispered, her eyes glued to my father. "Patrick, don't let your anger take you too far. This family is all we have."

At the sound of my mother speaking his name, my father's body shuddered, and all his breath left him in a single drawn-out exhale.

I watched him—waited for his next words.

He spoke them slowly, so I would not miss them. "You will join the United Irishmen, or you will find yourself on the street." He glanced at Sean, and it may have been my imagination, but I believe it was harder for him to say these next words, to include my brother in his threats. "Both of you will go."

"No!" my mother cried, rushing to gather Sean's head in her arms. She clung to her youngest child, tears streaming down her face as she pleaded with her husband. "Patrick, please. You can't do this! Your own children!"

"No children of mine will support the British," he grunted stubbornly.

I watched Sean. He was just raising his head, still cradled in my mother's arms, but I could see the determination on his face. He was my younger brother, but when it came to action, he was always the first to respond.

"Mam," he whispered, "let me up."

"No," she gasped, clinging to him more tightly. "No, Sean."

Gently but firmly my brother pried her arms away, and then he pushed back in his chair and stood to face our father. His voice was nearly a whisper. "I've always believed in the cause, Da."

"Then why haven't you joined?" my father demanded, seeming unsoftened by both my mother's tender display and my brother's calm words.

"I've been waiting." Sean glanced at me, and now it was my turn to look at the tabletop. "First for Patrick, like you assumed. But also for Mother." He reached out and took her hand but then focused right back on father. "I didn't want all the men in her life disappearing."

While my mother's quiet cries filled the room, my life flashed before my eyes. First, the way I'd always pictured it. Slowly aging in this house, eventually marrying—perhaps even Sarah McKenna, like I'd often imagined—and quietly growing old with my paintings.

But even as I envisioned it, I knew it was an impossible dream. Perhaps there had once been a time when such a fate would have been possible. But no longer.

I stood, suddenly drawing every eye to me. "I will go. I'll join the cause." Though my father had been yelling mere moments before, his face was already softening in victory—his lips were twitching, preparing to speak.

I held up a quick hand, halting his words of praise. "I have one condition," I stated.

My father's eyes narrowed while he waited, his lips pressing firmly together. I purposefully avoided looking at my mother, my brother. "And it is?" he grunted.

There was no surrender in my stance. "Sean stays here. He's too young."

"Nonsense!" Father burst out. "Mere boys are joining—"

"Sean will stay here," I repeated firmly.

Suddenly I was back on the grass, the memory of that vivid moment fading as the pain began to come back to me.

I was not in the kitchen, staring my father down. I was dying on a roadside that had turned into a battlefield the moment we'd ambushed the British cavalry.

Ironically enough, it had been my first major battle.

It would be my last.

My senses were returning, now that the killing stroke had been dealt. The bullet that had ripped through my chest and pierced my heart had pushed me harshly to the ground. I never saw the soldier that shot the rifle, and yet he'd had the power to take my life. It seemed so unfair.

It had been so shocking, so abrupt; I hardly felt the pain after the initial bite of lead. Slowly the shouts of men and cries of beasts had faded. I was alone with my thoughts.

I was now becoming aware of the pain. The searing, burning hole in my body. My shirt was drenched in blood. My blood. My hands were covered in the sticky substance. I tried to tell myself it was paint. Only paint.

I swallowed with herculean effort, choked on the blood in my throat, and shuddered with the realization that I was living my final seconds.

The worst part was that this sacrifice—my life—meant nothing. The rebels would possibly win this battle—perhaps they already had. They would acquire the needed cannons and boost their morale with the victory. There would be losses, of course, but they would be acceptable. I was a necessary casualty. My unachieved dreams were nothing compared to the greater good.

But then there was the true tragedy. Sean. My brother. He had refused my help. He wanted to come with me. He wanted this. He thought I would look after him. Protect him. And now, so early in our fight, I was leaving him.

He was here, somewhere. Was he lying nearby? Also struggling for breath? Or was he chasing away the last of the British? Was he already celebrating the victory, scanning the cheering rebels, looking for my face?

Each labored breath I fought for expanded my lungs briefly, only to rattle free an instant later, leaving my body oddly empty. I could feel my heartbeat slowing with each escaped breath. Each exhale racked my body with pain, and a childish whimper escaped my lips.

My loss would be mourned by my father, but he would be more proud of my death than he had been of my life. For some reason, I couldn't even imagine my mother's reaction. Perhaps that was a gift from God. I don't think I could have endured that pain.

The blood was saturating the ground beneath me.

I fought for breath, but no air entered my lungs.

My body shuddered one last time and then went still.

My heart stopped.

I felt it beat feebly for the last time. Then nothing. My heart was a second ball of lead in my body—lifeless, hard. There was no air in my lungs. No life in my limbs. No thoughts left to think.

Nothing . . .

And there on the roadside, alone in the middle of a crowded battlefield, I died.

one

I stared in the mirror, frowning deeply at my reflection.

Perfect. The first day back to school, and my makeup had never been so reluctant to cooperate with me. Once there was a time I would have been completely devastated by this. I would have seriously considered staying home. Just a week ago, I wouldn't have bothered with the makeup at all.

But today was different. It *had* to be different.

I fought to even out my mascara, then gave a last finishing brush to my foundation. I scooped up my long dirty blonde hair into a high ponytail, held it there a minute, then decided to leave it down. I'd always wanted thick hair, but I'd inherited my mother's thin and soft locks. They bounced around my shoulders as I let them go, finally settling just under my shoulder blades.

With one last glance in the mirror, I sighed and turned, leaving the small bathroom behind.

I stepped into the hallway, moving for the large staircase. I kept my eyes on the steps as I descended, but even without looking I could imagine perfectly the pictures that hung on the wall. The snapshots of my life had always been the same—same frames, same memories, same people.

Me and my younger sisters gathered around the inflatable pool in the backyard, five or six summers ago. Skipper, our old golden retriever, had been caught in the background. It was the last picture we ever got of him, before he died. Next on the wall came Jenna's first piano recital, then Josie's first soccer team. Me, showing my first watercolor painting, next to a picture of Grandma and Grandpa Stevens. Then the Bennett family, one Easter day years ago, complete with Grandma and Grandpa Bennett. (Grandpa Bennett was giving me bunny ears.) There was nothing surprising in the collection of pictures; every aspect of every snapshot was familiar.

Hanging on the center of the wall was the largest portrait. It depicted a kind father, skinny and bookish looking, small glasses perched high on his long nose. A woman stood at his side, her slightly curled hair billowing past her shoulders in gorgeous dark blonde locks. She had a small face and bright blue eyes. Their three daughters stood in front of them, each beaming in simple joy.

That was the picture I was avoiding most of all, and I refused to even glance at it as I reached the bottom step. I pulled my lips back into what I hoped resembled an easy, confident smile and then I moved toward the back of the house.

Grandma Bennett was frying eggs at the stove, and Grandpa Bennett was sitting at the kitchen table, reading the paper. They both looked like their son—thin and bookish. They were in their midsixties, and had moved in the day after the accident.

Grandpa looked up when I came in but didn't set aside the paper. He only craned his neck around the side of it. He smiled at me, the wrinkles on his face pulling tighter together as he did so. "Hey, how's the most beautiful girl in the world?"

At his warm words I felt my smile grow a bit more genuine, and I had to admit that as awful as things were, I was grateful to have my grandparents. While I took the seat across from Grandpa, I tried to think of a witty reply. And if not witty, then at least believable. I didn't want them to know how much I was struggling right now.

But before I could think of a good reply, Grandma turned around to answer her husband. "I'm doing very well, Henry." Her voice was low and just a little rough. It was one of the most comforting sounds in the world, and no one could read *If You Give a Mouse a Cookie* better than her.

"She loves me," Grandpa whispered conspiratorially to me, then ducked quickly behind his paper, chuckling as Grandma shook her spatula in his direction.

I watched Grandpa behind the paper and Grandma turn back to her cooking, and it wasn't hard at all to imagine two different people doing the same tasks. Once it would have been Jenny Bennett at the stove and David Bennett would have been the one crouched behind the day's newspaper.

I swallowed hard and ordered myself to stop. Today wasn't going to be like this. I wouldn't *let* it be like this. Only, it was so hard not to think about them, because their memory was still so alive . . .

To distract myself, I reached for the pitcher of apple juice sitting on the table. While I poured myself a generous amount, Grandma lifted the pan off the heat and carried it over to the table. She dumped the scrambled eggs onto an empty plate and asked, "How'd you sleep, honey?"

"Good," I lied easily, before putting the glass to my lips.

She didn't seem to notice the lie. "I'm glad." Grandma smiled, scraping the rest of the eggs off the pan with the spatula. As she turned back toward the stove, she paused to grunt at her husband. "Henry, put that down while the girls eat. The world and all its troubles will still be there."

"I'm nearly done," he grumbled from behind the paper.

I grabbed the top bowl from a small stack on the table and pulled the plate of steaming eggs toward me. I spoke automatically, "Thanks, Grandma. It smells great."

"You're welcome, honey. Have you seen your sisters yet?"

I started to shake my head but then we all heard the loud barreling down the stairs and the shrieks of eleven-year-old girls in harsh competition.

"No fair! You started on the second step!"

"You started moving before I said go!"

"You had the head start!"

"You're the one who moved first!"

I held my glass of juice and watched as my sisters burst into the kitchen, not seeming to care that they were making a spectacle of themselves. They were twins, but dressed nothing alike. Jenna preferred pinks and lime green. Josie stuck to blues and browns. Jenna spent her time reading and playing the piano, and Josie played basketball with the boys next door. Physically, they were identical, except that it was always easy to tell them apart by their noses. Jenna's was straight and perfect, while Josie's was a bit crooked. She'd broken it playing football when she was eight.

Josie reached the table first and snatched up a bowl before sitting next to Grandpa. Jenna was still glaring at her twin. "You started on the second step!"

"You moved first," Josie countered with a shrug, heaping the eggs high.

"Only to make it fair!"

Josie shook her head and grabbed for the juice. "You cheated first, loser."

Grandma put the pan back on the stove and said in her too-cheerful voice, "The next one to make a sound helps with the dishes." We all knew what that voice meant—she was serious.

The twins might have their disagreements, but where work was concerned, they both agreed that it was best avoided. They were quieted instantly and instead settled for mute glares as they both got their breakfast.

In the sudden silence, Grandpa's page turn was amplified, and Grandma spoke without turning away from the sink. "Henry, you've just won a date with the dishes."

"Hmm?" Grandpa asked, distracted.

The twins snorted into their food, and even my smile was real. For a fleeting moment. But all too soon reality came back to me, and I was that depressed girl again.

Everything in this kitchen was exactly as it had been my whole life—except for two major differences. My parents had been replaced by my grandparents—a huge change in anyone's book. Then there was the other major difference—also a pretty big one, if you ask me. Because ever since the accident, I'd gone psychic.

At least, that's the best word I'd come up with to describe it. (Psychic was better than insane, anyway.) Since the moment I'd woken up in the hospital, I could see auras. At first I tried to tell everyone—my grandparents, the hospital staff. But then reality set in, and I realized that they might not let me go home. Unless, of course, I assured them that everything was normal. So one morning when the doctor gently asked about my new "sight," I pretended I didn't know what she was talking about. They all assumed it had been related to some kind of head trauma, and a week later I was sent home.

I'd actually grown pretty used to it. The perpetual swirl of colors around people was now almost easy to ignore. And so now—two months later—as far as my family was concerned, I was perfectly normal.

Only one other person knew about my strange new vision, and that was my best friend, Kellie Pearson. (Or Lee, as she'd preferred ever since the third grade, when Jimmy Bates had teased her for being girlie. Lee had beaten him up to prove her point, and also changed her name.)

But though I pretended to be normal, I knew I wasn't. After almost an entire summer of ignoring the strange light show and the gold lining that everyone had around them, there were still times that I couldn't help but focus on the auras that revealed so many emotions.

Jenna was shoving a piece of toast in her mouth. The usual thin golden thread outlined her body, and the blue color of content swam around her. Josie looked much the same, sipping her juice. Only mixed in the blue was a tinge of red. I'd come to think of that as her competitive streak. It was almost always present in her, even when she was asleep.

Grandpa was still hiding behind his paper, but his visible curling fingers were surrounded by many colors. Green, which I'd come to decide was uneasiness, mixed with blue and flecks of yellow happiness. It was easy to imagine that whatever he was reading was making him worry—or maybe he was thinking about the accident too. I didn't need to see auras to know that Grandpa thought often of his son's untimely death.

Grandma was as she always was. Equal amounts of blue and yellow. And then—just at the edge—gray. She was still mourning the loss of her only child, and though she was a positive person, that sadness never left her completely.

Not for the first time, I glanced down at my own arm. But all I saw was the regular lightly tanned skin. For some reason, I couldn't see my own aura. At first, I'm not going to lie, I felt a little cheated by this fact. But later I decided it might be for the best. It would only be depressing to see what I was feeling: gray, more gray, some brown for pain, and then maybe the smallest bit of white—hope that things wouldn't be like this forever. That someday I would wake up and think of something else other than the car accident. That my first thought in the morning wouldn't be covered in pain and loneliness.

"You girls better hurry," Grandma called from across the

kitchen, breaking through my thoughts. "You don't want to be late your first day back."

I drove the twins in my car. It wasn't anything fancy—an older and slightly rusting Hyundai Elantra, maroon in color. My parents had given it to me for my seventeenth birthday. At one time it had been new, but that time was long past when they'd bought it. But it was fairly priced and surprisingly reliable. All in all, I loved it.

The girls took their regular places in the backseat, and I pulled out of the driveway carefully. Some people would probably consider me a boring driver because I was so cautious now, so slow, but I would never take car safety for granted again.

"Pass me your iPod," Josie demanded, leaning forward against her seat belt.

Without taking my eyes off the road, I waved a hand toward my backpack on the seat beside me. "It's in there."

Josie groped for the backpack and finally managed to drag it into the backseat. I heard the zipper pull, and seconds later my sister let the bag thump to the floor. "Any requests?" Josie asked, already tapping and sliding her fingers on the dial.

"No Taylor Swift," Jenna said, nose buried in a book.

Josie found what she was looking for and leaned forward to plug in the iPod. Seconds later the beginning strains of "Love Story" filled the car.

"Make it stop!" Jenna groaned.

I ignored their ensuing argument, not bothering to point out that they were *both* missing the song that had inspired the fight in the first place. But all of this was usual, so I ignored them with little effort.

I drove down the residential streets of the subdivision, heading to Lee's house. I'd been picking her up since the day I first got the car, and I had to admit that I felt the nostalgia. Here we were, starting our senior year in high school. All too soon this routine would end; we would graduate and move onto college. Our lives would go their separate ways.

As if I needed another excuse to feel depressed.

Lee had been my best friend since second grade, when my family first moved into the neighborhood. Though our personalities were as different as night and day, we understood each other. Lee always made me find something to laugh about, which was an invaluable talent lately. Her parents were divorced, and she lived with her mom. Every couple of months or so Lee would go through a new fashion phase. Summer had been the '70s for her, with the occasional '60s outfit thrown in. (She actually made a really good hippie.) This month she was rocking the gothic style. Next time? No one really knew. My personal favorite had been the '20s. Lee had not only worn the beads and dresses, but even the hats. She looked like she'd just stepped out of an old silent movie. That bespoke the type of dedication people just don't see today—except maybe in terrorists, or nuns.

I pulled up to the familiar house, and in seconds Lee was closing her front door and crossing the yard. Her hair had once been brown; of course, it had also been blonde, white, blue, purple, and magenta. Today it was black as pitch. It hung in long sheets on either side of her face, which looked unnaturally pale due to all the cosmetics. She'd applied her makeup religiously, smearing black lipstick over her usually pink lips, and the shadows around her eyes were impressive. She'd even gotten a nose ring, which I thought was taking it a bit too far, personally. But that was Lee—she loved to make people stare.

Her clothes were also perfect for the part—the leggings, the boots, the black sleeveless top. She never did anything halfway. But unlike most goths, who were surrounded by gray auras, Lee's was a mixture of blue and yellow.

She opened the passenger door, nodded wordlessly at the twins, then sank into the seat.

"Hey," she greeted me, slamming the door and instantly reaching for the iPod to find a new song. The twins were so deep in their argument, they didn't even notice.

"Hey," I returned, cautiously pulling away from the curb and into the empty street. "The nose ring is . . . a good touch."

"Hurts like a mother," Lee informed me, starting a song with lots of thudding bass. She turned up the volume, settled back in her seat, and then looked at me for the first time. "In a word, *don't*. Ever."

"I wasn't planning on it," I assured her, cracking a small smile.

"So," Lee gusted, slapping her hands on her knees. "Here we are—seniors. Weird, huh?"

"Yeah. It really hit me this morning."

She bobbed her head but didn't say anything. Aside from the music and the twins, we drove in silence. But things were never awkward with Lee. She always knew exactly what I needed.

I dropped the girls off at the nearby elementary school and wished them good luck. Josie didn't say anything, only shouldered her bag and walked quickly toward the soccer field. I decided not to mention that the bell would be ringing soon.

Jenna sighed and shoved her novel into her backpack. "You too, Kate. And don't worry, *I'll* have a good day, as long as the Nameless One stays away from me." With that she slipped out of the car, shut the door, and walked toward the school.

Lee whistled lowly. "Were we ever like that at that age?"

"I think we were worse," I said simply. I glanced out my window, searching for a break in the traffic so I could pull away from the curb. A van rolled slowly past, and I found my opportunity to slide in behind.

As I started inching toward the parking lot exit, Lee turned in her seat to stare at me, quieting the music as she did so. "So, how you doing?"

I shrugged a little, keeping my eyes on the cars around us. "I'm still psychic, if that's what you mean."

"I didn't mean that," she hinted delicately.

I nodded once, braking as the SUV in front of us stopped to let some obnoxious boys dart toward the school. "I know."

"Are you at least *talking* to Aaron again?" she persisted, unwilling to drop the subject. Best friends could be annoying that way.

I exhaled loudly. "We texted for an hour last night." I shrugged a single shoulder. "I guess we'll see what happens in person."

"You're just going through a rough patch. It happens in all relationships."

"He said I was taking too long to recover," I said stiffly, my voice pained despite my best efforts. "He said they're gone, and I should just move on. Focus on *us*. On *now*."

"So he was a selfish idiot. So are all guys. At least Aaron isn't always a jerk. He's actually a decent guy most of the time."

"I know," I said, inching past a slowly turning car. The moment the car had completed the turn and we were clear, I lurched quickly past them. "We'll just have to see how today—"

My words clogged in my throat and I gasped, fiercely slamming in the brake and clutch. The car stopped violently and Lee screamed, grabbing for the dash. My seat belt bit into my body painfully, reminding me of old bruises. I blinked rapidly and stared at the idiot standing in front of the hood—the one who had caused my gut-wrenching panic.

He was way too old to be a student at the elementary school but too young to be a teacher. Probably in his early twenties—maybe twenty-one. He had dark brown hair and the brown skin of a Hispanic. He was dressed in jeans and a blue T-shirt. He was peering directly into my eyes through the windshield, looking calm, even though just a split second before he'd stepped right in front of a moving car.

Lee was cursing in her seat, slipping back into a habit she'd been struggling to break since she was fifteen. For once, I wanted to join her. I could have killed him!

"What's wrong with you?" Lee panted, her voice mixed with fear and some anger. "Warn me the next time you decide to randomly test out your brakes, okay?"

"What?" I broke my gaze with the idiot so I could look over at my best friend. "But didn't you—?" I couldn't think of what else to say—the words seemed crazy enough in my head. I gaped at her a second, then glanced back out the windshield. I completely lost my breath.

The man was gone.

two

Lee hadn't seen anyone. According to her, I'd just stopped talking and slammed the brakes for no reason. I tried to describe him to her, but Lee just stared blankly at me until I stopped talking. I guess there are limits to what best friends will believe, and invisible Hispanic guys definitely cross that line.

Someone honked behind us, and without a word I resumed driving.

My heart was still hammering in my chest, and as I quickly scanned the school grounds I fought to regain my breath. I knew a college-aged Hispanic should stand out in this crowd, but I didn't see him. It was like he'd disappeared. Or—worse—like he hadn't been there at all.

I tried not to let Lee see how shaken I was as I merged onto the road and headed for the high school. She didn't question my ability to drive, or my sanity either. I wanted to tell her that for a girl who believed in psychics, you'd think she'd put a little bit more credence into invisible people.

But I didn't. For some reason, I couldn't. Because as much as the incident had scared me, this was my day to prove to myself and to my friends that I could be normal again. I couldn't mess this up. No matter what.

Five minutes later, we were locking our doors and staring up at the familiar brown buildings. Lee seemed to have completely forgotten the elementary school incident and was texting calmly as we walked from the car. I didn't want to think about what had happened, or even admit to myself that I'd seen an invisible man, but I couldn't forget the rush of pounding adrenaline. It was an awful feeling because it was so familiar. I found myself unconsciously rubbing my shoulder, where the seat belt had bit into my body.

Lee suddenly touched my arm, pulling me out of my thoughts. She offered a tentative smile, and her black fingertips gently massaged my tense muscles. "I'll see you second period, okay? You gonna be all right?"

I blew out my breath and forced a smile. "Yeah. Perfectly fine." She raised a disbelieving eyebrow, and I relented. "I just . . . that adrenaline rush was . . ."

"It's okay. Cars make you nervous now. Totally understandable. Don't even worry about it." She pulled a face and drew back her hand. "Off to English, I guess. Enjoy American lit."

"Thanks. See you in history."

She offered a quick wave while she turned away, flipping open her phone once more.

I continued moving toward the large front doors, trying to pull in a few deep, bracing breaths. Several people called out to me, asking about my summer. I responded with a forced smile and simple one-word answers: *Fine. Great. Fun.* Anything but the truth.

Once inside I moved for Mr. Benson's American literature class. It was an AP course, and I was pretty excited for it. Or rather, I had been. Before . . .

My father had taught English at the nearby college, and he'd even begun to dabble in fiction writing before he died. He'd always loved the written word, and he'd tried to pass that love on to his daughters. Jenna and I had caught on to the magic eagerly, but Josie was more athletic in temperament. She was the odd one out when it came to the Bennett family.

I had never read a classic unless he'd first shared it with me, and we'd both been excited for this class. But now he was gone, and I wondered if I'd dare read Melville or Poe without him.

I found the classroom easily because I'd taken English from Mr. Benson last year in the same room. I took a seat toward the front of the room, nodding to the two other students present. I knew them both, but not well.

A short minute passed. Then Aaron stepped into the room.

He was everything a girl could want in a boyfriend. Tall, strong, good looking, dashing smile, gentlemanly, athletic, and trustworthy. He lived in the same subdivision as me, but on the opposite side. He and his family had moved in only four years ago. We'd started dating just over a year ago, when we were both barely seventeen. His passion was basketball, but he enjoyed pretty much every other sport as well. He'd decided against playing football this year to concentrate on swimming instead. He was smart and he knew what he wanted from life.

I was lucky to have him, and I knew it.

But ever since the accident, our relationship had been different. Strained. He was getting frustrated with me, and I had to admit that I understood. I wouldn't want to be with me, either. Put simply, I just didn't want to do anything anymore. He'd ask to talk. I'd say no. He'd want to go see a movie. I avoided him. He wanted to take me out to eat. I was never hungry.

He was such a positive person. He couldn't seem to understand my lingering pain. Once I'd been released from the hospital, he thought things would get better. They hadn't. The only reason I hadn't let him go was because I needed stability in my life—the kind of stability a wonderful boyfriend could offer. Completely selfish, I know. But I still loved him. I was sure of it. Even if things didn't feel the same anymore. I mean, a single event couldn't change my feelings for him.

So why was I feeling a shadow of doubt?

All these thoughts flashed through my mind as I watched him move toward me. He smiled a bit tentatively as he took the seat next to me. "Hey, you look great today," he told me quietly, leaning in to kiss me briefly.

I felt nothing when his lips brushed mine. Once, I had. But now . . .

I faked a smile when he drew back. "Thanks, Aaron,"

He glanced around the room. "Smallest class I've ever been in. What kind of thing did we sign up for? If I have to read Moby Dick, I swear . . ." His voice trailed off into silence. We were both remembering the last time we'd been together. The words that *both* of us had said.

Three more students filtered into the classroom during our awkward stillness.

Finally Aaron turned back to face me, his voice low. "Hey, I was wondering if you wanted to do dinner tonight?"

"Sure," I said, wincing inwardly at the lack of excitement in my voice. "That would be fun." I insisted, trying to make us both believe it.

I could see the frustration in his green eyes, but his smile was caring. "We'll go to The Malt Shop. You love their cheese fries, and—trust me—something unhealthy will really do you good."

My smile was more natural this time, and it was obvious that he could tell, because his athletic body slowly relaxed.

Aaron's aura was the bluest I'd ever seen. He was so sure of his life—so content with what he had. Sure, he had a little green, and the tiniest bit of competitive red—but he was really the calmest person I knew. I honestly couldn't imagine my life without him.

A few more students filtered in before Mr. Benson stepped into the room and closed the door behind him. He had large glasses and stuttered occasionally when he got excited. He taught several classes here but often said that this was his favorite.

I straightened in my desk and focused on Mr. Benson, hoping some of his pink excitement would rub off on me.

"Welcome to a new year!" he said enthusiastically. "M-Most of you know me already, but if not—I'm Eric Benson. Let's circle our desks together—I want to see everyone."

Minor confusion ensued for a moment, but soon we had twelve desks forming a sloppy, oblong circle. Mr. Benson joined the so-called circle, sitting near the door with a sheaf of papers clutched in one hand. "All right, first off I'm going to pass these around. I want you to tell me your favorite book—American classic or not—and why you like it so much. Also, add your name and email address, and what you want to learn from this class. It doesn't have to be in essay form, but remember I'm an English teacher and I cringe at badly developed ideas." That said, he passed the stack to the left, and a red-haired girl pulled out a blank sheet and passed on the rest.

Mr. Benson continued to talk as he watched the papers go around. "Now, r-right off the bat I'm going to tell you that I want this class to be fun. I want this to be about you guys, so I'm going to need your participation. Do the assignments, and be ready to discuss the readings. D-do that, and you'll get an A for sure. Now, I know some of you from previous English classes, but let's all introduce ourselves anyway."

In the usual way, introductions were made. After I introduced myself, Mr. Benson asked how I was doing. I could tell by his aura that he was sincere, but I kept it to the one-word answer, and he didn't press me for more. The introductions continued with barely a hitch.

When Aaron got the stack of paper, he pulled out two sheets before leaning around me to pass the stack on. He then kept one piece for himself and handed the other one to me. I knew I should appreciate his thoughtfulness. Instead, I found myself fighting back a surge of frustration. He actually leaned around me rather than hand me a stack of *paper*? Did that seriously just happen?

Still, I was trying to save our relationship, not completely bomb it, so I just sighed, nodded some thanks, and then bent toward my backpack to get a pencil.

While I was leaning down, the classroom door suddenly opened. I sensed everyone turning to view the latecomer, but I wasn't able to follow their gaze immediately.

A deep and resonant voice filled the room. It was low, but powerful, and carried an unmistakable Irish accent. "Excuse me. Is this American literature?"

Finally my fingers wrapped around my pencil, and I drew myself back up. My eyes fell on the newcomer, standing almost awkwardly in the open doorway. A broad shoulder kept the door propped open, and a long-fingered hand curled around one strap of his bag, keeping it from sliding off his shoulder. He wore a light blue button-up shirt, sleeves rolled to the elbows. He had beautiful skin—not white, but definitely not tanned. His eyes were pure blue, and surprisingly penetrating. His jaw was perfectly sculpted, and his high cheekbones were prominent and strong. His nose was long, and dark brown hair curled onto his forehead. His pale-but-not-pale skin was covered with a very light dusting of freckles.

Mr. Benson was twisting in his desk, fighting to view the door at his back.

"This is," he assured the boy in the doorway. "And you must be the transfer student Mrs. Jems mentioned. What was your name? O'Connor?"

"O'Donnell," he said, his Irish accent strangely hypnotic. "Patrick O'Donnell."

I knew I was staring at him, though he had yet to even glance in my direction. I could feel Aaron's eyes on my face, though, and I knew I needed to stop openly appreciating the new guy. So I pressed down the top of my mechanical pencil, forcing the lead out. I stared at the white paper resting on the desk in front of me, trying to get a grip. I traced out my name, focusing on each individual letter while struggling to remember what the real assignment was supposed to be.

Mr. Benson was speaking again. "Well, Patrick, you haven't missed much at all. Grab one of those desks and join the circle. Right now we're . . ." He proceeded to re-explain the assignment, and I quickly began writing, glad when Aaron finally stopped staring at me and started his own work.

I didn't have a favorite book—whatever I was reading at the moment was generally the best book I'd ever read. But since thoughts of my dad were swimming in my mind, I found myself saying my favorite was *Peter Pan*. It had long been a favorite of my dad's. He'd read it to me often when I was young—a chapter every night. As I grew up, I started to read it to him. To me, it was a story that inspired the reader to have fun, no matter the circumstances. To never let life's struggles get you down. Never lose your positive spirit. Though I wasn't sure if I'd followed the story's promptings in my own life, I decided to describe the possible moral anyway.

A few sentences into my explanation, I heard his low voice beside me. "Can I slide in here?"

I glanced to my right and saw Patrick O'Donnell standing next to my desk. His deep gaze—riveted firmly on my face—reminded me of this morning, with the invisible man. The stare was just so intense, so *real* and undeniable. It was like a tangible thing. All I could do was stare right back at him, thinking that his eyes were the clearest blue I'd ever seen.

And then Mr. Benson was interrupting us with a hesitant cough. "Kate—could you make room for Patrick?"

I jerked my eyes away. "Um, yeah," I told them both, fighting the flushing of my skin and losing miserably. I stood and pushed closer to Aaron, who was watching the exchange a bit too closely. Of course that didn't help the blushing, and I was very grateful that I'd left my hair down today so it could slide over my shoulders and shield my red face from view.

I resumed my seat and didn't look in his direction. But I could hear Patrick fit his desk in beside mine before tossing his bag to the floor, up against the chair. He sat down, searched briefly for a pencil, and then set that pencil to paper.

I watched him through my peripheral vision and was shocked when he didn't move again. I'd never seen anyone sit so still before. He didn't shift his weight, stretch his legs, or raise his head. He was immovable. Truthfully, the stillness was making me nervous. He certainly wasn't doing the assignment.

A few times during class I felt his intense stare through the curtain of my hair, but I never once acknowledged his attention. Call it uneasiness, or a way to avoid more blushing. Regardless, I didn't want to be caught in his enchanting gaze again. Not with my boyfriend sitting right next to me.

With class nearly over, Mr. Benson called for us to pass our papers to the right. Some people had filled a complete side and had written more on the back. My small handwriting had managed to fill one side, but I'd decided against writing more. I felt like I'd rambled enough about my father for one day. Aaron handed his paper to me, along with the others from that side of the circle, and then I handed the stack on to Patrick, with mine hidden neatly on the bottom. I don't know why I didn't want him seeing my work, but I didn't.

That's when I saw his page.

It was blank, except for two elegantly written words.

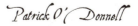

Patrick O' Donnell

I stared at those words until Patrick passed the stack on. And then I couldn't help but stare at him. He'd been sitting so intently and he'd written only his name? What sort of person took an AP class, and then didn't do the easy assignment—even a little bit?

As I watched him return his pencil to his bag, I realized something even more disturbing than his lack of work.

Patrick O'Donnell didn't have an aura. Or rather, it wasn't like any other aura I'd ever seen. There was no gold lining, no soft cloud of color pulsating around him. He was outlined in a simple silver thread, and there was no color emanating from him. It was impossible to know his mood, discern his emotions.

I'd been freaked out by the colors so long, I hadn't realized that there might be something more unsettling. What did this absence of aura mean? Was something wrong with him? Or was it a problem with my vision?

No . . . A quick glance around the room reassured me of that. Mr. Benson was surrounded by the familiar gold lining, and a cloud of yellow and tinges of pink hovered around his body. The redhead beside him—Andrea—was gold and gray, tinged with some purple jealousy.

I focused back on Patrick. Silver, then . . . nothing. I'd never seen anything like this before, and I was honestly freaking out. The hairs on my arms and neck were rising in some instinctual warning. It was like not only my vision but my body was screaming at me: He's different! Something's wrong!

That's when I got my second punch in the gut. Patrick wasn't the first. The Hispanic in the elementary school parking lot—the one Lee hadn't been able to see—he'd been the same. Silver outline, no . . . mood-aura. How had I not realized that before? Why hadn't the anomaly struck me before now?

But though their auras—or lack of them—were similar, the boy sitting beside me was very different from the Invisible Man, mostly because Patrick O'Donnell wasn't invisible. He was sitting next to me—turning toward me now—staring at my stare. And Aaron, sitting beside us, could see us staring at each other. So he was real. He was here. That left only one question.

What in the world was going on?

three

The instant the bell rang, I rose to my feet. When I moved my heel caught on the edge of my bag, and I stumbled back, off-balance. Aaron caught my arm even as my pencil went spinning through the air.

Suddenly Patrick was on his feet. With one hand he caught the pencil as it made its decent, and then he held it out to me on his open palm.

"Thanks," I mumbled, reaching for the pencil and not daring to look up into his eyes.

"Of course," he said, his accent lilting his voice into a gentle cadence. Then he turned, stooped to grab his bag, thrust the strap over his shoulder, and walked out the door into the seething hall.

"You okay?" Aaron asked behind me, slowly releasing my arm.

I glanced up at him and nodded. "I think so. Just lost my balance for a minute."

Aaron's brow was furrowed as he glanced toward the open classroom door. "He's kind of a weird guy, isn't he?"

I shrugged and bent to retrieve my backpack. Aaron's question would be better left unanswered. I stuck my pencil into my bag, then started walking toward the door. I was anxious to reach history so I could tell Lee what had happened. I wanted to know what she would think about silver auras, because personally I was drawing a blank. All I had to go on was my gut feeling, which kept telling me that something was wrong with Patrick O'Donnell.

Aaron followed close behind me as we left the room and entered the hall. At the first intersection we began to move our separate ways with a promise to meet up for lunch. Or rather, Aaron suggested it and I nodded a quick agreement.

The history classroom was almost full already, with still two minutes before class. I hesitated in the doorway, scanning the room quickly for Lee.

Her dark long hair was easy to spot, there in the back corner. I took two steps toward her, then stopped when I saw who Lee was sitting next to—Patrick O'Donnell. Just at the sight of him and his strange silver aura, the hairs on my body rose once more. I wanted to sit as far away from him as possible, because that's what instinct told me would be safest. But then, seeing the way he was staring at Lee . . . I couldn't abandon my best friend. If something truly was wrong with him, it seemed that I was the only one who could recognize it. I would have to risk the proximity in order to protect Lee.

I hurried through the desks and sat directly in front of Lee, who looked up at me with a smile that definitely didn't go with her gothic appearance. "Hey, Kate. You'll never believe where this guy's from—"

"Ireland?" I asked, turning in my chair and glancing toward those bright blue eyes that were just now focusing on me.

"Wow—how'd you know?" Lee took a double take of Patrick. "I mean, he's not a red head and he's not drinking beer." Patrick looked toward her with a cocked eyebrow, and Lee raised a defensive hand. "No offense, of course."

"None taken," he assured her in his deep but lilting voice. "And actually, most Irish people have brown hair."

"Seriously?" Lee asked. "What about the beer part? Isn't that true?"

He cracked a thin smile at her. "Maybe a little."

"We've actually already met," I interjected, unwilling to have this stranger focused exclusively on my best friend. Not until I understood more about him, anyway.

Lee looked back at me, looking far too interested. "Really? When?"

"First period," Patrick explained, retaking control of the conversation. "We have American lit together." He turned back toward me. "She must have guessed the Ireland part, though."

My arm hairs were sticking straight up, but I forced a smile. "Well, between the name and the accent, I thought it was a reasonable guess."

He nodded his dark head, giving me that.

Then the teacher walked in, and I turned toward the front of the class. Only then did I realize my back would be left exposed to him the entire hour, and I'd be unable to keep an eye on Lee. I sighed deeply, hoping the time would pass quickly.

The bell rang at last and Patrick told Lee good-bye before walking toward the door. He didn't even look at me, thank heavens.

Lee sighed hugely. "Oh my Oreos—did you *see* him!?" Normally Lee's habit of using random words to replace profanity made me laugh—right now, I was too freaked to even smile. "I've never seen such gorgeous eyes. And his body! Goodness, he's got to be the fittest guy I've ever seen in my life. Did you *see* him?"

"Yeah, I did—and guess what?" I hissed lowly, careful not to let anyone else hear. "He doesn't have an aura."

Lee cocked her head at me, eyebrows raised. "Seriously? Like, no colors whatsoever?"

I nodded quickly. "He's outlined in silver—not gold. And where there's usually color—nothing!"

Lee considered this, her eyes narrowing slowly in thought. "You've never seen this before? Not in anyone?"

I nearly brought up the Hispanic man, but something stopped me. Maybe it was because my saner half realized that trying to use an invisible man as proof probably wouldn't do either of us a bit of good. "No. And, honestly, I thought I'd lost my sight or something, when I first realized he didn't have one." I shook my head, deeply frustrated. "And every time I hear his voice I get all . . . weird."

"Oh, I was feeling that." Lee grinned.

"No—not like a good weird. He made me uneasy."

"You're just freaked cuz you can't see into his soul, psychic." She patted me on the shoulder, sympathy in her eyes. "Look, don't let this ruin your first day back. I mean, maybe it would be nice to have a friend you can't read, or whatever. Come on—the bell's going to ring soon."

Without waiting for me she turned for the door, and reluctantly I followed. We walked down the emptying hall together until she reached her lab. I continued on alone to trig. Upon stepping into the room and searching for an empty desk, I wanted to scream when my eyes met his.

Again. Three periods in a row! And the only empty seat was right behind him. The last place I wanted to go was closer to him and his strange aura, but what choice did I have? It's not that I believed he was evil or anything, but I couldn't deny the way my body reacted to him. The tightening in my stomach, the rising hairs, the loss of focus when he stared at me . . .

I quickly walked past him and sat down. I knew he knew I was there, but he didn't turn around. He was chatting with the girl beside him. She was a cheerleader named Virginia. She was a total blonde, and she always looked perfect. She was giggling at something he'd said and leaning closer to him from across the small aisle. Though I was close, I couldn't tell what she whispered to him. But watching her perfectly sculpted eyebrow raise, and her gorgeous eyes get larger, and her lips twist meaningfully . . .

well, it left little to the imagination. She flirted with everyone, but this time I was really bugged. If only she knew what I knew.

Which was what, exactly? He had no aura? Could that really be a bad thing? What if there was nothing unnatural about that? Maybe, he was like me. Maybe if you could see auras, no one else could see yours.

I don't know why I was irked by that thought, but I was. Though it was a weird, often scary quirk, it was kind of cool. And I felt special with it. I *liked* thinking I was the only one with this gift. Making lemonade out of lemons, looking on the bright side—whatever you want to call it. Since I was stuck with the psychic thing, I intended to like it. But no matter which way I looked at it, the possibility of having to share this special ability with someone else took away a lot of the appeal. I was no longer special. Just Kate.

And now I was being melodramatic.

I rolled my eyes at myself and stooped to retrieve a notebook from my bag. Lee was probably right. I was just going overboard with this whole thing. Maybe he wasn't psychic. Without being able to see his aura, there was no way to judge. And just because he didn't have an aura, well, that didn't make Patrick O'Donnell a dangerous alien. He was different. Nothing more.

I straightened, setting my notebook on the desk with one hand while gripping my pencil with the other. I heard Patrick murmur something low, but I couldn't make out the words. I didn't *want* to. I was done being freaked by him. Done spying on him. I certainly wasn't one to judge what was normal and what wasn't.

The teacher entered the room, calling us all to attention. That's when I noticed Virginia.

She was sitting straight-backed, staring precisely ahead. Her body, which had been twisted strategically toward Patrick, was now facing perfectly forward. I'd never seen her abandon fresh meat so quickly—not in all my years knowing her.

I watched her all through class, glancing every once in a while to Patrick's broad back. Virginia took studious notes the whole hour and didn't once flash a flirty smile toward the boy beside her. In fact, it was almost like she couldn't see him. Like she'd forgotten about him completely.

All at once, my worries were back. Something was definitely wrong with Patrick O'Donnell if he could get Virginia to turn away with only a few words.

Lunch finally came. And with it, I hoped to escape Patrick O'Donnell. He was in every class I was. Somehow, I always had to sit near him. For some reason, I would at times find him staring at me and other times he'd ignore me completely.

I entered the cafeteria, waited in the long line, bought my lunch, and made my way to the back corner table. I sat next to Aaron, who was already eating.

"Hey, Kate, how's the day going?" he asked through a bite of apple.

"I think I'm ready to be done," I said shortly, placing my tray next to his.

Aaron's best friend, Jaxon, laughed from his place across from me. "Come on, girl, you still got two hours to go!"

"Thanks, Jaxon," I muttered. I turned to Aaron. "You remember that weird guy from lit class?"

He stared at me, still chewing his apple. "What weird guy?"

"You know—the new kid. Patrick O'Donnell."

"Oh, the Irish guy, right!" Aaron reached for his milk carton, poking the straw in and then taking a huge sip. "What about him?"

I started peeling the plastic wrap off my tuna sandwich. "He's been in every class with me."

Jaxon snickered, his dark skin tightening with his grin. "Lucky you, girl—I heard he's a looker."

· · · ☀ s e e r s

"Jax, knock it off," Aaron said dimly, setting his milk aside so he could look at me. "Is he bothering you?"

"No. Most of the time he doesn't even look at me. I just . . ." My words drifted and faded. I had nothing to add to that. I was trying to save my relationship with my boyfriend. Now was not the time to tell him I was psychic, or something equally bizarre.

Aaron was looking at me intently, worry creasing his brow. But before he could ask me anything else Lee set her tray next to mine, ending the potential conversation. I hurried to take a bite of my sandwich, expelling my breath while I chewed.

"Hey, guys!" Lee declared loudly as she settled onto the bench. "Mind if I invite a cool new guy to the table?" she asked.

I choked—literally. Aaron patted my back gently, like that would help anything. It was Lee who finally got smart and pushed my boyfriend's hand away, so she could firmly pound my back.

"Kate?" Aaron asked, rising to his feet in aggravation. "Are you all right? Do you need me to get something?"

"Here," Patrick's lilting voice soothed at my other side. "Drink this." I blinked through tears to see the water bottle he was proffering toward me. Mutely I took it, uncapped it, and took a few generous swallows.

Several coughs later, I was waving everyone back into their seats. "I'm fine," I gasped. "Really. Sorry."

Lee patted my back one last time, then sat down between me and my new stalker.

Aaron sat back down but kept staring at my face, looking worried. "You sure you're okay? You're a bit pale . . ."

"She just choked on a school of fish and a wheat field—how would you feel?" Lee glared distrustfully at my sandwich. "I knew that stuff was unhealthy."

"I think you're exaggerating," Jaxon stated, staring at her huge slice of pepperoni pizza, dripping in grease.

Lee glared at him. "An-y-way, everyone, this is Patrick O'Donnell."

Jaxon nodded. "I'm Jaxon. Pleased to meet ya, Ricky."

"Patrick, please," he corrected.

I snorted a little, and Lee elbowed me. "Ow!" I protested lowly. "Choking here."

"So, Patrick," Aaron said loudly. "You're from Ireland?"

Patrick nodded and took a bite from his sandwich. I don't know why it unsettled me so much to see that he was eating tuna on wheat—just like me. "Yes. Wexford County."

"Uh, is that near Dublin?" Aaron asked uncertainly.

Patrick gave a half nod, as if considering. "Pretty close, I suppose."

"When did you move to the States?" Lee asked.

"A few years ago." He took another large bite.

"When did you move to New Mexico?" Lee asked, still fishing deviously for his life history. I wanted to roll my eyes, but somehow I resisted the urge.

"Oh, just earlier this summer. Two months ago, or so."

I swallowed hard, then set my sandwich down and reached for the water bottle. I didn't want to think about what I'd been doing two months ago.

I felt Lee's hand on my knee, and I knew her thoughts were with mine. I'd been in the hospital two months ago. My parents were already deep in the ground.

"Why haven't we seen ya around?" Jaxon asked.

Patrick shrugged. "I'm not much of a social person, I guess."

"Well," Lee grinned at him. "We'll have to change that now, won't we?"

I glanced around at my friends, completely shocked. I was sure he'd somehow hypnotized Virginia earlier, and obviously Patrick's hypnosis was working on everybody but me.

four

School was finally over. I hurried to my car, sure that Lee would meet me there. As for Patrick, I wondered how I'd survive the rest of the semester. It was like he'd stolen my schedule or something. He was in every class I had. Even choir! I hadn't seen him sing a single note, but there he was, standing with the basses. I hate to admit it, but I literally fled from the choir room as soon as the bell rang. It wasn't that he was openly hostile, but he was just always . . . there.

And then there was the way everyone acted around him—and the way he acted around *them*. He could be friendly when he wanted. But more often than not, he was staring into space, a pensive frown on his face. I wasn't sure what his intentions were yet, but one thing was certain: he was manipulative, and I was fairly certain he was hiding something.

I hurried out to the car to find Lee already waiting. "Pretty good first day, huh?" she asked. "I mean, you and Aaron were talking like normal, and then that new guy . . . swoon."

I got into the car without a word and reached over to unlock her door. Once she was inside she stared at me, looking a little surprised. "You still think something's wrong with him?"

"I *know* something's wrong," I corrected stubbornly. "He's in all my classes. It's like he copied my schedule or something."

Lee's eyes lit up. "Even choir? He can sing too?"

"I think you're missing my point."

"What point is that?"

"He's stalker creepy."

"He is not."

I pulled out my iPod and tossed it to her before I forced the key into the ignition. "Look, can you just trust me that he's weird? Doesn't *anyone* else see that?"

"Nope. But then, we're not psychic."

"Does that mocking response mean you're not going to trust me?" I asked, looking behind me and shifting into reverse so I could back out.

Lee's mouth twisted a little as she searched for a song. "Well, I sort of already invited him to my party this weekend."

I groaned, shifted to first, and started to make my way out of the parking lot. "Really? He could be a psycho or something."

"Then we'll have to start a psych club or something." Lee grinned, finally finding a loud song with a driving beat. The blasting music sort of killed conversation, so I drove to the elementary school while Lee texted.

I dropped Lee off at her house, then headed for home. The twins were in the backseat arguing about who got to watch what when they got home, and when I suggested it might be easier if they just liked the same things like normal twins, I got yelled at.

By the time I pulled into the driveway, Josie was so angry the red swelled around her like a very real, very tangible cloud. I'd noticed that about kids—they're more controlled by their emotions than adults. Jenna was slower exiting the vehicle, so she was still present when I shut my door and caught sight of him, standing in the middle of the street in front of our house.

It was the Hispanic guy from earlier, and he was staring at me with a huge grin. Though he was good looking, the eeriness of the moment made him creepy. Fortunately, ever since the accident, I'd become very good at faking, in an attempt to keep from freaking everybody out. And so with a super calm voice I asked Jenna if she knew who he was.

Jenna turned to face the street, following my gaze quickly. "Uh . . . who?" she asked. "Mr. Sorenson?"

I saw that our neighbor across the street was working in his yard. Jenna saw him but didn't see the Hispanic guy standing twelve feet away? The one staring right at us?

His silver lining was familiar to me by now, after all my time with Patrick today. But seeing it on this guy only made me more wary of Patrick. In what ways were they similar? Why could everyone see Patrick but only I could see this man?

I didn't want to freak my sister out, so I decided not to talk to him. I grabbed her arm and tightened my grip on my bag. "Oh— right—Mr. Sorenson. Come on, I think I smell cookies." I pulled her into the house but luckily she didn't think it odd. Homemade cookies would have warranted almost any sort of behavior, even running and screaming.

Josie had left the front door open so we were able to walk right inside. But before I closed the door, I forced myself to look back out into the street. I shouldn't have been surprised.

It was empty.

Once I was holding two gooey chocolate chip cookies, I hurried up to my room. I shut the door, turned the lock, and dumped my backpack on the bed. I walked to the window, which overlooked the front yard. I took the first bite of chewy goodness, and it practically melted in my mouth. I watched the street as I swallowed, but it was completely empty. But just the memory of that man—his smile, his aura, his invisibility—had me shivering despite the heat of the afternoon. Whoever he was, he knew where I lived.

I finished my cookies and reached into my pocket, plucking out my phone. In seconds Lee was answering.

"What's up?" she asked. I could hear the TV in the background and the sound of her setting a glass down. I knew her house as well as my own, so I could easily picture her curled up on the brown couch in her living room, the low coffee table holding an array of snacks.

"I know you're going to think I'm crazy," I started, still staring out the window.

Before I could go on she interrupted. "I *know* you're crazy. So spill."

"I just saw him again."

"Who?"

"The Hispanic guy—the one who stepped in front of the car this morning at the elementary school."

"The invisible one?"

"He's not invisible to me. I came home, got out of the car, and there he was—standing in the middle of the street, staring at me."

I heard the couch wheeze as she shifted. "Kate, there was no one in front of your car this morning. I would've seen him."

"I know," I groaned, finally turning away from the sunlight to fall across my bed, which squeaked in protest. "But something's going on. And I'm not gonna lie—I'm freaking out."

"Look, don't freak out. You want to stay at my house tonight?"

I sighed and rolled on to my back. "No. He'd probably just find me over there."

There was a short silence, then Lee spoke softly. "You're the one with the special vision, Kate. If you say you saw someone, I believe you."

Her faith meant a lot, but it didn't erase my unease. "Thanks. But what if I really am going crazy? Or what if he's a ghost or something?"

"You don't believe in ghosts."

"I didn't believe in auras, either."

"True." Lee hesitated, then spoke slowly. "Does this guy . . . have an aura? I mean, can you tell if he's angry about something, or . . . ?"

I stared at my white ceiling—one of the most colorless places left in my life. "Not a normal one. He's outlined in silver."

I could hear Lee turn off the TV, and I knew now I had her complete attention. "No colors?" She asked.

"None."

"But that's like—"

"Patrick. I know."

"That doesn't make sense, though," she protested. "I mean, I can see Patrick. They aren't the same."

"But they both have strange auras—strange auras that *match*."

"This is getting kind of weird."

There was a short silence, then Lee spoke again, more firmly than before. "Have you tried talking to the Hispanic? I mean, *can* he talk?"

"He looks real, if that's what you mean. And no, I haven't had the chance. Jenna was with me in the driveway, and I didn't want to freak her out."

"Maybe we should talk to Patrick."

"And say what?" I exhaled heavily, allowing my frustration to show. "Ask about his aura? See if he knows any invisible people?"

"Maybe we shouldn't be so pointed. We can treat it more like an undercover mission."

"You're serious?"

"Aren't you?" she asked, sounding almost offended. "You're my best friend and you're being haunted by an invisible guy. I think we should take this seriously."

"Wait, I thought you liked Patrick."

"I still have a hard time believing he could be evil or anything, but if he has the same aura as this invisible guy I think we'd be stupid to not ask questions. Look, my mom's going to be home soon—I better go. Let me know how your date goes tonight, and call me if you see that guy again."

"'Kay. Thanks, Lee."

"Not a problem. Talk to you later."

"Bye."

I ended the call but continued to stare up at the ceiling for a long time. I wasn't thinking of one thing in particular—just my life in general. *Then* versus *now*. Before the accident, my life had been so simple. So normal. I played the piano, I sketched, I read books, and I loved my friends and family. Now I was a psychic, being haunted by a man only I could see, and stalked by an Irishman who may or may not be dangerous.

My college experience was going to be great. I could tell.

A couple hours later I was checking my email when there was a knock on the bedroom door.

"Come in," I called, barely glancing away from the screen.

The knob jiggled, and I heard Grandpa's voice. "It's locked."

I sighed, clicked back to my inbox, then stood and crossed the room in a few long strides. I turned the lock quickly and pulled the door open. "Sorry, Grandpa."

His thin face was lifted in his usual smile, and he waved my apology aside as he stepped into the room. "A girl needs her space, I suppose." He moved for my bed, then lowered himself onto it with a groan. "Your grandmother is a slave driver. The backyard's looking good, though. Have you seen it?"

"Not yet," I admitted, sitting at my desk but turned toward him.

"Well, it may be my last work, so I hope she enjoys it."

I smiled, and he slapped his hands against his knees. "So, how was the first day?"

I lifted one shoulder in a half shrug. "Good. It was nice to get back into a routine."

His kind eyes shined behind his glasses, and the similarity between him and my dad nearly took my breath away. "You know," he said lowly, "I'm glad you can lie and be brave for your sisters, but you can tell me what you're really feeling."

"What do you mean?" I asked, stalling.

He regarded me firmly. "Sweetie, you're your father's daughter. That boy had so many thoughts in his head; he rarely told everyone what he was thinking. He learned to trust me, though. I want you to know that you can too."

I sighed and turned back to my laptop. I knew it was rude, but I didn't really want to talk right now. "I'm fine, Grandpa."

I could imagine him bobbing his head, the light catching the lenses of his glasses. "Well, you know where to find me if you need me."

I nodded silently, still staring at the bright screen.

"You know," he said broadly. "I'm glad you're going out with the Phelps boy tonight. He's a good kid."

"Yeah. I'm really lucky to have someone like him. My mom really approved."

"Are you . . . you know . . . serious with him?"

I blinked, then turned to face him. He was actually blushing a little. "Grandpa, how much is Grandma paying you to talk to me?"

"Nonsense! I can't talk to my granddaughter?"

"About my boyfriend?"

"Maybe she promised me another cookie before bed."

I smiled with him, but then he reached across the small space to take my hand. "Just because your parents approved doesn't mean you have to love him. You understand that, right?"

Sometimes my grandfather's perception shocked me. This was one of those times.

He released my hand, patted my knee, then wished me good luck on my date before closing the door behind him.

five

Aaron was there right on time. The twins made kissy noises from the kitchen as I called a good-night to my grandma. There was a time I would have been embarrassed, but not tonight. Maybe it was because I knew Aaron was used to them, or maybe it was just because I didn't care anymore.

I shut the door firmly behind us and walked with Aaron to his car. The warm early evening breeze rippled through my loose hair, tossing it back over my shoulders. I noticed that Aaron had showered and changed into nicer clothes for our date. Dark jeans and a black button-up shirt opening to reveal a white tee underneath.

I was wearing exactly what I'd worn to school: light jeans, frayed at the bottom, and a simple red theme top. I hadn't even worn any jewelry or body spray. I hoped he didn't notice because I didn't want him to realize I wasn't really trying.

As usual, he opened the door for me, and I slipped into his family's SUV. He hurried around, and then we were on our way, driving out of the residential area.

"How's your afternoon been?" he asked, eager to fill the silence.

"Pretty good. Yours?"

"Yeah, it was all right. I got work off so I could help my dad fix the fence. I told you Derek backed into it with the car, didn't I?"

"Yeah, you told me."

"Dad was pretty upset. Luckily the fence took most of the damage or dad would've really killed him."

I nodded but couldn't think of anything else to say. Once upon a time it hadn't been like this between us. Words had come easily, and those rare times when there was a silence, it hadn't been awkward. I knew that I was the one to blame. I was the one who was seeing things differently—auras aside, even.

Aaron turned left onto a busier street, and I searched desperately for something to say. "You're going to Lee's party this weekend, right?" I asked the first thing that came to mind.

He nodded, glancing over at me before focusing more firmly on traffic. "I was planning on it. She always makes 'em fun. A good way to break into school again."

The silence stretched between us, tense and deep. I was about to reach for the volume on his stereo, intent on filling the deepening void, when Aaron spoke at last.

"Hey, I wanted to apologize—for those things I said last week." His voice was halting but sincere.

I forced a smile and pulled in a deep breath. "Yeah—don't worry about it. I was just having a rough day."

"I was a real jerk," he insisted, eyes trained firmly ahead. "I didn't mean any of it. I had no right to tell you how much time you need."

"It's fine. Let's just forget it."

His lips pressed together and he nodded, braking at the red light. Once stopped, he reached for my hand, which I easily surrendered. His warm fingers wrapped around mine were comforting, but nothing more. For me, at least. But watching Aaron's aura become overpowered with yellow, I guessed he viewed the contact a bit differently.

While we waited for the light to change I glanced out my window, and wished immediately that I hadn't. Standing on the sidewalk was the invisible man. He was leaning against a light pole, grinning in at me. His teeth seemed whiter in the coming darkness, but his silver outline was just as mystifying as ever.

Our eyes met, and slowly mine grew into slits. Whoever he was, I wanted him to get a message: I wasn't intimidated.

His smile widened, and he offered me a sweeping bow.

"What are you looking at?" Aaron asked, peering around me with interest.

"Uh—nothing," I stammered, forcing my eyes away from the invisible man. "Green," I hinted, just before the car behind us honked. As Aaron pressed the accelerator and we crossed the intersection, I glanced into my side mirror.

The sidewalk was empty, except for the glowing yellow circle of light on the cement.

As we waited in line to order, I pulled out my phone and sent a quick text to Lee. *Saw him again.*

Aaron ordered for me—a double cheeseburger, cheese fries, and a Sprite. He then got the same for himself, except he exchanged the Sprite for a root beer.

It irked me that he didn't even ask what I wanted, but I sighed when I realized it was exactly what I would have ordered for myself, if given the chance.

"Something wrong?" he asked, catching my expression as he turned away from the cashier.

I shook my head. "Nope. Want some ketchup?"

"You bet." He grinned. "I'll get our table."

I slipped my phone back into my pocket and moved to the condiment counter. I grabbed a few small paper cups off the large stack and then held the first under the ketchup dispenser.

"Hello," a lilting voice said beside me.

I pushed too hard on the pump and ketchup spilled out of the cup and covered my hand. I turned quickly, my eyes darting up to meet Patrick's clear blue ones right beside me.

"What are you doing here?" I demanded. The fact that I'd been caught off guard made my voice rougher than I'd intended.

He blinked once, then held up the empty cup in his hand. "I think I'm waiting in line for the ketchup—if there's any left," he added, gesturing with his chin toward my dripping palm.

I ignored him while I jerked a handful of napkins free of the dispenser and hurried to clean up the mess. I tossed the pile of ketchup and napkins into the trash beside me, then reached for a new cup.

"Want me to do that?" he asked.

"No, I don't need your help." I knew I was growing snappy, but it felt good. I had a lot I wanted to snap about, and it seemed that fate had conveniently placed a target in my path. That, or he really was stalking me.

"Do you come here often?" I asked, focusing on the pump as I filled first one cup, then another.

"No. This is my first time."

"Hmm."

I filled a couple more, intent on letting that be the end of the conversation. But before I could finish he was speaking again.

"So, it's Kate, isn't it?"

I didn't answer him.

"Don't we have two classes together or something?"

"Try every single one," I hinted meanly, scooping up my ketchup cups and refusing to look at him.

"Really?" He sounded surprised, but when I glanced up at him it seemed like his eyes were laughing at me.

"Really," I stated. My phone vibrated as I turned away sharply and marched toward the corner table, where Aaron and I always sat. He was waiting with our drinks, and he stood to help me juggle the ketchup. I sat down across from him and pulled out my phone while Aaron sipped his drink.

Which one? Lee had asked.

Both, I tapped out.

"So," Aaron said loudly, "Lee told me you're thinking about applying to some school back East?"

I shut my phone and sat it on the bench beside me. Internally, I was groaning. What had possessed Lee to mention that bit of information to *Aaron* of all people? This was not an argument I wanted to take on tonight.

I pulled in a deep breath and forced a smile. "Yeah," I said, reaching for my drink. "But I'm still not sure. I just think it would be cool to live out that way."

He shrugged. "I don't know. I always pictured us staying local. State, or something. They have a pretty good art department here, don't they?"

"They do," I agreed. "I'm just not sure that's what I want to do anymore."

"You've always wanted to teach art," he protested. "Wait," he cut me off. "You're thinking of going professional? I always told you your sketches were amazing."

"No," I broke in. "I'm just not sure I want to focus on art anymore."

He stared at me, like he wondered who I was. I'd broken the perfect picture he'd crafted in his head, and I could see that it bothered him. "But what else would you do?" he nearly stammered.

I shrugged and played with my straw, pulling it out and then pushing it back into the ice cubes. "I don't know. I've been thinking about a writing career. I thought I might talk to Mr. Benson about an English major."

Aaron's stare grew even more disbelieving. I stared right back at him, unwilling to apologize or take back my words.

Eventually Aaron cleared his throat and nodded. I guessed he'd decided that he didn't want to argue about this either. "That sounds good. It's good to have multiple options." He took another sip of root beer, but I could tell he was still bugged.

A waitress arrived with our food, and we began eating without further discussion.

I kept glancing around, but I couldn't see where Patrick had gone. In all honesty, I was surprised he wasn't sitting in the booth next to us.

Aaron and I didn't talk much, but when we did we kept it simple.

Just before I finished my burger I caught sight of Patrick again, heading for the door this time. His head was bowed, and he held a slim silver phone to his ear. I watched him intently as he moved, because something was different about him. At first, I couldn't tell exactly what. But a split second later, I began to get an idea.

He was moving quickly for the door, and his face was hard. He wasn't walking like a leisurely teenager. He was taking large strides with deep purpose. He suddenly looked a lot older than a high schooler, and when he reached the door and glanced back at me, his intense stare matched the invisible man's perfectly—only Patrick wasn't smiling.

He looked right at me, and our eyes caught and held from across the restaurant. Still staring at me, he murmured a few words into the phone. Then he pulled it away from his ear and shoved it into his pocket without breaking my gaze.

"You okay?" Aaron asked from across the table. I turned toward him and saw the confusion on his face. "You were like, in a trance or something. Are you sure you're feeling okay?"

"I—Patrick's over there—by the door. I was just surprised to see him here."

"Patrick O'Donnell?" My boyfriend's tone was deeper suddenly, and he straightened in his seat to get a better view of the entrance. "Where was he?"

"The door," I repeated, turning as I spoke. There he was, still standing before the door. Still staring at me.

"Where?" Frustration was leaking into Aaron's voice. "There's no one by the door."

I watched as Patrick O'Donnell swallowed hard and nodded slowly to me. I felt my entire body break out in sweat. He was standing there clear as day. But Aaron couldn't see him.

"I guess it wasn't him," I whispered slowly, riveted on Patrick's smooth face.

I heard Aaron slowly return to his meal, but I continued to watch Patrick. I couldn't believe what was happening to me. I didn't *understand* what was happening to me.

Patrick abruptly turned away, pushing almost roughly against the glass door. He rounded the corner of the building, and I lost sight of him as he was swallowed by the coming shadows of night.

Aaron wanted to go see a movie, but I wimped out and asked him to take me home. The day had been a long one, and luckily he understood that something was up with me so he didn't argue.

He drove me home, and I was happily surprised to see no invisible man, and no Patrick O'Donnell. I thanked Aaron for dinner on the porch, and even initiated our good-night kiss. It was a fast one, I knew he wanted more, but I couldn't focus on kissing at the moment. My skin was crawling, and I wanted to get safely inside before I saw anyone else I wasn't supposed to.

Once in my room, I called Lee. She was as confused as I was when I told her Aaron couldn't see Patrick.

"Something really weird is going on," Lee sighed.

"Tell me about it." I glanced at the clock. It wasn't even eleven yet, but I was exhausted. "I think you're right, though—It's time to investigate Patrick O'Donnell."

"Seriously," she agreed. "And make sure your doors are locked."

I wondered if locks could keep invisible people out.

six

I was one of the first people in American lit the next morning. Andrea—the redhead with perhaps the most jealous purple aura I'd ever seen—was sitting across the prearranged circle from me, reading some dark vampire novel.

I had just settled into my own seat when Patrick O'Donnell entered the room. His gaze went right to me, and he offered one of his small smiles. He took the desk next to me and then spoke quietly.

"How was your dinner last night?"

I stared at him, barely keeping back all the accusations I wanted to chuck at him. Like how he turned invisible, or who the heck his creepy friend was. "Great. Yours?"

"Great," he copied me, then lowered his voice further. "Look, this might seem kind of strange, but, could I see your hand?"

I blinked and instinctively pushed my hands beneath my desk, tightly gripping my knees. "Why?" I demanded shortly.

He stared deeply into my eyes and spoke smoothly, his voice carefully low. "I wanted to see if they turned red from all the ketchup you spilled."

My eyes narrowed. "Is that supposed to be your idea of a joke?"

He shrugged. "You're not too friendly, are you?"

"Maybe you're *too* friendly. Did you ever think of that?"

He leaned back in his chair to regard me expansively. "I get the feeling that you don't like me very much."

"Really? How observant of you."

His lips quirked in what I almost thought was his first genuine smile. "Is there a reason behind the dislike?"

"Maybe."

"Are you going to tell me?"

"Probably not," I returned smoothly, leaning away from him to pull out a notebook and pencil. A few more students trickled in—including Aaron. He eyed Patrick strangely when he passed behind him but was smiling his regular charming smile when he sat at my other side.

"Hey, Patrick, Kate told me she saw you last night at the malt shop." My boyfriend wasn't very good with subtle.

"Yeah, I popped in for something. I was really just in and out."

Aaron pulled his backpack onto his desk and began digging through it. "Sorry I didn't see you. I know what it's like moving to a new area and feeling like an outcast. It bites."

Patrick shrugged. "I've gotten pretty used to it."

"I can't imagine moving to a new country. Do you miss Ireland?"

"Sometimes," he admitted. I waited for him to elaborate, but he didn't.

Then Mr. Benson came in, and the conversation ended as class began. We got a reading list, and I was surprised by how unfamiliar I was with the titles. Most of the author names I knew, but Benson explained that he wanted to read the lesser-known classics. First up would be *The House of the Seven Gables*, by Nathaniel Hawthorne. I'd read *The Scarlet Letter* before, but I'd never even heard of this one.

Class ended, Aaron kissed me good-bye, and I walked toward history. I didn't realize Patrick was walking beside me until he spoke. "How long have you two been dating?"

I gave him a weird look as I pushed through the crowded hall. "I don't see how that's any of your business."

He shrugged. "Curious, that's all."

"Over a year. Why?"

"Just curious," he reiterated.

"So . . . how come you're stalking me? Just curious," I added when he glanced up at me.

That quirky smile was back. "You noticed?" At my pointed look, he actually laughed, though the sound was low. "I'm a certified lunatic, and a serial killer. You're going to be my next victim—if you don't choke to death on a sandwich first."

His words did get a slight smile from me, but I wasn't ready to be all buddy-buddy just yet. "So you admit that you did get into all my classes on purpose?"

"All part of the grand design," he reassured me with a grin. He caught the closing classroom door and pulled it open for me with one hand.

I paused in the hall and peeked up at him, realizing that he wasn't much taller than me. "What's up with guys opening doors for girls anyway?" I blurted suddenly, thinking of Aaron's overly gentleman behavior. "I mean, it's not like we're weak and unable to twist a knob."

Patrick cocked a single eyebrow as he studied me. "Maybe it's not about weakness, but respect. Gentlemen open doors for ladies. That's how it's always been."

"What if I'm not much of a lady?" I challenged.

He shrugged characteristically. "Maybe you're not. But I've always been a gentleman."

I looked into his eyes and was captured by the sudden intensity I saw there. They were truly the bluest eyes I'd ever seen. Pure and beautiful. Deep, but clear. I wondered if they were his greatest weapon when it came to hypnosis—I was certainly becoming lost.

He stared right back at me, probing, searching . . . I could see the look of concentration on his face as he searched my eyes. For what, I couldn't imagine. I was starting to feel dizzy, and I realized I'd locked my knees and was no longer breathing. But I couldn't move. Not because he'd hypnotized me—at least, I didn't think he had—but because I didn't have any desire to break the contact. I felt like we were sharing a moment. Almost like we were becoming one. It was the weirdest sensation, but after the numbness, pain, and fear I'd experienced since the accident, it was the most exhilarating and peaceful moment I could ever remember having.

Someone coughed beside us. Patrick broke the gaze and turned at the sound—I was only a split second behind him.

Lee's long black hair lay in sheets against either side of her face, and her dark makeup made her look all the more serious as she stared at us. "Kate? You okay?"

I nodded quickly—too quickly. The dizziness brought spots of color into my vision—well, more color than usual, anyway. I didn't speak or look at him as he held the door for me and Lee. I marched to a desk in the back corner and was relieved when Patrick moved to the opposite side of the classroom.

Lee sat next to me and hissed in my ear. "What were you doing with him? It looked like he was looking into your soul or something."

I let out my breath in a low, steady stream and hazarded a glance across the room.

He was watching me, a thin smile on his face.

"Kate?" Lee demanded lowly, slapping my arm to get my attention.

"What?" I jerked my eyes away from Patrick and focused on her.

"What? *What?* Honestly, you're scaring me. Patrick equals freaky aura, remember? If you can't protect yourself from him, how are you supposed to protect me?"

"Nothing happened. I mean, he opened the door for me, and . . ."

"And . . . what?"

"Nothing. I think you're right. I don't think he's evil."

Her brow raised in a disbelieving sort of way, and I hurried to clarify. "He's still weird, and mysterious, but I think I just got a look into his soul or something."

"Well, he was certainly boring into yours, so it's only fair."

"Seriously, Lee, I think he's okay. I don't know, it's almost like . . ." I couldn't stop my eyes from wandering back across the room, and my voice was a mere whisper. "It's almost like he knew I was afraid of him, and he was . . . letting me know he's safe. Does that make any sense?"

Lee regarded me with an almost disgusted look. "No. But nothing in your life makes sense anymore."

"Tell me about it," I sighed, watching Patrick as he bent to get a pencil.

"Well," Lee snorted. "I guess I'm not uninviting him to my party then, am I?"

I shook my head slowly, still watching him. "Nope. I think your undercover mission was a great idea—and it starts now."

"Yippee," Lee cheered dully.

I sat next to Aaron at the lunch table, still looking over my shoulder, watching as Patrick paid for his meal. I wasn't afraid of him. I was positive that he'd let me look into his soul or whatever, so I could see his intentions. I knew he meant me no harm. But the whole experience left more questions than anything else. If he wasn't here to hurt me, then why was he here? Perhaps even more important, why did he let me glimpse his soul anyway? Did he somehow *know* about me?

There was only one sure way to get these answers; I intended to befriend him. I wasn't quite sure how that would go down, since he annoyed me half the time, and his unexplained presence still sort of unnerved me—not to mention I had a boyfriend. Still, it was the only way I felt I could safely get my answers. I refused to just walk up to him and start demanding answers— why he was here, who he really was, if he knew about my abilities, why he'd gone invisible at the restaurant, if he knew an invisible guy, and why his aura was silver. No, I would be cool and collected about this. I would be so cautious and subtle, he wouldn't know what hit him.

I started poking at my lasagna, but I was focused on Patrick as he and Lee walked toward us.

I was grateful that Jaxon was deep in conversation with Aaron, so my boyfriend couldn't read too much into my sudden fixation with the good-looking Irishman.

I was just about to turn back to my food, so I wouldn't look too interested, when I saw Patrick stop—speak briefly to Lee— and then turn and walk in the opposite direction. My forehead crinkled as I watched him walk around the crowded cafeteria. Where was he going?

Lee sunk on the bench next to me, and I kept my voice extremely low so no one else would hear. "Where's he going?"

Lee shrugged. "I don't know. He just said that he wanted to sit at another table today."

"Another table? Why?"

She shrugged again. "Maybe he's not really stalking you."

"He just wants me to think that," I grunted, turning once more to follow Patrick's movements.

In a second I spotted him. He was sitting at a sparsely occupied table, the one closest to the cafeteria ladies. He was sitting with the special needs students.

He was laughing at something and reaching to help a larger kid open his water bottle. He seemed perfectly at ease, and the small cluster of special needs students seemed to warm right up to him, though I'd never seen another student sit with them before.

I couldn't keep my eyes off his back as he ate and joked with the teenagers around him. I probably would have stared at him the whole time if Lee hadn't elbowed me just in time for me to turn around before Aaron could notice. I might thank her later, once the bruise disappeared.

"So, Lee," Aaron said, laughter still lacing his voice from his conversation with Jaxon. "Is this party going to be like all your others?"

She swallowed a gulp of Coke before answering. "Super awesome? Of course."

"Are you going to actually invite people you know?" Jaxon asked. "Cuz, seriously, last time I didn't know half the people there."

"That's what makes it fun," Lee countered. "I mean, if it's just the same old crowd, how are you supposed to make new friends?" She turned to Aaron for help. "Support me on this. If I remember right, you met Kate at one of my parties."

Aaron cleared his throat and nodded. "True. I guess I won't rip on it too much."

"Thanks, I guess . . ." Lee looked at me purposefully, but I didn't know what to say. Slowly I ate my food, wondering the whole time what Patrick O'Donnell was up to.

seven

The first week of school went by quickly, all things considered. It had been one of the most eventful weeks of my life, and I was glad when Saturday came around. Honestly, I didn't know how much more I could take.

Patrick continued to be everywhere. I even caught a glimpse of him in the grocery store, but he was gone before I could talk to him—plus I didn't want to leave my grandma standing alone by the frozen foods. He was in all my classes, and we even talked a little. Not enough to get to my questions, but enough to learn that he was indeed coming to Lee's party Saturday night.

As for the invisible man, I didn't see him once the rest of the week. I didn't know how to feel about this, actually. Of course I was somewhat relieved, but it was almost worse not seeing him because I was left to wonder where he was instead.

Aaron and me ... we were pretty much the same. I don't think he noticed my sudden interest in Patrick, but he couldn't have been completely oblivious. Maybe he just thought I was being friendly.

Aside from seeing each other at school, Aaron and I didn't hang out much. Thursday night he came to my house for dinner and to play board games. He and Josie were the last survivors on Monopoly, sheer desire to win keeping them both in the game far longer than the rest of us. Finally Josie tried to wriggle out of a payment by trading Park Place with three hotels—more than fair, she insisted evenly. Grandpa and Jenna started a low chorus of "Fight, fight, fight," but Grandma pretty much insisted that the game end there. Though the two weren't happy about it, Aaron and Josie shook hands and called it even. But just to be safe, I decided we probably shouldn't do another game night any time soon.

I spent Saturday with Lee, trying to get her house ready for the party. Her mom was out of town at a weekend business conference. She was usually gone every couple of weekends, which made this annual party possible. I still wasn't sure how she managed to pay for all the food, but Lee knew how to throw a party. While Lee set up her mom's impressive sound system on the large deck in the back yard, I covered the fence, shrubs, and railing in strands of Christmas lights—colored and plain white.

Then we filled some coolers with ice and sodas. Each guest was supposed to bring some sort of snack, but even without that, Lee probably had it covered. Her party would be bigger than prom.

The official start time was seven, but it was pretty much a "come when you want" thing. Once I'd helped with the setup, I hurried home to change. I thought about wearing a summer dress but settled for just jeans and a brown top. I could've been more exciting, I know, but at least I added a necklace.

Grandma ordered me to be home by midnight, and she also assured me that she would be up waiting for me. Grandpa opened the door for me and told me in a whisper that Grandma was asleep by eleven every night and not to worry about it.

I shook my head fondly at him and then I was gone.

I had to park several houses away, and by the time I was at her neighbor's house, I could clearly hear the booming music. I knew from experience that the neighbors wouldn't complain until ten, though. I moved right into the backyard through the open gate and was shocked like I always was by how many people were already crammed into the yard.

The music was loud, and with the darkening sky above, the lights in her yard were pretty spectacular. The swimming pool was covered with a tarp, but almost every other space was occupied by people. Some, I knew. Many, I could have sworn I'd never seen before. Several groups had to be made up of college students, and once again I wondered where Lee found these people.

I could see Lee on the deck talking loudly to a group of goth boys in front of the stereo. I thought about going to her, but then decided it wasn't worth it—the deck and stairs were packed. Instead I moved back around the swimming pool, where there was actually some breathing room.

I pulled out my phone and sent a text to Aaron, to see if he was here yet. A minute later I got his reply. *Just left. C u soon.* There was also an emoticon of a pink heart, and I couldn't help but smile. Aaron could be predictable, but he was always cute.

"Quite the crowd," someone spoke beside me.

I shut my phone and looked up quickly to see—of course—Patrick O'Donnell. He looked great. He was wearing the familiar light jeans and button-up shirt—only instead of the usual blue, this shirt was dark green. His brown hair curled onto his forehead. It was somewhat raggedly cut, but it looked good. I wondered why I'd never particularly noticed it before, but then my eyes caught his and I remembered why I got distracted around him.

"She doesn't really know all these people, does she?" He sounded almost concerned.

I chuckled softly and shook my head, forcing my eyes from his. "No. I doubt she knows half."

He nodded once and then held out a Sprite. At my wondering look, he shrugged. "I was only going to make the trek once, so I got two. Trust me, you'd die of thirst before reaching that cooler."

I took the can with a quick thank-you, and proceeded to pop it open. We both sipped our drinks for a moment, letting the music and the roar of the laughing crowd wash over us.

Finally I found my voice. "So, how are you liking school?"

He shrugged. "Some classes are better than others. I've never really liked math."

"I'm with you on that." I chuckled and took another quick drink before continuing. "It's a pretty good school, though."

"The teachers are good," he agreed. "And the students are really quite nice."

Something seemed weird about the way he said that, but I couldn't put my finger on it. Besides, his accent made everything he said sound a little different.

"Have you lived here your whole life?" he asked.

"Mostly. I was born in California."

"That's a beautiful state," he commented.

"Yeah. I wish I could remember more about it, though. I moved here when I was seven or so."

"Not too long ago." He shrugged, taking another drink.

"I guess." I straightened, and forced myself to look at him. "So, have you started our reading assignment? In lit?"

"*The House of the Seven Gables*, yeah. I finished it this morning. Sort of bored, I guess."

"You're done with the whole book?"

He nodded. "It was a slow day. What about you?"

"I'll finish chapter ten by Monday," I laughed, slightly breathless for some reason. My drink was cold. That was probably it.

He grinned. "What do you think of it so far?"

"It's pretty good," I admitted slowly, considering. "Better than I thought it would be. The symbolism is pretty cool."

"There's a lot of that," he agreed. "It's a good book. Not the best, but not bad."

"So . . . What *is* your favorite book?"

He bit his lower lip and squinted into the crowd. "Hmm . . . could you have picked a harder question?" He shook his head, then shrugged. "Would you laugh if I said *Peter Pan?*"

"Seriously?" I asked, completely shocked.

He nodded, still looking toward the deck. The Christmas lights shined and reflected in his eyes, making them appear all the more mysterious. "Sure. It's got a boy who never grows old. What could be more fascinating than that? Forever young and happy. You have to admit, it's a great idea."

"I agree, but . . . I've never heard anyone pick that as a favorite."

"You've read it?" He sounded a little surprised.

"It's one of my favorites," I admitted. "The Disney version isn't so bad, either."

"I haven't seen that," he said, before hurrying to take another drink. For some reason I got the impression that he'd said something he hadn't meant to.

I pressed my lips together, then decided to ignore that for now, and just enjoy the conversation. Though I knew he wasn't normal, I was really enjoying his company. Of course, I told myself that I was only pretending to be friendly. This was all part of the plan to make him slip up and reveal something devious. "You've never seen *Peter Pan?*" I tried. "That's like, child abuse. It's a classic. I think they really captured the magic of the story."

"Despite being a Londoner, J. M. Barrie knew how to enchant an audience."

I chuckled again, and my fingers played with the condensation on my soda. "You sound like you don't like the British."

"Has anyone ever liked the British?" he teased.

"Come on—they're polite, they've got great accents, and they drink a lot of tea. What's not to like?"

"They've been at war with pretty much every country," he pointed out. "They tried to rule the world."

"Wasn't that the Germans?"

"Them too." He laughed.

"I can't believe we're at a party, talking about this."

"And immortal flying boys," he added, his lips twisting into a breathtaking half grin.

I laughed again, and that's when Aaron stepped into our bubble. "Hey," he said, glancing between us. "Sorry I'm late. Dad just doesn't know when to stop, you know?"

I swallowed hard, assuring myself that the disappointment I felt at Aaron's intrusion was only because I was making progress with Patrick.

"Don't worry about it," I told him, keeping the smile firmly on my face. I gestured to Patrick with a small wave of my hand. "We've just been talking about school. Can you believe he already finished *The House of the Seven Gables?*"

"Really?"

Patrick shrugged. "I didn't have anything else to do." He finished off his drink and then excused himself to find the trash. I watched him disappear into the thick crowd, and then Aaron spotted Jaxon. Without asking me he took hold of my elbow to guide me through the thick tangle of people, and I fought to cover my sigh while I let him lead me.

I stood with Aaron and his friends, and I kept my eye out for Patrick. But between all the people and their multi-colored auras, it was hard to see anyone specific. There was a moment I saw a flash of silver, and I guessed it was his strange aura. But when I tried to focus on it, it was gone. I soon gave up on trying to spot him, and instead I craned my neck to get a better view of the deck. I knew Lee would be around there somewhere, and she'd be the perfect excuse to get away from sports talk.

There she was, still standing by the stereo. The goths she'd been entertaining were gone, and now she was only talking to one person. I felt my stomach drop.

She was talking to a Hispanic man, with a silver aura. It was him! The invisible man! He was here, talking to her!

"I'm going to find Lee," I told Aaron quickly. I don't know if he really heard me, but he didn't stop me as I shrunk out of the circle and headed for the deck. I was soon swallowed up by the pounding music and the thick crowd.

I wasn't sure what I was going to do, but a plan of action didn't seem necessary at the moment. This was the man who'd been haunting me, and now suddenly he was talking to my best friend—someone who hadn't been able to see him last time. I may have decided against interrogating Patrick O'Donnell, but from this invisible man, I was going to get my answers.

I pushed up the wooden stairs of the deck and forced my way to the back corner. "Lee!" I called, knowing she probably wouldn't hear me, so close to the speakers. I wormed around a small group of giggling girls and then bumped right into my best friend.

"Whoa!" She laughed, reaching out to steady us both. "Hey there. It's going great, huh? This has to be one of my best ever!"

My eyes darted around us, but he was gone. I couldn't let him get away! "Lee, that guy you were talking to—where did he go?"

"Toni?" She asked, smiling. "Oh goodness, I wish you could have met him. But he said he had to run."

"Did you see which way he went?" I asked.

Her eyes narrowed as she recognized the worry in my voice. "Yeah, he went that way. What's wrong? Are you okay?"

"I'll explain later," I promised, already moving for the stairs. Once free of the deck, I pushed in the direction she'd pointed. I elbowed through the last of the crowd, and then found myself in the empty side yard.

The gate was still open, and with the sun completely gone now, there wasn't much light over here. Going from surrounded by body heat to empty night forced a shiver through my body, though I wasn't cold. In spite of myself, my footsteps slowed and

I actually paused at the corner of the house. The music was still pounding loudly, but it was oddly distant now that I was nearly to the front yard. I hesitated, then followed my instincts. I peered cautiously around the corner of the house, like you see in the movies, and I wanted to gasp at what I saw.

Two men stood in the front yard. Their heads were bowed, and they were obviously having a heated discussion. They were both outlined in silver, and though their voices were low, I heard every word.

"Come on," the invisible man said in a dark but eerily playful way. "I was just having a bit of fun."

"I'm not laughing," Patrick said thinly, his voice incredibly deep.

"Look, just because you're mad at me about *that* doesn't mean you should ruin my Saturday night. For a while there, I thought I was teaching you how to be loose. Come on, man."

Patrick seemed unmoved. I found myself shivering again at the sound of his voice. "I'm counting to five. And you better be out of my sight, or I swear . . ."

"No you don't. I've never heard you curse."

"One."

"Seriously? You're counting? What am I, six?"

"Two."

"Who made you my mother?"

"Three."

"Come on, man. It was supposed to be funny!"

"Stay away from Kate."

I shuddered at the menace in Patrick's even voice. It was hard to imagine he was the same person I'd been laughing with not even hour ago.

Patrick continued thinly. "I'll forgive you for your other misdemeanors, but if you come near her again without my permission, you'll regret it."

"For being an angel, you could be a bit more angelic."

"Toni, go home. Now."

"Sheesh, could you be any more boring?"

"I'm really not in the mood for this right now." He abruptly turned away, and I shrank back against the house, my heart pounding as he headed back toward the party—toward me. Still completely mystified about what I'd witnessed, I turned and darted away before Patrick could see me.

I pushed back toward Aaron, knowing that he'd be just where I'd left him. My heart was beating almost painfully against my chest, and I kept hearing snatches of the conversation I'd over-heard. I was beginning to wonder if Patrick really was such a good person after all.

One thing was certain. He and the invisible man knew each other.

eight

Patrick tried to approach me once, but before he could get too close I asked Aaron to come dance with me. I was still unsure about what I'd witnessed in the front yard, and the last thing I wanted was to be alone with Patrick O'Donnell. Aaron led me closer to the speakers, where a small portion of the crowd was dancing, and I didn't see Patrick again. Or the invisible man. Who wasn't so invisible, it seemed.

I knew that Lee probably expected me to come back and explain my strange behavior, but something kept me from seeking her out. Maybe I was just too overwhelmed with the weirdness of it all. These seemed more like scenes from a movie, not my life. So I danced with Aaron for a while before announcing that I was ready to call it a night.

Aaron was a little disappointed, but his aura was still mostly blue as he walked me to my car. He opened my door for me, but before I could get in he grasped my wrist. Looking at his hand, I could see that the blue was being quickly replaced by green uneasiness, and tinges of brown—pain.

"Kate, are you all right?" His voice was soft, and for the first time I realized how tense my body was.

"I'm fine," I whispered automatically.

"No, you're not." He snorted out a laugh that held no happiness. "Kate, you've hardly said a word to me all night. You don't even look at me when we talk anymore."

I bit my lower lip, then lifted my head. Our eyes met, and I could see the hurt on his face.

"I just want to know what you're thinking," he begged softly. "I want to help you. But I can't be there for you if you won't let me in."

I wanted to look away from the pain I was causing him, but I forced myself to keep our gaze steady. Slowly I began to speak. "I'm sorry I've been so distant. I know it's not fair to you. I just . . ." I shrugged helplessly, and fought the stinging of tears in my eyes. "It's just so hard, okay? It's not like I can just magically wish all of this to go away. I changed that day. And I'm still trying to adjust."

He ducked his head, and I knew from his aura that he was worried he'd pushed me further away. I gripped his hand, our fingers intertwining easily. "Aaron, this isn't about you. Honestly, I'd be a complete wreck without you. I love you." More or less, that was the truth.

His eyes lifted, and he watched my face closely. "I love you too," he whispered. Then he leaned in and kissed me.

This wasn't the gentle peck I'd grown used too lately—the one that I didn't notice. No, tonight I could feel the warmth all over my body as our lips melted together. He held me tightly and kissed me tenderly. I grew dizzy in his arms, and I didn't want it to end. I tried not to think about anything—I just relished the moment. I knew that he loved me. Despite all the crazy things happening in my life right now, Aaron Phelps loved me. He was kissing me, making me breathless.

When we finally broke apart, I was gasping, and so was he. He cradled my head in both his palms, his fingertips gently pressing my hair back so he could kiss my forehead.

"I love you, Kate," he whispered. "And we'll make this work. Because we're meant to be together."

I kissed him again. I wanted to feel that glorious feeling

again. I wanted to be a normal girl, desperately in love with her boyfriend. I wanted to be that perfect couple that Aaron saw so clearly.

Once the kiss was over and I was in the car, Aaron gently shut the door and I watched his aura—practically swimming in blue and yellow—knowing that no matter how badly I wanted to be normal, I wasn't.

I started the car and Aaron wandered back to the sidewalk, in the direction of the party, several houses away. I shifted into gear and slowly eased out from between two other cars. Once I was on the street, I pulled a sharp U-turn and headed back toward my house. Picking up speed I glanced out my rearview mirror. I could still see the glow of lights that marked Lee's party, but I found myself focusing on a man just stepping on the sidewalk, several houses away from Lee's. He had a silver aura, and— though it was dark—I knew it was Patrick. I just didn't have the same icy feeling as when the invisible man was watching me. But I also knew that he'd seen everything, and I found myself blushing.

I focused back on the road ahead, and for the first time this week, I let the tears fall.

Monday afternoon found me in the cafeteria sitting next to Lee, alone at our usual table. Aaron and Jaxon, along with several other athlete buddies, had decided to drive down to our rival school during lunch. I didn't ask any questions, but Jaxon let it slip that he had plenty of paint in his truck.

Without the guys, and with Patrick sitting with the special needs kids now, I assumed Lee and I would have a meal alone.

I'd avoided her the rest of the weekend, and she'd been so busy cleaning up the yard after the party that she hadn't had an opportunity to regale me with questions about the mysterious

Toni. Honestly, I'd been so weird lately, she probably just chalked this up to my latest mental breakdown. Still, I didn't want to talk about it. Because if I told her that Toni was actually the Invisible Man, it would lead to the conversation I'd overheard between Patrick and Toni, and I wasn't ready to admit out loud that I might have been wrong about Patrick being good. Because, despite what I'd heard and seen, there was a part of me that was still entranced by him and our brief conversation at the party. Talking and laughing with him had been so natural and easy. So comforting. I didn't want to admit to anyone—maybe even myself—that I was afraid to lose that.

Luckily, we weren't alone for long. But it was with mixed feelings that I watched Patrick approach us.

He didn't seem as happy as usual. He was walking toward the table slowly, and I was reminded of the first time I saw him, standing awkwardly in the doorway to American lit. That awkwardness was present now as he glanced between me and Lee. It was obvious in his eyes, his stance—he wondered if he belonged here anymore.

I supposed that meant he knew I'd seen him spying on my good-bye with Aaron on Saturday night, or maybe it was because I'd avoided him most of the night. I hoped it wasn't because he somehow knew that I'd been the one spying on him.

"May I join you?" he asked formally.

I stared at him, unable—unwilling—to answer.

"Sure," Lee said into the short silence, casting a strange look at me.

"Thank you," he murmured lowly, before taking a seat on my other side. Pinned in by the two of them on my bench, I felt trapped.

"So," Lee said slowly. "What brings you back to this table?"

He glanced up from his lunch, which remained untouched. "They had a field trip today—they won't miss me."

"Well, I think that's really nice that you'd sit by them," Lee said, still stealing overt glances at me, begging me to start talking, to stop being so weird.

"Actually, it's nice of them to let *me*," Patrick explained, his fingers playing with his fork, but not picking it up. "It's probably the only table in the whole school where everything you are isn't judged. You can wear anything, say anything, and no one's trying to measure you. They're just glad to have you."

"Wow." Lee looked taken aback by his intense reply. Actually, she looked kind of stunned. "You make the rest of us sound like creeps."

He looked up at her, his blue eyes worried. "That wasn't my intention. I only meant that—"

Lee waved his quick words away. "No, no, I understand. Maybe I need to start joining you." Her phone vibrated, and she pulled it out of her pocket with the speed of any texting addict. She flipped it open, glanced at the screen, and then tapped out a rapid reply even as she spoke. "Oreos, I forgot. I promised Mr. Walton I'd help organize the music library—you know, to get my grade up? Mom says I can kiss the thought of a car good-bye if I get anything less than an A in band." She sighed loudly and snapped her phone shut. She looked up at both of us, forcing a smile. "I already know I'm not going to practice, so Walton told me I could make it up by going through years worth of unsorted music. Lucky me, huh? At least he likes me, I guess. If you can call such a punishment favoritism."

She stood, pulling her tray up with her. "Well, guess I'll see you guys later. Wish me luck." Without waiting for a response she walked away, leaving me alone with Patrick.

I took a quick bite of my mashed potatoes and slid a few inches away from him, pulling my tray with me.

I didn't look up when he sighed deeply, or even when he angled himself toward me. "Kate, what's the matter? Did I do something wrong?"

"What makes you think anything's wrong?" I grunted, staring at my food and propping my elbow nearest to him on the table to better cut us off.

"You. You're acting like I've got some kind of disease or something." His voice sounded far too accusing, considering the fact that there was more off about him than there was with me. But I didn't point that out. I just shoveled another spoonful of potato into my mouth.

He sighed deeply and picked up his fork, only to stab his chicken. He didn't bother to eat it, though. "You avoided me, at Lee's party. I just want to know why. Because I thought we were getting along just fine. Did I offend you somehow? Do you *like* the British?"

I let my elbow slip off the edge of the table, and I turned to stare at him, fighting to keep emotion from twisting my face. "I do. I *do* like the British. They have a great sense of humor."

"So, you're shunning me because I mocked the English?" The disbelief in his voice was almost comical.

"No."

"Then why?"

I bit my lower lip, knowing I'd regret anything I blurted out at this point. Not that that stopped me, of course.

"Look," I hissed suddenly, leaning toward him. "I know about you. I know that you're different. I know, because *I'm* different too. I can see auras. You know, read people's emotions. But not you. You're different. You have a silver aura, and I can't see your emotions." I waved my hand in the space between us, back and forth, groping for the right words. "And this, this *friendship* you're trying to achieve, well, it's not going to work. I was playing along because I was curious about you. But now, I just want you to stay away from me—and from all my friends. You got it?"

He was staring at me; his eyes blinked slowly. He didn't look as scared or as nervous as I sort of imagined he would, but he didn't look angry either. He just looked . . . surprised? Maybe a little unsure. I suppose he'd never been confronted like this before, but I could understand that. It was a first for me too.

"Kate . . ." his voice trailed off, and in his momentary hesitation I stood, gripping my tray tightly as I walked away.

"Wait!" I heard him call out behind me, but I didn't stop. I dumped my mostly uneaten meal into the garbage and deposited my tray before turning on my heel and walking firmly out of the room. I wasn't entirely sure about where I was going. Just away from Patrick.

I heard him stumbling along behind me, but that only caused my step to quicken. I wanted to end this conversation as strongly as I'd begun it. I was going to have the last word—even if it meant getting in my car and driving home. Forget about school. Defying Patrick in all his weirdness was worth a few absences.

"Kate, please!"

I hated that we were making a scene. I was in the hall now, lined with lockers and cliques of students eating on the floor. I stepped over and around their legs and was soon pushing on the doors out of the school. Once under the sun, my mind started to clear. I was a bit angry at myself for losing my control with him, but I was also somewhat relieved. There would be no more pretending. That also meant no more conversations with Patrick O'Donnell, but I should be happy about that part.

Students were sitting on the grass in small clusters under the patches of shade offered by the scattered trees. From my peripheral vision I knew that some were glancing up at me and my abrupt entrance into the yard, but they quickly turned back to their normal lives. Lucky them.

Behind me I heard the door burst open, then begin to swing closed. He was still following me, but at least he'd stopped calling my name.

I quickened my step, but refused to run. A fast walk was acceptable, though.

I felt him coming up behind me, and my body tensed, though I refused to show it. I lifted my gaze and stared straight ahead, unwilling to show any sign of weakness.

He drew up beside me, matching his long strides to mine. "Kate, will you let me explain?" he asked, his voice not quite a whisper, but pretty close.

"No. Stay away from me." Before I could veer away from him, he was grabbing my arm, keeping me close to his side. "Let go of me!" I growled, glaring up at him. We were still walking, but slowing down as we neared the parking lot.

"No," he said firmly. "Not until you listen to me."

"Why are you here?" I demanded.

I guess I expected him to say something like, "I'm here because I really am a normal kid, just trying to make it through high school." Something like that, anyway. Some sort of denial that he was different. At the most, I expected him to admit to being psychic too, but that our meeting was purely incidental.

At any rate, the last thing I expected was the answer he really gave me.

We'd stepped off the curb and were standing at the edge of the parking lot. He yanked my arm, pulling us both to a stop. I was looking up at him, trying to keep my face as hard and smooth as possible. He was staring down at me, his face calm and almost emotionless.

His eyes bored right into mine and his lips slowly but deliberately moved. "I'm here for you."

nine

I stared at him, my mouth dropping open. He met my stare evenly, his clear blue eyes flicking across my face, fighting to measure my reaction.

I blinked, and my voice broke despite my best efforts. "You *are* stalking me? Why?" I attempted to jerk my arm away but his grip was like iron.

"Please, you don't understand," he spoke quietly and quickly. His rushed words hardly made sense. "Normally this doesn't happen. You're different. I didn't mean to scare you—I was supposed to be reassuring. Once I opened myself to you, I thought I'd cleared all doubt—it usually works."

"That day, when you opened the door for me?" I broke in, desperate to understand. I couldn't lie to myself—I was scared, and growing more so every passing second, but this exchange was strangely exhilarating. Now I understood why people jumped out of airplanes.

"Yes." He nodded once, the motion clipped and harsh. "I was trying to get close to you, by showing you I meant you no harm."

Meant? I may not be a straight-A student, but I recognized the use of past tense. I tried pulling my arm away again, this time putting all my body weight into it. He hardly wavered under the strain—only tightened his grip. I was stuck.

I kept pulling anyway, leaning away from him even as I

glared bravely into his pale face. "Why me? What do you *want* from me?"

"You can see auras," he stated firmly. "Ever since your parents died."

"How did you know that?" I gasped loudly. "How could you *possibly* have *known* that!?"

"I know a lot of things about your family. Things about *you*."

I used my fingernails to start clawing at his restraining hand, but he only snatched that wrist too. He sighed deeply, gripping both my wrists.

"I'll scream," I threatened, still gasping from the adrenaline rush.

"No, you won't," he countered. "Because you want answers."

"Let go of me."

"No. You have to listen to me, and we can't talk here."

"I'm not going anywhere with you."

He jerked my arms, pulling me closer to him. I was still straining to lean away but he lowered his face toward mine, his voice extremely deep. "Kate, I won't hurt you. That's not why I'm here."

"Then let me go!" I nearly cried.

"I can't do that. We need to talk."

"Who's Toni?"

He blinked in surprise—whether from the words, or the demanding way I said them, I don't know. But it was enough. The split second of surprise was all I needed. I pushed with all my might, my fear and adrenaline lending me strength. I crashed into his chest and he fell, initially pulling me with him. But then his arms shot out instinctively to catch himself, or at least to cushion his fall. That was my moment. I fell onto the curb but was already rolling away from him. I felt my elbows grind painfully against the cement but then I was lunging to my feet and darting into the parking lot.

I heard him scrambling on the ground and then pounding

after me, his breath coming in even pants as he ran.

I was faster, but only just. I spotted my car and aimed for the passenger door, knowing that Lee hadn't locked it—she never did, unless I verbally reminded her, which, luckily, this morning I hadn't. I slammed into my car, clawed for the handle and yanked it up. The door opened, and I all but jumped inside, jerking it closed behind me. I slapped my hand against the lock, just before Patrick's hands landed on the window.

"Kate!" he called through the glass, his eyes panicked. "Please—open the door. I'm not going to hurt you, I promise. I would never do that. Please."

"Stay away from me!" I yelled, crawling backwards over the emergency brake and into the driver's seat.

"Kate, please, this is important. Have you seen anyone else with a different aura—aside from me and Toni?"

I reached into my pocket and pulled out my keys. My hands were shaking, but I tried to ignore that as I fitted the key into the ignition. I could feel my phone in my pocket, and I was grateful I hadn't left it in my locker with my backpack. The small device offered a sense of security. All I had to do was push a few buttons and I could be connected with reality again.

I started the car and shifted into gear, not bothering with my seat belt. The car started to roll forward, but Patrick just walked alongside it, palms still pressed to the window.

"Kate—have you seen anyone with a black aura? Kate?"

Once clear of the other cars, I pressed more firmly against the accelerator, and Patrick started jogging next to the car to keep up with me. "Kate, listen to me. It's only a matter of time. If you see anyone with a black aura you need to get—"

I reached the exit and launched into the street with more speed than I'd used since the accident. But it had the desired effect. Patrick's hands slipped away from the car, and he stopped running after me.

As I shifted into third, I looked into my rearview mirror. He was standing in the empty road, watching me with his arms hanging at his sides. His piercing eyes seemed to find mine. He was already receding into the distance—how could he possibly see my eyes in the small mirror?

It wasn't until I rounded the corner and merged onto another street that I noticed the trembling. I was shaking all over. With weak fingers I fought with my seat belt until I heard the loud click that signaled its locking into place. Then I leaned back in my seat and sucked in deep breaths. My body was beginning to slowly relax, even as a part of my mind grew more and more terrified.

I wondered what Patrick had been trying to tell me, what he would have told me if I hadn't run away. But I'd done the logical thing, hadn't I? He'd restrained me, chased me, threatened me—right? My heart was throbbing inside my chest, each beat slightly less painful than the one before it. Yes, my body was sure that I'd done the right thing. But my mind couldn't stop hearing Patrick's words, over and over—an endless echo meant to haunt me.

It's only a matter of time.

I drove straight home, and was relieved that my grandparents were gone. I had the house to myself. I parked my car and walked inside—careful to turn all the locks safely back into place. I went straight to my room, still clutching my keys. I laid on my bed and stared up at the ceiling, my mind reeling with a million different thoughts.

Patrick knew about me. He'd known about me before I'd told him anything. He was here for me. Why? And black auras? *More* strange people were going to come into my life?

It's only a matter of time.

I kept an eye on the clock, and when it was time, I headed

back out to my car. Once inside I locked the door again, needing the security in my current condition. I was completely freaked. I drove back to the high school, hoping Lee would be ready and waiting. I didn't want to linger. But my worry was unfounded—Lee was there, and Patrick wasn't.

She must have been a little surprised to see me already in the car, but she didn't seem to realize I'd been gone. She climbed in and immediately started talking about the band teacher and how awful organizing the music library was going to be.

I nodded occasionally, and she didn't appear to notice my lack of interest. After she'd exhausted that subject, she turned on some loud music. I wanted to talk to someone about what had happened, but I couldn't find the words. I opened my mouth several times, but nothing came out. So I drove in silence.

Once at the elementary school, I pulled next to the curb and waited for the twins. My eyes scanned the parking lot—despite my fear of seeing something I'd rather not—but all I saw were the usual swirling colors. No black. And, almost more important to me, no silver.

Jenna tried opening the back door, but it was locked. Lee turned around and unlocked it and Jenna slipped inside, sliding all the way over. Josie was right behind her, the two of them continuing a conversation as they shut the door and put on their seat belts. I started to inch my way out of the parking lot.

"I still think she's weird," Josie was saying, shoving her backpack to the floor.

"I think she's awesome," Jenna argued happily. "You just hate her cuz you're getting bad grades already."

"It's school—who cares?"

"Maybe you *should* care."

"That's the best comeback you've got?"

"What was wrong with it?"

"It was *so* not cool."

Jenna leaned forward, pushing her head up between the two front seats. "You guys heard about Ms. Rhodes, didn't you?"

Lee turned down the sound just slightly. "Ms. R? She's still teaching here? She's an old bat."

"That's just it—she's not teaching anymore."

Lee glanced back at Jenna. "She retired?"

My mind was focused on other things, but I found myself listening to the conversation in spite of myself.

Jenna was shaking her head. "Nope. That's the weird thing. She was there the first couple of days, then she just disappeared."

Josie shoved her head up beside Jenna's, her eyes rolling. "It's not *that* exciting. She didn't show up Thursday, so we have a substitute until the school can get a hold of her."

"She's not answering her phone?" Lee asked.

Jenna bobbed her head. "Kinda freaky, huh? Someone was going to go by her house today, but I never heard what happened."

"She probably just lost her mind and forgot what day it was," Josie argued. "Can we talk about something else?"

"What if she was murdered or something?" Jenna asked quietly, and though I could tell she was trying to be nonchalant about the whole thing, some fear was leaking through. "I mean, people get murdered every day. It makes sense that it would happen to someone we know eventually."

"Who would murder an old sixth-grade teacher?" Josie snorted, settling back into her seat.

Lee shrugged, pushing her long black hair over one shoulder. "Probably any of her past students."

Josie laughed, but Jenna broke in, "Anyway, until she gets back we have a cool sub. Miss Avalos. She grew up in Mexico, and she tells some really awesome stories."

"I think she's pretty lame," Josie argued.

"Just cuz she actually teaches us something—expects us to answer . . ."

The argument continued, but I tuned it out. I had more important things on my mind than missing elementary teachers and cool or lame subs.

In fifteen minutes I was back in my room, lying on my bed. I could hear the twins downstairs, and I knew that my grandparents would be home soon. My grandpa was so good at reading me, I knew he'd start insisting I tell him what was bothering me. And I wanted to—I just wasn't ready yet.

So I called Aaron.

"Hey," he answered on the second ring. His voice was so surprised and happy, it was easy to picture his aura. "What's up?"

"Do you want to go out tonight?" I asked, getting right to the point.

He was quiet for just a second, but I knew that was only because he was taken aback. For months he'd been the one forcing me to do everything, and then suddenly out of the blue here I was, asking him out.

"Of course," he finally answered, his smile even more evident in his voice now. "What do you want to do?"

"Anything," I said, staring up at the ceiling, almost blinded by the pure and boring white.

ten

We went to a movie, but I couldn't have repeated the name of it. There were some battle scenes, and occasionally the theater would burst into laughter. But though I was sitting in one of the best seats in the house with Aaron holding my hand, I wasn't really there. I was convinced at this point that I'd been wrong to run away from Patrick so soon. I should've learned more about him. Now he probably thought I was a terrified target, and that couldn't be a good thing. I needed to confront him. The only problem was, I was scared to. I'd joked about him stalking me, but he really had been. According to him, that was the reason he was here. Did he need me for something? Was he here to get my help? But why would he need *my* help? Did he want me to see how angry his mom was, or help him manipulate his dad's emotions? Such simple explanations seemed ridiculous.

But what else could he want with me? Was he psychic too? Did he hunt down other psychics and kill them so he could be the only one? And what was his relationship to Toni? Were they friends or enemies? Should I be telling all of this to the cops? What if I was being followed right now? And what about the black-aura people? Black meant bad people, right? Or was that just in the movies?

And then, of course, my endless questions always brought me back to one fact: Deep down, I knew that Patrick O'Donnell was good. I'd seen that for myself. I'd felt it. And as I stared at the large movie screen, I just kept seeing him—his image when I first saw him, looking awkward and unsure, poised to enter the classroom. Him sitting with the special needs kids, helping one of them open a water bottle. His pure blue eyes, staring into mine as we stood in the doorway and shared an almost magical moment. Lastly, his panicked expression as he stared through the car window, begging me to listen.

Patrick O'Donnell, I decided there in the theater, was not dangerous. Had he scared me? Almost out of my wits. Did he mean me harm? Not at all.

But then, why was he here?

The movie ended, and Aaron continued to hold my hand as we stood and made our way out to the main aisle. Once in the crowded lobby he asked me if I was hungry. I nodded, and he led me out into the cool evening air. He drove to a slightly fancier restaurant than we would usually frequent, and I guess that was sort of his way of letting me know that he appreciated my newfound enthusiasm. It was a small Mexican restaurant, and I understood exactly why Aaron had chosen it—we'd had our first date here. This was his way of showing me that we were back on track. If only I could've believed him.

We sat at a small table in the corner and placed our orders. Then we proceeded to snack on the chips and salsa, and I attempted to shake myself from my deep and all-too-absorbing thoughts. Now that the movie was over, I would need to be better company. I didn't want to ruin this evening for him, since it obviously meant a whole lot to him.

"Thanks for this," I said suddenly, and he looked up with a slow smile.

"You're welcome. And thank you, for asking me." He hesitated, then continued carefully. "It's been a long time."

I knew he was talking about my initiating a date, but for

some reason I kept thinking about how—at least for me—our relationship was still far from how it used to be.

"I'm sorry," I replied, dipping another tortilla chip into the thick salsa. He waited for me to finish it, and then he reached across the table. I responded by placing my free hand on the red table cloth, and he gently wrapped his fingers around mine, squeezing tenderly.

"Don't be sorry," he insisted lowly. "You're doing your best, Kate."

I wasn't sure why his words bothered me, but they did. I decided to change the subject. "So, what did you guys do to our dear rivals today?"

He pulled back his hand, grinning as he reached for another chip. I knew not just from his aura that—in his mind—everything was back to normal. "You know that huge wall they have—Senior Row? Well, it looks a lot less red now, and a lot more blue."

My lips tugged in a tentative smile. "Are you missing football?"

He nodded, licking some salsa from his lips. "More than I thought I would. But the team still lets me hang around."

"They miss you too."

"Maybe my tackle." He took another chip, and I did too.

By the time our food came, Aaron was in a deep conversation about sports, and I was pretending to be interested. When we were finished Aaron held my elbow to lead me out of the building.

As we walked in the parking lot toward his car, I just kept staring at his hand around my arm. It was so . . . possessive. But I felt guilty just thinking the word. I knew that wasn't how he meant it.

He held my hand during the drive to my house, and after pulling into the driveway he leaned over and kissed me gently. But as he got out of the car and rounded the hood, coming to open my door for me, I couldn't help but picture Patrick O'Donnell. Maybe it was seeing Aaron's face through the window that triggered the memory, but it was enough to pull me back into my reality. The worries and thoughts I'd held at bay through dinner came rushing back, and I wondered how best to face them. Because no matter what I thought about Patrick, I was going to have to face him tomorrow. And despite my recurring insistence that he was good, I was still more than a little scared of him.

Aaron walked me to the porch, kissed me again under the golden light, and then moved back toward his car. I didn't wait to watch him drive away but opened the unlocked door and stepped into the house instead. The kitchen light was on, but before I could decide to walk toward it, Grandma's voice was calling out to me.

"Kate, is that you?"

"Yes," I assured her, walking across the dark wood floor and heading for the kitchen. A part of me was wishing I could just crash in my bed, but at least it was Grandma, and not Grandpa—the one who would be sure to realize something was wrong.

She was sitting at the kitchen table, sipping a cup of tea and reading a book. She looked up when I stepped into the room, and her smile was genuine but distracted. Just by looking at the extra yellow in her aura, I knew she was reading a romance, and I couldn't help but smile. Some people could find enjoyment in the simplest things. I wished, not for the first time, that I could be more like her.

"How was your date?" Grandma asked, her rough voice soothing in the otherwise quiet house.

"It was really nice. I needed it, I think."

She nodded. "You certainly did. He's a good boy."

I nodded to her book. "I'll let you get back to that."

Grandma sighed, shifting her weight in the chair as she did so. "Good idea—your grandfather will be down any minute now, and I can't read while he teases me." She focused back on the page before her, and I turned and retreated up the stairs.

Once back in my room I followed my regular routine—only this time I kept my light off. I didn't want to see any colors. I didn't want to think. The dim light offered by the moon filtered through my window, adding a comforting glow to my surroundings. In minutes I was curling up on my bed and pinching my eyes closed. But my brain wouldn't stop thinking, and I couldn't banish Patrick's face from my mind.

As I slowly fell asleep, it was almost like he was watching over me. His clear blue eyes were riveted on me—a silent observer. My last conscious thought was that I should be scared, or at least a little uneasy under his unwavering gaze. But I wasn't. I only felt peace.

eleven

I took my seat in American lit five minutes before the warning bell. I was completely alone, and absolutely nervous. I caught myself biting my thumbnail, and that's when I decided to doodle while I waited for him to show up—because somehow, I knew he would, despite everything that had happened yesterday.

I set my pencil to paper, and then let my mind focus on the issue at hand—Patrick O'Donnell. I was hoping that he'd get here soon, so we could have a few minutes to talk before the rest of the class showed up. In my mind, this was the perfect place to try and understand what had happened between us, because he couldn't really do anything to hurt me if the rest of the class started walking in on us. It was a public place that afforded us a couple minutes of privacy. Not that I thought he would hurt me—that strange feeling from last night had yet to leave me. The assurance that he was watching over me was still real, though it didn't make a whole lot of sense.

My stomach was reacting to all of this by doing strange flips every couple of seconds. A part of me was still convinced that being alone with him—even for a minute—was stupid after that display in the parking lot. But my more confident side completely refused to act like a scared little girl. I wanted some answers, and I'd go crazy until I heard his explanation. I didn't know what to expect from him, since I'd seen so many sides of him now, but I wasn't going to run away from this anymore. At least not until I understood what was going on.

He cleared his throat a bit loudly, and I looked up, fighting to keep the fear off my face.

Patrick was biting his lower lip, hesitating in the doorway. He looked so harmless, so . . . sorry. I felt my body tighten, and I straightened in my desk, my eyes glued to his face, watching for the first sign of hostility.

"May I come in?" he asked in a thin whisper.

He doesn't want to hurt you, a small voice in my head reassured. But the lingering peace I'd felt just a moment ago wasn't quite as prevalent, now that his eyes were on me.

I nodded once but didn't take my eyes away from him.

He stepped slowly into the classroom, moving cautiously toward me. All that was missing were the raised hands—other than that, he had the surrendering look down. His bag hung from one slightly raised shoulder, and his eyes somehow managed to hold a combination that I could best describe as guarded openness. He walked slowly, gauging my reaction to his presence. I must have passed the test because he took his usual seat next to me, though he was careful not to come any closer. His eyes never left my face.

I refused to say the first word, so we sat in cold silence for a moment, just staring at each other.

His lips pressed tightly together, and then he spoke lowly. "I'm sorry about yesterday. It wasn't my intention to scare you."

"Well, you sort of did," I snapped reflexively.

He winced a little and nodded his head. "I know. And I'm sorry."

"You pretty much attacked me," I reminded him, my voice still harder than usual.

He squirmed in his seat. I don't know why, but I found it

kind of . . . cute. He looked completely repentant—not a look a girl generally saw on a guy. "I know. I didn't mean to let that happen. I lost control—I thought that—"

"That what?" I demanded.

His eyes pierced right into mine, and I stopped breathing under his intense stare. "I thought you were going to run away from me," he said thinly, a deeper emotion throbbing as an undercurrent to his words. I almost thought it was fear. Whatever it was, it kept him from sounding creepy.

I wasn't going to let him know that, of course. I actually felt like I had the upper hand right now, and I wasn't willing to let him know he'd won that easily.

I leaned back in my chair, regarding him with what I hoped was a stern look. "Listen, I don't know what your problem is, but you need a doctor." He blinked, and his brow furrowed in confusion. "You're cryptic and creepy," I explained. "And whatever it was that happened yesterday . . . it's not normal."

He glanced over at the wall, his eyes lingering on the clock a second too long—I knew he was avoiding my gaze. Then he turned back to me, pleading etched on every line of his angular face. "Kate, I promise I can explain everything, but this isn't the place."

"What did you mean about people with black auras?" I asked, ignoring his attempt to end the conversation.

The skin around his eyes tightened and his strong shoulders stiffened. "Have you seen anyone?" he asked, the hesitation that had made me feel powerful fleeing from his demeanor in an instant.

My lips pressed together, and I just stared at him and his sudden mood change.

"Kate," he said, leaning toward me. "This is important. Have you seen anyone with a black aura?"

The bell rang harshly, and the sound made us both jump.

The rumbling of voices from the hallway that had been distant before became louder—harder to drown out. Our time alone was coming to a fast close.

Patrick's eyes were quite clearly filling with worry. But before he could open his mouth again, I spoke firmly. "I have questions. If I meet you later, can you give me answers?"

He nodded eagerly, though his body was still tight with concern. "Yes. I can."

I hesitated, then decided I owed it to myself to ask. "Can I . . . ? Will I be safe with you?" I hated how the worry I'd been feeling slipped into my words. Instead of powerful and unconcerned, they sounded weak and fearful.

But Patrick's face relaxed, and his beautiful eyes became soothing. He nodded once, his eyes not leaving mine. "You will always be safe with me."

And though it defied reason, I knew he was speaking the truth.

My lips cracked apart, my mind unable to stop my heart from asking the question. "Who are you?" It sounded better than the alternative—What are you?

He offered a small, half smile. "Someone you can trust."

What kind of answer was that! I shook my head a little, still not breaking our gaze. "No, not that. Are you—?" For real? Human? Some kind of mental person? Any of those could have easily been understandable ends to that question. Unfortunately, I wasn't able to ask any of them, because just then Aaron stepped into the room.

He was followed quickly by a couple other students, and they effectively ended the conversation. Patrick turned away from me, reaching into his bag to pull out a notebook and pencil.

I turned back to my own paper, where I stared in shock at what I'd "doodled." It wasn't a doodle, first of all—probably not by anyone's definition. It was a sketch. One I'd done without thought, though the sure lines hardly looked accidental or unconscious. It was far from finished, but the image was obviously a face. Patrick's face.

I felt my cheeks redden, and I slapped the paper over, hoping Aaron hadn't seen it. I saw Patrick glance over at me and the sudden sound I'd made. I prayed he hadn't caught a glimpse of it either.

Aaron tossed his bag to the floor, and then sat next to me, grinning hugely. "Morning," he said, leaning over to kiss me. I surrendered my lips briefly, but as I pulled back, I sensed Patrick turning quickly away. My face was really burning now, knowing that he'd watched.

My boyfriend didn't seem to notice our audience of one, or even my blushing discomfort. Judging by his aura, he was still completely immersed in happiness over our date last night. "Hey, you didn't answer any of my texts this morning."

I forced a smile. "Yeah, I've been busy. Sorry."

"No worries. So, I was thinking, maybe you want to do something tonight? Last night was great, by the way."

Internally I was grimacing that Patrick was hearing all of this. I hardly knew anything about him, and he was overhearing everything about me. It didn't seem fair.

"Um, I don't really know what's going on tonight," I hedged. "I'll call you after I know."

"Let me guess, your grandparents are getting upset with me for stealing you every night." He winced, partly coming down from his cloud of exuberance. "Yeah, guess I didn't think about that. Your parents were always okay with me, so I just assumed . . . But we could always just hang out at your house if they don't want you going out again."

"Yeah, maybe," I said, with barely any enthusiasm at all. Apparently it was enough to fool him, though, because he was instantly back to grinning.

"Okay, sounds good. We didn't have another chapter to read, did we? Because I totally haven't touched this book since Monday's assignment . . ."

I hate to admit that I tuned him out, but I did. I had too many other things on my mind to make room for mundane complaints.

Actually, I didn't hear a thing all through class. I was only aware of the guy next to me—the one that wasn't my boyfriend. I couldn't keep from stealing looks at him, even after he caught me once. Our eyes met, held for a second too long—but not long enough—and then he looked away.

My heart was beating with an urgency I hadn't felt since my first crush, years ago. It was stupid, but undeniable. And it was getting harder and harder to keep my eyes off him.

I told myself it was only because I was intensely curious. I had so many questions, and Patrick had the answers. That's what fascinated me. It wasn't his appearance, or his voice, or the way he looked at me that kept me from looking away. It was the mystery around him that captivated me. Not his laugh, or the way he sat with his shoulders hunched, like he was keeping a deep secret.

In short, I wasn't attracted to him. The only reason I kept looking at him was to assure myself that he was real. That he was different. That he was here, sitting next to me. There was no other reason. And to prove it to myself, when class was over, I initiated the kiss with my boyfriend, and it was with Aaron that I walked out of the room, forcing myself to keep my eyes forward and not look back to see if Patrick was watching us or following me.

I managed to stay ahead of him, and I was equally relieved and sad when he seemed to take my hint and sat on the opposite side of the room for second period.

I saved a seat next to me for Lee, who came in a minute late. Still, she beat the teacher, so it wasn't that big of a deal. A minute later class started, and I tried to focus on taking notes.

When history finally ended, Lee led the way to the door. I followed, keeping my eyes trained safely forward. I refused to be caught staring at Patrick again—I'd managed to make it all through class without him catching me, and I intended to keep it that way.

So, naturally, he sidled right up next to me without my realizing it, and before I could look up, he discreetly slipped a folded piece of paper into my hand. Then he turned away, not even giving me a moment's chance to get lost in his eyes. I watched his back as he retreated down the crowded hallway. I knew he was going the wrong way, because we had every class together, but I wasn't going to say anything.

I pushed my way to my next class, my fingers curling around the small piece of stiff paper. My fingers teased the sharp corners, and it took all my self-control not to open it right then and there. Somehow I held off until I was settled in the back corner of third period, and for the moment I was alone. I took advantage of the privacy, and, with trembling fingers, pulled back the folds until I was clutching an entire sheet of paper.

There was a ridiculously small amount of writing on the note, but seeing his neat handwriting caused my stomach to flip. I was such a girl.

I shook my head at myself, frowning as I scanned the words.

Kate,

I'm sorry for scaring you. Call me when you're ready. Until then, I will keep my distance. Promise me that you'll call if you see anything unusual. Please don't tell anyone about this.

Be careful.

Patrick

At the bottom was a phone number. It was an area code I didn't recognize, but considering this was Patrick, an obscure area code wasn't the weirdest thing about him. Like the fact that he could go invisible, and that he had an invisible friend. (I still sort of wished I'd gotten that answer this morning, but time *had* been limited. Little things like how he managed to become invisible hadn't seemed that important, comparatively.)

I quickly refolded the note and shoved it into my pocket. But even though I wasn't looking at the words, I still saw them.

The more I learned about Patrick O'Donnell, the weirder he got. Honestly, this whole experience was starting to seem like a surreal dream.

Part of me was upset that he'd given me his number, because now if I called him today, I was going to look desperate. But I wanted my answers. If I didn't solve this puzzle soon, I was going to go insane. (Unless I already was insane, and that was the reason I was going through all of this.)

The rest of the day, I was distracted. I never saw Patrick again, so I suppose he wasn't lying when he said he was going to keep his distance. But that didn't mean I didn't keep an eye out for him. During the rest of my classes, and countless times during lunch, I found myself craning my head around, hoping to catch a glimpse of him.

For really the first time, I began to wonder what Patrick was. I'd assumed that he was human. But suddenly I found myself wondering . . . what if he wasn't? What if he was something else? I mean, I trusted him when he told me I would be safe with him, but what did I know about him, really? Practically nothing. And his apparent friendship with Toni, the Invisible Man, was equally disconcerting. Whatever Patrick was, Toni was. That thought alone caused me more worry than almost anything else. True, the conversation I'd overheard at Lee's party hadn't been exactly ominous, but just the fact that it had taken place was strange enough.

I didn't want to think that they were on the same side, because Toni had been haunting me and scaring me out of my mind since the first moment I'd seen him, standing in front of my car.

Needless to say, my day was both long and maddening. The second the final bell rang I left the choir room behind, swinging by the band room to drag Lee away from any potential distractions.

"Whoa, hold your horses!" Lee snorted at my impatience, as she lazily cleaned her beat-up clarinet. "What's the rush?"

"I don't feel well," I told her, knowing it wasn't really a lie.

Lee finished dismembering her clarinet, and then hurried to stash it in the instrument room. I could feel Lee's stare on my face as we walked silently out of the room and into the hall. She didn't speak until we were in sight of the exit.

"Kate, you've been acting really weird since Saturday."

"You make that sound like a long time—it's only Tuesday."

"Still."

I reached the doors a step before her and pushed one open. Lee was right behind me, and once we'd descended the few steps, she drew even with me again.

"Look, a friend can be worried, okay? Do you want to talk about it?"

I thought about Patrick's note and his plea to not tell anyone. But it wasn't that that stopped me from telling Lee—it was my desire to keep at least one area of my life sane. "I'd rather not," I told her, my eyes trained forward.

Lee shook her head next to me. "Look, I don't want to be one of those friends that get all annoying or anything, but maybe you should just end it."

I looked up at her, my eyes confused. "End what?"

Lee shrugged, her eyes defensive. "I mean, yeah, he's a great guy, and you guys have been together for a long time, but if he's driving you crazy . . . Maybe you just need to dump him."

"Aaron?"

"Sure. You're not happy, are you?" she asked, turning on me.

Now it was my turn to be defensive. "Well, things haven't quite gotten back to normal, but—"

"Kate, honestly—can you look at me and tell me you're happy?"

I didn't even bother to waste the energy it would take to look at her—I just kept walking toward my car. "I know it hasn't been easy, but things are getting better."

"You can't lie to me, girl. I know you too well. And I thought you knew you could tell me anything. Since when have you tried lying to me instead of spilling?"

I unlocked her door, since it was closest, then I walked around to my own. She'd gotten in and unlocked mine before I was completely around the car, so I just climbed in. I lifted my keys, but she snatched them away before I could set them in the ignition.

"Lee," I protested, letting my hand fall to smack my knee.

"Nope, we aren't going anywhere until you fess up." She had her elbow resting near the window, the keys dangling from her fingers, mocking me.

I groaned and thrust my head back against my seat, wincing when the impact was a bit more than I'd bargained for. "Look. I know you're trying to help, but I'm just . . . all right." I leaned forward, grasping the wheel as I turned my head to look at her. "I don't know that I was actually thinking about ending the relationship or anything, but I was having my doubts. And then Saturday night, Aaron and I . . ."

"You had another fight?" she asked.

I shook my head slowly. "No, the opposite—we kissed. I mean, seriously kissed, for the first time since everything happened."

"And . . . ?"

"And it was wonderful," I sighed, the frustration evident in the sound.

"And that's bad because . . . ?"

"Because I thought things were making sense. And now I'm all confused again. Because everything else feels the same as it did before, but now I know that I still really care about him. I know that it's me holding us back."

"I thought you'd admitted to that before."

"Well, I knew it was me—I just . . . now it's undeniable."

"And you feel like you're not being fair to him?" she guessed slowly.

I nodded glumly, sliding my fingers over the wheel, tracing invisible patterns. My eyes followed my movements, and I felt Lee watching me too.

"So," she said at last. "What are you going to do?"

"I don't know," I admitted in a whisper.

"Maybe you should talk to Aaron about this. Let him know you're confused. Let him know that you're worried about being unfair to him. I bet he can clear everything up."

"You're right. I know that. I just . . . "

"Easier said then done," Lee finished for me.

I cracked a smile. "Yeah. Something like that."

She gave me a smile in return, and not for the first time I was amazed by what a wonderful friend I had. The brown threads that colored her aura were pain—pain she felt for me. There was something comforting about that—actually seeing her empathy.

She suddenly handed me the keys, and I started the car. As we put on our seat belts, she leaned back and added jokingly, "Maybe it's time to tell him about your psychic-ness, eh?"

"No, no," I laughed. "Not even close."

She laughed with me, but I knew from her aura—the sudden uneasy green that was slowly invading her usual yellow and blue mix—that she hadn't been completely joking.

twelve

I decided not to call Patrick that night. I didn't want to seem desperate. He already thought I was crazy scared and I didn't want to make myself look any worse in his eyes. Not that I cared much about what he thought of me. It was more because I wanted to remain a calm, powerful, and collected psychic when I finally got my answers from him.

He wasn't in school Wednesday, but I should have known he wouldn't be. His note had been clear. I didn't see Toni either, but I hadn't since the party, so that wasn't too shocking.

Surprisingly, my short conversation with Lee had made me feel a lot better. True, we hadn't broached the subject that was really bothering me, but even just talking about Aaron had helped me feel more like the old me. As opposed to yesterday, or even since school began, I was able to concentrate on something other than Patrick O'Donnell. It felt good.

So good, that I put off calling him again. And again. Before I knew it, it was Friday, and I still hadn't called him or seen him.

Lee's mom was out of town again this weekend, so I was planning to spend a couple nights with Lee. As I was packing a small overnight bag, I saw his note, sitting on my desk where I'd left it days ago. I stared at the neatly folded paper for a long time, knowing I should call him now and set up a time to meet. I should get it over with—just get my answers, demand that he leave me alone, and then go back to my somewhat-normal life.

I went so far as to unfold the note and take out my phone, but I couldn't make myself dial. In the end, I just typed his name and number into my phone, saving Patrick O'Donnell as a contact. Then I refolded the note and shoved it into one of my desk drawers. I shouldn't be the one sweating—let him wonder what was keeping me.

Besides, I should be able to have one fun weekend with my best friend. I'd face Patrick O'Donnell next week.

I finished packing and then headed downstairs. I heard some noise in the kitchen and hoped it was my grandparents. I was anxious to get to Lee's, so we could spend as much time as possible together.

"Grandma?" I called out, just before entering the kitchen.

"Nope, just me," Grandpa said from behind his paper. He was sitting in his usual place, and his coffee remained untouched.

I stepped up to the table, shouldering my bag. "I'm going over to Lee's—I'll be back sometime Sunday. Could you pass that along to Grandma for me?"

"Sure can do." Grandpa's voice was lacking its usual level of amusement, and for the first time I really noticed his aura—at least what was visible around the paper.

It was almost completely green—the darkest green I think I'd ever seen.

"Grandpa, is something wrong?" I asked, fighting the knot of fear in my stomach.

He lowered the paper slowly, eyes lingering on the words until it was lying flat on the table. Then he removed his reading glasses and squinted up at me.

"Have you heard about those freak accidents happening down in Santa Fe?"

I shook my head slowly, knowing he'd continue without much prodding.

He humphed and reached for his coffee mug. "Not surprising. It's not like school teaches you anything important." He took a quick sip and then spoke quickly, eyes back on the paper. "For the past couple weeks, strange things have been happening down in the capital. Mysterious deaths, mostly. Freak accidents. The paper's started calling it 'The Death Train.' And it seems to be moving."

"Freak accidents?" I repeated, my skin prickling.

He frowned, still focused on the paper. "Yep. It started with some construction workers—some car broke through a guardrail and killed two of them. At least, that's what they're saying the first one was. But listen to this: 'The Death Train seems to be picking up speed, and moving meticulously through the city. In addition to the unfortunate workers at the construction site in . . .' blah, blah blah, . . . there it is—'there have been six other victims apparently caught by this haunting and unexplainable phenomenon. The last of which was found yesterday in her home—a middle-aged woman living alone, Annette Jones. She was found yesterday morning in her bed. She apparently strangled herself in her sleep, using her bedsheets. Police who visited the scene offered no further explanations, and there seem to be no leads. Officials are interested in any help the public can give. At this time, no suspects are being declared—all deaths seem to have been purely accidental.'"

Grandpa looked up, and I could see the worry as clearly in his eyes as in his aura.

I shrugged a little, though I couldn't lie—the article was freaky. "I don't understand, Grandpa. Why are you so worried? I mean, they're just accidents, right?"

Grandpa slowly shook his head. "I don't know . . . it appears that way, but—you know what they say—nothing is ever quite as it seems."

I felt my brow furrow. "You think someone's behind these deaths? Like a serial killer or something?"

He shrugged and took another drink from his mug. "Maybe."

I felt a reflexive chill go through my body, but before I could open my mouth to press him for more, Grandma was clearing her throat behind us.

I jumped a little at the sound. "Henry," Grandma scolded loudly. "What are you trying to do? Scare her out of her wits? I think you quit the army a bit too soon, old man. I've always thought so." She reached between us to fold up the paper and snatch it away.

Grandpa—though still surrounded by green—was smiling as he winked at me over Grandma's shoulder. "I guess she's forgotten that I came back to marry her."

"Oh no, I remember," she grunted, tossing the paper to the counter and then moving for the coffee pot. "I still think you'd have been a bit saner if you'd had the chance to shoot at a few more things before coming back, that's all."

Grandpa rolled his eyes at his wife, then turned back to regard me. I guess I hadn't completely managed to rearrange my pale face because his eyes grew soft as he looked at me. "Never you mind, Kate—I'm just an old fool, getting excited over nothing. Go on—have fun at Kellie's."

"What?" Grandma whipped around. "Where are you going, young lady?"

I sighed and tightened my grip on my bag. "Lee's mom is gone again, so I was going to stay with her so she won't be alone. I'll be back Sunday."

"Why am I always the last to know?" she asked. Before I could answer, she threw her hands in the air. "Never mind. Shoosh. Go on, have fun. But next time, tell me before I buy enough steak to feed three growing girls, hmm?"

"I think I can take care of her share," Grandpa assured her, patting his protruding waistline with a smug fondness.

"I got a salad for you, dear."

His eyes narrowed. "Charlotte, I refuse to eat like a rabbit."

"That's what you get for eating like a carnivorous wolf for the past sixty years."

"You're exaggerating, woman, and you know it."

I excused myself from the room with a small smile, but they barely seemed to notice. They squabbled like, well, only an old married couple can. They were so different from my parents, but in many ways, quite similar. It was equal amounts of wonderful and horrible to have my grandparents as a constant reminder of my parents' absence.

The short drive to Lee's house gave me an opportunity to think about the mysterious accidents in Santa Fe. True, the city was miles and miles away, but something that unexplainable and creepy didn't have to be close to freak a person out. For a moment I wondered if Lee had a paper, or if she'd let me look it up on her computer. But then I remembered that I was going for normal me this weekend, so that meant no worrying about a news story. I was going to enjoy this time with Lee, end of story.

Lee was ready with the PlayStation already on when I got there. And we proceeded to spend far too many hours dueling each other on Guitar Hero to be considered healthy.

In a word, the evening was great. Exactly what I needed. We played, talked, watched movies—it was like old times. I didn't once think about Patrick, or Aaron, or the Death Train. It was just me and Lee, and a lot of overdue girl time.

That night we watched older chick flicks until two in the morning and then fell asleep on the floor in front of the TV. We ached a bit more than we used to in the morning, and Lee joked about us getting old. It was perfect.

Saturday was pretty much more of the same, except we went swimming for a couple hours before Lee announced she wanted to go shopping. She didn't have enough black tops, and she said she could always use some more gothic accessories.

So we drove into the city around three in the afternoon, and were soon walking around in the mall. It wasn't as big as some malls, but it was enough to satisfy the general shopping urges. Since I'd never gone shopping for the gothic look, I followed Lee to the second level and into a dimly lit store. The lights were on, but the overwhelmingly black merchandise must have absorbed all the light, because it was pretty hard to see. The music wasn't really my style, nor was the carefully arranged assortment of clothing.

In minutes I was looking for an excuse to get out, and I found it when I saw a stand in the main area of the mall, selling sunglasses. I told her where I was going, and she nodded without looking up from between two shirts that looked really similar to me.

I couldn't keep the grin off my face as I made my way out of the store, noticing once again how yellow Lee's aura was, compared to the other customers and even the clerks.

Stepping out of that store was like stepping back into the living world. I felt like I could actually breathe again. I headed for the sunglasses and began browsing for the perfect pair. I was halfway around the cart when I felt someone step up behind me. I tensed, but he was speaking before I could turn around. It was a voice I knew, though not well.

"Hey there. Thought that was you."

I spun around, clutching a pair of large sunglasses, and found myself face to face with Toni, the Invisible Man.

He was grinning from ear to ear, and for the first time I noticed that we were the same height—I might even be a little taller. He had dark brown hair, and dark brown eyes, and his mischievous look was all too familiar. As was his silver aura.

"So," I said slowly. "Are you visible right now or am I talking to myself?"

He laughed a bit too loudly, and shoved his hands into his pockets. "I sure am, beautiful. So listen, uh, I'm sorry I haven't actually had a chance to introduce myself. I'm Antonio Alvarez. You can call me Toni."

"I'd rather call you gone," I retorted, turning back to the cart.

He chuckled. "You're funny, eh? I thought so. Sorry about scaring you, though."

"You didn't scare me."

"Patrick told a different story."

I replaced the sunglasses I'd been holding, then I turned back to him, adopting the stern face I used when addressing my sisters. "Did he? Well, you didn't."

"Whoa, now, let's not get feisty," he said, grinning and shaking his head. "I just thought I'd apologize if I scared you at all—you know, with my whole mock haunting thing."

I stared at him, not buying his apology one bit.

He squirmed a little under my stare, but then his joking manner was back. He pulled out his hands, raising them in defeat. "Listen, no need to get upset, beautiful. I'm new to this whole thing, all right?"

"What thing? The going invisible thing?"

"Oops." He paused with a small wince. "Eek, I'm in trouble now." Then suddenly his grin was back. "But yeah, that."

"So, are you mock haunting me *now?*"

"Not at all. Is it illegal for me to come to a mall or something?"

"Is that how invisible people spend their Saturdays?"

"That or sitting at home, bored. What do you think I'd choose?"

"I don't know—I don't know you."

He grunted a little, but it wasn't a negative sound. He was enjoying himself. "You pretend too, though. Also, while we're on the subject—are you going to call him or what?"

"Who?" I asked, though I knew very well who he meant. After all, Patrick was really the only thing we had in common.

Toni rolled his eyes. "Look, I can tell that you're a tough girl or whatever, but you really need to talk to him. There are some things you've got to know—for your own safety."

His eyes suddenly widened, and he leaned quickly toward me, reaching out—I flinched, but he was reaching for a pair of glasses that had caught his eye, not for my throat. "They're amazing!" he gasped, cradling them in his hands. "I've been looking for a pair like this for . . . for years!"

I tried to calm my pounding heart by pressing a hand to my chest, and I couldn't keep the glare off my face. "What's your problem?"

He glanced over at me, still fondling the glasses. "At the moment? No *moolah*. Can you lend me fifteen bucks? Plus tax?"

"Why would I do that?" I asked, too shocked by his asking to sound appropriately upset.

"Cuz you're beautiful *and* nice?" he tried.

"Not going to work," I assured him.

That mischievous look was back. "I guess I could just go invisible and steal them."

"You're a creep," I said, even as I started to dig through my purse. "You owe me," I told him, though I wasn't sure what made me say the words. Heaven knew I never wanted to see him again.

"Sure, sure, just hand it over," he said greedily, hand open and waiting. I started to hand him the money, then I glimpsed the price tag. "They're thirteen, you creep—not fifteen."

"Whoops. My dyslexia." His grin only widened. "It's betting getter, though. Get it? *Getting better*, betting getter, eh?"

I didn't laugh at his joke, but for some reason I still handed him the money he needed. "Don't try to swindle me again."

"Swindle? People still use that word? What sort of nerd are you?" He saw my face and reevaluated his next words. "Very well. Never again. But by again, do you mean that you would *like* to see me again?"

"Just pay for those glasses and get away from me, all right?"

I watched him carefully, just to be sure he'd actually pay for them and not just pocket the money, but as soon as the money was safely out of his hands I turned and started walking back toward the store where I'd left Lee.

Toni was right at my heels. "Didn't you want a pair?"

"Not anymore. You spent my funds."

"Want some ice cream? My treat."

"Why are you trying to be nice to me all of a sudden?"

"Truthfully? I want you to call Patrick so he'll go back to school, so I can have some time alone without his brooding company. That, and you're beautiful."

"Why would I go anywhere with you? I don't even know what you are."

"Ouch." He clutched his shirt near his heart, grimacing. "That was a little harsh, don't you think?"

"You're not human," I stated.

I shouldn't have been surprised by his answer, but the easy way he said it made the words seem more out of place than they already were.

"Nope, I'm not—but does that mean I'm evil? No." His eyes suddenly brightened, and he stopped walking. "Is that your hot friend? The goth one?"

I followed his eyes and saw Lee paying for her few purchases at the counter, several yards away from us. She hadn't seen us yet, but that would change any second now.

"Go away," I hissed, stepping in front of him to better block his view of Lee. I waved a hand at him, looking urgently over my shoulder at my best friend as I did so.

"You're kidding, right? I've been wanting to talk to her for a whole week!" He moved to take a step forward, but I grabbed his arm in my harshest grip.

"Ow!" he protested. "Why *do* that? *Why?*"

"Disappear *right now!*" I ordered, tightening my grip on his arm.

"Lee!" he called, grinning as he stepped around me. "Yo!"

I released him because I refused to look like an idiot in front of Lee, but I know he didn't miss my seething look. Not that it bothered him at all. He only smiled and stepped around me.

I turned with him to see Lee carrying a large bag. Of course, it was black.

"Hey!" She grinned, looking a bit too pleased to see him. "I wondered if I'd run into you again. Toni, right?"

"Exactly. And you won't *believe* how badly I've been wanting to run into *you*." He took her hand and actually kissed it. He then turned quickly back to me. "Your friend here was just telling me that you guys were getting hungry. My treat?"

"I thought you said you didn't have any cash on you," I inserted darkly.

"Posh," he said, shrugging me off. "I've always got a little something to spend on beautiful girls. What do you say?" I didn't miss the fact that he was pretty much just staring at her.

It was true that I believed he was pretty harmless at this point, but I still didn't want to leave him alone with my best friend. So when Lee gushed a much-too-happy yes, I reluctantly followed them, feeling more than a little shut out as Toni held her arm and Lee laughed at almost everything he said.

Once at the food court, Toni led her toward a Chinese place. As he pulled her chair out for her, he handed me her shopping bag—extra proof that I was the third wheel here. Rolling my eyes a little, I took my own seat and then Toni went to get our food.

Lee turned surprised but happy eyes toward me. "Kate, seriously, what just happened?"

"A creepy Hispanic guy just kissed your hand," I said dully.

"Don't be racist—it's so not you." But she wasn't upset with me. Her eyes were wide and pleased. "He remembered me! I can't believe that just happened. That's the sort of thing that happens to popular girls—or to you. Not me. He held my arm!"

I sighed but didn't reply—what was the point arguing? She wasn't going to listen. Besides, I didn't want her to know that he was the Invisible Man. If she found out about that, she would have to find out about the rest. And *that* wasn't happening.

"'Kay, I know this is sort of cheating," she whispered, leaning over the table toward me. "But, what's his aura like? Is he as happy as I am?"

I regarded her aura carefully. "Actually, I'd say you're more excited than happy. You're as pink as Barbie's favorite ball gown."

She slapped my arm, but before she could question me again about his aura, he was returning.

Once Toni was back, we all began eating a nice late lunch/early dinner of ham fried rice and orange chicken. During the meal *I* became the invisible person. Toni and Lee talked nonstop to each other and seemed to totally forget about my existence. As a result I finished much sooner than they did, and I was left to watch them flirt with each other.

I used a lot more concentration and precision to crack my fortune cookie than was absolutely necessary and carefully studied my fortune.

Good things are coming your way.

Ha. Like I believed that. Between Toni and Patrick and troubles with Aaron—I really doubted there was a lot of good in my future. Still, I folded the slip of paper and slid it into my purse. It would go in a wooden box that sat on my bookshelf, containing a hundred other fortunes.

As I was bending over, my phone vibrated, signaling a message. Lee was still talking animatedly with Toni, but as I flipped open the phone and saw it was from her, I realized that she was more proficient in the texting art than I'd ever imagined.

Plz!

That was all, but it was enough. I closed my phone and glanced up, and Lee was turning toward me. "Kate, I know we had our plans, but—could you meet me back at my house? Toni can take me back later."

I looked between them—Lee's silent pleading, Toni's grin and rapidly bobbing eyebrows. "Sure," I said at last, perhaps a moment too late. I looked between them again, then took the more-than-obvious hint to stand. My purse was balanced on my shoulder, and I picked up Lee's bag with the other hand. "I guess I'll—I'll see you guys later then."

Lee smiled thankfully, and Toni's grin impossibly widened. "Can't wait—it was good to run into you again, Kate." His words could have been ominous, but looking at his cocky face I only wanted to roll my eyes.

I turned away from them, hoping that I was right in assuming he wasn't dangerous as I slowly walked away. For a moment I debated wandering the mall a little longer, but I knew Lee wouldn't want me running into them again, so I decided just to head back to her house. I walked around a small group of whining children and their distressed mother, then circled the large fountain that dominated the main floor of the mall. The floor was crowded and noisy, and the pounding of the water made it seem even more chaotic.

But despite the crazy surroundings, somehow I heard the footsteps behind me. Call it heightened senses or stalker-awareness, but I was distinctly aware of the sound of someone following me. I glanced cautiously over my shoulder, but I couldn't see anyone directly behind me. I was about to turn back around when I noticed—several long paces behind me—a large, middle-aged man.

He had tanned skin and was dressed well in lightly colored slacks. It almost looked like he'd just got off from a day at the office, even though it was a Saturday. He had a phone pressed against his ear, but so did half the other people around us. No, there were really only two things that made this man different from the others. For one thing, he had a thin black aura. For another, he was staring right at me, slowly tracing my steps.

thirteen

Aman with a black aura was following me.
He was smiling a little as he caught my eye and realized I knew what he was doing.

My throat constricted, and I had trouble breathing. I bit my lower lip and quickened my step, but not too much—I was trembling so badly I worried I wouldn't be able to run if he tried to chase.

My heart throbbed against my chest, my wide eyes searched for an answer—for a safe getaway. A distant part of me was wondering if Toni was somehow responsible for this, but I didn't let myself pursue that avenue of thought for long. Instead, I did the only thing I could think of doing—I snatched my phone out of my pocket, and in a short second it was against my ear.

It rang three times, and I was starting to really panic when there was a sudden click. I heard his lilting voice, sounding confused.

"Hello?"

"Patrick," I said, forcing myself to sound calm. "It's me."

"Kate?"

"Yeah. So, um . . ." I glanced back over my shoulder, and sure enough, the man was still following me, though there were a couple emo boys between us now. It was a small relief to see that he wasn't closing the distance between us, only maintaining it. "I'm sorry I haven't called before now."

"No, that's fine—I told you to take your time." His voice, though he tried to mask it, was laced with excitement. Though normally I might have blushed at the thought that he was glad I'd called, I was too nervous about my situation to care about girlie things like that.

"Look, I think I have a problem," I said, talking the instant he'd stopped. "You know how you told me about those black auras?"

There was a very slight pause, and then, "Where are you?" His excitement was gone in an instant, replaced by a serious tone that bordered on dangerous. "What's going on?"

His protective words made my body thrill in unfamiliar ways, and I had to swallow hard before I could speak. "I'm at the mall. There's a man—he's following me, and he has a black aura."

"Kate, I need you to listen to me very carefully. Do not let him near you. Don't touch his skin, no matter what."

"What should I do?" I asked. Despite my hard efforts, fear underlined my words, and I hated that.

"Are you with anyone?" I heard something slam on Patrick's end, and I imagined it was a door.

"No. I was with Lee, but then—Toni—they're hanging out somewhere . . ."

"Toni's there?" Patrick's voice was surprised, along with a balanced mix of exasperation and gratitude. "Can you find him?"

"I don't know—they left—I'm almost to the outer doors."

I heard muttering, and though it probably wasn't meant for me, I heard the words anyway. "Of course he'd take the car. I'm going to kill him . . . Kate—" His voice was suddenly louder. "I'm going to call him. I want you to keep walking, and—"

"No, wait! I don't want Lee to know what's happening!"

"Kate—"

I overrode his protest. "No. I don't want her to know. I can't have her know."

"I . . . Kate, I'm running, but I'm not going to get there in time to do—"

"I can make it to my car." My voice was growing more confident. "I shouldn't have even called, I overreacted—"

"Kate," he interrupted firmly. "Don't hang up." He sighed loudly—somehow it sounded like a silent curse. "How close is he?"

I glanced over my shoulder and blinked in surprise. I stopped walking and scanned the crowd, but it was as if he'd disappeared.

"Kate?" Patrick's voice was tight, and I could hear his pounding footfalls.

"He—he's gone," I said, hardly believing my own words.

There was a very brief silence, and then he was speaking quickly. "I want you to go to your car. If you see him, scream. Cause some commotion—just don't let him get close to you."

"Why?"

"I'll explain la—"

"Right now," I cut in, my fear channeling into anger. "You'll explain right now."

He groaned loudly. "Of all the—look, can you just wait for five minutes?"

"No. What does he want? Who is he?" I was starting to lose it, and the people around me seemed to notice. I ignored the few weird looks and continued darting through the crowd a bit too quickly to be considered normal. In seconds I was outside, hesitating on the sidewalk as I stared out across the vast parking lot. Where on earth had I parked?

I knew Patrick was reluctant to say anything, but I guess he decided that appeasing me was better than refusing. Smart of him. "He's a Demon."

"A Demon?" I admit, I was disbelieving. I randomly chose a row and started fast-walking past the line of parked cars.

"Yes. I know it hardly makes sense, but—he can't hurt you. Demons can't touch humans unless humans first touch them. A safety precaution, not that they haven't found ways around it."

"What does he want with me?" I asked again, spotting my car two rows over. I cut between some SUVs and all but ran toward my car. It looked like the most inviting sanctuary I'd ever seen. Amazing how it had been my escape twice now in the same week.

Patrick's intense running was beginning to reveal itself in his voice. He was starting to sound winded. "He wants your help—I'll get into all that later, though. Are you to your car yet?" Though I don't know what he thought he'd achieve by still running toward me—he'd made it perfectly clear that he was far away from here—the thought that he was still running caused my stomach to flip.

"Almost—" A car honked loudly at me, and I hopped around the hood, probably less affected by the near-miss than I should've been.

At last I was at my car. I dropped Lee's bag to the ground as I dug in my purse for my keys. "Come on, come on, come on," I muttered. Patrick didn't comment on my ramblings. But then, he was busy panting.

Finally I heard them jingle and a second later I snatched them up. As soon as the door was open, I was jumping inside—Lee's bag caught up and thrown on the passenger seat almost as an afterthought. "I'm in," I gasped into the phone, slapping the lock back into place with an open palm.

"Good," he said, sounding extremely relieved.

"Did Toni do this?" I couldn't help but demand, now that I was relatively safe. "Was this some sort of trap?"

"No. Toni may be irresponsible, but he couldn't have known a Demon was there."

"Why not?" I asked sharply. I didn't like how he was shooting down my theory without any consideration.

"Because Guardians can't see Demons."

"Guardians? Seriously, what is going on?"

"Kate, can you come get me? I'll explain everything, I promise."

I sat in the driver's seat, breathing hard—more from the adrenaline rush than the actual hurry to get to safety. For a moment, I wavered, wondering if it was really such a good idea to be alone with him. Then I saw the black aura man—the Demon—just coming out of the mall and I caved.

"Where are you?" I asked Patrick, forcing the key into the ignition and keeping my head low as the Demon scanned the lot.

fourteen

We remained on our phones until we made eye contact a few minutes later—he was walking on the sidewalk, and I was pulling up to the curb beside him. He closed his phone without a word and smoothly moved the last steps to the idling car. I shut my phone a half-second after he did, but continued to hold it as I leaned over to flip his lock open. As I drew back in my seat, I took in his appearance with a quick glance through the window.

He looked like he always did—faded light jeans and a blue button-up shirt with sleeves rolled at the elbows. I noticed that he had a bracelet on his wrist, and I wondered if he'd always had it and I just hadn't noticed. It appeared to be homemade, and it looked like some dark kind of leather braiding. His thick brown hair was somewhat shaggier than usual, but his clear blue eyes were as captivating as ever. His strong jaw was tight with worry, and as he opened the door and lowered himself inside, I found myself staring at his muscular body—so lean and hard and powerful. I hated to admit it to myself, but I felt infinitely safer with him in the car than I had for a long time. And I wasn't just referring to the Demon from the mall or any of the other strange things that had started happening since I'd met Patrick. I hadn't felt this relaxed and safe since my parents had died.

Not that I was completely relaxed in his presence. My heart

rate—which had just managed to slow down—had picked up dramatically the moment I turned the corner and caught sight of him. Now I was trying to control my breathing before he could notice. Luckily he was currently breathing hard enough for both of us, so it masked my own unsteady breaths. Still, I strictly ordered myself to get a grip.

He turned to me, his intense gaze studying my face, scrutinizing for any sign that I'd lied, and that I really wasn't okay.

I stared right back at him, wordlessly searching his face for any sign that I'd made the wrong choice in coming here. But it didn't take a hard look to know that I hadn't made a mistake. The worry on his face was undeniable, and his eyes . . . well, I got swallowed up by the now-familiar crystalline blue.

"Are you all right?" he asked in a low whisper, his gaze still locked on my face.

I nodded a bit shakily. "Yeah. I mean, I still don't know what's going on, and I still have the creeps, but . . . I'm here."

His eyes lingered on my face a second longer, and then he was looking away, reaching for his seat belt and glancing around the empty street.

We were in the more industrial area of town, which was usually dead no matter what time you came, due to the hard financial times that had caused pretty much the whole area to shut down. But on a Saturday afternoon, we were completely alone. It was common knowledge that gangs met around here and drug deals went down at night, but . . .

My brow furrowed as the questions escalated in my mind, forming dangerous answers. "Wait a minute—what are you doing out here? And without a car?"

He forced his seat belt into place and then looked back up at me. He replied calmly, though his eyes hinted at uneasiness. "I live here."

I felt my eyes widen. "You what?"

"Toni and I." He clarified. "We live several blocks to the northwest, in an abandoned warehouse."

"Since when?" I demanded. "What about your par . . ." but I couldn't finish the question, and my eyes narrowed. Of course he wasn't normal—he wouldn't have parents and a real house. I just hadn't pictured him living in a vacant building on the west side—and especially not with the Invisible Man.

"What are you?" I demanded at last, though I could have used a harsher tone, I thought, once the words were out. I almost sounded scared. *Was* I scared? Of Patrick? For a short moment, I honestly wasn't sure.

And then he spoke—his voice still gentle, trying to force me into an ease he obviously wasn't totally feeling. Still, just the sound of his voice assured me that he didn't intend to hurt me.

"Kate, I'm a Guardian."

Personally I thought he should have sounded a bit more uneasy about revealing such a deep dark secret, but he didn't. He almost looked relieved to be finally telling me.

Not that his words meant anything to me. *I'm an alien from outer space* would have been more believable, because at least I'd know what I could expect from him: brain sucking, human annihilation, world domination, that sort of thing. In all honesty, Patrick's revelation had revealed nothing.

Well, almost nothing.

"You're not human?" I asked, my fingers curling more tightly around the steering wheel.

I watched his eyes flicker, and I knew he hadn't missed the tense action. His voice contained more caution than before. "I was, once."

Just what was I supposed to do with that? He wasn't clearing anything up.

I swallowed hard, trying hard to keep the edge in my voice. I needed to exert some authority—let him know that I was still in charge of this conversation. "What happened to you?" I asked, hoping it was a legitimate question.

He shrugged a single shoulder, his voice still calm. "I died."

I blanched, despite my best intentions. "You're dead?" I half-gasped. "Like a ghost?"

"Not quite."

Was he fighting a smile?

I blew out my breath and forced my eyes closed. I shook my head before letting it fall back against my seat. "I can't believe this is happening to me," I moaned.

"Denial is always the initial reaction," he assured me, in what he must have supposed was a soothing voice. "I promise, this isn't all as bad as it seems."

I opened my eyes and rolled my head against the seat to regard him. "Really? Because right now things aren't looking so good. Demons, Guardians, ghosts, auras . . . I think I liked it better when I just thought you were a weird Irishman. Or even an alien."

"Um, thanks?" He chuckled softly but briefly. He bit his lower lip and then nodded toward the front of the car. "You're wasting gas. Let's go somewhere we can talk."

"Where?" I questioned, my body tensing in fear so quickly that my voice caught.

He shook his head once, his clear eyes open and reassuring. "Anywhere that will make you comfortable, Kate. Preferably a place where we can safely discuss things, without being overheard."

I considered briefly, my inner voice screaming for me to kick him out of the car and drive away at top speed. But my curiosity and—I'll admit it—my desire to keep Patrick close (along with all the mixed but wonderful feelings he inspired inside me) won out in the end. I shifted to first and pulled back onto the deserted street. I pulled a sharp U-turn, and headed back toward town, a destination—the *only* destination—firmly in my mind.

Patrick didn't say anything as we drove, and I didn't bother to fill the silence. I wondered how much more my life could change in a single year, and then decided I didn't really want to know. Still, I had a feeling I was about to find out.

Patrick sat with one hand curled over his wrist, his elbows resting on his knees and his eyes staring out the passenger window. He didn't ask where I was taking him, and he only made one comment the whole drive. I'd pushed the power button on the radio, hoping that the sound would help to alleviate the oppressive silence, and I asked if he minded the music. He said that he didn't and then went right back to quietly gazing out the window.

I could only guess that he was organizing his thoughts. My one wish was that I could empty my reeling mind.

Before I was quite ready to be there, I was pulling through the familiar gate on the tree-lined road, which was really more like a driveway. If Patrick found it odd that we were driving into a cemetery, he didn't say so. Maybe he recognized the sense in me choosing the place that would take me closer to my parents, and maybe he didn't. Either way, I wasn't going to talk about my reasons for choosing this particular spot.

I navigated through the winding roadways, loving the instant comfort that came with the secluded area. Short and round pine trees dotted the acreage, and a carpet of green grass spread around the varied headstones and shrubs. I steered toward a newer section of the grounds, stopping when I found a good place to pull closer to the edge of the grass. I wasn't completely off the road, but another car could squeeze past if they were careful. Not that it was a really busy place, of course.

I pulled up the emergency brake and twisted the key, shutting off the car and cutting the wave of sound created by the radio. In the sudden silence, I turned expectantly toward him, feeling jittery.

He was still looking out his window, his breathing normal again. He didn't seem to be sitting on the edge of his seat, like I certainly was.

Finally he undid his seat belt and glanced over at me. "Should we walk?" he asked me quietly.

I nodded once and then curtly opened my door. I left my purse and Lee's bag behind, but I pocketed my phone and keys.

Once I was standing outside, I said automatically, "Lock your door. My car's pretty old school—no automatic locks." It was the same explanation I'd intoned a hundred times, but something was different this time, not that I could put a finger on the strange emotion I was feeling.

Patrick locked the door easily and then thinly smiled over the roof of the car at me. "That's okay. I like old things." He shut his door, and I followed suit a heartbeat after.

He pushed his hands deep into his pockets and then watched me carefully, wondering what I would do next.

I took a deep breath, pulling in the warmly scented air—freshly mown grass, bright sun, sweet flowers—and then I walked around the hood of my car, moving slowly. The quiet, peaceful surroundings prompted my careful mood despite my current situation—standing here with Patrick, unsure of who or what he was, unsure of what he was about to tell me, and certainly unwilling to think about how my whole life would be affected.

Once I was standing in front of Patrick I hesitated, then finally gave in and waved a hand vaguely around us. "Um—let's go that way."

"I'll follow you," he said simply. But he spoke with such sincerity, I wondered if he meant something more.

I started walking, weaving my way between the headstones, and he fell into step beside me. "So," I said. "Is this like, reverse psychology? You making me feel like I'm in control or something, even though I'm not?"

"I just want you to be as . . . comfortable as possible. This isn't exactly an easy thing to digest."

I glanced over at him, but the low breeze lifted strands of hair into my face, brushing across my eyes and obscuring my view of his face. I raised a hand and combed the errant hairs back behind my ears, then nodded at him. "Okay—I'm listening."

He pressed his lips together and looked ahead of us, considering, then slowly he began. "You knew something was different about me the first time you saw me. Or rather, my aura. Mine was the first silver aura you'd encountered, and so confusion would—"

I shook my head, interrupting his words. "No. I'd seen Toni. The idiot stepped in front of my car. I thought I'd gone insane, because Lee couldn't see him."

Patrick blew out his breath. "Right. Toni was . . . not supposed to show himself to you. He's sort of, well . . . he has disciplinary issues. That's why he got paired up with me, actually. I'm supposed to teach him self-control."

"You've got your work cut out for you,"

He gave one of those half grins. "Yeah, thanks." He ducked his head, sighing deeply. "Anyway, I was *supposed* to be the first person you saw. Then I was supposed to befriend you."

"Make me comfortable?" I guessed easily, some sarcasm leaking into my tone.

He nodded but didn't take his eyes off the ground. "Exactly. And I thought it was working, until you avoided me last Saturday."

"I saw you, talking to Toni," I said softly, lost in the memory. The sight of them, the feeling of fear and distrust building inside of me as I watched them together . . . "I heard you two in the front yard at Lee's, and . . . all my worries about you came back."

He was quiet for a short moment, and then—his voice almost overcome with regret—he continued. "And then I acted horribly, solidifying your fears. You surprised me with your accusations at lunch, and I was anything but reassuring as I chased you down. I was just so worried that you'd run away and I wouldn't have the chance to warn you."

"About the Demons?"

He finally looked up at me, his expression grave. "Yes."

I straightened, almost unconsciously lengthening my stride at the same time. "In the parking lot, you said that you came here for me. What did you mean? And how did you know about my . . . abilities?"

He spoke in an exhale, the words obviously somewhat rehearsed. "When a person has a very threatening near-death experience, they are literally changed. They see things differently, because they *are* different now. A Seer is split between worlds. They live on two separate planes of existence, which barely manage to coexist."

"I'm still human, though?" I asked, my voice uncharacteristically timid.

His eyes slid over to me, a thin smile twisting his lips. "Of course. You're just—special. You're a Seer, Kate."

"A Seer?"

"Because you see auras. You can discern the difference between beings—discern which plane a being exists on by the color of their aura."

"I sort of guessed that's what it meant," I told him, a little too snidely perhaps.

He held up a hand in defense. "I'm sorry. I didn't mean to offend you. I just wanted to clarify. I want this to make sense."

I sighed deeply, trying to let the fight leave me completely. My shoulders relaxed, and my voice was almost contrite. "Sorry, I'll try not to do that again. I just—I get snappy when I'm off-balance."

His response was hurried. "Don't apologize—you have a lot to take in. You've earned the right to be snappy." He hesitated—I thought he might say something more. He didn't.

We took a few steps in silence, then I dove back in. "So, everyone who almost experiences death is able to see auras?"

"Most," he allowed. "But only a select few are actually considered Seers. When we find you—as in, anyone who survives death—we Guardians keep an eye on you, to determine how severe your sight is. Generally, a person who nearly suffers death loses the ability to see auras before they regain full alertness. Most leave the hospital unchanged, with only a glimpse at the other plane—the colors—and that is hardly ever remembered. Unless the accident was extreme, in which case, the sight lingers. Sometimes it takes days to disappear completely, but by the time it does most people forget they ever saw anything unusual, and those who remember the auras force themselves to forget. Some people—like you—are quite obviously Seers, but sometimes Guardians are able to take that sight away. Some—again, like you—can't be blinded."

"You tried to . . . take my ability away?" I don't know why I was so mortified at the thought, but it just seemed so . . . invasive.

He nodded, watching me carefully. It was now that I realized we'd stopped walking. "That day I held the door for you," he said slowly. "I was trying to achieve one of two things. I either wanted to take your special vision away, or assure you that I meant you no harm. Blinding a Seer—if they can be blinded—is a simple enough thing. Guardians have a few special talents—the ability to let others feel our essence, or soul—which is generally the best way to assure Seers of our sincerity—and also the ability to draw a veil over Seers with imperfect or weak sight." He bit his lower lip. "I couldn't block your vision or manipulate it in any way. It's too strong. But I hope I was able to convince you that I mean you no harm, Kate."

I decided to ignore that last part, and so I started walking again. He followed slowly, and we fell into step again. "So," I began gradually. "Since you're still around, I guess that means you're not done with me. So what do you want?"

One eye squinted a bit, as if he wasn't sure how to put things delicately. "Mostly, I'm here for your own protection. Until you decide what you want to do," he added more quickly.

"My protection?"

His voice was suddenly strained, and he wasn't looking right at me anymore. "Guardians aren't the only ones who hunt for Seers," he said at last.

"You mean the Demons?" I asked, but it was really more for clarification than an actual question.

He answered me anyway. "Yes."

I hesitated. "When you say Demon, do you mean like, of the devil?"

He thought about that, and then pointed toward a spot on the grass. "Maybe we should sit down for this part? It might take a while."

He waited for me to lead the way, which I did after a moment's pause. Once we were seated on the lumpy ground, Patrick began to speak.

"As you've probably noticed, the world isn't exactly what you thought it was. There's more going on than most people realize." He was slipping into these words more easily, like he was used to this part of the conversation. Like he'd gone over this a hundred times before. I wasn't sure how I felt about that. For some reason, I didn't like to think of Patrick watching over other Seers. Especially female ones.

Was I actually feeling jealous?

Knock it off, my inner logic hissed, *and pay attention!*

"When you die," Patrick said carefully. "You are given a choice. You can go on to Heaven—which is actually any and every definition of paradise—or you can become a Guardian.

"Paradise is what most people choose—it's the logical choice. You move on to a better existence, and you get to live with your friends and family forever. You continue to do the things that made you happy here, and you're basically surrounded with peace and joy. There's no sorrow or pain."

I couldn't stop myself from cutting in. "You mean, my parents are alive still? They're just in Heaven?" Of course I'd been raised on Christian beliefs, but this was actual proof that my faith hadn't been in vain.

He nodded gently. "We don't stop living when we die here. We just exist somewhere else. Just as the sun doesn't disappear or cease to exist at night—it's just in another place. Or, more specifically, a different plane. One that even a Seer can't penetrate."

I flashed back to their funeral—to the words that had been said by so many. "So my parents really are in a better place?" I whispered.

His hand twitched on the ground between us, but he didn't touch me. "They couldn't be happier, I'm sure. Someday, you'll be reunited with them."

Patrick was quiet for a moment, letting me absorb this.

"Can I . . . ? Can I talk to them?"

The pity was clear in his eyes. "No. I'm sorry. Once you've made the choice, there's no going back. They can't return to the earthly plane. At least, not visibly. Their memory and some of their essence remains, but they've moved on. You won't see them again until you move on too."

I nodded, trying to show him that I didn't care that much anyway, but I wasn't fooling him. I decided to ask another question that would steer the conversation away from my parents. "What about kids? When they die—are they given the choice?"

Patrick shook his head quickly. "No. Those who die in infancy, or as young children, go immediately to Heaven. And actually, they remain their death age until their parents join them in Heaven. Then their parents are able to finish raising them, having all of the experiences that they missed out on before death's separation. Of course, there are differences; Heaven is perfect, after all. No sadness, or pain, or sickness."

"Wait—you don't stay your same age after you die?"

"You become the perfect age after you die—twenty-five. Unless you died young, as I mentioned before."

I blew out my breath. It was a lot to take in.

He watched me carefully, then—at a silent look from me—he took up the story again. "Since all choices are final once you're dead, not many people choose to become Guardians. Because once you've signed up for that, you can never move on. You can never go to Paradise."

"But *you* chose it," I said, sounding almost accusing.

"Yes, I did. So did Toni, though we both had very different motivations." He shook his head a little, as if recalling some distant memory. I couldn't tell if it was amusing, or sad. But then the moment was past, and he was back in storytelling mode. "A Guardian's job is to return to the earthly plane, mostly human. We have a few notable differences, obviously."

"Like being able to go invisible?"

He nodded once. "Right."

"How do you do that, anyway?"

He shrugged a little. "It's sort of our default mode, actually. It takes effort to be visible—I just have to think about going invisible, and, well, it happens. That's how all of our . . ." He searched for the right word.

"Quirks?" I offered.

His half grin was back. "Exactly. That's just how they work."

"But I could still see you," I protested, my brow furrowing.

"Seer," he hinted delicately.

"Oh. Right." I'd almost forgotten. "So I can see you, no matter what?"

Patrick nodded. "Touch me, talk to me—for you, I'd appear completely normal. Because when I'm invisible, I'm not on the earthly plane—I'm on the . . . Guardian plane, which you can still interact with."

I briefly wondered if he was invisible now, but I felt too weird asking that particular question. So I asked another one. "What else is different about you? Aside from being invisible?"

"Well, we're sort of immortal."

"*Sort of?*"

"We don't age and we can't die."

"Sounds like complete immortality to me," I said, awed. I shook my head, as if to clear it from all these impossible things. "So, you're immortal and you can go invisible—anything else I should know?"

He considered that, while subconsciously toying with the bracelet on his wrist. "Not anything that immediately comes to mind. Those are the big things."

"So wait a minute—how long have you been a Guardian?"

He answered without having to think. "Since 1798."

I blinked and nearly choked. "But that's . . ."

"A really long time," he agreed, a small smile cracking his face. "I know. Eternity is longer than you ever imagined, trust me."

I was still full of questions about him, but I could tell that he was eager to get on with his explanation, so I told myself not to interrupt anymore. There would be another time to hear more about his personal history. I hoped.

"Guardians have really only one purpose. One reason for existence. And that's to protect humans."

"From the Demons?"

"Yes. But that becomes difficult, because we can't tell the difference between Demons and Humans. Only a Seer can do that."

"So, you enlist the help of Seers to help track down these Demons?" I guessed, not really liking where this was going.

He nodded and deftly plucked out a blade of grass, pinching it tightly between his fingers. "But sometimes Seers would rather . . . not get involved? That's a good way of putting it. Either way, we try to protect them too. Because where a Seer is, Demons are never far away."

"May I ask why that is?"

"Demons want to find Guardians almost as much as we want

to find them. They try to enlist Seers too, and since there aren't that many to go around, well . . . There's usually a bit of a fight." He tossed the sliver of grass aside, and then shifted his position—pulling one bent leg up to his chest.

"Are Demons like, Guardians gone bad?" I asked, pulling both knees up to my chest and wrapping my arms tightly around them. "Can they go invisible too?"

"Demons exist on the same plane as Guardians. We're the middle plane, I guess you could say. Our plane separates the earthly from the heavenly. But I'm getting off topic. Demons are immortal, and they usually spend more time invisible than not, since that takes less effort than going visible, but that's pretty much where the similarities between Guardians and Demons end. They are completely different from us."

"They were once human?"

"Until they met death." He shifted his weight again, moving to stretch out his legs and lean back on his hands, which were balanced against the ground behind him. His strong, lean arms tensed, taking his weight easily. "It takes a lot of evil to become a Demon. I mean, a person can lie and steal their whole life, and still get the choice between Guardian and Paradise. (Just for the record, most of the shadier people choose to be a Guardian, so they're closer to the life they knew. Something about the idea of Heaven scares them.) Anyway, unless you're a murderer, or something equally as bad, you're not in danger of becoming a Demon. But when a human with a corrupt heart dies, they aren't given a choice. They're sent to some sort of probational prison, until everyone who knew them is dead. Then they're sent back to Earth, where they usually try to get even by corrupting humans."

"That's very thoughtful of the Man in Charge—to let them come back."

Patrick cracked a smile. "I don't try to understand or judge. I'm just here to help keep them under control."

"So you're like . . ." *Parole officer* didn't sound very flattering, so I went with my next thought. "A guardian angel?"

He frowned, though I could tell from his somewhat exasperated expression that he'd heard the comparison before. It was obvious he didn't appreciate it any more this time around. "That's where humans got the whole concept, but we prefer just Guardians. Some of us—like Toni—aren't exactly angelic material."

"So, you're more like the Demons' prison guards? That kinda stinks that you can't tell who's a Demon and who's not."

"Well, we can always keep an eye on the suspicious ones and then see if they go invisible. Then it's a pretty educated guess." He shrugged. "You're right, though, it makes it a little tough."

"So, that Demon in the mall—he wants me to be his eyes? So he can avoid Guardians?"

Patrick nodded but spoke quickly. "But trust me, the last thing you want is to work for a Demon. They're not exactly . . . stable. Driven by hate and revenge, they care little about others."

I raised my eyebrows at him. "Well, I guess I'll scratch 'go find a demon to serve' off my to-do list for the day."

He laughed once and shook his head. "This limits your career options, I'm sure."

"Back to the drawing board," I agreed with a small smile, pleased with myself for making him laugh.

He plucked another piece of grass from the lawn and absently began to twist it around his fingers. He continued to watch me, waiting for me to bring us back to the important conversation.

I searched briefly for a good question, and was instantly overwhelmed by them. I picked the easiest to word. "Why are the Demons afraid of you? I mean, it's not like you can kill them or anything. They're immortal. Why be intimidated?"

"They are immortal, so technically they can't *die*. But we can still take care of them." Patrick drew up his right leg and pulled the cuff up, away from his shoe. Then he pulled out a dagger that had been sheathed against his calf and looked at me, as if this would suddenly make everything clear to me.

I couldn't help but flinch at the sudden appearance of the weapon, but that didn't stop Patrick from balancing it on his palm and holding it out toward me. It wasn't in a threatening manner at all, but still it made me uneasy. It was obviously not a butter knife he had balanced on his open palm. "We only use it on Demons that have threatened a human soul or have endangered a Seer's life," he assured me quietly. He paused, and then allowed, "Generally, anyway."

"What good does it do, if it doesn't kill them?" I asked, still staring at the blade. It wasn't too long—maybe the length of my hand—but it was chillingly sharp. The hilt was lightly decorated, but equally small. Yet size wasn't everything. It still looked deadly to me.

"A stab in the heart banishes them from Earth forever," Patrick explained. "Most remember their first time in Prison well enough to know that they're better off here, so usually they don't give us a lot of trouble. Some, though, are too consumed with revenge to care. Others follow a higher order than themselves." He shrugged. "Bullets aren't effective, but a knife will do the trick every time."

"What do you mean about a higher order?" I wondered if he was trying to be cryptic on purpose, and thought briefly about slapping his arm.

"Well, we Guardians are pretty organized. We have leaders we report too, we have a system for finding and protecting Seers; it only makes sense that Demons—at least some of them—would organize themselves too."

"So, there's like a Demon government, or something?"

"A Demon King, or Lord as he prefers, but close enough."

I shivered despite the warmth of the day. "That's not creepy or anything," I muttered.

Despite our topic, Patrick seemed completely relaxed. "It's

really nothing to be worried about. He keeps his head low, and he always uses underlings to do his bidding. Honestly, you'll never have to worry about that side of the Demon world."

"So, what side *do* I need to be worried about?"

Patrick nodded a little and resheathed his dagger. "Good question. As you've already experienced, local Demons will take an interest in you for a while."

"For how long?" I asked, inwardly shuddering at the thought of being stalked all over again. The fear I'd felt at the mall had yet to completely disappear, and I wasn't exactly looking forward to going through something like that again.

"It depends on how desperate they are; how badly they want a Seer. But don't worry—Toni and I are here for exactly this reason. I've been assigned to be your Guardian, and I don't take that responsibility lightly. As long as you need protection, I'll be here. The more you're willing to help us hunt them down, the sooner you can go back to your old life—unless at that point you decide to become a full-time Seer for the Guardians."

I gave him my best "are you serious?" look, and he seemed to get the point, though he only smiled. "It's something to think about," he said in defense of himself. "You could help a lot of people."

"I guess I've just never considered Demon-hunting as a possible career path," I said evenly.

He chuckled, and then suddenly rolled to his feet. Towering over me, I was struck once again by how truly breathtaking he was. He offered a hand, which I took. He helped hoist me up, but once I was standing, he dropped my hand. I was almost startled to feel the tingle that filled my empty palm, and I wished more than anything in that moment that he would wrap his fingers around mine again.

Stupid.

We started wandering back in the general direction of the car, a careful distance keeping our bodies from touching.

He was quiet for probably a full minute before he spoke, casting a covert glance in my direction. "You know, I've always wondered what people like you are thinking right now—after hearing all that."

I exhaled loudly and kicked a rock out of my path. "Honestly? I'm not really thinking about anything in particular." I stopped speaking, but he remained silent, as if waiting for more. I finally gave in and continued. "I guess I don't know what to think. I'm being haunted by a bunch of immortals. It's weird."

He nodded. "I can understand that. Becoming a Guardian wasn't exactly an easy switch for me, either. But soon enough the weirdness becomes reality, and your life seems normal again."

"Really?" I asked doubtfully.

He shrugged a single shoulder. "More or less."

I let my eyes wander the cemetery, surprised like I always was by how peaceful and cut off from the world it seemed. Somehow, it made this conversation more believable.

"So . . . You said over the phone that Demons can't touch humans?"

Patrick didn't answer right away. "That's true," he admitted at last. "But don't let that make you complacent. It's a pretty useless protection, if you ask me."

"I thought you didn't judge?"

He smiled at my tentative smile, and then he scratched his chin. "Yeah, I suppose I did say that. Still, it isn't the best defense a human could have. Demon's aren't able to harm a human until a human's skin first comes in contact with the Demon's skin. The idea is that since a human has to initiate the contact, they must want Demon association, so they're getting what they deserve." He shook his head. "More often than not Demons use a handshake, but others have gotten really creative. So if you can help it, don't ever touch anyone with a black aura. Please," he added, as if he really did have to beg.

seers

I could see the car now, but it was still a ways off. "I'm sorry I have so many questions, but—I'm afraid I'm going to miss something important, so . . . is there a reason I can't see your emotions? I mean, there's your silver aura, but . . . Usually I see colors."

He was nodding before I'd finished, his eyes trained straight ahead. "Demons and Guardians can hide their emotions from Seers. I'm not really sure why, but it takes little effort, and it's kind of just . . . the natural thing to do, if that makes sense. Hiding a part of ourselves makes us feel less vulnerable to the all-seeing beings that you Seers are. "

I nodded once, to show that I understood, and then moved on to my next question. "So what now? What am I supposed to do?"

"For now, continue doing what you've been doing. I'll continue to be around you as much as possible, for your own safety, and if you see anything unusual, let me know. Toni and I will take care of the rest. You just point out any Demons that you see."

"You make it sound easy," I complained, though I wasn't as annoyed as I pretended to be. True, all of this was more than a little unsettling. But walking calmly through the cemetery next to Patrick, well . . . it wasn't exactly an awful way to spend an afternoon.

I tried to remember the existence of Aaron, my boyfriend, but Patrick was speaking again, and I was riveted by his words.

"You know, I think you've taken all of this in better than anyone else I've ever heard of."

"Really? Are you remembering the parking lot scene?"

"I couldn't really forget it, but yes—that included."

I bit my lower lip, wondering if it was really the time to broach this topic. "So, how many times have you been a guardian angel to Seers?"

He groaned, but it was a joking, playful sound. "You're going to keep calling me that, aren't you?"

"Guardian angel? Probably." I smiled, stepping up to the

passenger door, digging in my pocket for the keys.

"Hmm . . . I'll have to come up with something for you—so we'll be even."

"Good luck." I unlocked his door and then moved around the car to my side. Before I could reach my door Patrick was inside, and opening my door for me. He pushed it open with his fingertips, and then leaned back into his seat so I could get in. I whispered a quick thank-you, and put the key into the ignition. Before I could turn the car on, Patrick spoke.

"Kate," he said, and the sound of his voice so close to me caused my stomach to flip.

I glanced up and saw him watching me—a grateful look on his smooth face.

"Thank you," he said softly. "For believing me."

I forced a smile. "Well—after that Demon and everything else that's happened, I didn't have a lot of excuses to doubt."

"Still," he reached over, and I held my breath as his fingers lighted upon the back of my hand, which was resting low on the steering wheel. His touch was gentle, yet so electric. His fingertips lingered against my skin, giving that strange electricity plenty of time to travel through my wrist and down my arm, warming every pore and raising every hair. It continued on to my heart, and then down to my stomach. It felt like my entire body was reacting to that smallest of touches, and I wondered if he knew it. I hoped he didn't. It wasn't safe for anyone to know they held that much power. I was literally melting, and at the same time so alert and alive. My heart pounded, my breathing became more rapid.

"Thank you," he whispered fervently.

And then it was over. He pulled back and busied himself with his seat belt, giving me a second to recover. Not that a complete recovery was possible in so short a time, but I was able to shake myself enough to put on my own seat belt and start the car.

Still, it would be a long time before I felt normal again.

fifteen

Patrick was afraid of overwhelming me, so he asked me to just take him home. But I quickly assured him that Toni and Lee wouldn't be done for a while yet, and I didn't want to be alone right now. (I didn't tell him that last part, but I'm pretty sure he understood what I was thinking.) And so he asked what I wanted to do, like I had any idea of what I wanted right now.

I thought about taking him to get something to eat, but the last thing I wanted to do was be seen with him in public. What if I ran into Aaron, or my family—pretty much anyone who knew me? I didn't want to face that now—preferably never, though I knew such a wish wasn't very practical.

In the end, I asked him to show me where he'd been living for the last couple months.

While he directed me through the streets, taking us back to the industrial area, he asked me questions about myself. My likes and dislikes, mostly. He kept it pretty basic, but he looked interested in everything I said. I think it was just his way of "keeping me comfortable."

Colors, movies, books, foods—the usual things. I tried to squeeze in my own questions, but he was an expert at avoiding personal questions. (If your favorite color could be considered personal, anyway.)

I still believed that he was infinitely more fascinating than I was, and I was dying to learn the rest of his story. But it wasn't the sort of thing I felt comfortable flat-out asking him. "How did you die?" It seemed like a pretty uncouth question all the way around. I knew he was deflecting most of the questions that would lead to his personal life, and so eventually I gave up. I figured that I'd learn it all eventually. It sounded like he was going to be in my life for a while yet.

I definitely had mixed feelings about that.

Soon enough he was telling me to pull into a badly paved driveway, between two large brown buildings. I inched slowly forward, the long shadows of late afternoon making the path seem even smaller than it was.

It wasn't a pristine road by any means, and it took all my concentration to dodge the potholes without running into the sides of the buildings. Finally we emerged out of the alley and I found that we were in some kind of asphalt courtyard, mostly boxed in by brick and cement buildings.

Patrick pointed straight ahead. "That's the one. You can park anywhere."

I parked right in front of the most obvious double doors, which were boarded up. Glancing up, it appeared that most of the windows had been shattered by rocks or other objects. All in all, it didn't really look like home sweet home.

"You've been living *here?*" I asked, unable to keep the shock from my voice.

He chuckled and undid his seat belt. "Don't worry—I've lived in worse." He opened his door, locking it again before I could remind him. I followed his lead, this time bringing my purse with me just in case. The area seemed deserted, but still. I figured Lee's purchases could fend for themselves for a while.

He was already at the doors by the time I'd locked my car and turned to follow him. He waited until I was closer before opening the door on the left. On closer inspection, I realized that the boards weren't actually fastened to the building, so it basically was a door with some boards stuck on it.

"Immortal people don't lock up?" I asked, raising a questioning eyebrow.

"Sometimes. But since we're already dead, what more could someone do?" He teased, waving me inside the open door.

Some light filtered in through the upper windows, but the large room I found myself in was still a little too shadowy to be considered comfortable. And homey it definitely was not. It was a cavernous factory floor, which had been mostly cleared out years ago. Cobwebs, some scattered crates, and several large objects or machines I couldn't identify littered the wide floor. It was easy to imagine that this room was the entire first floor of the large building. The cement floor was hard and littered with bits of dirt and debris. Still, there was an obvious trail that led straight across the room, to a wide staircase that went up.

"Could use a little help," I admitted at last, hearing him coming up beside me.

"That's a gentle way of putting it," he returned smoothly, hands going deep into his pockets as he surveyed the room with me. "Honestly, though, the second floor is better. That's where we actually live."

I followed him as he moved across the floor, stirring up dust as we went. I still couldn't believe I was here. It was pretty much the last place I would have expected my Saturday with Lee to take me. Strangely, though, I didn't mind. All my fears that Patrick was in any way dangerous had fled, and I felt completely at ease. Aside from the occasional thoughts of Aaron, I was actually enjoying myself. True, that might have just been my mind's way of protecting itself from all the insane information I'd digested today, but still.

We moved up the stairs slowly, and I could feel Patrick

looking over at me almost constantly, watching for a negative reaction, I assumed. I don't know what he expected me to do, but I continued to just look at my surroundings, awed despite myself. I still didn't understand everything about Patrick and the Guardians, but I understood that he was here, living in this dump because he wanted to help people. To help me. It was a humbling thought.

The second floor looked like a completely different building. Instead of open and spacious, there were empty corridors and a lot of doors. This must have been where the supervisors had hung out all day, in their comfortable offices.

Patrick led me down a short hall just off the second floor landing, and then paused briefly before opening a door.

"Okay," he said, grinning his famous half grin. "Don't judge too harshly. Toni's not exactly neat."

"And you are?" I teased.

"I'm not going to deny or agree with that statement," he said, twisting the knob and pushing the door open.

This time he stepped in first, but I was quick to follow.

The room was fairly large, though sparsely decorated. There was a broken couch that sagged dangerously close to the floor on one side, and a low table in front of it. The table was pretty dented and scuffed up. Old newspapers and a couple grease-stained pizza boxes that appeared empty, lay on top of the table. Next to the torn couch was a small, broken bookshelf. It held a few books—mostly Patrick's school stuff, I realized with a quick glance. I could recognize them because I had the very same stash on my bedroom floor.

It was easy to see why they'd picked this room to be their living space, because the four windows that lined the back wall were still intact, though extremely dirty. Also, there were two doors on both the left and right walls, leading to smaller offices, or rooms. All were closed, except one on our left. Patrick hurried in that direction, shutting it before I could get a good look. I spied the end of a mattress, but that was all before I was just staring at a closed door.

He offered a somewhat embarrassed smile. "That's just my bedroom. Trust me, not much to see."

I glanced around the room again, spying a microwave in the corner, sitting on a stool. One of those really small fridges hummed next to it. "You have electricity?" I asked, surprised.

"Yeah. We try to avoid using lights in here though—the windows would make it obvious we were here," he added in simple explanation. "But Terrence set us up pretty nicely as far as utilities go. Everything works, but we're pretty off-grid, which fits our needs of lying low. We don't exactly want Demons knowing where we sleep—or humans, for that matter."

"Terrence?" I asked, stepping toward the windows.

"He's a Guardian, but instead of Demon-hunting and human-protecting he specializes in getting the Guardians in this area set up. You know, find them low places to live, help get them settled, that sort of thing. There are quite a few like him, positioned in all the corners of the world. We call them Overseers or Supervisors. He's a really nice guy—I'm sure you'll meet him sometime."

"So not all Guardians are like you and Toni?"

"Is that relief I hear?" He almost laughed. He stayed near his door, leaning against the wall with folded arms, and watched me as I stood next to the couch and looked out the window. I got a nice view of the building next to us—shattered windows and all. "Great view," I told him anyway, craning my neck up to see if I could catch a glimpse of the sky.

He laughed again, and I tried to memorize the sound. It was beautiful and relaxing. It made my body tingle, and I wished he'd do it again. "Yeah, basically this place is the Ritz."

I turned around and resumed the conversation, my mind still struggling to wrap around everything about my new world. "So

Terence helps you Guardians, who protect Seers, who are supposed to help you hunt Demons, to protect the Humans?"

He nodded once, fingering the black bracelet on his wrist. "It's confusing, I know. All you need to focus on for now is that there are Guardians everywhere, and with the help of Seers, we keep humans safe from the Demons."

I nodded once, showing that I understood that part. And really, it did sort of make sense. Some Guardians worked to support the other Guardians who did the actual guarding work. Still, I had lots of questions about how the whole network operated.

Patrick suddenly leaned away from the wall, and his arms dropped to his sides. "I don't know what we've got, but do you want something to drink? Or eat?"

"Immortal people eat, then?" I asked, forcing my deepening thoughts to a lighter but still intriguing topic.

"Ha ha." He opened the fridge long enough for a foul smell to escape, then quickly closed it, pulling a sour face. "Sorry about that." He straightened abruptly, and though he still looked perfectly at ease, I got the impression that he was somehow nervous. "Um, yeah, we can eat. I mean, we don't have to. We never actually feel hunger, but eating is fun. It doesn't ever effect us negatively."

I looked at all the pizza boxes. "Obviously."

"Toni enjoys it more than others, quite frankly. If I'd remembered it was this bad, I wouldn't have invited you over."

"Don't worry about it, really," I assured him, seeing that despite his joking tone, he was actually afraid I might be offended by the place. "In a weird way, it's exactly what I expected. I mean, minus the glamorous mansion and fancy furniture part."

"Thanks," he grinned. "At least this stuff was all free."

"I think you still paid too much for the couch."

"It's comfortable," he defended.

My phone vibrated, and it was loud in the sudden silence. I pulled it out quickly, and saw that it was Lee calling. Back to reality, it seemed.

I answered quickly, hoping Toni hadn't stranded her or something. "Lee, what's up?" I asked, staring at the floor and all the while feeling Patrick's eyes on my face.

"Goodness, girl, where are you? Toni and I just got back to the house, and we wanted to watch a movie." Her voice turned teasingly suggestive. "Are you with Aaron?"

"No," I answered quickly—too quickly. I wanted to hit myself. I couldn't tell her the truth, and Aaron would have been the best excuse.

Luckily she wasn't really listening. "Well, bring him over too. I don't know what we're watching yet, but I just stuck a pizza in. See you in five?"

"Make it ten."

"Gotcha. See you then." She hung up without waiting for my good-bye, and I closed my phone slowly, looking at it like it was some kind of strange device.

"What's wrong?" Patrick asked, mistaking the consternation on my face for panic.

"I guess Toni and Lee are having a movie night at her house. She wants me there—with Aaron." I immediately regretted mentioning my boyfriend's name out loud, because some of the easiness that I'd been getting used to faded from Patrick's face the instant I said it.

"Oh." He unconsciously pushed a hand into his hair—a nervous habit, I guessed. "Well, you should go. Sorry I kept you as long as I did. Probably not exactly the way you wanted to spend your day."

"Actually, I'm just glad to understand it all. Sort of." My weak joke tugged a small smile from him, but I had a feeling I wasn't going to hear that wonderful laugh again.

"So," I began slowly, unsure of how to continue. He gave me an encouraging nod, and I found my voice. "We just pretend everything's normal, right? I mean, we go back to school, do what we always do . . . that sort of thing?"

He nodded for real now. "Yes. And let me know if you see anything unusual. Call me night or day, whenever. I'll have a talk with Toni and make sure he doesn't steal the car again."

"The car—is that courtesy of Terrence, too?"

He smiled. "Yes, why do you ask?"

"Well, I was hoping you hadn't picked that out too," I teased, gesturing toward the couch with a small wave of my hand.

"Yes, it actually runs," he assured me, taking the joke in stride. "Come on," he said suddenly, and I knew that my time with him was over. For tonight, anyway. "I'll walk you to your car."

sixteen

Once I'd pulled back onto a main street, I called Aaron. He was more than happy to meet me at Lee's for a movie, though I warned him her date was really bizarre.

It felt a little strange for me to drive away from the warehouse and leave Patrick standing in that deserted courtyard. It almost felt like I was abandoning him, after everything we'd gone through that afternoon. But what else could I have done? It was time to try and return to my regular life, no matter how weird it felt. He'd said that was what we needed to do.

Aaron and I pulled up to Lee's house at virtually the same time, and he greeted me with a happy kiss in her driveway. I couldn't help but wonder what it would feel like to kiss Patrick, since his mere touch had filled me more than Aaron's kisses ever had. Of course, I regretted that thought instantly and vowed not to revisit it for the rest of the night.

There was another car in the driveway, but I was too distracted to notice much about it, other than the fact that it was blue. Aaron pulled me up onto the porch, and I took a deep breath, trying desperately to calm my racing thoughts. I needed to concentrate. No one could know that there was anything different about me. I mean, Patrick had said as much, but I didn't want my friends to know I wasn't normal anymore.

Toni opened the door for us, and though he gave me a

knowing grin, he didn't say anything other than a natural "hi." He didn't single me out any more than Aaron, and I was grateful to him even though I still considered him to be a little creep. A little creep that was also an immortal Guardian.

Lee was in the back of the house, and I went to help her, leaving Aaron and Toni to introduce themselves and pick a movie. As soon as I stepped into the kitchen, Lee started talking about how wonderful Toni was and how he was the funniest guy she'd ever met.

"He's a freshman over at the college," she continued, as she opened the oven to check the pizza. A short second later she was closing the door and resetting the timer for three minutes. She turned back toward me, watching as I opened a cupboard and lifted down four plates. As soon as I'd set them on the counter, she was speaking again. "Isn't he hot? I mean, I still can't believe he singled me out like that."

"You're not giving yourself enough credit," I told her honestly.

She blew out her breath loudly and moved for the cups. "Maybe. But honestly, doesn't he just crack you up?" Her question was obviously rhetorical.

"So what else did you guys do?" I asked. Though I was gathering dinner supplies in Lee's kitchen, my mind was still in an abandoned warehouse, firmly captivated by a pair of perfect blue eyes.

"Well, after we ate, we window-shopped for a while, and then we went driving in his car. I just still can't believe that a college guy would go for me, you know?"

"Do you want me to make some punch or something?" For the life of me, I couldn't focus on the conversation Lee was trying to have. Not that she really noticed. She was walking on sunshine, far above me.

She kept craning her neck around, trying to look into the living room.

I finally rolled my eyes and grabbed her arm, pulling her toward the door. "Just go—I'll manage this."

"You sure?" she asked, looking at me for really the first time, though she was still glancing past me with more frequency than would normally be considered polite.

"I'm sure."

With a wordless grin, she was out the door, and I was alone. For a few minutes.

I was searching the pantry when I heard someone step up behind me. "Need a hand?" Aaron asked.

I turned around, forcing a smile. I really needed to stop thinking about Patrick. But that was impossible after everything I'd learned today. About him, and me, and the world in general. Still, I needed to try.

"Yeah—maybe you can see the napkins somewhere."

Just then the timer sounded, and I left the pantry-conquering to Aaron so I could tend to dinner. I pulled out the pizza, switched off the oven, and started to hunt down a pitcher.

"Found them," Aaron suddenly declared, emerging with a small stack of napkins clutched victoriously in his raised hand. He set them down next to the plates and cups and then moved to lean against the counter next to me, watching as I filled a clear pitcher with water.

As I mixed the punch, Aaron made conversation. He told me about swim practice and how he only seemed to be getting slower and slower with the backstroke. "I'm going to have to really improve if coach is gonna let me compete. I'll probably be in the pool more this week than out of it, just trying to get my speed back."

I nodded but didn't comment. I was staring at the punch I was stirring. I'd subconsciously picked blue, not that it was the right shade for his eyes. Not even close.

"So what did you do today?" Aaron asked.

I continued to stir, but I threw a quick smile in his direction. "Not much. Lee and I pretty much wasted the whole day, then we went by the mall to pick up some new shirts for her goth look."

"Sounds relaxing."

"Yeah . . . It was." *Despite everything . . .*

He stuck his thumb out toward the pizza. "Want me to cut that?"

"Sure." I mentally shook myself. "The pizza cutter should be in that second drawer—the one by the fridge."

As Aaron ambled across the kitchen, Toni and Lee suddenly stepped inside. They were each holding two movies, and they needed help narrowing the choices down. We started eating our pizza while we argued about which movie to watch. Once we'd finally decided, we moved the rest of our food into the living room, where we all crashed onto the long couch.

Of course, I use the term "we" very loosely. I was pretty quiet, and I remained very distracted the entire night. I think Aaron noticed that something was bothering me, but he was so used to my weird moods by now that he didn't say anything. Toni and Lee, well, they didn't notice much of anything besides each other.

As soon as the movie was over, Aaron was ready to leave. I hated to think I'd ruined the evening for him, but I knew that I hadn't fulfilled his expectations very well. He kissed me good-bye and then thanked Lee a bit too loudly for a great evening. Clearly, he was trying to send a message to Toni, who slowly got the point of my boyfriend's lingering.

Toni said his good-byes to Lee, and to me—adding a wink that clearly signified he knew where I'd been, though I wasn't sure how—and then the boys were gone.

Long after Lee had fallen asleep, I remained awake, staring around the dark room. It would be a long time before I found sleep, and even when I did, my brain continued to work throughout my dreams.

Monday morning found me in American lit, several minutes before the warning bell would sound. I wasn't alone, though. Patrick was already seated at his desk, ready and waiting for me. I took my usual seat next to him, my small smile somewhat embarrassing, but impossible to stop.

"So, I'm guessing all that wasn't a dream," I said, by way of a greeting.

He cocked his head a little, a smile in his eyes. "A strange hello, but . . . I'll take it."

"How was the rest of your weekend?" I asked.

He shrugged, his eyes never leaving my face. "Yours?"

"Pretty calm, after Saturday." I leaned down to pull out a notebook and something to write with. I needed an excuse to look away from him, if only for a second. I had to stop the blush from coming and exposing me for the silly twitterpated girl I was.

Once I straightened in my chair, he spoke, his voice back to business. "I spoke with Toni, and told him to back off a little from Lee. I assume that's what you want?"

I nodded. "The less involved she is, the better."

"Well, I talked to him, but I can't promise anything. He's not exactly . . . easy to control."

"How long have you two been partners?"

He considered briefly, his eyes glancing toward the ceiling. For a strange moment, I wondered if he was avoiding my gaze, the way I'd just done with him. "Phew, time flies. He's been with me for almost twenty-three years now." He looked back at me in time to see the shock on my face, and he smiled kindly. "Immortal, remember? Time doesn't have quite the same connotations that you put on it."

"It's just hard to imagine—I'm only eighteen."

"Extremely young," he agreed with a grin.

I shook my head in wonder. "I still can barely digest the fact that you've been alive for . . . how long was it?"

"I was born in 1780. I died in 1798. So I guess technically I've only been alive for eighteen years too."

He was close enough that I could elbow him, and I did so without thinking. It wasn't until I pulled away that I realized that probably was a weird thing to do to someone I hardly knew. True, we'd shared a lot in the past little while, but that didn't really merit the camaraderie I was feeling. (Not to mention all the other things I was feeling.)

Patrick didn't seem to mind, however, so I tried not to let it embarrass me. Still, I would be more careful in the future.

"You know what I meant," I said, trying to draw the attention away from the slight pause that had yet to grow awkward. "I mean, what's it been like? Seeing the world change in so many ways . . . The technology alone must have been amazing."

"It's been rather interesting," he said. "Cars, computers . . . still, I think there are things in the past that were better."

"Like what?"

"Times were simpler," he explained. "Not necessarily easier, but . . . I think people were happier."

"The more people have, the more they want—that kind of thing?"

"Exactly."

I considered that for a moment. It was pretty obvious that he didn't want to talk about his personal life, but I was dying to know all the same. I decided one more veiled question couldn't hurt. "Families were stronger back then, I bet. More love in the home?"

A strange shadow crossed his face, and he looked down at his desk. "I think love is one of the only constant things through time. It was all pretty much the same. Emotions are complicated, no matter when you lived."

My curiosity was piqued by his tone, but I knew he didn't want to say anything more. He'd only said that much to keep me from prying further.

But before I could think of anything else to add, Patrick was looking up, a slight smile back on his face. "So, I thought you should know—I'm not in choir. I mean, not technically."

"Huh?"

"Choir. Last hour? I'm not really in the class."

"But I saw . . ." Realization dawned. "That's why you wouldn't sing. You were invisible!"

He nodded. "It was just another test—to see if you were indeed a Seer."

"So you can't sing?" I asked teasingly.

He grinned but didn't answer my question. "I just thought you should know, so you don't try talking to me there. You'd look like a crazy person."

"You're still going to come, even though you never participate?"

He didn't answer because just then Aaron walked in, a second before the bell rang. "Hey," he called, looking carefully between Patrick and me. "Lee said you'd be here. Why so early?"

I reached down toward my bag, then pulled out *The House of the Seven Gables*. "Thought I'd try to get the last of the reading assignment in before class. Have you finished?"

He seemed to relax a little, and I saw in his aura the tinge of purple jealousy and green uneasiness die down a little. But they didn't leave. "Not even close. I can't get into this book at all. It's just kind of . . . dumb."

I turned slightly away from Patrick to watch Aaron take his seat on my other side, and I wished for not the first time that I could see Patrick's aura when I felt him lower his head. I wondered what he was thinking about this intrusion, and my turning away from him. He did understand that I wasn't shutting him out, didn't he? I hoped he did.

Aaron was speaking to me, a little bit louder than was neces-sary, since I was sitting right next to him. "So, do you want to do something after school?"

I said the first thing that came to mind—usually not a good habit for me to get into. "What about practice? You know you want to participate in the meet."

"Yeah, you're right, but . . ." He sighed, catching sight of my serious face. "All right. Fine. Maybe another night this week." He reached down to dig in his backpack, and I leaned back in my seat, fighting the urge to sigh aloud.

Sitting between two guys you've just offended is not really the most comfortable place to be.

seventeen

Lee led the way into the cafeteria, through the line, and up to the table. It wasn't until she was sitting down that I realized it wasn't *the* table. As in, the place where we always sat.

Five special needs students were already eating lunch, but most looked up to watch Lee as she sat down, a big smile on her otherwise gothic face. "Hey, guys, can we sit here?" Asking a bit late, in my opinion, since she was already making herself at home at the table.

A very skinny boy with glasses and a skin condition started bobbing his head before returning to his sandwich—head still nodding a little, as if he couldn't stop it.

"Psst!" Lee mock-whispered to me. "I think it's impolite to stare, hon."

Trying not to imagine what Aaron would think, I took a seat at the end of one of the benches—across from Lee, and right next to a girl dressed almost completely in purple. Her hair was pretty short and ramrod straight. She turned to smile at me, and I found myself relaxing. Her nose was incredibly small, and her rather flat face was very round. I know it sounds awful to say, but she actually looked pretty. I know I shouldn't be surprised, but I was. I guess I'd never actually taken the time to look closely at this particular group of kids. Not that that didn't make me feel really guilty or anything . . .

I started to unwrap my sandwich, looking at each of them in turn, but focusing on their auras. I didn't see a bit of green or purple. There was no gray depression or red anger. There were only positive colors—pink excitement, as a larger girl with almost dazed eyes enjoyed her chocolate chip cookie before finishing the mac and cheese in front of her. Blue contentment as the skinny boy sipped some chocolate milk. Yellow happiness as the girl beside me picked up a snack pack of chips.

"Lee," I whispered in awe. "They're almost like little kids. Their auras . . . they're so *happy*."

"Hello," a boy with a nasal voice said to Lee, speaking loudly and trying to lean around the person between them—cookie girl. "Hello."

Lee smiled at him and nodded quickly. "Hi."

He extended a slightly curled hand, pushing it past the nose of the girl, who didn't seem to mind. "Hello," he repeated.

"That's Trent," Patrick said suddenly from behind me, and I jumped a little as I whirled around to look up at him. He was standing almost right behind me, with a large boy I assumed he'd been helping through the line.

He glanced down at me, then focused back on Lee. "He'll keep saying hello until you tell him your name and shake his hand."

Lee took Trent's offered hand. "I'm Lee," she said, keeping her voice clear and distinct. "It's nice to meet you, Trent."

"Hello!" He grinned hugely, shaking her hand several vigorous times before finally letting go and returning to his mac and cheese. "Spaghetti?" he asked eagerly.

"Maybe tomorrow, Trent," Patrick assured him, moving around the purple girl next to me, and sitting on her other side. The large boy he'd helped moved to the opposite corner of the table, and another boy—very thin but with the happiest aura I'd seen so far—came and settled into a seat on Patrick's free side.

"Hey, hey, what?" the purple girl asked, watching Patrick like he was her only friend in the world.

"I'm just telling Trent he might get spaghetti tomorrow," Patrick explained. Then he addressed me and Lee. "This is Bianca." He then went around the table quickly, starting with the skinny boy with the skin condition. "That's Mark, and that—" he pointed to the larger girl eating her cookie, "—is Olivia." The large boy that had followed him came next, "This is Jason, and that's David," he pointed to a boy on the end, who was eating his apple slices with a lot of concentration, his glasses almost sliding off his nose. "And this," he nodded to the boy directly on his left—the one who was almost drowning in yellow happiness, though outwardly he was really just calmly eating a salad and staring off into space. "This is Landen."

"Spaghetti?" Trent asked again, looking up from his food expectantly.

Patrick shrugged. "Sorry, Trent."

Trent sighed loudly. "Darn." Then he brightened. "Maybe next time!" He started to eat, moving on from his momentary disappointment without a thought.

Bianca pushed her small bag of chips toward me. "Please?" she asked, staring right at me.

I set down my sandwich and hurried to help her open the bag. As she took it back, she offered a quick, "Thank you!"

Mark was scratching a red spot on his chin, and he was gazing at me from across the table. "You're pretty," he said.

I blushed, hardly knowing what to say. "Thank you," I finally managed.

He had wire-rimmed glasses, and he pushed them right up against his face, still smiling at me. "You're *very* pretty," he insisted.

Unsure of how to react, I glanced down at my sandwich.

Should I ignore him, since I'd already responded once? Or did I have to say something before he got his feelings hurt for being ignored?

Suddenly Patrick spoke, his soothing voice low. "Yes, Mark. She is."

I could feel Lee's eyes on my face as I leaned closer to the table and looked past Bianca. I knew I shouldn't let her see my interest, but I wanted—almost needed—to see the look on Patrick's face.

He was staring at his lunch, absently toying with the edge of his sandwich. After a seemingly eternal moment, he finally glanced up, catching my stare. He held my gaze for a moment that was probably more intense than Lee should have witnessed, and then he quickly looked away. He picked up his sandwich and took a large bite, chewing firmly until Jason handed him his water bottle, silently asking for help.

As he twisted away from me to help Jason, I finally dared to meet Lee's probing eyes from across the table. She had a strange half smile on her face and understanding in her eyes. She mouthed a very long "*Ohhhhhhh.*" Then—at a harsh look from me—she focused back on her lunch before Patrick could turn around and catch her. A smile continued to tug at the corner of her mouth, though, for the rest of lunch.

As for me, I was left trying to convince myself that he really hadn't said that. I mean, it was only to keep Mark from saying it again and again, right? Patrick was just trying to save me embarrassment or even save Mark. He hadn't really meant anything by the simple words. He certainly hadn't looked at me *that* way . . . had he?

Was it even possible that he felt a small measure of the attraction I felt for him? Honestly? I mean, he was like . . . over two hundred years old, not that he looked it. And aside from the fact that he was incredibly old, I wasn't anything special. I mean seriously, I was just another Seer to him. He'd been helping damsels in distress for two centuries, for crying out loud. I'm sure he'd seen plenty of beautiful faces over the years. What could possibly make me attractive to him? It made sense that my heartbeat quickened when I was near him. He was breathtaking, mysterious, and my protector. I mean, that was why he was here. But to think that he felt anything for me seemed like a completely ludicrous assumption.

Logically, I knew I should be a little weirded out by the fact I was reacting this way toward a severely old man. But I wasn't. He wasn't ancient, or creepy. He was Patrick.

Just Patrick.

And I needed to get a hold of myself before I fell any deeper. Because though I knew who he was now, I still didn't know much of anything about him. Not really.

All through lunch, Mark—the one who'd called me pretty— kept going on and on about some video game, telling us all about the different levels, and how good he was getting. David—the other boy with glasses—argued that there was no way Mark was that good.

For the most part, everyone else was pretty quiet. I know I was, and Patrick hardly said a word. Lee ate quickly, and then excused herself. She was hoping to finish organizing one of the drawers in the music library before next period. She told us goodbye, her eyes lingering on me, still dancing in new understanding. I wanted to shake her.

When lunch was over, an older man—Mr. Donner—came to help lead the kids to their next class. He gave a grateful look to Patrick, who seemed embarrassed by the silent praise. He and Mark shared a secret handshake, he touched Landen's shoulder as the extremely silent and happy boy wandered away, and then we were alone at the table.

"You're right," I said, and he looked up questioningly. "They're awesome."

He smiled a little. "I'm glad you think so." He stood, pulling up his tray with him. "Come on—we're going to be late to biology."

We almost were. There weren't two empty seats together, so for really the first time all day we weren't actually together. As I was pulling out my notes for the class, I accidentally pulled out my lit notebook. Seeing the cover suddenly reminded me of the sketch I'd been working on last week—the one of Patrick. A quick glance around the room assured me that everyone was safely focused on our teacher, Mrs. Johnson. I couldn't resist—I opened the notebook, and quickly found the right page.

The unfinished face of Patrick O'Donnell was staring up at me, looking as pensive on paper as he did in life. True, his eyes seemed harder in this than I would have drawn them now, knowing the truth about him as I did. Without actually meaning to, I began to amend my mistakes, and I continued the sketch.

I was completely absorbed in my work, and for the first time I regretted that I hadn't taken an art class this semester. In the end, I suppose I'd been avoiding my talent since my parents died. I don't really know why.

Slowly the face came to life before my eyes. I'd always been good at capturing emotion, and the lines of his jaw seemed perfect. I tried a few different things with his eyes, but I couldn't get them quite right. I finally decided that it was the best I could do with a sketch, and moved my attention to touching up his hair.

The bell rang, startling me. I set my pencil down and closed the book quickly, like I was hiding something. Which, admittedly, I was. I didn't want anyone even *thinking* that I might be drawing a lifelike rendition of Patrick O'Donnell.

I shoved my stuff back into my bag and looked up just in time to see Patrick walking quickly out of the room, his phone at his ear. Puzzled, I stood, slinging my backpack over my shoulder. I made my way through the students still in the room, but by the time I was in the hall, I couldn't see Patrick anywhere.

I just stood there for a moment, letting the traffic of rushing students slide around me. Eventually I decided that my standing there was dumb. So I turned and headed for the choir room, growing more and more worried every second.

It was pretty easy to assume that Toni had been the one calling Patrick. But was something wrong? Why else would he have left without giving me a reason? I knew his exit hadn't been planned, or else he would have mentioned something to me. Or would he have? Was I wrongly assuming that I was somehow part of the Demon-catching team? I mean, true, I was the one who could see them, but did that mean I was going to be involved in everything that went on in that crazy world? Probably not.

Choir seemed to be extra long. I just kept looking at the clock, waiting for the bell to ring. It didn't. At least, not for a long time.

Five minutes before we'd be released, I couldn't stand it any longer. I pulled out my phone, sort of ducking behind the girl in front of me.

Where r u? I sent him, pushing the buttons a bit too fiercely.

I sort of expected him to ignore me, but my guardian angel was quick to reply. Not even a full minute had passed before I was looking at his words. *Is something wrong?*

I rolled my eyes and answered quickly. *No. Where r u?*

Two-minute wait this time. *With Toni. Explain later.*

"Of course," I muttered to myself. The girl next to me shot me a weird look, but once she saw my phone, she understood. I wasn't talking to myself. Not really.

A minute later the bell rang, and I was one of the first ones out. I walked the short distance to the band room, where Lee was standing with another senior named Rodney, who was a bit of a nerd, but in a good, cute kind of way.

"He offered to help me clean a few drawers out, and he'll take me home after." She shrugged. "Less work for me in the long run, right?" She leaned closer, and her voice was really low. "I'll call you once I'm home, though—you have a *lot* of explaining to do."

Like that gave me something to look forward to.

I walked out to my car alone, but someone was waiting for me once I got there.

Aaron was reclining against the driver's door, his arms folded tightly across his chest. When he saw me approaching, he leaned away, though his arms remained folded.

"Hey, aren't you supposed to be in the pool?" I asked, hoping that my voice sounded as carefree as I needed it to be.

"Yeah, soon—I wanted to tell you good-bye." He waited until I'd stepped up to him, and then he leaned down and kissed me. "I missed you at lunch," he said, drawing back out of the kiss.

I winced. "Sorry about that. Lee wanted to sit with the special needs kids for a change."

"Yeah, I saw that. Patrick was there too, wasn't he?"

My eyes narrowed, and I saw his mouth tighten in response. His aura—rapidly turning a dark shade of purple—proved his next words to be a lie. "I'm not worried or anything, I just want to know what's going on with you two. You guys always seem to have a lot to talk about."

"What do you mean? I'm just trying to be friendly."

"Sure, I understand. It's just that . . . I'd really appreciate it if you'd sit with me at lunch, okay? It doesn't look good for my girlfriend to spend more time with some random guy than with me."

"Aaron, you're jealous."

"No, I'm not," he argued, though the flaring purple around him was clear. "I'm only trying to make sure everything's still okay between us."

"Of course it is," I assured him, my fingers nearly strangling the strap of my bag. "Just because we're together doesn't mean we can't have other friends, right?"

"I wasn't saying you couldn't. I only meant that I think it's weird when you talk more to Patrick than you do to me." He sighed deeply, and if I couldn't see the purple still surrounding him, I would have thought he was letting the fight go. "Look, if you're really worried about him being friendless, maybe Jaxon and I can start hanging out with him too, all right? You don't have to be his only friend."

"Well, I didn't see anyone else lining up for the job."

"Kate, that's only because he started acting like a loner."

"By sitting with the special needs kids at lunch? Is that a bad thing to you?"

"Of course not! Look, can you just let this go? I don't want us to fight over something as stupid as this."

I pushed past him, drawing out my keys.

"Ah, Kate, come on . . ."

I opened the door and climbed in. Only after I was reaching for the door did I look up at him. "I don't want to have this fight either. So I'm going to go now, and try and forget that you said that. Good luck at practice. I'll see you tomorrow." I pulled the door closed, refused to look at him again as I started the car, and backed slowly out of the parking space.

I didn't glance back as I shifted into gear, or as I drove away. I would never know if he stood there watching me go, or if he turned and left the instant my door closed.

eighteen

Jenna and Josie climbed into the backseat, neither of them commenting on Lee's absence. Josie just busied herself with hooking up my iPod, and Jenna grumbled loudly about a boy who kept looking at her all through lunch.

"I mean, that's not creepy or anything," she groaned sarcastically. "The worst part is that I heard from Marci who heard from Sara who heard Brenna tell Danny that Nick likes me! Ugh! Nick Palmer. I mean, could I have a more disgusting guy like me?"

"Hey, isn't he the one who beat you at the spelling bee last year?" Josie asked.

"*Barely*," Jenna drawled. "It's only because I got the word *hygiene*." She said it like it was a disgusting word. "I mean, what sort of person expects a ten-year-old to know that one?"

"Nick Palmer knew it," Josie pointed out.

"He had the nerve to embarrass me in front of the entire school, and now he actually dares to *like* me?"

I glanced in the rearview mirror at my sister. "You know, I thought I had problems, but you're right—you're in trouble."

She sighed loudly. "Yeah, thanks."

What I wouldn't give to be eleven again.

I got home and decided to work on some homework I'd been avoiding. It was the sort of distraction I needed, and it kept me busy for a good hour and a half. Just as I was putting things away and wondering what I should do next, Lee called.

She didn't waste a second.

"Okay, I saw that look between you and Patrick. What's going on? I thought you were still scared of him and his aura! Are you taking the whole undercover ops thing a little too far? What about Aaron?"

"Calm down, it's not like that at all. We just sort of—well, I guess we're kind of friends now."

"What happened? Last I heard, you didn't trust him. Why the sudden change of heart?"

"I don't know. We just started talking—at your party. He's a good guy."

"What about his aura?"

"Well, it hasn't changed, but . . . I think he's pretty normal." It was a complete lie, but I knew Lee wouldn't catch it.

"Well, you certainly had a moment during lunch. I mean, what was that? You were totally flirting with him!"

"I was not. I didn't do anything!"

"Yes, you were. And so I repeat: what about Aaron?"

"What about him?"

"He's sort of your boyfriend, remember?"

"Yeah, I do. Being friends with Patrick doesn't change that."

Her voice held laughter. "I think Patrick has more than friendship on his mind."

"No way. I mean, he knows I'm taken."

"Well, that wasn't a 'we're just friends' look. It practically *seethed* with meaning."

I pressed my fingertips against my desk. I wanted to believe her words, but I knew I had to deny them. "It wasn't like that. Honestly. Aaron and I are perfectly happy together, end of story."

"You can lie to yourself, but you can't fool me. I know what I saw. But, you know, if you're sure that you don't reciprocate any feelings . . ."

"Not even close," I assured her.

"Good. Then why don't we do a whole double date thing this Friday? You and Aaron, me and Patrick."

"What about Toni?" I asked quickly, knowing he was my only possible weapon.

"What about him? He's a college guy. I'm not really holding my breath on a relationship, so I might as well snatch up the most gorgeous available guy at school. Unless, of course, you'd rather I kept my distance . . . ?"

I wanted to grind my teeth together, but I knew she'd hear that and guess my thoughts—and that's exactly the sort of thing I was trying to avoid. "Not at all."

"Then it's a date. Be sure to tell Aaron as soon as possible."

I had a call coming in on the other line, and a quick glance showed me it was Patrick. "Hey, Lee, I gotta run—Grandma's calling me."

"'Kay. I'll see you tomorrow."

I hung up with a quick good-bye and switched lines. "Hello?"

"Hey Kate, it's me—Patrick."

"What's up?" I asked, trying to sound uninterested.

He got right to the point. I guess immortal people don't enjoy beating around the bush as much as regular human beings. "I'm sorry I left like that. But Terence was at the warehouse, and well . . . I needed to speak with him. I hope it didn't alarm you, though."

"Nope. Not at all. Why would it?"

He spoke slowly, and it was easy to imagine him pacing in front of his dilapidated couch. "Well, you've had a lot of new things to process, and security is important when you're surrounded by things you don't understand. I just wanted to apologize because I promised I'd be around, and then suddenly I wasn't."

"Well, I was fine. You don't have to be around every minute."

"Of course. I'm sorry if I've offended you."

I sighed a bit too deeply, and then shook my head—though of course he wouldn't see that. "No, you haven't offended me."

"Are you mocking my speech?" he asked, that small smile evident in his words.

I laughed once despite myself. "For a two-hundred-and-something-year-old, you actually do pretty good."

"Um, thank you. I think."

I hesitated. "What's that like, anyway? I mean, really? Do you like . . . know everything?"

He chuckled. "Not even close. I believe it's impossible for one person to know everything—no matter how long they live." He paused, gathering his thoughts, then slowly continued. "When you die, you keep your maturity level forever."

"That explains Toni, I guess," I joked, trying to digest what he'd just told me.

"Yes, it does."

"How old is he?"

"I believe he was born in 1812."

I shook my head in disbelief. "That's so weird."

"What's weirder is to think that we're some of the younger ones."

"So, even though you've lived for so long, you still act eighteen?"

"As opposed to being a boring old sage? Yes."

"So it's kind of like the whole Peter Pan thing. Live forever, but never grow up."

He chuckled. "Yes, in many ways. Of course we still have experiences, but they don't age us. If that makes any sense at all."

"No, it sort of does." His light laugh was contagious—I couldn't keep the smile from my own face.

"Kate!" Josie screamed up the stairs. "Grandma says come down and help with dinner right now!"

"What was that?" Patrick asked, deeply curious.

"Just Josie—my sister. I have to go."

"She has . . . quite a voice."

"Yes, she does."

"Kate—" As soon as he'd started, he stopped.

"Yes?" I prompted.

There was a short, deliberating silence. And when he finally spoke, I knew that they weren't the words he'd originally wanted to say. "I'll just talk to you tomorrow."

I bit my lower lip but decided not to press him. "All right. Have a good night."

"You too," he returned. And then he was gone.

nineteen

The rest of the week passed by quickly—just more of the same. No Demon sightings, though. Aaron and I continued to be tense around each other, though we'd both tried to make amends. I didn't go early to American lit anymore, and he and Jaxon joined us at the special needs table during lunch. But though we both made efforts, things just didn't feel right. I wondered if they ever would again, but I knew I shouldn't be thinking things like that. I needed to be positive. Then, of course, a small part of me had to wonder if I wanted this relationship to last in the first place.

I didn't linger on that thought, though.

Lee was all excited about the double date for Friday, and Aaron tried to pretend that he was too. But after he'd learned that Patrick would be there, well . . . he just wasn't very happy with me—like it was entirely my fault. Patrick wasn't looking forward to it either, but he was perhaps the best pretender of us all. I was probably the worst. The night had disaster written all over it, and by the smirks Lee sent me, I knew she knew it too. I wondered more than once why I considered her my best friend.

But despite my misgivings, Friday night arrived undeterred. Patrick had agreed to drive, but I knew that was only because he didn't want anyone knowing that he lived in an abandoned warehouse. Originally Aaron had suggested that each guy pick up their date, and then we could just meet at the restaurant. But Lee wouldn't have any of that. She was going all-out for this thing, and I wanted to strangle her for it. I knew she was trying to make a point. She wanted me to admit that I had feelings for Patrick—and that was certainly not happening. I mean, friends as good as Lee sometimes know more about you than you do yourself, but sometimes they just think that they do. It was an unfortunate thing, but I supposed I'd just have to make the best of it.

While I waited for them to pick me up, I loitered in the kitchen, trying to tell myself I didn't need a cookie, but craving the sugar just the same.

Suddenly I heard Grandpa's voice behind me. "Just take one already," he stage whispered. "Resistance is futile."

"*Star Trek* again?" I pretended to be horrified. "Grandma would be appalled."

He moved around me and lowered himself into his usual seat at the table. "She likes 'em just as much, despite her teasing. Sometimes arguing is just another way to show love."

I took his advice without thinking, taking the two long steps to the cookie jar with a sigh. "You're an awful influence on me."

"I think your figure will survive."

"Grandpa!"

"Get one for me too, huh?"

I frowned as I handed his over, and then asked if he'd like some milk. He nodded once, and I hurried over to the fridge, pulling open the wide door with one tug.

"You look cute tonight," Grandpa said by way of conversation. "Going out with Aaron again?"

I glanced down at my clothes, feeling a little guilty at how much I'd actually tried this time—and knowing the reason why. Because I hadn't gotten this dressed up since I'd first started dating Aaron. I was wearing a new pair of dark jeans—the kind that are really flattering, though you don't like to say so and brag.

My layered maroon and brown top tied in with some cute brown boots I hadn't worn for a long time. And a necklace with varying sizes and colors of stones complimented the outfit. I'd curled my loose-lying hair, so it actually had some volume. I didn't use much makeup, but my mother had always said the trick wasn't to hide, but accentuate, and I'd followed her advice perfectly.

"You're letting all the cold out," Grandpa reminded me, and I snatched up the milk and hurried to close the fridge.

I returned to the table, milk in one hand, two cups in the other. I poured us each a glass, and then took my seat across from him. We ate for a short moment in silence, then Grandpa cleared his throat.

"So, is it a date with Aaron?"

I nodded, and pulled another bite-sized piece off my cookie. "Yep. We're doubling tonight."

"Are you *nervous*, girl?"

I glanced up, hating that I was so easy for him to read. "A little. What gave it away?"

"You're biting your lip. You only do that when you're nervous."

I pressed my lips together, then shoved a piece of cookie in my mouth.

"Why're you nervous?" Grandpa pressed.

"I don't really know," I said slowly.

I could feel his eyes on my face, but I didn't meet them. I sipped my milk, then noticed the morning paper still lying on the table beside us. "Anything new that I should know about? School's useless, remember?"

He blew out his breath, and then shoved the last bit of cookie into his mouth. "Well, the Death Train's still moving, but that's about it."

The Death Train. I'd nearly forgotten the mysterious string of accidental deaths. "Still unexplainable?" I asked, taking another quick drink.

He nodded and reached for the paper. "Yes, but it's really start-ing to puzzle the police. There've been two more accidents, but there's something very calculated about them. The weirdest part is that they're progressing geographically in the same direction."

"What do you mean?"

"It's almost like the deaths are marking a trail. The most recent death took place at a gas station just outside of Santa Fe. Some people are starting to worry that it's some kind of pos-sessed serial killer with inhuman powers."

"What do you think it is?"

He shrugged. "I wouldn't dare guess. Hope it stops soon, though—cuz if it keeps moving in the direction it's going now, it's going to cut clean through our town."

He caught the worry on my face and waved a quick hand, dropping the paper back to the table at the same time. "Now, now, don't go getting all worried—your grandma would kill me."

There was a firm knock on the door, and I quickly stood. I moved to take my cup, but Grandpa spoke quickly. "No, I'll take care of this mess. You have some fun tonight. Don't keep the poor boy waiting."

I smiled. "Thanks, Grandpa."

"I love you, sweetheart."

"I love you, too." I pulled in a deep breath and straightened my shirt as I walked out of the kitchen. I heard Grandpa's quick— "Don't be nervous!"—and then I was opening the front door.

My breath was knocked out of my body.

It was Patrick standing on my doorstep. His hands were deep in his pockets, his shoulders hunched slightly inward. His mouth was parting in an actual gape, though it was small. His blue eyes were serious but widening as they trailed over my body. When they returned to mine, they were almost glowing with an emotion I can best describe as wonder.

He was wearing a crisp pair of jeans—light like usual—and

a black button-up shirt, rolled characteristically to the elbows. I'd never seen him in black, and the effect was impressive. He'd very recently showered, and the scent of clean soap lingered on his skin. His longish hair was slightly damp, causing it to appear darker than it really was.

He swallowed hard, and the lump in his throat bobbed against his open collar in a very masculine way. His mouth snapped closed as an afterthought, and he straightened up with a quick motion.

"Kate."

It was all he said, but, strangely, it said it all. I was humbled by his appraisal of me, and a thin blush bloomed over my face.

"Hello, Patrick." His name nearly got stuck in my throat, which only caused my blush to deepen. Why couldn't I speak as smoothly as he did?

His eyes ran over my face, taking in the added color, before he finally turned to the side, pointing across the yard to his idling car with one open hand. "Um, Lee said it was all right if I escort you to the car—we'll be picking up Aaron next."

I absently scratched my left temple, pushing a wide curl back as I did so. I knew the motion looked nervous, even as I did it, but I couldn't help myself. "No, um, that's fine. Thank you."

He nodded once, and then rolled awkwardly onto the balls of his feet. "Shall we?" he asked at last, slight unease twisting his lips into a thin smile.

"Oh—right." I closed the door quickly and joined him on the porch. We walked together down the few steps to the sidewalk, then followed it to the driveway. We walked mere inches from each other, but never touched. In an effort to distract myself from him, I took in the sight of his car—a rather new looking Nissan Altima, midnight blue in color.

"Nice car," I commented, glad my voice didn't crack this time.

"Thanks." He cast me a quick smile, but we didn't have time to say anything else. He opened the back passenger door for me, since Lee was already in the front, and I climbed inside. He closed it for me, and while he walked around, Lee peeked over her seat at me. "He cleans up pretty nicely, huh?"

"Stop it," I hissed, knowing she'd know exactly what I was talking about.

Patrick opened his door and sank inside while Lee turned back around. "Kate looks really nice tonight, doesn't she?" she asked him loudly.

I wondered if all gothic people were this rude and annoying, or if I'd just gotten lucky.

He nodded once but didn't verbally reply. A muscle in his jaw was working, though, and I don't know that I'd ever seen him this tense. My heart was thrilling at all the possible reasons for his stoic behavior, even as I ordered myself to stop thinking like that. I needed to concentrate on Aaron. This was my chance to prove to him and to Lee that Patrick and I were only friends. Maybe I could even succeed in proving it to myself, though I highly doubted I'd be able to ignore the intense emotions he inspired in me.

My thoughts ended as I watched him shift into drive, and we pulled away from the curb. He never once glanced in his rearview mirror. It was like he was afraid of catching my eye. I wondered briefly if he'd ever been in a situation like this before, or if it was as alien to him as it was to me. I took a small measure of comfort in that thought.

Still, I knew that I'd already entertained too many thoughts about him. It was time to focus my attention on someone else. And so I settled back into my seat and glared at the back of Lee's headrest, hoping she'd get a lethal dose of my negative energy.

Her diabolical plan was all too clear at this point. I'd originally thought she was merely going to force me to watch Aaron and Patrick interact with each other. A torture, true, but one that I could have handled. I could pretend indifference for an evening. But no, that wasn't enough for her. She was going to dangle him in front of me, goad me with her eyes, taunt me with small remarks meant to make us all squirm. She wanted me to reveal my attraction to Patrick in front of my boyfriend. It was her way of helping me free myself, or see the light, or something similarly messed up. Well, it wasn't going to happen. I wouldn't let it.

Patrick wasn't making this any easier, it had to be noted. It was like he was intentionally trying to make himself even more desirable than usual. As if his probing glances and quiet words weren't enough to drive a girl crazy.

Lee was going to pay for this.

"You know," Lee said suddenly, breaking the short silence. "These cars must be really popular or something." She glanced over her shoulder at me. "Remember Toni? His car was exactly like this. Same color and everything."

I was able to keep my face smooth until she turned back around—then I grimaced to myself. Of course! How dumb could I have been not to realize that Patrick's car and Toni's car were one and the same? I was trying so hard to keep my two new worlds separate, I hadn't realized that Lee had spent time in the very car Patrick was going to be driving tonight.

I glanced in the rearview mirror, desperate to see if Patrick was freaking out like me.

But he was still avoiding me, it seemed—completely focused on the road. "Toni?" he asked Lee, sounding perfectly curious. He was a good liar. I should try to remember that, even though I trusted him almost implicitly at this point. A part of me wondered how that had happened, after our rocky beginning.

"Just this college guy I went out with last weekend," Lee explained, not bothering to hide her excitement at the words college guy. "He was at my party, and I ran into him at the mall last Saturday. He's a freshman."

"A freshman, huh?" There was the slightest twinge in his voice, and I knew he was fighting a smile. "A mature guy, then?"

I barely hid my snort, but luckily Lee was talking again.

"Don't get jealous or anything—nothing's going to happen." Lee pointed quickly. "Turn on this street."

Patrick followed her instructions perfectly, and before I was ready, we were pulling up to Aaron's house.

He was already outside, throwing a Frisbee toward his two youngest brothers, who were eagerly jumping up and down, reaching and pushing for the flying disc.

Aaron yelled something to them and then lightly jogged over to the waiting car. He opened the back door and slipped inside, leaning over to kiss me briefly before closing the door.

"You look great, Kate," he said, his voice heavy from playing with his brothers. He put on his seat belt and glanced toward the front of the car. "You too, Lee. And, Patrick—thanks for driving."

"It wasn't a problem," Patrick said, some deeper emotion throbbing behind his words. He twisted the wheel and let off the brake, and we were back to driving, an awkward silence pervading the atmosphere.

Surely he didn't need to be holding the gear shift so tightly—or at all, since his car was an automatic. His knuckles were turning white. He was making me even more nervous.

Lee leaned forward against her seat belt and began pushing buttons on the stereo. "What kind of music do you like, Patrick? You don't have any presets."

"I'm fine with anything." His answer was short but still polite.

"Okay." She shrugged and looked at us in the back. "Any requests?"

"Nope, anything's good." Aaron spoke a little too quickly, and I got the distinct impression that he was trying to seem carefree. But I knew him too well—he was just as tense as I was.

"You've planned everything else," I told her, my eyes belaying my pleasant tone, though she was the only one to catch it. "Why don't you choose?"

She grinned at my reaction, her black lipstick stretching. "Okay."

Knowing what she was going to pick, I silently prayed that Patrick didn't mind hard rock. Then again, he wasn't actually old, right? So maybe it wouldn't bother him too much . . .

Tonight was shaping up to be just the disaster I'd imagined.

Surprising me at first, Lee stopped on a completely unfamiliar station. There was no pounding bass or ear-splitting screams. But all too soon her ulterior motive became clear, and I fought the urge to growl aloud. Big Band love songs. Perfect. As if this night couldn't get any more awkward . . .

Catching the mood of the music, Aaron reached across the empty seat between us to take my hand. I sent him a thin and somewhat shaky smile, hoping that he wouldn't read too much into it.

His shoulders relaxed marginally, and I watched as his aura slowly lost some of its purple color, to be replaced by blue contentment. "You do look beautiful," he whispered. He bit his lower lip and then leaned in to kiss me again. For real this time. There was nothing cursory about it, or habitual. It was deep and sincere, and when he finally drew back, I could feel the blush on my face. A blush that only deepened when Aaron glanced out his window, and I was clear to steal a fast look in the rearview mirror—and meet a pair of tight blue eyes.

As soon as Patrick realized I'd caught him staring, he flashed me a quick smile. It was meant to be that "oops, sorry, don't mind me" kind, but there was nothing reassuring or real about it. It was more like the "I know I shouldn't have looked, but I couldn't help it" kind, and a split second later he was focused back on the road.

I cleared my throat and stared out my own window, nibbling on my thumbnail until I tasted the clear nail polish and quickly pushed my hand—the one not in Aaron's grip—back into my lap.

The drive was awkward, but I had hopes that the date would

only go uphill from here. The beginning was always the worst, right? It only made sense.

I wonder why I didn't quite believe it.

Lee had chosen perhaps the most romantic restaurant possible in a fifty-mile radius. It was an Italian place with lots of candles, soft music, and fake ivy crawling over gray stone walls. It was like the cherry on top of this nightmare sundae, and I had to dimly appreciate her dark sense of humor.

We had to park in virtually the farthest corner of the lot, the restaurant was so popular. Once the car was stopped, Aaron opened his door and quickly walked around the back of the car to get mine for me. He took my hand to help me out, and then continued to hold it tightly, our fingers intertwining out of habit.

Patrick—carefully keeping his eyes away from mine—stepped out of the car and then rounded the hood lithely. He held Lee's door for her but didn't offer his hand. That didn't seem to bother Lee, who grinningly exited the car and straightened her black top. Once the doors were closed and locked, Lee started leading the way, and Patrick hurried to walk beside her, hands in his pockets.

Aaron and I fell into step behind them, and I took this opportunity to pinch my eyes closed and pray for a miracle.

Unfortunately, we navigated the parking lot in perfect safety, and I really doubted that I was going to come down with a serious illness in the next couple of minutes. It looked like I was stuck here. Lee was going to regret this.

We entered the restaurant, waited to be seated, and then in minutes were led to a quiet table for four, set against a back wall. I sat next to the wall, frowning briefly at the fake ivy an inch from my face. A strand of plastic leaves had never offended me before, but tonight was a first on many fronts.

Aaron sat next to me, and Lee sat across from him—leaving Patrick the last seat, directly opposite me. He sat slowly, and I could tell from the way he blew out his breath that he would rather be anywhere but here.

I could understand that.

He reached absently for his leather bracelet, spinning it slowly around his wrist. I tried to remind myself not to watch every little thing he did.

We deliberated a while and then finally placed our orders. Aaron actually let me speak for myself, which I was grateful for. Some breadsticks were deposited in little baskets on the table, and our server promised to return with our drinks in a moment.

Lee—looking completely unaffected by the havoc she was wreaking—reached for a breadstick and took a large bite. "Mmm, these are so good," she told us, her eyes lingering a little longer on me than anyone else.

Aaron followed her lead, if for no other reason than to break the ice.

I sighed and reached for one in the basket in front of me—the same breadstick Patrick reached for at the exact same moment. Our fingers brushed, but he was quick to pull away. "After you," he insisted softly, and I hesitated only a second before snatching it quickly away. Aaron was just turning, and I didn't want him to see my hand hovering that closely to Patrick's.

While I nibbled on mine, though, I couldn't stop myself from looking up through my lashes. Sure enough, Patrick was staring at me, slowly chewing his bite of breadstick. Though I knew it was wrong to acknowledge it, I could feel the warmth of his legs, just inches from mine beneath the table. I knew he was noting the same thing, just by the way his chewing slowed and his eyes grew even more serious.

Luckily, our drinks arrived at that moment, and it was the distraction I needed to escape his eyes.

twenty

All in all, dinner went well. There wasn't a whole lot of conversation, and Lee and Aaron did most of the talking. Patrick only spoke when asked a direct question, and I wasn't much better. But somehow, we made it through. Lee and I both insisted on paying half the bill, and it was expensive enough that the boys didn't put up much of a fight. Aaron did insist that we do something else though, so he could in some way pay me back. Lee liked the idea. For the record, Patrick said nothing.

As we made our way out of the restaurant, we had to pause in the lobby area for a large group of young couples to enter. We stood back away from the door, pressing against the wall to let them through the small path. Aaron was in the lead, and he leaned back into me to avoid getting hit by a woman's swinging purse. His lean in turn caused me to push back—right against Patrick's hard chest.

My whole body tingled, and I heard Patrick's rapid intake of breath right above me. I wondered wildly what *that* meant, even as I tried not to get too comfortable there. His bare arm brushed mine as Aaron pulled gently on my hand, oblivious to what was going on behind him but hoping to make it through the doors before anyone else came through.

The lights weren't very bright, but our eyes had had plenty of time to adjust. So I found it a little odd when my eyes played a trick on me. As I was walking through the open double doors, I thought I saw a man with a black aura just entering.

As soon as the night air hit my skin I twisted around, trying to catch sight of him again, to prove to myself that his black aura was real. But all I saw as the doors moved to swing closed was the boisterous group we'd had to wait for, and an older couple—a man and woman—both with harmless blue and pink auras.

"What is it?" Patrick asked lowly, right beside me. He'd seen my hesitation and sudden swerve of interest, and I could feel him tensing.

Deciding I'd mistaken the older man's blue aura for black, I just shook my head and turned my attention back to walking. Aaron's grip on my hand was firm as he led the way back to the car, Lee and Patrick right behind us.

Patrick didn't question me, but he was silent and frowning when we reached the car. I felt stupid for causing that brief scene, and I hoped he'd forget it, and not let it ruin the rest of the night. There were plenty of other things that could do that.

Once in the car, Lee suggested we catch a movie.

I opened my mouth to protest, knowing I couldn't survive that much longer, but Aaron was already agreeing it was a great idea.

Patrick mutely started the car, and my mouth clamped shut.

We stood outside the theater for a long time, trying to choose which movie to see. Patrick didn't care, Lee wanted a chick flick, and Aaron wanted action. I expressed a desire to see a new horror movie. I hated scary movies, and Lee knew it, but it sounded better right now than any other option. Plus, it would give me an excuse to scream.

I got a few weird looks from Aaron and Patrick, but it was starting in three minutes, so debate time was limited. Lee almost looked happier about this turn of events than if she had gotten her way, so she wasn't complaining. We hurried inside, bought tickets, and then took our seats in theater seven.

There weren't very many other people in the theater, and we were able to get good seats in the middle. Lee orchestrated everything so I was wedged in between Aaron and Patrick, and there wasn't time to move because the lights were already dimming.

It always took a while to grow used to the subtle glows of peoples auras, and being in an otherwise dark room made them that much harder to ignore. I tried to focus on the previews, but we hadn't even been sitting a full minute before Lee leaned over Patrick to ask me if I wanted to come with her to the bathroom.

I gave her a nod, excused myself to Aaron in a whisper, and then stood. Patrick stood at the same time, pushing back against his seat to make room for me to slide past. I think he was hoping to avoid our touching, and I inwardly thanked him for that, even though I was mildly disappointed. Or maybe I was grateful *because* I knew that disappointment was a bad thing for me to be feeling.

I followed Lee slowly out of the dark theater—even darker because the first preview had just ended, and the screen was black. I blinked against the brighter light in the wide hall and stepped around a pile of popcorn that had been spilled.

"So, how are we enjoying the night?" Lee asked, not bothering to keep her voice low. Even though the corridor was deserted, I sent her a scowling look.

"All right, you've made your point. Can you knock it off? Please?"

"What point was that?" Lee questioned, a finger tapping her chin in mock confusion.

I ground my teeth together, then admitted it in a burst. "I'm attracted to Patrick O'Donnell. Are you happy now?"

"Uh-huh." She grinned and pushed into the empty bathroom. "Now the *real* question is, what are you going to do about it?"

She stepped up to the mirror, taking in her appearance with

a careful eye. She brushed a finger over some of her eye shadow in an effort to touch it up.

I threw up my hands. "What? What am I supposed to do?"

She twisted around to face me, leaning against the counter. "Personally? I don't know. But that thing that you and Aaron have been lacking? That's exactly what you and Patrick have."

"And what would that be?" I asked, trying to sound snappy.

Lee's smile only grew at my attempt to sound upset. "Chemistry. And girl, do you and Patrick ever have it."

I shook my head at her and then moved to the nearest stall.

It wasn't until we were both washing our hands that my resolve to be silent snapped. "Okay." I rounded on her, shaking my wet hands into the sink. "So it's not like that changes anything. Aaron and I have been together for a long time—I can't just end that."

"Why not?" She moved for the paper towels. "You're not happy. And Aaron deserves better than half-commitment."

"I love Aaron."

"There are different types of love," Lee reminded me, sounding gentle for the first time tonight. It wasn't the "ha ha in your face" tone she'd been using, anyway. "Look, I only did all of this because I'm your friend. You were in denial. I was just helping you open your eyes."

"Patrick doesn't like me," I blurted without thinking. "I mean, we might have a tentative friendship, but reading anything else into it is just silly."

"Why?"

"Because I really don't know anything about him. His past. What if he's, you know . . . already taken? What if he likes someone else?"

Lee just stared at me as I finished drying my hands. She waited until I'd tossed the used towel into the overflowing trash to finally speak. She was a fan of the dramatic pause.

"Kate," she said frankly. "He hasn't been able to take his eyes off you all night."

I swallowed hard and looked down, pretending to straighten my necklace.

"Honestly, watching him watch you—and vice versa—has been driving *me* crazy. The way he looks at you . . . it's so honest. So . . ." She searched fruitlessly for the perfect word, before finally shrugging. "At the risk of sounding corny, all right, it's adoring."

"As in, he adores me?" I asked, unable to keep the shock out of my voice. Her word choice was just so . . . un-gothic.

She bristled, looking uncomfortable with the seriousness of the conversation. "Look, I just mean that you owe it to yourself, Aaron, and Patrick to do something, okay? Because just as this night has been torture, your whole life is going to be that way unless you start really thinking about what you're doing."

I sighed, finally lifting my head to regard her. "You know, in a very weird way, I can see that you're doing what you think a good friend should do. But now, I would really appreciate it if you let me take the lead on my life, okay?"

She held out her hands. "No, no, please, take the wheel. It was getting way too confusing for me." She smiled slowly. "Still, you have to admit that my plan worked flawlessly."

"Yes, you're a criminal mastermind," I said wryly, turning to pull the door open.

"Good pick for the movie, though!" she commented happily, following close behind me.

"Yeah, I'm going to give myself nightmares for a month," I predicted as I stepped out into the hall—and walked right into someone.

My hand that had kept the door open for Lee fell, landing on the stranger's hand, which was coming up to steady me. Our skin brushed, and I looked up quickly, embarrassed for actually running into someone.

It only took a second to recognize him—his low smile. It was the man from the mall. Or more correctly, the *Demon* from the mall. His large body was familiar in a spine-tingling sort of way, even though I'd never seen him up close before. Also eerily familiar was the black thread that outlined him—the most colorless aura I'd ever seen. He was wearing the same clothes he'd worn at the mall—the office-worthy attire.

After digesting who he was—*what* he was—I felt my face pale. He was here, following me. Even now, he was grasping my arm, because I'd first touched his skin. Whatever shield or protection that normally kept a Demon from hurting a human was gone. Patrick had warned me that Demons could get creative when trying to get past the thin defense. I guess standing outside a restroom, waiting for an unsuspecting human to crash into them made this Demon one of the creative ones.

But did he think he'd just found another human, or was he in fact aware of my being a Seer? What other explanation was there?

All of this happened in a split second.

Lee was still stepping out of the bathroom, pushing into my suddenly halted back.

The Demon was grasping my arm, keeping me from falling despite my unbalance and Lee's further pushing. "I'm so sorry," he said, his voice strangely high-pitched. "This is entirely my fault."

"Don't worry about it," Lee grunted, not aware of my panic or inability to talk. She stepped around me, and as she did so the Demon released my arm and took a step back.

He nodded to us—his smile widening as he focused briefly on me—then he turned and continued walking down the hall.

Lee didn't seem to notice that anything terrifying had just happened. She just kept walking back toward the theater, a few steps behind the retreating Demon.

I jerked my feet into motion, trying to keep my face from

revealing my fear. I stumbled a little as I fell back into step with my friend, my mind racing, unsure of what to do.

Patrick. I needed to get to Patrick. He needed to know that a Demon was here.

"Kate, you okay?" Lee mistook the reason for the lingering fear on my face. "Come on, I'm sure the show won't be that bad."

I forced a smile but didn't say anything.

We were almost back to the theater.

I watched as the Demon turned down another hall, heading for the lobby. He didn't look back, but he didn't have to. I knew he was feeling very smug, even without the aid of swirling colors.

Lee opened the theater door but allowed me to go in first since my seat was the furthest down our row.

The movie was just starting—I could tell that by the soft, haunting melody that filled the room. It was a song that should be beautiful, but since it was appearing in the opening credits of a horror film it was anything but. I halted a few steps into the theater, because it was too dark to see where the stairs were, let alone which row was ours.

After a moment the screen shifted from a dark woodsy area to reveal an old-style schoolhouse placed in an open meadow. The sudden white in the screen lit up the faces in the theater, and my eyes were drawn to Patrick's face, his gaze riveted on the screen. I gripped the handrail and started up the stairs, Lee right behind me.

We were still a couple rows away when Patrick looked over— Aaron copying the motion a half second behind him—and saw us. We side-walked into our row, pushing quickly past the other seats. Patrick stood for me again, allowing me to slink past easily.

Once we were all seated again, Aaron took my hand, and I fought to steady the pounding of my heart. It was maddening, having Patrick right next to me but not daring to speak. It was too quiet. Aside from the tantalizing strains of ghostly music and the usual sound of ripping candy wrappers, the theater was silent.

Aaron leaned over to me, assuring me I hadn't missed much. I nodded but I didn't look away from the screen.

Soon enough, I knew, the children in the movie would start screaming—probably when their teacher got possessed or something. That would be my moment to tell Patrick what had happened.

Before the screaming could start, though, there was a flash of light in the bottom left corner of the screen. Someone was entering the theater.

My lurching stomach knew who it would be before my eyes caught sight of his familiar black aura. He was standing at the base of the stairs, waiting for his eyes to adjust. At least, that's what anyone else catching sight of him might think. But the screen was bright enough for me to look down and see his face, and he was watching me.

He had the familiar grin, and he was placing a single piece of popcorn into his mouth. He raised the small cup of popcorn to me in some mock salute, and my breaths became more rapid despite my attempts to stay calm.

I jumped when everyone in the theater suddenly screamed, along with all of the children in the fictional school. I heard Aaron chuckle weakly beside me, and his hand tightened around mine, reassuring me that everything was okay. If only he knew.

I leaned back in my seat, unable to tear my eyes away from the Demon.

Patrick was suddenly whispering to me, though his body had barely inclined toward me. "Kate, are you all right?"

I shook my head just slightly, and I could feel his eyes on my face now. "Demon," I choked lowly.

His body became hard, and he followed my gaze quickly, his eyes narrowed dangerously.

The Demon was still calmly eating popcorn, but at least he finally looked away from me to cast a small smile at Patrick. He started walking up the stairs toward us, his steps unhurried.

I felt Patrick tense—knew that he was about to stand—and I knew I had to stop him. He wasn't looking at me, so I laid my free hand on his knee, hoping to get his attention. He glanced quickly back at me, and luckily the theater erupted into screaming again at that moment.

"No, don't," I whispered quickly. "Don't make a scene."

"Is it the same one?" Patrick asked lowly.

"From the mall?" I clarified.

He nodded once, the motion harsh.

I nodded in return, hoping people would start screaming again soon. Patrick glanced back toward the aisle, and I followed his gaze. We watched together as the Demon skirted around our row, and then eventually moved to take a seat two rows behind us. I focused back on the screen, swallowing hard, but Patrick continued to strain his neck, unwilling to look away from the Demon sitting behind me.

I realized my hand was still on his knee, and I quickly lifted it away, stealing a peek at Aaron. Luckily my boyfriend was completely absorbed in the movie and hadn't noticed anything. On screen—we were now in a house—a closet door was just banging open. The theater jumped as one, and several girls screamed, though it was a false alarm.

I took the opportunity to whisper quickly to Patrick. "Turn around—he's not going to do anything."

For a moment I wondered if he'd heard. But then—very slowly—Patrick turned stiffly back to the screen. His jaw was clenched tight, and his hands rested on his knees. Belatedly, I realized they were itching to reach for the hidden blade he'd shown me before. I don't know if that made me feel better or worse. If nothing else, it made the whole thing very real.

It was agony waiting for the dialogue to start up again in the movie. A happy family was getting ready to move into a beautiful old-style house, and everything was pretty quiet. I wondered which characters—if any—would survive the two-hour movie. Finally, some louder music started playing as the family moved in.

It was finally loud enough that I could talk to Patrick unnoticed.

"What is he doing here?"

Patrick didn't take his eyes off the screen. "He's probably just trying to get close to you. But he can't do anything until you've touched him first."

"Um, about that . . ."

He glanced quickly at me, striving to keep the worry off his face but not succeeding completely. "What happened?" he demanded softly.

In a breathy whisper I briefly related what had happened in the hall. I would have thought it impossible for him to become any stiffer, but he did. By the time I was done, I had officially freaked myself out. If I hadn't been taking this whole thing seriously before, the panic in his eyes was enough for me to start worrying now.

"So why's he still here, if he got what he wants?" I ended my explanation by asking.

"He probably wants to talk to you," Patrick whispered thinly, eyes trained carefully on the screen, though it was obvious he was aching to turn around and check on the Demon.

Lee suddenly leaned between us, brow furrowed. "What are you guys talking about? I'm only getting every few words. Could you talk any quieter?"

Her movement got Aaron's attention. He straightened in his seat, turning toward me. "What's going on?" he asked.

I opened my mouth to say something, but then Patrick was

speaking quickly. "Kate was just asking me if I wanted anything to snack on."

Aaron glanced back at me, and I smiled encouragingly. "Yeah, I was thinking of going to get something. Anyone else interested in anything?"

My boyfriend shook his head. "No, I'm good. But would you like me to go get it?"

"No, I don't mind. You're more into this than I am." I looked over at Lee. "Anything for you?"

"Uh, sure—anything works."

I ignored her puzzled look and forced a smile. "Great—I'll be right back." I stood and pushed past them so quickly that Patrick didn't even have time to stand.

I was almost to the side aisle before I heard Patrick move to his feet. "I think I *do* want something," he said by way of explanation, and then he was only steps behind me.

I gripped the railing and moved down the stairs quickly, my back tingling uncomfortably as I imagined the Demon's eyes on me.

I was a little surprised that Aaron didn't follow me, but Lee was almost as creative as the Demons. I had a feeling she knew how to keep him there. And so in seconds I was stepping into the bright hall, and Patrick was only a half-step behind me.

I paused, but he gripped my elbow and propelled me forward, moving down the hall toward the lobby. Before I could ask about the rush, he spoke shortly. "He's following us."

I knew who he meant.

"What does he want?" I asked in a panicked whisper.

Patrick's face was deadly smooth. "I'm going to find out."

We still had a corner to turn before we'd make it to the lobby, but that's when he spoke.

"Please, this will only take a moment."

I shivered at his high-pitched voice, but not turning to face him was almost worse than the alternative. Patrick stopped walking, twisting back around. He continued to hold my arm, keeping me close to his side.

"What is your name?" Patrick demanded, sudden authority in his voice.

The large Demon smiled, still holding his popcorn. "That's really not very important, Guardian. Compared to other things I know."

"So you know who I am," Patrick snorted. "Usually that causes a Demon some fear."

"I'm not normal." He focused his small eyes on me, and his smile widened. "I'm sorry to have given you that scare last week. But I'm sure you understand. Kate."

I couldn't stop the shudder that rippled through my body, and Patrick stiffened beside me. "Don't address her," he ordered thinly. "You'll speak only to me."

The Demon shrugged. "Very well. Be rude. I only came to pass along a warning. Consider it a kindness."

"Stalking someone isn't exactly nice," I flung back at him, hoping to appear more confident than I actually was. I think I came off as an ornery little girl.

The Demon smiled. "It was a means to an end. I knew you must be surrounded by Guardians by now, and they're not exactly the most welcoming bunch."

"There's a reason for that," Patrick said, his eyes almost more threatening than his tone.

"Now, now, I know the rules." He wagged a thick finger in Patrick's direction. "You have no right to threaten me unless I make the first move. Since I haven't hurt anyone, you can't touch me." He turned his attention back to me. "Personally, I mean you no harm. I've been watching you for weeks now, as a favor for some other Demons. I owe them, you see, and was passing along some information. But I have no desire to get on the bad side of the Guardians." He cast a pointed look in Patrick's direction. "Tonight was merely my way of setting things right."

"What do you mean?" I asked.

The Demon ate another piece of popcorn before replying. "There's a dangerous Demon looking for you. I'm not sure why he's taken such an interest in you, but he has. And he's not alone. Hopefully you have more than one Guardian on your side, or you're in some serious trouble."

"Who's looking for her?" Patrick asked, his fingers tightening around my arm.

"I know him as Quin Romero. I don't know much else—only that he knows just about everything there is to know about Kate. And he's getting ready to make his move." The Demon focused back on me. "I've never seen a Demon so interested in a single Seer. Either he needs one quite badly, or . . ." He shrugged indifferently. "I'll let you figure it out."

"You expect me to believe that you came here to help us?" Patrick asked, incredulous. "After you forced her to touch you?"

"That was just for a bit of fun." He popped another piece into his mouth and then glanced at his watch. "I really better be going. I have places to be, you understand." He gave us each a last smile, then turned and walked away, leaving us standing there, the overpowering smell of popcorn almost sickening to my twisting stomach.

twenty-one

Lying on my bed in my dark room, it was almost hard to imagine that the events of the night had actually happened. I'd survived the double date and talked with my first Demon. Not that the talk had been very enlightening. He'd come to warn me, but had never really gotten much out besides the basic "watch your back" kind of thing. In reality, it ended up being scarier than no warning at all.

After the Demon had abruptly left us, it took a while before Patrick released my arm. But he stayed very close to me as I ordered a few different treats at the concessions counter—and for pretty much the rest of the night. Walking back toward the theater, I wanted to talk about everything that had happened, but it was clear from Patrick's dark and pondering expression that he'd rather not.

Just before reentering the theater, however, he spoke quickly. "Do you think you could come by the warehouse tomorrow morning sometime?"

I gave him a quick nod, and then he didn't speak directly to me the rest of the night.

The only upside of the Demon encounter was that nothing in the movie even came close to scaring me.

Needless to say, I didn't get much sleep. And when I did, I kept having this dream that I was in a movie theater, completely surrounded by people with black auras, and unable to get out. They were all speaking Spanish, and I kept hearing the name Quin Romero. It was probably the worst dream I'd ever had, though I didn't fully understand it.

I was glad when seven o' clock came around, and I could finally justify getting out of bed. It was late enough that I shouldn't be asked *too* many questions, but if Grandpa saw me I would probably get more than a strange look. After all, it was a Saturday, and I'd come in quite late last night.

I hurried to get dressed, settling for a plain white T-shirt and a pair of old capris. My hair wasn't completely flat, so I gathered it up in a ponytail, showing off the remaining curls to their best advantage. I skipped the makeup, even though I knew I'd be seeing Patrick. I kept feeling like I was taking too much time as it was.

Grandma was up, making homemade muffins. I think she's the only person I know who—without fail—wakes with the sun. She complained a little that I was leaving before the muffins would be ready, and I had to take two granola bars before she'd let me leave. (I told her I was meeting Lee at the mall, for an all-day shopping spree. I know, I shouldn't tell lies—but sometimes the truth is worse.)

She told me to have fun but to be home before five that night. Grandpa was taking her to the symphony, and I would be on twin duty.

So with the short delay, it was just after 7:40 when I pulled up to the old warehouse. It wasn't until I switched the car off that I realized that I hadn't even called. Not much I could do about that now, I finally decided. I snatched up my purse, locked the car, and then moved to the double doors. I pulled open the left one, and stepped into the darkish room. Every scuff of my feet echoed loudly across the floor, and so I found myself taking the stairs two at a time—anything to end the awful, empty sound.

Though I'd only been to the warehouse once, I knew which hall led to the right door without any hesitation. I stepped up to the closed door and then quickly knocked.

There was a pause, and I found myself needlessly holding my breath. And then I heard a couch offer a protesting squeak, followed by slow footsteps. The door swung open, and Toni grinned at me.

"Ah, an early riser. I like that in a woman."

I hardly knew what to do with such a weird greeting. "I, uh . . . sorry I didn't call first."

"Don't be silly—come in, come in!" He pulled the door open wider, stepping to the side as he did so.

I slid past him into the room but soon paused before the low table, awkwardly fingering the strap on my purse as I stood, waiting for something. Anything. Maybe I just wanted Toni to say something else—invite me to make myself at home. Not that an invitation would make me overcome my sudden shyness, but still.

I noticed that someone had cleaned the place up a little. Of course, I use the term *clean* very loosely. The floor needed to be swept, and a little dusting wouldn't go amiss. But the garbage that had previously littered the table and floor was gone.

Patrick's absence from the room was also duly noted, but before I could ask, Toni was waving toward one of the closed doors—Patrick's bedroom. "Our esteemed group leader still sleeps. He's not exactly a morning person." He strolled casually toward me, still smiling widely. "It's great to finally see you, Kate. I mean, when you actually know everything."

"Um, yeah," I said, uncertain if I should be offended by the way he said that—like I was completely dumb the last time we'd spoken.

He put out his brown-skinned hand, and I shook it a little hesitantly. But at his warm touch, I felt myself relax slightly. "Welcome to the team," he said happily. "This is pretty much my favorite part—the Demon hunting. This preliminary stuff—getting to know you, slowly telling you everything—that gets boring. But this—this is why we're here."

I released his hand and shook my head. "Easy for you to say. It isn't your life spinning out of control."

"Touché." He clapped his hands loudly together, and I almost winced at the unexpected sound. "So! How'd your whole first Demon encounter go? Patty didn't share many details."

"Patty?" I asked, smiling despite myself.

"He likes it. Secretly. *Very* secretly." Toni ambled back to the couch, then sat and faced a new-looking laptop that rested on the coffee table. Since it hadn't been there last time, I assumed it was courtesy of Terence's most recent visit.

"What are you doing?" I asked, curiously stepping closer.

"Research, mostly. It's another project—you wouldn't be interested."

Before I'd actually given my body the command, I was sinking into the couch next to him, my eyes searching the screen. It was a news article, but that wasn't what first caught my eye. It was the headline: *Death Train Continues to Advance.*

"I know this story. My grandpa was telling me about it." I felt my body stiffen, and the hairs on the back of my neck rose. "Is it . . . a Demon?"

"You're quick," Toni commented, impressed. "And, yup, it totally is."

A door opened suddenly, and I twisted around to see Patrick just coming out of his room. He had sleep lines crisscrossing against the right side of his face, and one hand was running through some very untidy hair. His blue eyes squinted a little, confusion on his face. He was wearing blue and white plaid pajama bottoms, and a gray T-shirt that was a bit too small for him. It tugged especially tight across his shoulders, outlining his strong muscles impressively.

"Kate?" he asked, his voice croaking groggily. "What's wrong? Has something happened?"

Before I could say anything, Toni was clearing his throat loudly. "Uh, dude, you're in your *jammies*. Don't embarrass the company."

"I heard your voice," Patrick continued, ignoring Toni and completely focused on me. He stretched open his eyes, as if that would help banish the lingering sleep, and then he expelled a heavy breath. "I was worried."

I knew I was staring at him, but I couldn't help it. I'd never seen his body like this—seen so much of his muscular arms. "I'm sorry—I should have called or something. I know it's early . . ."

He just shook his head, pinching his eyes closed briefly. "No, that's fine. I'm just glad you're okay." He glanced toward Toni, brow furrowed. "Why didn't you wake me up?"

Toni shrugged, turning back to the computer. "You just looked so darn cute and peaceful," he said, his words only partially laced with sarcasm.

Patrick swallowed hard and then rubbed a hand over his face—but not before I saw his eyes roll. Now that his initial scare was over, he was beginning to look slightly embarrassed. "Right. Well, um, I'm going to go and . . . get dressed." He hesitated, then turned suddenly, muttering something I couldn't quite catch. He stepped back into his room and firmly closed the door behind him.

I heard Toni chuckling, and I turned questioningly toward him. "What?" I asked.

He just shook his head, eyes on the screen, lips tugging into an unwilling smile. "Nothing at all, Kate. Nothing at all."

I wanted to question him further, but my eyes had followed his, and soon I was reading the article along with him.

A few short minutes later, when Patrick stepped back into the room—this time fully clothed, though he was wearing a brown T-shirt instead of the usual button-up—Toni and I were just finishing the last line of the article.

Patrick looked over at us as he moved toward the fridge. "Learn anything new?" he asked.

"Nope, not really—he's getting closer though."

"How can you know it's a Demon?" I asked, glancing between them. "I mean, they're just accidents."

"That's just what he wants humans to think," Toni answered quickly. "Terence knows it's a Demon, though. Whoever he is, he calls himself Far Darrig."

"Far Darrig?" I repeated the strange words a bit uncertainly.

Patrick broke in from across the room, where he was tossing some wrappers and things into the nearby trash can. "*Fear Dearg.* It's Irish." When he spoke the old Gaelic words, they sounded musical.

"He's an evil spirit in Irish legend," Toni said, eyes wide and voice haunting.

"Actually, he's one of the Good People," Patrick caught sight of my confused face over his shoulder, and elaborated. "A fairy. Like the fabled leprechaun. They're known also as Wee People."

Toni snorted, then apologetically raised his hand at Patrick's sideways look. "It's just hearing that word—especially in your beautiful lilting brogue. It cracks me up. Wee. Wee wee. *Wee wee . . .*"

"*Anyway,*" Patrick overrode his partner. "*Fear Dearg* exists in fairy tales as a mischievous fairy who enjoys playing practical jokes on humans—usually causing some harm and anxiety on humanity's part. He's also been called the Red Man, because in the stories he would wear a red cloak and cap."

Toni put his hands behind his head and reclined back into the couch. "Personally, I prefer Cinderella at bedtime."

"So this person, this Demon—is he Irish?"

"All the nuts are—no offense, Patrick." Toni paused, then

continued, his tone allowing. "But, if you *happened* to take some, that's okay too."

Patrick rolled his eyes but didn't reply.

I was still confused. "How do you know so much about this Demon, if he's still at large? I mean, you know his name, but these deaths didn't start all that long ago."

"Because," Toni spoke calmly, "this isn't the first string of freak accidents to ever happen. This has all happened before."

"It has?"

"Sure. Once in England, and a few years ago in China. Once in New York too I think—but that was in the late 1800s or so."

"Also in Australia," Patrick added, searching the nearly empty fridge. "Toni, did you eat all those apples?"

"Poss-i-bly?" He said it slowly, making the single word sound like a question.

Patrick sighed, then closed the fridge and turned to me. "Have you had breakfast?"

I nodded, and then he came to join us on the couch—thoughts of food forgotten—continuing the conversation despite the quick break. "There could have been other instances that we've missed, but whoever this Demon is, he's one sick guy. These killings are just a stalking maneuver for him. A way to make his real victim feel the fear of the hunt, and keep humans unaware but on edge. He basks in the hunt, obviously."

"You mean, he's after someone specific?" I asked, feeling my stomach tighten. "A Guardian?"

Patrick hesitated, debating how to answer me.

Toni didn't have that problem. "Actually, Terence said he usually kidnaps a Seer."

Patrick shot him a look, and Toni flipped his palms up, the universal sign for, *What did I do?*

"A Seer?" I repeated, fear coming into my voice against my will.

Patrick offered a final scowl to Toni, then he focused solely on me. "Don't worry about it, Kate. Terence just wanted us to keep an eye on things because it's happening near here. Other Guardians are handling it. We're like the optional backup, in case they need help. Besides, we have no indication that *Fear Dearg* even knows about you. You're still relatively new."

"What happens to the Seers he kidnaps?" I had to ask.

He sighed and lightly scratched one of the deeper sleep lines, high on his cheek. "Usually, they're never seen again."

"Except in Australia," Toni said quickly. "The Seer was found by her Guardians. I mean, she wasn't alive anymore, but . . ." His words trailed off, and Patrick took over.

"This is all unimportant. Right now, we need to focus on the immediate Demon problem."

I pulled in a deep, bracing breath, and then nodded my agreement. If I worried about anything else, I was going to have a mental breakdown. "Right. What are we planning to do about that, exactly?"

"Well," Toni said expansively. "The best approach to finding a Demon is to do sweeps—go to populated areas and set you loose on them. You find one, we question it. Quite simple, really. Or, of course, we could just wait for them to find you."

Patrick was shaking his head. "No, I was hoping you could do a search on the Internet for me. The Demon gave us a name."

"Oh yeah? You failed to mention that last night," Toni leaned forward, closing the news window and opening up a familiar search engine.

"How did you get Internet?" I asked while he rapidly clicked. "Doesn't that have to be set up by a company? Wait, don't tell me—Terence?"

"Actually, it was all me." Toni grinned. "Terence got the laptop, but I stole the Internet all by myself." He waggled his fingers, slightly above the keyboard. "These skilled hands can steal more than just tangible things, girl."

Patrick rolled his eyes, then said by way of explanation, "Toni was a thief, in his previous life."

"Oh," I shot the back of Toni's head a sharp look. "That explains a lot."

"Don't judge," Toni preached, eyes on the screen. "It was how I lived."

"And died, if I remember right," Patrick said, almost to himself.

"'Kay, what was the name?" Toni rapidly changed the subject.

I answered before Patrick could. "Quin Romero."

Toni's hands hovered over the keys but didn't move. After a brief pause, he was glancing over at us, eyes wide. "Are you sure?" he asked, nothing playful or joking in his voice.

"Yes," Patrick said, eyes searching his friend's face. "Do you know him?"

"I certainly hope not," Toni sighed, grimacing just a little. "But I did know a Quin Romero, back when I was alive. The first time, I mean. Technically I'm still alive, just—"

"And?" Patrick prompted.

"And he wasn't a very friendly fellow back then—I wouldn't be surprised if he turned Demon. He was sort of the guy who shot me."

I gaped. "Are you serious? He killed you?"

Toni shrugged. "I mean, it was years ago, but it's still sort of a sore spot for me." He shook his head, regret in the action. "I should never have gone back in the house. But I couldn't just leave the gold candlesticks. I mean, seriously, if you're going to rob a hostile drug lord, do it well, right?"

Patrick shook his head, brow furrowed. "If this is the same Quin Romero, what can you tell us? Is he as dangerous as the Demon from the theater claims?"

"And then some," Toni nodded. "If he's the Quin Romero

I know, he's definitely going to be a force to reckon with. He's quite the strategist, and dealing out pain is the only thing natural to him. He always had plenty of followers too, which I imagine hasn't changed much in death. In short, we're in epic trouble."

"Maybe it's not the same guy," I suggested. But I could tell by the intense concentration on Patrick's face that he didn't agree with me.

"He's probably come after me," Toni said, wincing. "I mean, revenge is his ultimate happiness. If he knows I'm here . . ."

"But he's after me," I said. "That Demon confirmed it, in the theater. He'd been spying on me, for this Romero man."

Patrick nodded, his eyes focused on the far wall. "Kate's right. This isn't about revenge. At least not yet." He thought for a short moment, then spoke firmly. "Toni, do the search. See if you can come up with anything in this area."

"I doubt I'll find his latest address," Toni muttered, but he started typing anyway.

For a few minutes, he came up with nothing that seemed helpful. Then he suddenly smiled and typed in a new name. *Selena Avalos.*

I leaned closer, curious, but unquestioning. I could feel Patrick beside me, also confused. "Ah-ha!" Toni laughed in success. "Look at this hit—Selena Avalos, currently employed by this esteemed city's educational board."

"Who is she?" Patrick asked quickly, still not following.

"One of Quin Romero's most faithful stooges, back in the day. Man, the first time I saw her . . . she's the most beautiful, perfect woman you've ever seen." Toni sighed happily, then continued quickly. "Of course, she's also evil and heartless—she just stood and watched Romero shoot me in the courtyard. But her smile is *really* something. We sort of had a thing going, before she betrayed me . . ."

I gave him a weird look, but he was back to tapping on the

keyboard. He continued to speak while he followed different links. "If Selena Avalos is in town, you can bet Romero is too."

"Avalos," I whispered to myself. Something about that name was so familiar. And then it hit me. "The sub!"

Patrick squinted at me, not following.

"At the elementary school—my sisters told me that they had a new teacher. A sub. Their old teacher, Ms. Rhodes—she just didn't show up one day, during the first week of school. Miss Avalos is their substitute right now."

"Now *that's* a coincidence," Toni said, though clearly he wasn't surprised.

"What's a Demon doing in an elementary school?" I demanded, a bit more sharply than I probably should have. "Teaching my *sisters*, for crying out loud!"

Patrick looked to Toni. "Can you find an address or something?"

"Already ahead of you, man—and nope, there's not one listed."

My mind was racing—dreading all the possibilities. "It has to be because of me, right? Oh my gosh, she's probably already gotten them to touch her—she could hurt them!"

Patrick shook his head, though the motion wasn't all that calming—his eyes were too tense to be soothing. "Relax, Kate. She hasn't done anything yet. For all we know, she's not with Romero."

"*Ha!*" We both looked at Toni, who smiled sheepishly. "Sorry. Was that out loud?"

Patrick frowned, staring at the screen, thinking, calculating. "This is a good thing," he finally said. "At least we have a lead. Someway to find Romero."

"What exactly are we supposed to do?" Toni asked. "Visit her at school—ask her where her boss is?"

"Even her lies could tell us something useful." Patrick pushed himself up off the couch and began to slowly pace the room. "Toni, what would Romero want with Kate?"

"Uh . . . probably a Seer?" Toni guessed. At Patrick's stern look, he amended. "I don't know—there's probably some personal reason." He glanced over at me. "Did you have family in Mexico in the early 1800s? Maybe your ancestor offended him once."

"Not that I know of," I said slowly. I was still thinking about Selena Avalos and her frightening proximity to my sisters.

"There has to be something else," Patrick pressed. "Toni? You got anything?"

"No, man, I got nothing. Just because the guy killed me doesn't mean we were buddy-buddy. I don't know how he thinks. He's a murderer and a troublemaker. And rich. At least, he was."

"Maybe we can use that to find him," Patrick stated. "We could search the most expensive hotels in the city."

Toni sent a doubtful look in my direction. "Are you sure she's ready for a mission?"

Patrick shook his head. "You could recognize him. Kate can stay here."

"What?" That pulled me out of my personal thoughts. "I'm not staying here. I'm coming with you."

"Kate—"

I stood so he couldn't tower over me. "I'm not discussing this, Patrick. These people are getting close to my family, and I can't let that happen. I *won't* let it happen. I'm going."

We stared at each other for a long time, neither one of us ready to relent. And then Toni stood, patting me on the shoulder. "Welcome to the team," he said.

"Toni—"

"Patrick, she should be there. It's a dangerous world she's a part of now, and she's got a right to help make it safer." He turned to me. "I'm guessing you don't have a knife on you?"

I paled just slightly but kept my face relatively strong. "No, I left all my weapons at home, under my bed."

Toni laughed a little, then shrugged. "No big deal. You can borrow one of mine."

"That won't be necessary," Patrick cut in. He sighed deeply, then shook his head once. "I don't know that this is a good idea, but you can come. As long as you promise to listen to me. Understood?"

I gave a firm nod.

Toni lightly elbowed my arm. "Well, if you're not going to carry a weapon, maybe you can come up with a list of hotels to visit? And if you're really good with the Internet, maybe you could look at recently sold homes in the area? The more expensive, the better. While you do that, Patrick and I will don our armor, eh?"

twenty-two

Their armor turned out to be nothing more than their regular clothes. I figured he was referring to their weapons, more than anything else. Still, by the time they were armed and ready to go—smaller blades hidden up their sleeves, in addition to the ones secured on their legs—I had a quick list of possible hotels. Since we lived in the Four Corners area, we had a few more hotels than the average city. I'd also found a few houses that had been sold in the last three or four weeks, but none seemed very promising to me.

Patrick led the way out of the warehouse, back to the first floor. But instead of going out the usual double doors, he led us across the factory floor, toward a single door in the back corner. This led to a small driveway, which we followed to a large shed. Swinging the wide doors open revealed the midnight-blue Nissan Altima, marking the shed as a makeshift garage.

Toni lunged for the driver's seat, but no one objected his wordless claim. Patrick held the passenger door for me, but I was slow as I moved toward him. My eyes were glued to the shiny hood of the new looking car, my mind completely boggled. I'd been so nervous about the date last night that I hadn't really registered how weird it was that they owned such a nice car, compared to the rest of the material things they had.

"So you live in there, but you drive *this?*"

Patrick shrugged, smiling a little at my surprise. "Terence wants us to blend in, and hardly anyone drives a rusty clunker anymore."

Toni leaned his head out the driver's window. "There was a time no one drove at all, and let me tell you—that really slowed us Guardians down."

"Besides," Patrick broke in smoothly. "Maybe the reason we live in an abandoned warehouse is so we can afford to drive like this?"

"It's a thought," I said, still amused. I moved for the open door and ducked into the passenger seat. "Still, it's not what I expected after seeing your couch."

Patrick grinned, then pushed my door closed. In one smooth motion he was opening the door behind me and climbing into the backseat. Then Toni shifted out of park, and we were off.

It wasn't until we hit the road that I began to really wonder what I'd signed up for. I'll admit, I was starting to worry just a little. I mean, really—Demon hunting? Can you blame me for having some second thoughts?

As we headed for the nearest hotel on the list, Toni punched a couple buttons on the stereo before groaning loudly. "Nice, man—is there a reason you deleted all my presets? And where's my hula dancer?"

"She's in the trunk," Patrick replied easily. "I had to make some changes. Lee was in the car last night, and it couldn't look *too* identical to the one you drove."

"That's the worst excuse I've ever heard to erase a man's presets and steal his dash ornament—but so be it."

"You should never have bought that thing anyway—if Terence knew that your allowance went to such stupid pieces of—"

"Who says I paid for it?"

Patrick sighed loudly. "Toni, please tell me you didn't steal it."

"All right—I didn't steal it."

I just shook my head—amazed that two immortal people would be arguing about such mundane things. It seemed unreal. Well, I guess no more unreal than anything else I'd seen yet.

"Toni, I'm supposed to be making progress with you."

"And you're doing great. I bought that pizza the other day. And Kate here can vouch for me when I tell you I bought *these*." He lifted up the pair of sunglasses from the mall to emphasize his point, and then he pushed them onto his nose.

"Yeah, with my money," I complained loosely.

Patrick groaned. "Seriously, Toni? You took her money?"

"Consider it an early payment for when I save her life. It's bound to happen at some point."

I laughed. "Toni, you've got to be the worst excuse for a guardian angel—"

"Her too?" Toni whined, glancing in the rearview mirror at Patrick. "Did you tell her that, man?"

"Nope," Patrick flicked his hands up defensively. "Not me. She got it on her own."

"Why do they always *do* that?" Toni griped to no one in particular. "I mean, it's like every Seer always cracks that joke. Like it's a conspiracy or something."

"Maybe you guys should change your name?" I suggested.

"To what? The Immortal Killers? It sounds like a bad '80s band." His eyes suddenly brightened. "Ooh! I love this song!" He twisted the volume up and sang loudly to the fast pumping words, completely forgetting the argument.

I rolled my eyes but started to laugh when I heard Patrick singing along to the chorus. I craned my neck around the seat to throw him a smile. "So you *can* sing?" I called over the music.

He only grinned at me, blue eyes shining, and kept on singing.

I turned back around but continued to listen to Patrick's voice. He was actually pretty good. I mean, *really* good. His pitch was right on, and he sustained his notes strongly. There was a resonant quality to his tenor voice that few regular people had. (I guess the reason he stood by the basses was because it was the easiest place for an invisible immortal to stand—or maybe his range was as impressive as everything else about him.)

We made it to the first hotel, and Toni parked smoothly in a pretty small space. He turned off the car and lowered the volume before winking at me. "You ready for this adventure?"

"I guess we'll find out," I returned, in what I hoped was an easy tone. I opened my door, cutting the music off. The others were quick to follow my lead, and soon the three of us were walking toward the hotel.

I was walking between them, and I noticed the twisted look growing on Toni's face. When he caught my questioning stare, he shrugged. "This place doesn't look fancy enough. We're not going to find Romero here."

"Maybe not," Patrick said lowly. "But we might find someone else." He cast a quick look to me. "Don't be nervous. Just look around, let us know if you see a Demon. Okay?"

"You're not going to . . ." I lowered my voice as we walked through the front doors and into the large lobby, "kill anyone, are you?"

Toni grunted. "I wish we'd get that lucky. We're only allowed to politely ask questions, unless we catch them in the act, or they attack us. Or if we've got witnesses against them. You'd think killing a Demon would be more simple, huh?"

"Truthfully? I wasn't sure what to expect. But I'm sort of relieved, I guess."

We walked right past the front desk, where the employees seemed almost overwhelmed with all the people trying to procure rooms. Still, I was kind of surprised that three people could slip past unnoticed. That's when Patrick whispered quickly. "Oh—I should tell you—Toni and I are invisible."

"What?" I choked lowly, almost stumbling. Patrick gripped my elbow to steady me.

Toni chuckled. "Maybe you *should* have had a bit of training first. I just didn't think you'd mess up a regular sweep."

"It's just a precaution." Patrick assured me. "But if you'd feel more comfortable . . ." Nothing seemed to change about him— no blurriness, no mysterious flickering—but Patrick cast me a reassuring smile after a split-second pause. "There. I'm visible now."

To me, he looked as solid as Toni did. It was really weird to think that the people around us would see only me and Patrick. "Can you guys warn me before you do that next time?" I asked in a hard whisper. "It's weird. How long were you . . . ?"

Toni shrugged. "I think I went as soon as I closed the car door. Habit. You, Patrick?"

"I'm not sure—around then."

I shook my head, and my phone vibrated suddenly. I pulled it out of my purse, which hung from my shoulder, and answered Patrick's quick glance. "It's probably Lee."

I flipped it open and saw that it was a message from Aaron. *Ur w/Lee?*

Still walking, I tapped out a quick answer. *@ mall, ya.*

Just as I was closing my phone, Toni said quietly, "You're here to pay attention, my young Padawan."

"Are invisible people supposed to talk?" I hissed, annoyed.

"You look like you're talking to yourself, you know."

Patrick led us down a hall, toward some elevators. He spoke thinly, eyes forward. "Toni, knock it off. She's got a life, okay?"

"You think I don't?"

I leveled a hard look at him, then addressed Patrick. "Can people hear him when he's invisible?"

Patrick shook his head and pushed the up arrow on the wall. "No. When we go invisible, it's like we live on a completely different plane or frequency. We can't be seen, heard, or felt by humans."

"But Demons can see you?"

He nodded. "And other Guardians. And Seers, of course."

"Can you guys . . . walk through walls?"

Toni answered that one. "Nope. That sucks, huh? Someone wasn't thinking . . ."

Patrick shook his head. "Just pretend like he's not here."

An older couple came up behind us, just as the elevator doors slid open. I stepped in with Toni, but Patrick waited for the older couple, courteously holding an arm out across the doors, to keep them from closing

The old man nodded gratefully, and the woman gave him a small smile.

Once we were inside, the doors closed, and Patrick asked which floor they needed. He obligingly pressed the number five, and then eleven.

Toni caught sight of my wondering expression, and he answered in an extra loud voice, just to further annoy me. "He doesn't want to draw attention to us by going up to the top floor, or just the next one up. He's picking a random place to start the search."

I bit my lower lip and focused on the elevator doors.

Patrick sent a quick look in Toni's direction, but he didn't dare scowl because the older couple might have gotten the wrong idea.

"We're here for our fiftieth anniversary," the woman explained, her words as slow and labored as her step had been.

Patrick smiled politely.

The old man nodded and took his wife's hand affectionately. "The kids paid for this. Isn't that something?"

"We told them not to overspend, but I think they did." The woman sighed. "I suppose though, between the five of them . . ."

The elevator stopped, and the doors parted. Patrick again extended his arm, and the old couple slowly made their way into the hall. "Thank you, young man," the woman called over her shoulder.

"Have a nice stay," Patrick spoke at last. And then the doors closed, and we were alone. I was deeply touched by Patrick's actions, but I decided not to say anything. I worried that whatever I said would be seen as corny or dumb.

The brief silence was short-lived, however. The elevator stopped at the seventh floor, and a couple girls joined us, one pushing for the twelfth floor. They were talking loudly about how disappointing some trip had been, and I tuned them out as my phone vibrated.

It was from Aaron. *Funny. Lee thought I was w/u. Yer G-ma is confused 2. Where r u?*

I let out a deep breath, closing my eyes briefly. Great. Like I needed this now. My boyfriend had just caught me lying to him, and now my grandma and best friend knew about it too. Unless Aaron had somehow covered for me? Maybe my grandma didn't know . . .

I saw the incoming call from her phone, and I knew my luck had run out.

"Trouble?" Toni asked, leaning against the wall beside me.

I only frowned. The elevator stopped, and the girls got out. The next stop would be ours. I debated about answering my grandma's call, and then quickly pressed the button.

"Hi, Grandma."

Patrick and Toni watched me as I listened to my grandmother's even words.

"Kate Bennett, I don't set many rules. But I do expect you not to go lying to me. Where are you? Aaron just called—he said he talked to Lee, and you're not with her. He's worried about you. So am I."

"I—I just had to get out of the house."

"Kate . . ."

"Please, try to understand."

There was a slight pause, and then her voice was more under-standing. "Are you at the cemetery, honey?"

I swallowed hard. "Yeah. But please—don't tell Aaron. I need to be alone right now."

The change in her voice was instantaneous. "You just take your time, sweetheart. But please—don't lie to me next time. I can take any sort of truth from you, but no more lies."

"Deal."

"Come home when you can. Should I be finding a new sitter for your sisters?"

"No, of course not. I'll be home in . . . a bit."

The elevator stopped, and I hoped she'd miss the little ding that signaled our arrival.

"Okay. I love you, sweetie."

"I love you too."

We said quick good-byes, and then I turned my phone com-pletely off. I'd feel guilty later, but I needed to focus now.

I could feel Patrick's eyes on my face, but I didn't bother to comment about the call. We stepped out of the elevator, and my first official day as a helpful Seer began.

We found nothing at the first hotel. We walked down every hall, through the dining room where breakfast was being served, and we even walked the grounds. It was true, it would have been easy to miss someone, but still—after just over an hour, Patrick suggested we move on to the next one.

We followed the same procedure and got the same results. There were no Demons in sight, no matter where we looked. Or rather, where *I* looked. I was the Seer, after all.

By noon we'd eliminated three hotels, and we stopped at a fast food place to grab something to eat. I wasn't that hungry, but Patrick insisted that we take a quick break. In an effort to make me eat, the two immortals also ate.

The break was relatively short, and we were at the next hotel about twenty minutes after we'd left the last one. I couldn't speak for them, but I was getting tired and more than a little frustrated. More than once on the walk toward this hotel I doubted if we were even using our time constructively. I mean, we were just guessing that we might get lucky enough to see something. It really wasn't the most reliable way to get results.

We entered the lobby, and I was just about to open my mouth and suggest we try hunting down Selena Avalos, the teacher, when Toni spoke suddenly. "We're not going to be able to slip past these guys. There's not a big enough crowd."

"Your suggestion?" Patrick asked, his step slowing beside me.

"I'll take care of it. You two work your magic, and I'll join you when I can."

"Don't get arrested," Patrick warned, but Toni was already stepping pompously up to the counter.

"Excuse me!" he declared loudly to the man seated there. "I have a complaint that I want addressed immediately!"

The clerk stood slowly, looking bored. His smile was entirely fake. "Of course, sir. What seems to be the problem?"

"Don't you take that tone with me. I know I look young and hot, but that's the plastic surgery. I'm old enough to be your father. So show some respect!"

I don't know if the young man at the front desk believed him, but his smile wavered, and his eyes became more alert. "Of course. Sorry, sir. Is there a problem with your room?"

"Ha! Don't get me started on my room. I just wanted to reprimand you about your food, and the lack of service. And when's the last time this rug was vacuumed? My asthma can't be ignored!"

Patrick and I walked past the desk and toward the elevators—I could barely hear the clerk's stilted, awkward defense, before Toni was going off about something else.

I just shook my head. "He's good, isn't he?"

"Don't tell him," Patrick begged, though his eyes looked somewhat impressed "His head can't afford to get any bigger." He pushed the up button, and the elevator dinged almost immediately.

We followed the by now familiar routine. Pick a floor, walk the halls—no Demons—pick another floor . . .

We'd been to several and were just getting off the elevator on the fifteenth floor when I heard his voice.

It was the Demon from the theater—there was no mistaking that strangely high-pitched voice. "I want some more towels," he was saying. "Do I look like a guy who likes drying off with a wet towel?"

I looked up at Patrick, but his narrowed eyes and suddenly stern face let me know that he recognized the voice too.

Now that the moment of confrontation was here, I was nervous. The elevator closed behind us, and I looked up at Patrick, worry leaking into my expression.

Patrick bit his lower lip and then pulled me aside, away from the Demon's voice. He pushed me gently into a small alcove, where two padded chairs sat against the wall, a table with a large flower arrangement between them.

"Stay here," he whispered lowly. "I'm going to follow him. I don't want you around if things go badly."

"But—"

"Once we're gone, wait for two minutes and then go down to the lobby. Find Toni, and then head home, all right?"

"But—what if he's not alone? What if you need help?"

He smiled just a little. "I've been doing this for a long time, Kate. Trust me. I'm just going to ask him a few questions."

I wanted to argue some more, but then we heard heavy foot-steps coming down the hall. Patrick ducked around the corner, hiding in the alcove with me. The footsteps came closer, and Patrick peeked cautiously around the corner.

I heard someone press the elevator button, and tried to push my fear away. Patrick wasn't worried. I shouldn't be, either. He knew what he was doing.

The elevator arrived after a brief wait, and then—a last, small smile in my direction—Patrick was gone. I looked quickly around the corner, but all I saw was Patrick darting into the elevator, a startled gasp immediately following his appearance.

Then the doors closed, and I was alone. I gnawed on my lower lip for a tense moment, clutching the corner of the wall for lack of something better to do with my hands. I still couldn't believe we'd found my stalker. But what did that mean for us, really? He'd tried to act haughty and creepy in the theater—and he'd succeeded, honestly—but there had been fear there too. If Romero was half as evil and dangerous as Toni claimed, I had a feeling that the Demon Patrick was hoping to get answers from was going to be very reluctant to betray his boss.

Before I'd consciously made the decision, I found myself heading toward the elevator—and then I turned and walked slowly down the carpeted hall instead. I didn't know what room was his, but when I spied a maid's cart outside an open door half-way down the corridor, I made a guess that this was it.

There was no one around—the hallway was completely deserted. I could hear the maid in the small bathroom, and I took a chance. I tried not to think about what my grandma would say if I got caught as I carefully stepped inside.

The room was nice, but basic. Two beds, a desk, a night-stand, and a dresser. The bathroom door was closed, and the only other door I assumed was a closet. That's what I headed for. I opened it slowly, and then pushed inside the small space.

I closed the door, and then tried to keep my breathing low and even.

I still wasn't sure exactly what I thought I'd find in his room, but I hoped I might find some clue as to why this Demon was interested in me—or rather, why Quin Romero was interested in me. If nothing else, I might find something about Selena Avalos, my sisters' Demon teacher.

I listened to the maid as she quickly and efficiently cleaned and restocked the bathroom. Then I heard her reenter the room, and then finally close the outer door. I strained my ears and waited for the sound of her cart rolling away, and then—once I was sure she was gone—I opened the closet door and stepped back into the room. I started with the suitcase in the corner, but soon discovered it was mostly empty. He'd probably been living here since he started stalking me and had grown quite comfortable. He wasn't living out of a suitcase, per se.

So I moved for the desk and searched the couple drawers. I found the customary Bible, which appeared untouched, but not really anything else of interest. He had a laptop on his desk, but I knew there was no way I'd be able to guess his password. So after checking the surface of the desk for any diabolic, hidden messages, I moved to the dresser. At first I avoided the top drawer, for obvious reasons. (I didn't exactly want to see Demon underwear.) But after searching the others and coming up with nothing, I gave in and opened the top one. Still, I found nothing of interest to me and my family. He looked like a regular business guy, who'd just extended his stay after some business conference.

I checked the closet and even the bathroom. But since the maid had just cleaned, there wasn't even any garbage for me to search through. (I was sort of grateful for that.)

I sat on the edge of one of the beds and thought about searching under the mattresses. Or maybe pulling up the edges of the carpet. Then I saw the nightstand. Somehow I'd missed it in my hurried search.

I fell to my knees in front of it, pulling open the drawers. I found a phone charger and some pens—other than that, the drawers were empty. On top of the small stand rested a single lamp and a blank pad of hotel paper.

I sighed and retook my seat on the bed. I couldn't think of anywhere else to look. I was more than a little discouraged. I was in the Demon's secret lair, and I still couldn't find anything that would help me understand what was going on. I was worse at this whole detective thing than I'd thought.

I prepared to stand and then suddenly stopped. I glanced back at the blank pad of paper, sitting calmly next to the lamp. I hesitated, wondering what had made me look back at it. And then flashes of movies came back to me. The stupid yet ingenious trick that had been used probably a hundred times—the one where the villain writes out an address or something on the hotel paper, and then tears off the sheet and leaves—not realizing that their pen pressed deeper, indenting the message on the paper below.

I reached over and snatched up the pad—and my heart soared. I couldn't believe it. There was something there—faint numbers or letters. Elated that the trick really worked, I opened the drawer and jerked out a pen. I pulled off the lid, and began to carefully run the pen back and forth across the page, hoping to highlight the hidden message.

It was more than I could have hoped for.

twenty-three

New Mexico, United States

I left Kate in the small alcove, trusting that she'd be safe while I pursued the Demon alone.

There were a few reasons I left her behind. Most obviously, I didn't want her to have to be in his presence again. I had felt her tense fear in the theater last night, when the Demon had first introduced himself. Kate had been so strong through all of this, and then—to see her fear—had really driven home the fact that she was in over her head. She didn't understand what was going on in her life right now, and she was scared. My protective nature kicked in automatically.

Of course, watching the Demon watch her had also led to this going-solo decision. I didn't want his beady eyes to touch her ever again—I didn't want him to smile that way at her, or speak in that confident tone toward her. Let him face me. It was my duty and right to be her guardian. I intended to do a good job.

When it came right down to it, though, I just didn't think she was ready to do this—to be an active part of Demon hunting. Besides, her presence would only serve to complicate things. If he ran and I was forced to chase, he would probably go invisible—it was the automatic trigger in our beings to become this way when trouble arose. A protective instinct.

In the end, I needed answers. And I would get them too. Whatever it took. No matter how heartless I had to pretend to be. I just didn't want her to see that side of me yet. Partially reasonable, but mostly selfish motivations

Luckily, it was time to focus on the Demon now—I was walking toward the elevator, almost there. Thoughts of Kate would have to wait. I knew that they'd be back.

They were never far from my mind.

I entered the elevator with more speed than was probably necessary, but I stopped just inside. The doors closed behind me, and the Demon's eyes widened as he adjusted to my sudden appearance.

"You," he nearly choked, standing against the back wall.

I smiled, though my hard gaze assured him that I wasn't in a friendly mood. "Me."

"You followed me?" he asked, glancing around the empty elevator. We were moving now, heading down. I saw that he'd pushed the lobby button, and I didn't bother to change it.

"You're going to come with me," I told him firmly, my eyes unblinking. "We have a lot to discuss."

His initial shock was wearing off. He shrugged his shoulders and straightened the cuffs on his sleeves. "I don't see the point. I've told you everything I could. Too much, actually."

"Do you know Selena Avalos?"

He smiled slowly, but his eyes glinted with unease. "I'm impressed. You do your homework, Guardian."

"Where is she living? A hotel, like you?"

"I couldn't really say. I've only met her a few times. Security measures, you see."

"You were willing to tell me about Romero. Would it really hurt to tell me where I can find him? I'd like a word with him."

"I'm more afraid of him than I am of you," he assured me.

"I'd like to change that," I said calmly.

He paled but not considerably. Nowhere near enough.

"Why is Romero interested in Kate Bennett?" I asked, my tone carefully sharp.

"He didn't discuss the reasons with me—"

"What's your name?"

He didn't want to answer. But after a short second, he spoke dully. "Call me Bill."

"How long have you been a Demon, Bill?"

He didn't know how to react to my conversational question. He'd been expecting something completely different—something more forceful. "For just about twenty years."

I snorted at his youthfulness, knowing it would offend him. "You remember Prison, then, don't you? Because I can send you back there."

He nodded once. "Yeah. So can Romero."

The elevator slowed, then stopped. The chime sounded, and the doors opened. "Walk with me." My voice left little doubt about the command. I stepped to the side, waiting for him to go first.

I guess I was expecting him to comply. A wise Demon would have. But his immaturity commanded his actions, and he charged me. I went invisible instinctively, knowing that he'd probably been in that state since he first saw me. He used his sheer bulk to push into me, forcing us both out of the elevator to crash against the hard granite floor. He was on top of me, and his weight crushed the air out of my lungs. I gasped for breath, and grabbed for a sure hold on him. I latched onto his arm, keeping him down on the floor beside me.

He was putting up more of a fight than I would have expected, and I couldn't afford for something to go wrong.

"Toni!" I yelled, knowing that no humans would hear the shout.

The Demon's efforts to escape my grasp became more urgent. We rolled on the floor, and he slammed a hard fist against my nose once he was back on top. My nose cracked, but I felt minimal pain—the regenerative immortal magic was kicking in, repairing the damage before it could become fully realized. No blood had a chance to escape before my nose was perfectly healed again.

But to avoid another hit, I released my hold on him. He might be large and heavy, but I was quick and strong. I was up before he could scramble to his feet. I stood over him, my arms raised defensively. He crouched on his knees, eyes darting from my face, to the potential exit I blocked.

"You're coming with me," I warned, my breath heavy and my voice hard.

"I don't think so," he returned. And then he lurched to his feet and yelled toward a human woman next to us. "Give me your purse! Now!"

I wanted to curse—he was visible! He was staging a robbery, making himself the center of attention so I couldn't pull him away unnoticed. I had to admit, I hadn't expected the move—especially after learning his age.

I watched as the woman handed her purse over, tears in her eyes. The Demon held her purse, tossed me a quick grin, and then bolted around me. The woman started screaming, and security stopped him before he could make it to the doors. The police would arrive in minutes—I could do nothing. I looked on in mute frustration from the sidelines, completely helpless to interfere.

I half expected Toni to show up beside me, but he never did. I guessed that Kate had slipped past me without my noticing, and Toni was already taking her back to get her car. I dreaded facing them both and telling them of my failure.

I stayed in the lobby for the seven minutes it took the police to arrive, handcuff him, and escort him to the car. Then I pulled out my phone—still invisible—and tried calling Kate. It went right to her voicemail, and I frowned, though it made sense. I'd seen her turn it off after talking with her grandmother. Still, I was disappointed. I liked having excuses to call her, even if I was reluctant to relate what had happened.

I called Toni next, already walking toward the front of the hotel. He answered on the second ring.

"Yo. What's up?"

"I'm through here. Can you pick me up?"

"Uh . . . Where are you?"

"At the hotel. The Demon got away—I couldn't get anything from him. Is Kate still with you?"

" . . . Should she be? I'm all sorts of confused right now."

I immediately stopped walking and turned quickly around, eyes scanning the busy lobby. "Where are you?" I demanded.

"I'm at the hotel too. In the little boys room, actually. Kinda awkward, huh? Anyway, you guys found a Demon, then? Awesome, I want to hear the whole thing."

My stomach dropped, and my heart began pounding rapidly. I started quickly back for the elevators—beginning to run when I remembered I was invisible. Something was wrong—she should have been down here over five minutes ago. What if I'd left her up there, and there was another Demon? The thought hadn't occurred to me before, and I cursed myself. Just because we'd never seen this Demon with a partner didn't mean he worked alone. "Toni, meet me on the fifteenth floor as soon as you can. Something's wrong—Kate should have been in the lobby by now."

"You left her alone? On her first mission? What's wrong with you, man?"

"Toni, just hurry, okay?" I hung up on him and slapped my palm a few times over the elevator button—shifting to visible with little effort or thought. I impatiently waited for an elevator to come—it seemed to take forever. I tried not to think about all the things that could have gone wrong. I'd never forgive myself if something happened to her—it would be entirely my fault.

The elevator arrived, and I jumped inside, jabbing the appropriate button. The doors finally closed, and I began to rise. Fortunately, the elevator wasn't called on to stop anywhere before reaching the floor I needed.

I stepped out, hesitating in the hall, unsure of where to go now that I was here. I checked the alcove—no Kate. I started down the main hall, but it was deserted. Only closed doors on either side. It was now that I began to really panic.

And then my phone vibrated, still clutched in the cage of my taut fingers. I jerked it open and placed it against my ear. "Toni?"

"Yup, it's me. I'm in the lobby."

"Toni, I can't find her—she's not here."

"Relax, dude, she's here. You just missed her—she came down as you went up. Way to overreact, though."

I relaxed so quickly I was almost dizzy. I swallowed hard and closed my eyes, trying to get a grip on myself. She was all right. She was with Toni. She was safe.

"That's good," I finally managed to say. Toni knew me well enough to know that I wasn't my usual self, but he didn't comment on it. For now. But knowing Toni, I'd be teased about my overreaction later.

"Yeah, it is—so's the information she got. Here, I'll let her tell you."

I turned back for the elevator as Toni's phone changed hands, and then I was hearing Kate's bright voice.

She sounded a little breathless but very pleased. Still, her first words were for me. "Patrick, are you sure you're okay? Toni said the Demon got away."

"I'm fine. He was just smarter than I thought he would be. But what's Toni talking about? What information?"

"Well," the excitement was back in her words, "after you left, I decided to search his room, if I could find it. Anything I might learn to better understand what's going on, you know?"

She paused but wasn't waiting for an answer—just trying to catch her breath. I'd reprimand her later for disobeying me.

"Anyway, the maid was cleaning his room—remember, we heard him yelling at someone? Anyway, her cart was in the hall, and she was in the bathroom. I hid in the closet until she left, and then I searched the room. At first there was nothing, really—and then I found a pad of paper. You know how in the movies bad guys always jot down addresses and stuff, and then the message gets imprinted on the paper beneath?"

"Not really," I told her honestly, pushing the elevator button. "But I understand the concept."

"So," she said triumphantly. "This means that even though we didn't get much out of him, we got this—Romero, @ 10pm. And then there's an address and a date—next Wednesday. He's going to be meeting Romero! And now we know where and when."

I smiled despite myself—my heart still working to stop pounding. "That's excellent, Kate. Good work."

We headed back to the warehouse, calling it a day. It was almost one, but we'd done just about everything we could. Once we were back in the car, I very gently told her not to ever deviate from the mission plan again—unless she had my permission. She agreed, but it seemed like a somewhat offhand promise to me. I didn't press her. I was too fascinated by the happy glow her eyes held. It wasn't something I'd ever seen in her before, and it was beautiful. It enhanced her entire appearance, and I didn't want to take that away.

Most Seers I'd come in contact with weren't exactly the happiest bunch of people. Many—like Kate—got their sight by nearly dying alongside others they loved very much. It was true that everyone had struggles in their lives, but it seemed that Kate was even more sorrowful than most. But it was the quiet way she mourned that had first captured my attention. It was unique, the way she was brave for her friends and remaining family. The way she tried so hard to please her boyfriend and look out for all those around her.

Kate was very special, there was no doubt about that.

Toni stopped next to her car, and she thanked him briefly before getting out of the car. I hesitated only a second before opening my own door. I saw Toni's quick, knowing grin, and then he pulled around the building, leaving us alone.

Kate threw me a smile as she moved for her car, as if she'd expected me to follow her. "Thanks for letting me come along. I know you could have left me behind just as easily today."

I shook my head and fell into step beside her, shoving my hands deep into my pockets. "No, thank you. This mission would have been a complete failure without you."

She shrugged, allowing that, and we shared a quick laugh. She pulled out her keys and unlocked her car. But she didn't open the door—she turned back to look at me, one eye squinted a little more than the other. It was a very cute look for her, and I found myself struggling to breathe.

"You are going to let me come, aren't you? On Monday? To question Selena Avalos?"

I bit my lower lip, then nodded. "All right. I can allow that."

"What about Wednesday?" she asked, her lopsided, squinty look still in place.

I straightened, shaking my head just slightly. "I don't think that's such a good idea. If Romero really will be there, then—"

"I'm coming." The squinting was gone. Her eyes were wide and sure. "I need to help—you can't understand how good it feels to actually do something about all this."

"That confrontation will be very different from the one with Avalos—"

"Well," she interrupted, rolling onto the balls of her feet, looking rather proud of herself. "It looks like I'm the one with the address, so you should probably let me tag along."

I frowned, eying her with mock distaste. Well, it was only partially mocked. A part of me genuinely wished she wasn't so brave and opinionated. "I think I preferred the 1700s. Women were less independent."

"So you like your women humble and boring?"

"I like women who respect my opinion, I guess."

She leaned against her car door, squinty look back in place. "How about a deal? Some equality of wills?"

"I'm listening."

"What if we see how Monday goes. And if I listen and be good, then maybe I can come along Wednesday. I'll stay in the car if you tell me to, and I'll be perfectly obedient—just like the women of the 1700s. How about it?" She extended a hand, and I sighed loudly before taking it, my smile finally breaking through as I flexed my fingers around hers.

"All right. We'll see how it goes. But can I hold on to the address in the meantime?"

She pulled her hand back, shock on her face. "Of course not! That's my insurance. You won't leave without me if I have it."

My hand was tingling. "I don't think I'd dare face your wrath, if I double-crossed you."

"Smart of you."

We laughed, and she fingered her keys. As I stared at her—the delicate curves of her face, her smile—she gazed into my eyes. The air changed around us—intensified. She seemed to feel the change too, and her smile fell. I could feel mine disappearing, too.

I wondered what was coming—what would happen. I knew what I wanted to happen. The thing I'd been dreaming about since I first laid eyes on her. But I knew that couldn't happen. It wouldn't happen. I couldn't let it happen.

Before I could lose my resolve, Kate got smart and ended the moment. She forced a smile and then opened her car. She tossed her purse over onto the passenger seat, hesitated, and then turned and embraced me quickly. I folded my arms around her, surprised at how easy it was to hold her. How natural it felt to have her arms around my neck, her breath puffing onto my skin.

I wanted to keep her close for much longer, but she was already pulling back, before I'd fully gotten used to the idea that she was actually hugging me. Her arms pulled away from my shoulders, and I caught a glimpse of her slightly pink face.

"Thanks again," she said, her smile friendly—just as her hug was meant to be. A quick exchange between friends. And maybe it had been for her. My own stomach was clenching with emotions that definitely went beyond the bounds of friendship.

But I tried to hide that, and I managed to match her parting smile. "Of course. And thank you, for everything you did today."

"Okay." Her lips pressed together, and then she turned and got into her car. I waited until she was safely inside, and then I shut the door for her. She manually rolled the window down, and then offered a last smile. The possible blush that I thought I'd glimpsed was gone—if it had ever been there at all. "I'll see you Monday then?"

"Monday," I agreed.

Then she started the car, and in less than a minute I was standing alone in the dusty courtyard, watching the dust settle in her wake.

Toni was lying on the couch, lounging back with the laptop balanced on his stomach. He didn't look up when I entered, but his words were obviously for me.

"You like her. A lot."

I didn't say anything. Only moved for my room.

"Seriously, I thought there was something before today, but now . . . now I know. That date must have been killer, huh?"

I opened my door and stepped quickly inside, completely intent on escaping his words.

"Tough with her having a boyfriend though . . ."

I shut the door and kicked off my shoes. I looked around the small room that had been an office, once upon a time. The furnishings were few—the utter basics. A mattress, set on the floor. A small desk, cluttered with books and papers. A dresser with my clothes. That was about it.

I pulled in a deep breath, telling myself that I shouldn't have this conversation. I should stay here, in this feeble sanctuary, ignore him . . .

I sighed, then turned and jerked the door back open. Toni was smiling smugly up at me, knowing all along that I'd come back out. I frowned at that—maybe I was too predictable.

"It's not like that at all," I said, as if I hadn't stopped the conversation by closing my door a minute ago. I forced my voice to keep calm, though my racing heart was most definitely contradicting the simple evenness of my tone.

The idiot actually laughed. "Really? You're going to deny it? I saw the way you watched her—spoke to her. Heck, even the way you stand around her. You've got it bad. So I reiterate—stinks about that boyfriend, huh?"

I ground my teeth together and then moved quickly toward him. He swung his legs out and moved the computer to the table. He was sitting by the time I reached the couch, and I lowered myself next to him. "What do you want me to say?" I asked softly, staring at the laptop.

"I want you to admit it, first of all." He shook his head, marveling at the situation. "Now I understand why you enjoy school so much. The world makes sense again!"

I spoke slowly, so he wouldn't misunderstand. "Kate is a wonderful person. I admit that she intrigues me—"

"Intrigues you? Seriously? Do you remember what century we're in these days?"

I just shook my head and pushed back against the lumpy cushions. "I try to give you an honest answer and you mock me. Nice."

"Look, I'm just trying to do you a favor. Because, maybe you just can't see it, but she's 'intrigued' by you too." His hands fell to his sides after making air-quotes, and I blew out my breath sharply, staring hard at the wall opposite us.

"I'm her Guardian. There's nothing more."

"You know, I was talking with Lee—when we were at the mall—and she mentioned that Kate isn't happy right now. With Aaron, I mean. I guess they've been in a rut."

"Your point?" I tried not to sound excited. I think I succeeded.

"Maybe you should make your move," he hinted.

"Why are you doing this?"

"Doing what?" he asked innocently. "Being your pal? Maybe it's because I like you. Maybe you're just a sorry chap who needs some serious help. Didn't you ever like a girl? Cuz you sure don't act like you know what you're doing."

"I think this conversation should have ended a few minutes ago." I lifted myself off the couch, but soon turned back to receive Toni's next words.

"You have a right to be happy, you know. You don't have to be all gloom and doom. I mean you're dead, but, so what? You can still be happy. You also have the right to go after Kate."

"Toni—"

"Lemme finish. Now, I'm not saying that it's going to work out. I mean, there's some obvious reasons why it's going to be strictly a short-term thing, but . . . you'll regret it forever if you don't."

I knew what he meant—it was one of the major things I had yet to tell Kate. Because while it's true that most people get to make the choice to become Guardians, Seers don't get that chance. It's like they've already done their time—given their help to the human race. They go straight to Heaven. Kate—when she eventually died, as all humans must—wouldn't get the choice. She would go to Heaven— the one place I would never be able to go.

Of course, I hadn't thought about this too extensively. Why ago-nize over things that wouldn't even matter? Because though I liked her—liked her a lot, admittedly—she was with Aaron. And even if by some miracle she came to like me and picked me instead of him, she would grow sick of this life. The life of a Seer was not one that people chose for long. Some Seers didn't want any part of it. Some made it six months before walking away. The longest I'd ever heard was twenty years. And once Kate was sick of it all, I'd never see her again.

Even in the best-case scenario—that she stayed, we fell in love, and lived a long life together—I wouldn't age, and she would. Eventually she would die, and we'd be separated forever. And if I thought I was miserable now . . .

It was better not to even try, I'd assured myself.

But it would be so easy to fall in love with Kate. I was already halfway gone, and falling faster and faster every time I saw her, spoke with her. I had to keep grabbing for the side of the cliff—anything to keep the inevitable fall from happening. I only hoped that she would get sick of this life quickly, because I knew that I couldn't hold off for long.

As with every time I let my imagination wander to the possibilities, I now forced myself to recall Aaron. He wasn't a bad guy. In fact, he was very kind to her. I'd watched that very carefully last night. But there was also something superficial to the actions. He did it because it was expected of him—not because Kate deserved it. He held her hand because he wanted too—not because he saw who she really was. There were times I got the distinct impression that he didn't know all that much about her. He didn't understand her nervous habits, why she smiled just slightly every once in a while, as if she was entertaining a humorous thought.

I wasn't intimating that I understood her—but I wasn't her boyfriend, either.

I knew I needed to stop torturing myself. So I pulled up a picture in my mind—a picture of Aaron and Kate kissing in the backseat while I drove the vehicle. It was a good one to remember. Painful, but effective. It stopped these thoughts, anyway.

Toni was staring at me, waiting for me to say something.

I finally spoke, my words quiet, my defensive edge gone. "I would love nothing more than to try, Toni. But I can't. Kate doesn't need that right now."

Toni sighed loudly and then plopped his feet up onto the coffee table, which creaked dangerously. "Fine. Sure. Whatever. Just thought I'd speak up, you know. Be your psychiatrist for once. But that's cool—I understand. All this time, I never realized, though . . ."

He waited, and I finally bit. "Realized what?"

"That you're a quitter. I mean, Guardians by nature are fighters." He shrugged indifferently. "But you know, that's fine. You're different, and I respect that."

"Good," I said loudly. "Then is that the end of the conversation? Am I free?"

Toni suddenly smiled. "It's another girl, isn't it? Some young Irish maid stole your heart, and you've sworn off love forever. You're a walking broken heart, and I've never noticed. A regular romance novel is your soul!"

I gave him a weird look and then turned back for my bedroom. "I'll talk to you later, Toni. I think I'm going to take a nap."

"Um, you may want to run a little errand before then."

I turned around, but only because I was curious about the devious change to his voice.

He plucked up a black, basic wallet that had been on the couch next to him. "Somehow, Kate's wallet managed to find my fingers. You should probably return it to her, don't you think?"

"You stole her wallet?" I walked quickly over and then snatched it away from his grubby hand. "What kind of sick matchmaker are you?" I cracked the wallet open, so I could be sure the cash pocket wasn't empty.

Toni leaned back easily, fingers laced behind his head. "If it works, I'd say I'm successful. You're going to go return it, right? I mean, after you wait an appropriately long time. I mean, you don't want to appear too eager to see her again. Am I right?" He nodded at my shirt. "I'd change if I were you, too. Brown is just not your best color, man."

I didn't know whether to yell at him or thank him. So I just turned and went back to my room, taking the wallet with me.

As I set it carefully on my desk, I wondered how long I'd stare at it before getting up the courage to go to her house.

twenty-four

New Mexico, United States

Once back home, I learned that Grandpa was out picking Josie up from a soccer game. Jenna was in her room, and Grandma was waiting for me in the living room. Generally not a good sign. I moved to sit next to her on the couch, the wide bay window behind us.

She didn't look upset—only concerned. "Honey, would you like to talk?" she asked softly, as soon as the initial greetings were out of the way.

I tried to give her a real smile, and I think she believed me. "Yeah. It was just a bad day. Lots of memories hit me at once, and . . ."

But she was nodding gently. "It's all right. I understand." The brown in her aura flared, and I instantly felt bad for lying—for inspiring the sudden pain she most obviously felt.

"Thanks, Grandma," I whispered, leaning closer and wrapping my arms around her slightly stooped form. She patted my back softly, but soon enough was pulling back.

"So," I winced. "I turned off my phone to avoid Aaron. Did he call you back?"

"Only once—and I told him I'd talked to you, and you were all right."

She must have understood my frustrated expression, because she suddenly took hold of my hand. "Now, don't start accusing him of tattle-telling and make a big deal about this. He was obviously concerned. He was at work, and Lee came by with her mom's car to get it inspected. I guess your Grandpa had talked to Howard, the head mechanic over there, about getting your car's oil changed. Aaron called the house to talk to Grandpa about the price, and he casually asked about you. I told him you were with Lee. He got worried, quite understandably."

I sighed, then decided to let the fight go out of me. I knew I'd forgive him eventually, so why not start now? Still, there was something about his actions that rubbed me wrong . . .

"I'm not blaming him," I told her, and she visibly relaxed.

"Good. Because he's a very nice boy, and you're great together."

I casually steered the conversation to school, and I talked with her for a few more minutes before I excused myself.

Once in my room I sat at my desk and started up my computer. While it loaded, I let myself think about the day's events. So much had happened since this morning—I'd learned so much. But for some reason, my mind stuck on only one image. The image that had been burned into my memory, and that I couldn't stop thinking about the whole drive back home.

I kept reliving the moment at my car with Patrick. That second when everything changed. When the air became charged as his eyes wandered my face, and I couldn't stop myself from getting lost in his intense stare.

My stomach was tight, and my heart pounded. I watched him watch me, wondering how a moment could last this long—feel this intimate, without touching or speaking. I was aware of his every breath, the tensing in his posture as the moment dragged on. I could feel a strange heat in my chest. I couldn't think of Aaron, or focus on anything but the blue in Patrick's eyes. I wondered what those strong arms would feel like around my body. I remember thinking about what it would be like to press against his lean figure. To be held by him. That was all. My wondering never took us farther than that.

And that's why—despite my better judgment—I'd hugged him quickly before escaping into my car. He'd looked surprised. But when I pulled back, I'd seen the pleasure in his eyes. Just thinking about my arms around him—his hands on my back—had me struggling to breathe. My head, pressed briefly against his . . .

My computer was ready, I realized. I mentally shook myself and tried to rid my mind of those dangerous fantasies. Dangerous because they so unarmed me, and also because I refused to get hurt. Belatedly, I realized that Aaron should have been reason number one.

I entered my password, pulled up a search engine, and then pulled out the carefully folded piece of paper I'd taken from the hotel. I typed in the address and soon found what I was looking for. It was a nightclub of some kind, located about thirty miles from here. I printed out some directions, and then folded them and put them in my purse. They'd be ready, when Wednesday came around.

Now I had Monday to worry about. But it wasn't really worry—more like a strange sense of anticipation. Selena Avalos was going to get a piece of me, that was for sure. I was ready to start striking back for the fear I'd been feeling. I just couldn't think too much about what Quin Romero would want me for. Then, of course, I was also worried about Far Darrig, the Demon killer that was on the loose—and headed this way. Patrick had tried to reassure me that I wasn't the target, and I think a small part of me believed him. After all, that made sense. In the Demon world, I was less than insignificant. But still, it was another thing I could worry about, so naturally I did.

I decided that while I was on the Internet I'd look to see

if they'd learned anything new about the Death Train, but I couldn't find anything.

And so I turned to homework, though I wasn't really able to focus.

Before I'd accomplished much of anything, I heard Grandpa and Josie return—long overdue, in Grandma's mind—and I heard Josie loudly giving Grandma the play by play of the game they'd barely won.

I tuned my family out, trying to concentrate and actually get something done. But it was a wasted effort. Grandma yelled for me to come down, and I looked at the clock—shocked when the time registered. It was nearly six. I'd been up here for hours.

I tucked my stuff away quickly and then headed down. Grandma was in the kitchen, wearing one of her nicest dresses for the symphony. She was getting a glass of water, which she didn't drink when she saw me. "Okay, I just ordered pizza—I got enough that the twins can make themselves sick. We won't be back terribly late. Make sure the twins are in bed by ten—I don't care what excuses they use. I expect you in bed not much later than eleven. Saturday or not. We should be back around then."

"Unless I kidnap her and we elope," Grandpa joked, entering the room.

I turned to smile at him, taking in the dark suit he wore. I usually only saw him in an old pair of comfortable suspenders or overalls, so the change was almost startling. "You look great, Grandpa."

"I look like a fish out of water," he complained, but it was in good fun. He smiled back at me, cocking his head slightly to the side. "You know, you actually look happy tonight, darling. I mean really, genuinely happy."

"Thanks, I think." I shrugged. "I feel pretty happy."

Grandma dumped her remaining water into the sink and then turned to us. "Right. Do you have your wallet, dear?"

"Yes, indeed."

"And you stopped to fill up after picking up Josie, right?"

"Yes, I did."

"Good." She nodded, satisfied. She could get so flustered, it was almost funny.

They both hugged me good-bye—Grandma kissed my cheek—and then they were out the door. Grandma came back a second later, though, to call up to the twins to be on good behavior. "I'm leaving my second pair of eyes here, just in case!" she threatened. And then she left, and I sighed in relief. Her stress had been rubbing off on me, and at last I could relax.

I went into the kitchen to get a drink of my own, and I'd just set the used glass into the dishwasher when there was a knock on the door. I closed the dishwasher and wandered back to the front door. I pulled it open and blinked in surprise. It was Patrick.

He had that awkward stance, the one that was growing very familiar. Only one hand was in his pocket, though—the other held my wallet. He followed my gaze and smiled apologetically.

"Toni, uh . . ." He shrugged. "I'm still working on him."

"Oh, um." I lifted a finger and scratched absently at my hairline. I was very aware of his stare on my face, catching every motion, every emotion. It was warming and unnerving, all at the same time. It left me slightly unsure of what to say. But I had to say something—he was waiting for me to say something. "Thank you," I forced out at last. "You didn't have to come all this way—I would have seen you Monday."

"I know. I tried calling, but your phone's still off."

"It is?" I patted my pocket, but it was still upstairs. "I guess I forgot to turn it back on," I said, sounding sheepish. It was a new sound for me, and I didn't really like it.

He smiled a half grin and then handed the wallet to me. I took it with both hands, trying really hard not to push my hair back behind my ear. I wasn't going to give into my nervousness.

My fingers ran uselessly over the corners of the wallet, flipping it over and over in my hands.

Both hands were now firmly in his pockets. "I didn't mind. It was an excuse to get away from Toni for a while."

"Yeah, um, I can't imagine living with him full-time." An honest answer, but it shouldn't have been that hard to come up with.

"It can be a challenge," Patrick admitted.

There was a short silence, and I honestly didn't know what to say. I didn't want him to leave, I realized. But that was exactly why I needed to let him go.

And then Josie was bounding down the steps, chanting, "Not supposed to have friends over, not supposed to have friends over!"

She reached the bottom of the staircase and then pulled the door open wider, so she could see who it was. "Wow. Hi. I'm Josie." She saw my wallet, then got a really confused look on her face. "Is he the pizza guy? Where's the pizza?"

The last was directed toward him, but before he could stumble out an answer, I was speaking. "He's a friend from school. Patrick, this is my sister Josie."

He extended a hand, his smile small but genuine. "Ah, the one with the loud voice."

Josie took his hand, smiling despite herself. "Flattery won't work on me, but I do take pride in my lungs. Does Kate talk about me often?"

"She may have mentioned you once." He shrugged a single shoulder, obviously teasing her. "I mean, older sisters avoid talking about younger sisters, right? It's perfectly natural."

"That doesn't mean it's nice," Josie argued. She elbowed me and then caught sight of his car on the street. "Nice ride. Are you one of those rich guys that move in from foreign countries with parents who are spies and have plans to make their children into terrorists?"

"Wow," he laughed shortly and blinked his wide eyes once. "Should I be offended? I'm not sure . . ."

"You just talk funny, that's all."

"Thanks."

"*You* said I had a loud voice," she pointed out.

He bowed quickly, the motion mostly from the shoulders up. "True. Truce?"

"Why not?" Josie glanced back at me, eying me strangely. "So, were you going to invite him in or make him sweat on the porch all night?"

Patrick spoke quickly, twisting slightly away from us, jerking a thumb back toward his car. "No, that's all right. I was just leaving."

"You just got here!" Josie protested. She rounded on me. "Is he staying or not?"

I stared at my sister's face, wondering if her sudden interest in him was a blessing or a curse. Then I decided to seize the moment. I'd be making amends to Aaron tomorrow anyway— why not really dig myself a hole, first?

I turned toward Patrick, a somewhat cautious smile on my face—but sincere nonetheless. "I guess that's up to him. He's welcome to, though."

He glanced between us—eyes almost sinking into mine, once they met—and then he smiled. "I'd love to."

twenty-five

An hour later the four of us were crammed onto one couch, laughing hysterically. The movie wasn't all that funny, but in our present mood, anything would have been hilarious.

The remains of our dinner cluttered the coffee table—only one slice remained, and there were a couple leftover bread sticks on the side.

Jenna was almost hyperventilating, she couldn't breathe. Josie was laughing so hard she was slipping off the couch.

Why the hysterics? Quite simply, Patrick was hilarious. For a guy who hadn't watched many movies, he knew how to enjoy them. He hadn't done it on purpose, but he'd certainly started a new fad.

While I was getting drinks and bringing in plates, Josie and Jenna fought over what movie to watch with dinner. Patrick tried to help out by turning on the TV, but he accidentally hit a wrong button on the stereo. We didn't realize until we started the movie that we were listening to a corny Mexican radio station while watching our movie.

The result was instant laugh attacks. Patrick was embarrassed at first—but soon he was laughing right along with us. He alternately switched through stations but always kept them classical or easy listening. The result was best when there was no singing, we soon learned. One of the best moments was during a shootout on screen, while listening to spa-worthy music.

That's what made Josie slip to the floor the first time.

Once that movie ended, Jenna was up, grabbing another. "Let's try it on *this* one!" she gasped.

My arms were wrapped tightly around my body, and I struggled for air. When our laughter would start to die, Patrick would switch to a new station. I told myself that I'd be prepared—that I wouldn't start laughing again. I honestly thought I might die from lack of oxygen if I went through another fit.

My resolve fled when he flipped back to a classical station, where the strains of the Wedding March accompanied a high-speed chase.

The twins literally rolled on the floor, and Jenna gasped about how much it hurt. Patrick's laugh was loud, and his face was almost completely red. He was shaking the whole couch, and I had to tightly grip the arm to keep from falling off myself.

I think I was laughing more from the three of them than the movie/music antics.

When the movie ended, we were all gasping, trying to get a hold of ourselves. But just as we started to quiet, Jenna would whisper, "Car chase," or Josie would croak, "Patrick moved the couch three feet!" and it would all start up again.

It probably took us a half hour after the movie was over to breathe normally—with only a few sudden bursts of laughter.

Aside from the pain in my midsection, it felt amazingly good to laugh. I hadn't ever laughed that hard in my life, especially not since my parents had passed away.

"When I can stand," Josie gasped from the floor, "I'm going to kill you, Patrick."

"I'm so sore," Jenna groaned. "I can't move!"

"I can still barely breathe," I complained, burrowing deeper into the plush couch.

"I can't believe how funny you all looked," Patrick gulped through another laugh.

"Us?" Josie rolled to her knees to regard him. "*Us!?* Did you *see* yourself? You were practically dying!"

I glanced down at the floor and then faced Patrick with a grin. "You did move the couch."

He snorted, his body rippling with a suppressed laugh. "I did not—that was all you!"

"Not even." I reached over to slap his arm, missed, and did a face-plant into the cushion, my arm falling uselessly to brush the floor.

That started them all laughing again, and it was a while before I was able to raise my head and speak. "All right, that's enough—you two were supposed to be in bed half an hour ago. Get."

"Ah, who cares? It's a Saturday, and Grandma's gone."

Jenna seemed to agree with her twin. "Yeah—let's watch another. What about an animated movie this time? A Disney classic. That could be awesome!"

"Robin Hood!" Josie yelled, naming her favorite.

"Get it!" Jenna urged.

Patrick blew out his breath, as if that would rid him of the giggles. He leaned forward, patting me gently on the back, where I was still face-planted next to him. He addressed the twins. "I think your sister's right. It's getting late. You don't want your grandparents to get back while I'm here—they might not let me come back."

Josie looked horrified. "Then go!" She lurched forward, clutching his leg. "Go, go, go!"

He just shook his head. "Not until you're in bed."

"Meanie!" Josie yelled into his leg.

But it worked.

In minutes they were telling us good night and heading

upstairs. Soft music continued to play out of the speakers, but Jenna had switched the TV off.

"Are you still alive?" he asked next to me, pushing the cushion down in an effort to free my nose and give me some air.

"Yep. But I hurt."

He chuckled. "I didn't know girls could make some of the sounds you made tonight."

As I pushed myself up, I slapped his knee, and then we were sitting side by side in the otherwise empty room, probably a little closer than would be considered good, seeing as how I had a boyfriend.

"You're good with kids," I said, more to break the short silence than anything else. "They really like you."

"They're fun girls."

"Yeah, I guess they are." I glanced over at him, hoping I wouldn't ruin the jovial mood that—while subdued—still lingered. "Did you have any siblings?"

He continued to stare at the black screen. "Um, yeah. I did. A brother."

"Older or younger?"

"Younger. But only by a little."

"Were you close?"

He nodded once. "Very."

"What was his name?" I asked tentatively.

It took a moment before he answered. "Sean. His name was Sean."

I bit my lower lip, deliberated shortly, and then laid my hand on his knee. He looked over at me, surprised by the contact. I smiled understandingly. "Is it hard to talk about him? About your family?"

His eyes moved over my face, and he nodded. "Yes. I know it was a long time ago, but still . . ."

He glanced away, and I kicked myself for bringing it up. Of

course it would be painful. He must have watched them die, while he himself never aged.

I was about to draw my hand back, but then he was turned toward me, speaking quietly. "I loved my family deeply. My father was sometimes hard for me to talk to during my last year of life, but I still loved and respected him. My mother was an angel. And my brother . . . he was my best friend." He hesitated, choosing his words carefully. "You probably don't know much about the time period—at least, not much aside from the American and French revolutions. But it was a hard time for Ireland as well. We were under British rule, and life wasn't easy. A rebellion began, and my father was swept into it like many were. He encouraged Sean and I to join, but I wanted other things." He cracked a very thin smile. "Don't laugh, but, I wanted to be an artist. A painter."

I regarded him with new admiration. "You paint?"

"I haven't for a very long time," he admitted. He tilted his head to the side. "Why are you smiling like that?"

"Um, I'm sort of an artist myself. But I prefer sketching to painting. I've always been better at that."

"You're an artist?" His initial surprise was mingled with light approval.

I shrugged a bit awkwardly. "Sort of."

"I would love to see some of your work."

"Only if I can see some of yours," I bargained.

A smile flickered across his face. "Very well. It's a deal."

I realized that my hand had been on his knee for too long. I pulled back but settled deeper into the couch, leaning even closer to him as I did so. I was just so . . . comfortable. "So, what happened?"

He shook his head slowly, eyes moving to the far wall as he continued with the story. "Sean and I joined the United Irishmen, and I died a rebel in my first major battle. In the history books, it's known as the Battle of Tubberneering. It was a success for the rebels, even if victory was short-lived."

I swallowed hard and looked down at my hand, picking at the seam on my jeans. "I'm so sorry," I finally said, unsure of what else to say. "That must have been . . . awful." I felt like an idiot for my poor choice of words. They were so inadequate.

He nodded once, still looking away. "I remember thinking that I'd failed my family. My father, for dying after so recently joining the cause, my mother for never returning, and Sean—for not being able to protect him like I promised I would."

I was burning to ask a question—one that I knew I shouldn't. It was perhaps the most personal question I could ever ask him. But I couldn't stop myself from whispering the words. "If you loved them so much . . . why would you choose to become a Guardian?"

He didn't speak for a long time. I was just opening my mouth to apologize for my rudeness when he finally spoke. "I became a Guardian to protect my brother—like I'd promised. I was with him every step of the war. I had to follow rules, of course—I could never show myself to him, or anyone I knew. That sort of thing is never allowed. But I got him through—at least until he and my parents had to flee for France. They were traitors and would be killed if found in Ireland."

He paused, and I could hear the clock ticking.

He shrugged. "And then I stopped watching them. It became too painful to watch my mother grow old and frail—to watch my father be driven insane by his patriotism. To see my brother get over my loss and move on. To forget I ever existed."

Before I could stop myself, my hand was back on his knee. He was looking toward me, and I tried to keep back the tears that were in my eyes. "You never forget those who die, Patrick. Just because you learn to laugh again doesn't mean you never loved them."

He watched my face, and when he spoke his voice cracked with emotion. "I know. It was still hard to watch them, though."

I rubbed his knee slowly, swallowing back my sudden tears. "I know. I'm so sorry."

He took a deep breath, and then watched my hand, gently moving against his leg. "Thank you, Kate," he whispered.

In the next moment I was hugging him, pulling him close as I tried to offer comfort for a pain I knew only too well.

A couple minutes passed with our arms around each other, and then Patrick forced a small laugh. "If your grandparents walked in on us now . . ."

I laughed and then pulled away, breaking the contact. "You're right. That would've been hard to explain."

But he didn't stand up, and neither did I.

I glanced down, catching sight of his leather bracelet. I'd been meaning to ask him about it, but I hadn't yet had the opportunity.

"Um, I hope I don't scare you off with the whole Inquisition thing, but, I was wondering . . . your bracelet? You wear it a lot, and I just wondered . . ." My voice trailed off, but he was smiling lightly.

"It has quite the past—like me, I guess. It was a gift."

I immediately pictured the face of a girl. That's why I was really relieved when he continued before I could say something dumb and reveal my thoughts. That would have been beyond embarrassing.

"Toni gave it to me, when we first became partners. He knew that we'd been paired up so I could try and . . . reform him. He gave me this to prove that everyone is a thief at heart."

My brow furrowed. "How?"

He almost rolled his eyes. "The idiot stole it from someone. I still don't know who, because he refuses to tell me. Since I couldn't return it right away . . ." He shrugged. "I like to keep it nearby, just in case Toni cracks or I finally figure out where he could have gotten it from."

"You'll probably be waiting a long time for him to fess up."

"You're right, I'm sure. We're already going on twenty-two, almost twenty-three years, so . . ."

I laughed lowly, awed by the sheer craziness of my life.

He smiled at my reaction, but once things had gotten quiet again he rose to his feet. "It's getting late. I'd better go."

I stood as well, though I didn't want to see him leave, and we walked slowly out of the room. "Thanks for coming," I said softly, glancing up the stairs as we walked past. I didn't hear anything up there, so I imagined the twins had already zonked out.

He opened the front door and then turned back to face me, his voice quiet in the dark hall. "Thanks for letting me stay. I had a really great time."

I nodded. "I needed that."

"So did I."

We stood in the silent entryway, just staring at each other. He was standing just inside the door, and the bright moonlight outlined him in a starry glow, emphasizing the silver in his aura. The darkness from the night outside added to his ethereal appearance, and I realized that I'd stopped breathing.

So had he.

He was watching me closely, his eyes warming every inch of me, though they never left mine. The air between us sparked and thickened. Intensified, and adapted.

He swallowed once, and then he was leaning toward me. And in that second, when I realized what he was going to do, I couldn't think of one reason to stop him.

His lips pressed gently against mine, lingering sweetly before he pulled back. A mere breath away he waited, pausing to see if I'd respond.

I did.

I took that final step closer, the one that would press our bodies together, and then I tilted my head back and I kissed him. Our lips brushed once—twice—and then his arms wrapped around my waist, pulling me closer as he breathed my name.

I pushed my fingers into his hair, still kissing softly. My hands wandered over the planes of his face, and I felt his hand on my arm, then my shoulder, then the side of my neck. There he held me in place as his lips explored mine. When he broke away for air, I opened my eyes to see his face—catch his expression.

He looked awed. Anxious. Eager. Pleased. Unsure. Conflicted. Elated. And so many other nameless emotions.

I must have looked pretty similar, because he hesitated briefly before reaching up to caress my cheek with the fingertips of one hand.

"I'm sorry," he whispered thinly, still slightly breathless. "I shouldn't have done that. Forgive me." And then—before I could think of something to say—he was releasing me, pulling away. He stepped out of the house, pulling the door closed behind him with a swift jerk. He'd moved more quickly than could be considered normal, almost like he was trying to run away from me without actually forcing his legs into a run.

I couldn't move. I was rooted into place. The feel of his fingers against the skin on my face, his gentle lips on my sensitive mouth . . . they held me there. The memory of his kiss had honestly left me reeling.

I heard his car door open, then slam closed. Those sounds triggered my steps. I walked slowly into the living room, pushed back the edge of the curtain, and watched his car as he lurched away from the curb and drove quickly up the street.

I wondered if he was as changed by the experience as I was.

twenty-six

Aaron called me late Sunday morning. We didn't talk for long. I kept up the same lie Grandma had unwittingly helped me craft—that I'd been at the cemetery. He tried to sound understanding after that, but I could still hear the hurt in his tone. For some reason, that made me mad. But I held my anger in check.

He asked me to go to the Fall Ball with him, the school dance that was taking place this Saturday. He apologized for not asking sooner, but I told him not to worry about it. We were a couple, after all—it wasn't like I was surprised that we were going together.

I thought about the formal dresses I had, wondering which one I'd pick if I wasn't able to get enough time to go shopping. I supposed that would somewhat depend on what happened with the Demon problem this week. My life lately was pretty unpredictable.

I finally said good-bye to Aaron and moved to the kitchen—where the family had congregated so the twins could tell Grandma and Grandpa all about Patrick and the fun night we'd had.

Grandpa wanted to try watching a movie Patrick-style right away, and the twins were willing—though they doubted it would be as funny without Patrick and his loud laugh.

I was hoping to escape with them, but Grandma started speaking before I could. "Who is this Patrick exactly? A friend of yours?"

"Yeah. He recently moved here from Ireland." Sort of true—except for the recent part. "He's a really nice guy, but he doesn't have a lot of friends. Lee's kinda crazy about him."

"Oh." She seemed to relax a little at that, which is of course why I'd said it in the first place. She changed the subject. "So I thought I heard you talking to Aaron? Is all that figured out?"

I suddenly flashed back to Patrick's kiss. "Yeah, I think so. I'm going to a formal dance with him this weekend."

"Really? That'll be nice. I bet he looks great in a suit."

"He does." I wondered what Patrick would look like in a suit, and then I realized for the hundredth time that I was thinking about him again, and I ordered myself to stop. But like many things, it was easier said than done.

Monday came, and I wondered what it would be like to see Patrick again. I wondered if it would be awkward, or be just like before we'd shared a beautiful kiss together. I couldn't decide which was more likely, or which one I'd rather have.

I got to American lit just as the warning bell rang—early, but not too early. Patrick was there, and I knew we'd have a brief moment alone.

He didn't look up as I moved to take my place beside him, and it wasn't until I was seated that he glanced up, a smile on his face. "Good morning. How are you?"

"I'm good." I noticed the drawing he'd been working on, and I smiled and leaned closer. "The twins? You drew them?"

He laughed. "At least you recognized them. It was my project yesterday." He winced. "I'm afraid I've lost a lot of my touch."

I studied the picture. It depicted Josie and Jenna, lying on the floor laughing with the couch behind them. "This is really good," I told him honestly.

He shook his head. "Not really."

"You captured the emotion."

He handed it to me, not commenting on the praise. "Maybe you could give it to them? A peace offering after all the pain I inflicted."

I laughed and carefully tucked it into my bag. When I looked back up I caught him staring at me. But even though our eyes met and held, and we each knew what the other was thinking about, it wasn't awkward like I'd feared. It was more like . . . we both felt something missing. And though we mourned its absence, there wasn't anything to say.

And then Aaron came in, and I broke our intimate gaze.

"Kate!" Aaron grinned and came quickly toward me, dropping a quick kiss against my lips that almost hurt—not because he was forceful, but because I knew now that there was so much more out there.

"You seem happy," I commented, hoping he wouldn't notice the hint of sadness in my voice.

"Of course I am. I'm with the most beautiful girl on the planet, plus I just found out from coach that I'm definitely competing in the meet this Wednesday! You're going to be there, right? I'm sure I can sneak you on the bus if you don't want to drive down."

"Um, what time is it?" I could feel Patrick next to me, trying unsuccessfully to look like he wasn't listening to every word.

"It starts at six or something, but we won't be up until eight most likely."

"It's a two-hour drive, isn't it?"

"Yeah, something like that. What, did you have other plans?"

"Sort of—I was planning a movie night with Lee." It was almost scary how fast the story came to me. Becoming a good liar had never been one of my goals in life, but somehow it had happened.

"Oh." I could tell from his aura that he was even more disappointed than he sounded—which was pretty impressive, because he wasn't really trying to hide it. "Could you guys do that another night or something?"

"I don't know—we've been planning it for a while," I lied. "I'll talk to her, though."

"Okay. That would really suck if you couldn't come."

"Yeah, it would."

Mr. Benson entered the room, and the conversation ended. But I could tell he was still pretty upset with me. I sighed. If only he could understand. I was trying to stop a group of Demons. It was slightly more important than watching a swim meet.

I wondered if the truth would even help the matter at this point. It seemed like all I was able to do anymore was disappoint him.

Patrick was going to come pick me up at my house, minutes after I dropped the twins off at home. Luckily it was timed perfectly so they were upstairs and didn't realize he was here—or else we might not have made it back to the elementary school in time to catch their Demon teacher.

As it was, we entered the parking lot just as I spotted a young and beautiful-looking woman unlocking her silver car. It was a Toyota Camry. Her black aura seemed strangely in conflict with her good looks and modest brown dress, but I pointed her out to Patrick, and he moved to pull into a spot one away from her.

She looked up as we approached, squinting through the windshield to catch a glimpse of us. Patrick pushed the gearshift to park, and then threw a warning glance at me. "Let me do the talking. If I tell you to get in the car, do it. Okay?"

I nodded that I understood, my hand itching to open the door.

He sighed at my eagerness and then switched off the car and opened his door. I waited until he was almost around the car before I opened mine—I knew he would have freaked out if I hadn't waited, because I was closer to the Demon.

She balanced a large bag on her shoulder, and she watched us with wide, gorgeous eyes. Her brown skin was almost more of an olive color, and she was exceptionally beautiful. Her face was long and perfectly sculpted. Her skin was flawless, and her lips were full and naturally red. Her figure was also impressive, and I was suddenly more self conscious.

Put succinctly, I understood why Toni had politely asked to stay behind. She was the perfect blend of beauty and danger. I was confident that no man would be able to resist her call—especially someone like Toni, who'd been under her spell before.

She watched us carefully, a small smile that didn't touch her eyes pasted on her face. "Well, hello," she said, glancing between us. "Let me guess." She pointed a perfect finger at Patrick. "You're the overprotective Guardian, and you," she flicked her finger toward me, like I was an unfortunate afterthought, "you're the helpless Seer. Pathetically easy to guess."

I forgot Patrick's order to keep quiet. "How'd you know? About what we are?"

"Well, I figured it was only a matter of time before someone checked on me." She smiled toward Patrick, and the smile was purely seductive. I hated her already. "You're either getting old or lazy. I've been here for weeks, Guardian."

"What's your name?" Patrick asked, seemingly unaffected by her demure smile.

"Selena Avalos," she replied, her voice beautifully husky, yet still thinly musical.

I glanced at Patrick, but he was focused on the task at hand. "What are you doing here?"

"Getting ready to get in my car after a long day of teaching small children. Is that a crime?"

His face could have been carved from stone, and his gaze was almost as hard.

She pretended to suddenly understand the question. "Oh! Oh, you mean in the city? Why, I'm doing exactly what you Guardians want every Demon to do—turn over a new leaf. I've been reforming myself. I went to school, got my teaching degree, and I've been looking for a steady job ever since. I'm only subbing now, but this position may yet turn permanent."

"What do you know about the disappearance of Ms. Rhodes?"

Her smile twisted, and then she laughed and wagged a slim finger at him. "You naughty boy—you know more than you're letting on!" She shrugged just a little. "I haven't a clue. I mean, you can't think that I had anything to do with her disappearance? I'm reformed, remember?"

Once again, I couldn't be silent—Patrick sent me a quick look, but at least he didn't stop me. "Why are you here?" I asked. "What is it you want?"

"Hmm," she considered me deeply, eyes sweeping over every inch of me—judging, and then grinning when she realized there was no competition between us—on any level. "You must be new to the trade, dear. You're never supposed to be that direct. You're a watch dog to us immortals—nothing more. Don't get uppity."

Patrick took a step toward her, angling his body protectively in front of me as he did so. "Miss Avalos, I think you better start talking before this gets unpleasant."

"What is there to discuss? I know your rules. Have I attacked you? No. Have I been caught doing anything wrong? Not at all. Do you have witnesses to some crime? I think not. So, if you'll excuse me, I have places to be."

She moved to turn, but I took a quick step toward her, which got her to keep her back from turning. Patrick grabbed my elbow, stopping me from getting too close, but I think my eyes conveyed the right message to her.

"If you touch my sisters," I growled, "you're going to regret it."

She stared at me—momentarily shocked—and then smiled demurely. "Ooh, she knows how to issue empty threats. I feel very frightened." She glanced over my shoulder, meeting Patrick's narrowed eyes. "You Guardians should learn to keep your Seers on shorter leashes. You might find you can get a word in occasionally."

Patrick stepped up beside me, fingers still wrapped protectively around my arm. He got close to her—close enough that she almost leaned back against her car. "If you know the rules, then you know I need a valid address, or some way to contact you."

She smiled, showing perfect white teeth. "I think the school works, don't you? Unless you want to spend an evening with me over the weekend, of course, then naturally I'll give you my home address."

I shouldn't have felt a wave of jealousy, but I did.

Patrick didn't waver, though. "Where are you living?"

"How about a number?" she asked instead. "Numbers are great, because then you can call me whenever the moment is right." She rattled off a phone number, paused, then repeated it.

"I got it the first time," Patrick assured her thinly.

She grinned. "Yes, you Guardians are pretty quick, aren't you? Well! Until we meet again." She nodded to each of us. "Patrick, Kate—it was good to meet you. Perhaps you'll have better manners next time, Seer."

We watched her get into her car, and then she backed up, offering a quick wave to Patrick before driving out of the lot.

"She knew our names," I stated in the thick silence, fuming.

He sighed. "She knows a lot more than she pretends."

"Why did we let her go, then?" I demanded, turning on him.

He released my arm and sighed again—more deeply this time. "Kate, I didn't want to. But I couldn't do anything else. We have no evidence that she's not who she says she is—a reformed Demon."

I snorted. "Yeah, because she played the part so well. What about my sisters?"

"For the time being, I think they're safe." He suddenly laid his hand against my arm, trying to offer comfort. "I promise, though, I won't let anything happen to them. We'll figure this out." He pulled back, and his eyes narrowed. "But as for you . . ."

"What?" I asked, my straight face designed to look innocent.

He narrowed his eyes at me, but I knew he wasn't very upset. "I thought I made it clear that I would be asking the questions."

"You weren't asking them fast enough," I told him defensively.

He smiled just a little, though it was obvious he was trying to be stern. "I was getting to them."

"Not the ones I wanted. Besides . . ."

"What?" he prompted, smile still lingering.

Only slightly embarrassed, I hurried to finish. "I thought maybe her looks and creepy smiles might get to you. I bet most men fall under her spell."

He laughed aloud and shook his head at me. "Trust me— you had nothing to worry about."

"Why not?" I asked, a bit irritated by his reaction. I thought I'd had a fair point.

His lips came together, the smirk still in place. But his eyes were serious, and I hardly believed the words that came out of his mouth. "Because I'm under another spell right now, and it's a lot more powerful."

I stared at him until I could see the seriousness begin to enter his eyes. Then I cleared my throat and turned back for the car. It was better if I didn't comment on that one—for both of us, I knew. "Um . . . yeah. Anyway, talking with her was a waste of time. We didn't get anything out of her."

Patrick was right behind me, jogging a step ahead to get my door before I could. "We got her number. Plus, we know that she's definitely a part of all this."

"I guess so."

He watched me get into the car, but once I was settled he continued to hold the door, until I glanced up at him.

He spoke sincerely, nothing joking in his expression. "Kate, everything's going to be okay. This is the sort of thing I've been doing for over two hundred years now."

And as I stared into his eyes at that moment, I completely believed in his ability to keep me and my family safe.

He closed my door, and then a minute later we were pulling onto the road, headed back to my house.

"Kate, can I make a suggestion?" he asked suddenly.

I watched him warily. "I guess."

He flashed a quick smile to me, picking up on my cautious tone and finding it humorous. "Maybe you shouldn't come Wednesday. Just have a normal night—go to Aaron's swim meet."

I was already shaking my head, turning to look out my window. "Can I ask you something, Patrick?"

He paused, and I surreptitiously stole a glance at him. He was watching the road carefully, obviously not wanting to hear my question. "All right," he finally sighed.

I continued to look out my window, but I could see a hazy reflection of him through the glass. "If I was a Seer with experience, would you take me along?"

I could almost feel him squirm more than see it in the window. "Honestly? Yes. But I mean no offense against you. It's just that the situation might get out of hand, and Toni and I—"

"So there's a need for a Seer?" I clarified. "That's what I thought. You need to know who the Demons are, don't you?"

He flashed me an annoyed look but turned quickly away

when he thought I'd missed it. "If you come, there can be no more disobedience. Do you understand?"

I gave him a slightly sour look. "I'll be a good little dog, I promise."

He laughed just a little, though there was a hard edge not meant for me. "Yeah, I guess I should have warned you about that. Most Demons don't really see Seers as, well, people."

"I got that vibe."

"I'm sorry."

I felt my heart lighten when I realized that he truly was. Not for the first time, I wondered what his aura would look like. He was just such a mystery—it was hard to imagine. I had a feeling, though, that his aura would be the most complex I'd seen yet. But after all, that only made sense—he was the deepest person I knew. Sometimes so predictable, and yet still so mysterious. It was such an intriguing combination.

But these thoughts turned me toward other thoughts— thoughts of kissing him—and I knew I needed to stop that train before it reached the station. No matter how much I didn't want to.

twenty-seven

It had taken a long conversation with Lee to persuade her to lie to Aaron. I told more lies of course—lies about going dress shopping, and Wednesday being the only night to do it to effectively surprise my boyfriend. She offered to come along—I had to plead with her to stay, in case he called her house. Aaron had turned into a regular Nazi when it came to me. Since I'd lied once, he thought I was making it my full-time occupation these days. Which, truthfully, I guess I sort of was. But still—it was annoying to have him checking on me all the time. It felt wrong to have my boyfriend call my grandma and ask where I was.

I'm still not sure if Lee actually believed me or not, but she agreed to stay home and pretend I was with her. When I told her she might have to lie to my grandma, she started protesting again. I had to resort to some blackmail before she reluctantly agreed to the lies.

"What else are best friends for?" she finally grunted.

I even parked my car at a grocery store so it would be out of the way, unable to mess up the lies I'd so carefully told.

And so Wednesday night found me, Patrick, and Toni in their car, thirty miles southwest of where I was supposed to be. Approximately.

I knew Patrick wasn't happy about my presence, but he was trying to make the best of it. I had purposefully promised myself that I would be on good behavior, no matter what Patrick asked me to do. Sit in the car? I could live with that. Don't ask questions? Not a problem. I was going to prove to him that he hadn't made a mistake in bringing me along.

Patrick had driven this time, and Toni was in the back, staring in appreciation at the building across the street. "This looks like the kind of club that's featured in the movies. You know? Pulsing lights, gorgeous women, great music, plenty of drinks . . . I'm psyched."

Patrick and I ignored him. "Kate, in the line—are there any Demons?"

I was already looking at the long line of eager people, hoping to get inside. It snaked back a long way, and at the head was a security guard of some kind, checking IDs.

"I count six," I said at last—double-checking quickly.

Toni whistled lowly. "We've got a hot spot, that's for sure. Should we call Terrence?"

Patrick debated slowly, deliberately. Finally he spoke. "He'll tell us to back off. We won't be able to get to Romero. We'll call him after the meeting."

"How are we getting past the guard?" I asked.

"Is he a Demon?" Toni asked.

Patrick answered before I could. "No. He's going to be a Seer. He's watching for Guardians. Romero will leave the instant they see us."

"So?" Toni asked, getting impatient.

"I'm thinking . . ."

I only waited a second before ending the short silence. "I could go in."

"That's out of the question," Patrick said at the same time Toni slapped his hands together, saying, "Excellent!"

"No." Patrick reiterated firmly. "We'll think of something else."

"Like what?" I asked, trying to hide the small bit of fear I felt at the thought of going in alone. "It's almost ten—Romero is in there."

"You don't even know who to look for," Patrick protested.

"Maybe I could find a back door or window—let you guys in?"

Toni looked impressed. "Not a bad plan, Kate. I like it."

"You couldn't get in anyway," Patrick pointed out, sounding a bit too relieved by his own words. "I'm sure you have to be over twenty-one to get in. Besides, a Demon hot bed is probably a pretty exclusive place."

I hated to admit that he had a point, but he did. I sighed loudly, falling back against my seat. "Then what are we supposed to do? Just go home?"

There was a sudden tapping on the back passenger window, and we all whirled around to face the door. The night was dark, but the few street lights let us know that the new arrival was a man. A man with a silver aura.

"It's a Guardian," I whispered, shocked.

Patrick pressed the automatic locks, and then the mystery man opened his door and slipped into the car with us.

He had dirty blond hair and light green eyes. He was tall and rugged-looking, probably in his mid-thirties. He was very tan and had a cocky half grin on his face. "G'day, mates—my Seer *thought* he saw two Guardians over here. Guess he was right." He had a very strong Australian accent that seemed to fill the entire car, making this moment seem even more unreal.

Patrick regarded the man strangely. "And you are?"

"Oh, of course, sorry about that—I'm Jack Williams. Terence sent me down and out this way, tracking Far Darrig. I'm guessing you've heard of him?"

At Toni's quick nod, Jack continued. "Anyways, my Seer just went inside, and he'll be getting me in soon enough—thought you blokes might just like to tag along."

And then he turned to me, seeing me for the first time. His eyes widened a little, and I guess I should have been flattered. But as his arrogant smile stiffened into place, I fought the urge to frown. "Well, 'ello, 'ello, 'ello. My Seer didn't mention you. You're quite the beaut, aren't ya?"

"Excuse me?" I asked, trying to look more offended and less taken aback. I think he enjoyed my reaction, but he was already turning back to Patrick.

"So what you blokes doing here? Hoping for a corker night?"

At Patrick's blank look, Jack tried to explain. "It's slang for something excellent." He glanced around at our unsmiling faces and then shook his head. "For a couple of immortals, you'd think you'd spend a bit of bloody time in the Outback."

Toni cleared his throat, and that brought us back to the issue at hand. "You and your Seer—you tracked Far Darrig to here?"

Jack nodded. "Sure thing. Some poor bloke bit it last night, just a few blocks from here—we're pretty sure it's that Demon who's responsible. Then my Seer got a look at this place when we driving by last night and nearly choked." He looked at Patrick, and leaned forward. "That means he was surprised," he mock whispered.

"So I imagined," Patrick said, no inflection in his words.

Jack leaned back against the seat. "So that's my story—we're here to scout out the place, see what's cooking inside. Interested in coming along?"

Toni glanced toward Patrick and then nodded quickly. "Sure. Sounds like fun."

Jack grinned and slapped his palm over Toni's knee. "That's the spirit. What about you?" he asked Patrick.

He barely contained a sigh, but he nodded. "I'm in."

"Me too," I said.

Jack grinned in my direction, but Patrick was already shaking his head. "You're staying right here. Where it's safe. We already have a Seer on the inside. There's no need for you to come."

Toni waved a quick farewell to me and then exited the car. Jack offered me a sympathetic nod. "Maybe next time, love." And then he was gone too.

Patrick turned toward his door, but before he could pull the handle I was reaching over and grabbing his arm. "Patrick, please," I begged softly, my fingers flexing around his halted elbow. "I won't be in the way. I need to go in there."

He glanced at my hand and, though it was too dark to know for sure, his jaw seemed to tighten before his eyes swept back up to my face. "Kate, I need you to stay in the car. I can't guarantee your safety any other way. There are too many variables."

"Jack, you mean?" I said wryly.

Patrick nodded once. "He's a big one. I'm not sure how he deals with Demons, but I have a feeling he doesn't understand the word *inconspicuous*."

I sighed, releasing his arm and sinking back against my seat, my arms folding tightly under my chest. "Fine," I grumbled. "I'll stay."

"Kate . . ."

"I know. I understand. Really, I do."

He watched me for a moment, and I think he was going to say something, but then Jack pounded the hood of the car. "It's time!" he said, a bit too loudly in my opinion. Then he looked more closely at the hood, appearing sheepish. His voice was quieter and more muffled. "Sorry, mate—I think I dented your bonnet."

Patrick sighed, opened his door, then cast a last look at me before getting out. "Please, Kate—I'm trusting you to stay in the car. Lock the doors. If we're not back in a half hour, or if anyone tries to get in the car, drive away. Toni and I can find another way home."

"All right," I promised reluctantly. He started to slide out, and my next words came out fast. "Please be careful, Patrick."

He tossed a glance over his shoulder, his leg stopped swinging out, and he smiled just a little. "I will." He swallowed, then tossed me a nod. "Lock the doors," he reminded me briefly.

And then he was shutting his door, crossing the street with Toni and the weird Guardian named Jack.

I locked the doors, wondering if all Guardians were as strange and diverse as the ones I'd already met. I watched the three Guardians move to the back of the line and then slip casually into a side alley that ran along the right side of the building.

I settled back in my seat, not looking forward to the wait.

twenty-eight

Ten minutes had passed. From my perspective, nothing had changed. There was still a long line waiting to get inside the club, and I could still barely hear the sound of thudding bass. I'd never been in a night club before, but I'd seen enough movies to imagine Patrick and the others wandering around a dimly lit room, flashing lights almost blinding them.

They were outnumbered. That was abundantly clear. And so what if they couldn't die? They could be kidnapped or held hostage. Though I'd been feeling pretty brave with them in the car with me, I was beginning to worry that coming here had been a mistake. We didn't know enough about Romero—but at the same time, we knew far too much. He was a ruthless killer—a heartless Demon.

I was dying to know what was happening inside the club. Had they found him yet? Would Toni recognize him? Would Patrick watch him or approach him? Would Jack ruin the whole thing?

I was so concentrated on my thoughts and watching the front of the building that I didn't hear the light tapping on my window right away. Once the sound registered I whipped around, cringing back instinctively—and with due cause.

It was the Demon from the mall.

I bit back a scream but only barely. I crawled away from the

window, into the driver's seat. I hadn't consciously made the choice
to drive away yet, but the Demon must've thought I had. He was
suddenly waving his hands, pantomiming for me to stop. He
pointed to the window, asking me with his eyes to roll it down.

I shook my head firmly.

He sighed, and for the first time I noticed how dirty and
rumpled his clothes were. He mouthed a single word—*please*.

Again, I shook my head.

He glanced up and down the street, making sure we were
alone, and then he put his face closer to the window, speaking
just loud enough for me to hear him. "I need your help," he said.
"I think Romero just tried to have me killed." His eyes were bulg-
ing, and I could sense his fear.

I swallowed hard and again shook my head. He wasn't coming
in here. No matter how well he acted the part of a desperate man.

He was growing frustrated—agitated. "I won't hurt you,"
he said through the glass. "Please—I promise." His harried face
brightened with sudden hope. "I can show you," he said, and then
suddenly I could see his aura.

It wasn't what I would have expected from a Demon. But I
guess, in a weird way, it was exactly right. Mixes of gray depression, and brown pain and regret. There was a streak of purple
jealousy, but it seemed out of place in his otherwise dark emotions. There was no blue. No white. Not the slightest hint of
yellow. I'd never seen more sadness and pain.

"See?" he nearly begged. "I mean you no harm. Surely you
can see that."

I just shook my head. "I'm sorry," I whispered, and I realized
I *was* sorry. No one should have to feel like he did.

He read my lips, and his face crumpled. He leaned against
the car, palms on the window. "So am I," he said. He straightened
just a little, though his hands remained in place. "Your sisters,"
he said. "They're in danger."

My breath caught, and I leaned forward. "What's going to happen?" I asked a bit too loudly, desperate for answers.

His eyes scanned my face, and the fight left his body. "Romero plans to use them against you. It's all going to unfold sooner than you could know. You must run, Kate. Leave all of this behind. The Demons, the Guardians—you want no part of this life. Take it from one who had no choice."

"You had a choice," I told him.

He nodded once. "True. I did. And so do you. Choose better than I did." He swallowed hard, and then began to explain everything. "Romero needs you to—"

He stopped speaking. His eyes grew wide, and then he slumped against the car, gasping once against the window, fogging the glass briefly. I watched in horror as he slid against the car, and then fell to the ground.

I was staring at a short man with a black aura. He held a knife that glinted softly under the yellow street lights, sharply contrasting the silver metal and the streaks of blood that now spotted it. This new Demon was staring into the car in confusion, but it was a cold and heartless gaze. He was wondering why I existed, wondering how he could most easily kill me—the witness to his crime.

I was frozen. I knew the keys were in the ignition. I knew I should jerk them, start the car, drive away from this place as quickly as possible. But I couldn't. I was caught in a terrible stare that I couldn't break, no matter how hard I tried.

The murdering Demon regarded me for a short while, and then he stooped toward the dead Demon's body. I assumed he was cleaning the knife, but I didn't care what he was doing. I felt completely sick, but at least I was free of his gaze.

I twisted the key, and the car roared to life. I was about to shift into gear when I heard Patrick's yell.

"Kate!"

I looked up quickly, saw him jogging toward the car, just crossing the street. He was focused on me—he didn't know about the Demon ducked on the other side of the car.

"Patrick!" I yelled in warning, grabbing for the door handle. I couldn't explain the sudden urgency that had me needing to be at his side, but I could feel the tears building up against my eyes and I didn't care about logic.

The lock was still in place, though, preventing me from running to the safety of his arms. Without thought, I slammed the button I needed, and suddenly all the doors were unlocked.

I opened mine instantly, practically falling out of the car. But I heard the passenger door open a split second behind me, and the car shifted as the Demon climbed inside. I screamed instinctively—I heard Patrick's footfalls quicken, though it might have just been my heartbeat. I tried to stumble out of the car, but my foot caught against the lip of the door and my face fell toward the asphalt.

The Demon caught my swinging arm—which had wildly brushed his skin first—stopping my fall. But he was trying to drag me back inside. It only took a split second for me to realize what he wanted: to pull me back into the car and lock the doors, effectively isolating me from Patrick.

I wasn't going to let that happen. I turned on the Demon, clawed at his face—flinching when I realized how close he was. His head was near my slumped shoulder—he was practically on top of me.

He yelled in pain and anger, and I watched in sick fascination as every cut I managed to inflict healed instantly. The torn skin barely had time to sting before it was smooth again. That more than anything made me scream again. It was so unnatural—so wrong. I was trying to stop an immortal being. What was the point?

I was gasping for breath, on the verge of hyperventilating.

And then Patrick was there. He grabbed my arms, my shoulders, yanking me out of the car and out from under my attacker. I could feel the bruises his hard fingers created against my skin, but strangely I didn't feel any pain.

My feet slammed against the pavement, finally free of the car, and one of Patrick's arms snaked around my waist, supporting me. His other hand pulled a knife from his belt, holding it toward the Demon, who was lying awkwardly across the front seats.

Patrick was breathing hard and rotating me to the side of his body, trying to shield me from whatever would happen next.

"Get out of the car." Patrick ordered the Demon menace in his hissing voice. *"Now."*

The Demon stared at Patrick, obviously murderously angry at the sudden turn of events. He too was breathing hard, but despite his anger he was smiling. It was a cold, awful smile. I shuddered at the sight, but couldn't pinch my eyes closed.

The Demon slowly shifted his body until he was back in the passenger seat. And then he was slipping out of the car, straightening on the other side. Once the car was between us, he bolted down the sidewalk, darting into an alley—confident in the knowledge that Patrick wouldn't leave me to go after him.

"I'll get him!" Toni yelled suddenly from somewhere behind us. I jumped at the unexpected voice, and Patrick's arm tightened dramatically around me.

Toni darted past us, his head slightly ducked in an effort to gain more speed. He bolted past the car and pounded into the dark alley, vanishing from view.

I was still struggling to breathe and the unshed tears were frozen in my eyes. My heart was pounding, my body shaking despite my Guardian's secure hold. Patrick shoved the dagger into his belt, and then he twisted me to face him, hands running up and down my arms.

"Kate?" he asked breathlessly, his blue eyes deep with emotion. "Are you all right? Did he hurt you?"

I shook my head, but with all my trembling I didn't know how believable it looked.

"What happened?" he demanded.

It took more effort than I thought it would to form words. I had to force each sound out, and even then it was hard to understand—even for me. "I was in the car. And then he came—the Demon from the mall. He wanted me to open the car. I wouldn't. He showed me his aura." I ducked my head, trying to get control of myself. "There was so much pain. But I couldn't let him in." I looked up, gasping through the tears that had finally decided to fall. "That Demon—he killed him. He was trying to tell me something, and then he just killed him." My voice broke, and I couldn't say anything else.

Patrick gathered me into his arms, pulling me tightly against his body. "It's okay," he whispered soothingly into my hair. "I'm here now. You're perfectly safe."

I clutched at his stiff shirt, buried my head deeply into his chest. Still, the images of death and pain didn't disappear. Maybe they never would. "I could've saved him," I mumbled tearfully. "I should've let him in. He was so afraid . . ."

"Shh, you did exactly what you should have done," he assured me, one hand rubbing up and down my back. His head lifted until his chin was resting on top of my head, as if that could help reduce my shaking. "It's okay. You're safe now." He swallowed hard, and I could feel the pounding of his heart. I knew he was only pretending to be calm—his body was definitely telling a different story. But I let him pretend, because I needed the security his calm offered.

And so Patrick held me while I cried, and for the first time I began to wonder if I really had what it took to be a Seer—even for a little while.

✺

Jack came strolling out of the club minutes after Patrick and I had stopped talking. He must have noticed my tear-stained face, but he wisely didn't comment on it as he approached.

A young man with large glasses trailed behind Jack, and I guessed that was the Seer. He appeared to be in his early twenties—maybe twenty-two.

Jack informed Patrick that the Demons had fled, and then he thanked us for a great time. I didn't say anything, and Patrick's voice was low when he asked Jack if he could dispose of a body.

"Happy to," he said easily. He nodded to me. "Hope to see you again sometime, miss."

Patrick told him where he could find the Demon body, and I was sure to keep my eyes closed until I heard the sound of Jack and his Seer driving away.

Patrick ran a hand over my hair, smoothing it down. "Come on," he whispered. "You should sit down." He helped me into the car—the backseat, thankfully. I didn't want to be anywhere near the front of the car right now.

He slid in next to me, closing the door behind him. And then he gathered me back into his arms and held me tightly.

"I'm so sorry," he whispered in the thick silence, his breath falling against my neck. "That was the last thing I wanted you to see."

"I don't know if I can do this," I breathed thinly.

He was quiet. His fingers lightly traced comforting patterns on my arm, but he didn't say anything. I focused on the circles he traced, and slowly my breathing became more even.

"He said my sisters are in danger," I said at last.

His answer was low and instant. "I'll have Toni start following them at school."

In my mind, I kept seeing the Demon's wide eyes, slowly

going lifeless as he slumped against the car. The last puff of breath against the glass.

"What happened inside?" I asked, desperately needing the distraction.

He seemed to debate for a short moment, but thankfully he started talking. "Jason—the Seer—helped us through a back window. I told them we were looking for a Demon named Romero. We split up and wandered the crowd. Luckily the lights were so bright and colorful, I don't think any Seer could have picked us out as Guardians.

"Toni spotted him, sitting at a table in the corner, surrounded by people. I didn't want to approach him, because I didn't want to have to just walk away—like what happened with Avalos. I wanted to end this. So I waited, and then the moment came. Romero was talking with Bill, the Demon from the mall. Money changed hands, and then Bill was dismissed. I thought about going after him, but then moved closer to Romero instead."

Patrick's shoulders shrugged around me. "And then we were seen. Romero's men attacked us, and he slipped away. I'm sorry."

"What do we do now?" I asked softly.

His arms flexed around me, pulling me even closer. "Now I'm going to keep you safe. Maybe we scared Romero tonight, maybe we didn't. But Toni and I are going to keep a constant watch over you and your family. We'll never be far."

I closed my eyes, leaning my head against him, wondering if that would be enough to keep my world from spinning.

I'd composed myself by the time Toni returned. I mean, I wasn't happy and smiling, but I wasn't an emotional wreck either. I'd seen a man murdered—I had a feeling I wasn't going to be myself for a while yet.

Toni got into the driver's seat, looking a little surprised that it was already running. He glanced back at us, focusing on me. "You all right?" he asked, sounding genuinely concerned.

I nodded a little, still wrapped tightly in Patrick's arms.

I was grateful that Patrick didn't ask Toni if his hunt had been successful—I knew just by looking at Toni that it had been. I didn't want to hear about it. My stomach felt sick, and I just wanted to go home.

Patrick drove my car home from the grocery store, and Toni followed us to my house. Patrick walked me to the door, and I didn't care if anyone saw—I needed his support.

"You should be safe tonight," Patrick whispered, as we stepped up to the porch. "But if it would make you feel better, I can stay. No one would see me."

But I just shook my head, my eyes not quite on his. "Thank you. For everything. But I think I need to be alone. I need to pretend that everything is normal."

He nodded once, respecting my wish. But before he released me, he set his hands gently on either side of my face, softly forcing me to meet his gaze. "Call if you need anything, Kate. Please."

My eyes focused on his, and I felt some of the tenseness drain out of my body. It was like his empathy was a living force and could actually take away some of my fear and pain. And maybe he had that ability. He was a Guardian. He wasn't normal. Was anything in my life normal right now?

"Thank you," I whispered again. And then I pulled away and entered my dark house, shutting the door behind me—on Patrick, on the horrible night I'd had, on everything.

If only it really could hold everything back.

twenty-nine

"Are you okay?" Lee asked, watching my face carefully.

I'd just dropped the twins off—getting a thumbs up from an invisible Toni who'd arrived earlier. It did help put my mind at ease, knowing that the twins wouldn't be alone. But still, just the fact that they needed an invisible immortal watching over them made my skin crawl.

I pulled back onto the street, heading for the high school.

Lee was still patiently waiting.

"I didn't get a lot of sleep last night," I finally told her. It was the truth. Maybe it wasn't the only reason, but it was true nonetheless.

"You look sick," Lee told me gently.

I nodded. "I know. I looked in a mirror."

"Really?" She tried to act surprised. I barely cracked a smile, and she sighed, regarding me carefully. "You know, I may not understand everything about you, but I know enough. And you may not tell me everything that's going on, but I've seen enough. There's something you're not telling me, and it's killing you."

I wanted to confide in her about everything—I really did. But I didn't know where to start—I wasn't even sure I'd be doing her a favor by telling her. Besides, we were almost to school. There was no time. And so I told her the only thing I could think of—the thing I'd been dying to tell her since it had happened.

"I kissed Patrick."

She stared at me, blinking rapidly. "Wow. That was fast. How did it go?"

I sighed. "Too good. It was . . . perfect."

"What are you going to do about Aaron?"

"I don't know yet."

She nodded once in understanding, and then she laid a hand on mine, balanced on the gearshift. "I'm here for you, Kate. Whatever you need. Remember that, okay?"

"Thanks. I will. You're the best."

"I know I am." She smiled.

Surprisingly, school went pretty well. I mean, I was still freaked out and exhausted, but I felt better after admitting to Lee about cheating on my boyfriend. It was kind of like that drama gave me something to focus on, instead of everything else that was happening around me.

Aaron didn't say much to me. He was still upset about the meet I'd missed, even though he'd done well. I didn't feel like repeatedly apologizing, so I didn't. I don't think that made him any happier with me.

Patrick kept a careful eye on me throughout the day, but he managed to keep his distance at the same time. He didn't reference last night or any of our other problems. For that I was grateful. The day was like a break from the Demons, and I needed that break.

Still, the worry was there. A constant presence in the back of my mind.

I spent the evening in my bedroom, talking to Lee. I still didn't want to tell her about Demons and Guardians, but we talked a lot about Aaron and Patrick. I told her all about his evening over here, with me and the twins. I blushed a little as I described our kiss and then his apology. I was still a bit confused by that reaction. Why was he sorry the kiss had happened? Hadn't he felt the magic of that moment?

By the time we fell asleep—both of us squished on my twin bed—I had a better grasp of my feelings. I knew I needed to talk to Patrick and see if he cared for me like I was coming to care for him. But before I did that, I needed to break it off with Aaron. Because regardless of what Patrick decided, I was no longer in love with Aaron. Lee felt pretty confident that we could remain friends, but I knew that even that would take a while. Still, neither of us were happy—that was clear to me now.

Friday morning, while Lee grabbed us some Pop-Tarts, I glanced down at the newspaper that Grandpa had been reading. He'd left it lying there, while Grandma had ordered him to help her pack. Her best friend, a weird but cute old woman named Lilly Gibbs, had fallen yesterday sometime, breaking her leg. She was older than Grandma by almost ten years, but she acted younger most of the time. (Her cat had climbed up a tree, and the almost-eighty-year-old woman decided to climb up and help get him down.) She'd insisted that she was perfectly capable of caring for herself, but Grandma intended to at least spend the entire weekend at her farmhouse. She lived about fifty miles away, in a small country town.

I think Grandpa just wanted her gone already. He was anxious to have the house to himself and not be bothered every five seconds by her endless plans and preparations.

The twins were fighting upstairs. I could hear their heated voices, but not the individual words, which was fine by me. I concentrated on the paper, my eyes scanning the article quickly. The Death Train was moving closer. It told of a man who had died mysteriously, not quite thirty miles from here. It was like Jack

Williams, the Australian Guardian, had said—Far Darrig was getting closer to his target. I pitied whoever it was, even while a dim part of me wondered if I was uselessly pitying myself. But since Patrick didn't seem to believe the Demon was after me, I would trust him. It was all I could do right now, that or lose my mind with fear.

I yelled for the twins to hurry, and then thankfully took my Pop-Tarts from Lee. "We're walking out the door!" I warned, calling up the stairs.

"We're coming!" Josie nearly screamed. "Keep your shirt on, all right?"

Jenna ran down the stairs first, a deep scowl on her face.

"What's going on?" I asked.

"Nothing." Jenna grunted, pushing past me to open the front door. "You'll just take her side anyway." She marched outside, and I rolled my eyes to Lee, who was grimacing.

"Some days I'm kinda glad about the whole only child thing. Today is definitely one of those days."

Josie was stepping heavily down the stairs, a frown wrinkling her brow. "Yeah—I'd sign up for that," she told Lee. And then she pushed past me and jumped off the porch.

I sighed and followed them, but with less energy. Lee fell into step beside me, and we met Grandpa on the walkway. He was heading back inside, after carrying out some of Grandma's bags, and he looked confused.

"What's eating them?" he asked.

"Just another day at the Bennett house." I shrugged.

Lee shook her head. "Don't ask me, Mr. Bennett. I'm only a visitor here."

He reached out and tapped her nose, like he used to do when we were six. "I think not. You practically lived here your growing up years. Hate to break it to you, but you're part of the Bennett madness."

"Thanks, I think. Maybe." Lee stepped past him, moving for the car.

Before I could follow, Grandpa was reaching for my arm, keeping me there with a light touch. "Kate, I was thinking maybe we could talk after school. You know, about some things."

I could see the seriousness in his eyes, and his aura, even if I didn't understand entirely what he was getting at.

"Sure," I said slowly. "I'd like that."

He smiled. "Good. Have a nice day at school, doing whatever it is you do these days."

"Thanks. You have a good day too."

"Will do."

My car horn honked behind us, and I frowned in the direction of the driveway, seeing Josie just sinking back into her seat.

"Bye, Grandpa."

"Bye, honey."

I dropped the twins off at school, but only after giving them a stern lecture on fighting over stupid things. The result of that was two sisters who were now more angry with me than each other. Neither one said good-bye as they climbed out, and I heard the invisible Toni, who was waiting on the sidewalk, say, "You're great at that, Kate—maybe you should be a counselor or something."

Josie slammed the door, and I shook my head—at the twins, and at Toni.

My morning classes went well. I was just glad it was Friday. Aaron was in a slightly happier mood. He kept talking about the dance tomorrow and how excited he was. Jaxon and a few of his other sports friends were all going as a group with their dates, and they had a lot of fun activities planned for the day. He was telling me all about it during lunch, but I found it hard to concentrate while I was very aware that Patrick could hear every word.

"Maybe I can pick you up around noon? We're going to have

a picnic at the park, and then do this whole scavenger hunt thing. Then we might play some more games, maybe catch a movie before dinner. Then I can bring you back home and you can have plenty of time to do whatever, get ready—you know, that stuff. Then we can go to the dance."

"Sure," I said. "It sounds like fun."

Lee didn't need a ride home—she'd be staying to work on the music library, which she'd been avoiding for the entire week. Rodney, the band geek, was helping her out again and had offered to take her home. I thought about teasing her, since she'd had a crush on the dark-haired drummer for years but decided against it. I just didn't have the energy after putting up with the talkative Aaron and silent Patrick.

While I was walking to my car I got a phone call from Toni.

"Your sisters are getting into a blue minivan," he hissed urgently. "I repeat, a blue mini van!"

I frowned in confusion, then realization dawned. Still, I asked him to read me the license plate, just to be sure. He did. "Should I intervene?" he asked, sounding eager to do so. I knew he'd been bored out of his mind the past couple days.

"No—I forgot about that—they were invited to a party. The woman driving is Mrs. Collins. And I'm pretty sure she's safe," I added sarcastically. "Besides, what evil Demon would drive a minivan?"

"Well, excuse me for taking my job seriously," Toni grumbled at my light teasing.

"Thanks for being concerned," I told him sincerely. "It means a lot that you're keeping an eye on them."

"Yeah, yeah. I've had enough of this school—I'm calling Patrick. Unless you want to give me a lift?"

"I was hoping to just head home, but . . ."

"Fine. Whatever. It's not like I'm important or anything . . ."

I sighed and unlocked my car. "That's not what I meant."

"Of *course* not," he said expansively. "But really—don't worry about it. Patrick's probably already on his way."

I got in my car and prepared to say good-bye and end the call. But he wasn't done yet.

"Lee isn't with you, is she?"

"You still smitten with her?" I asked.

"She's unique and a hottie. What's not to like?"

"Good-bye, Toni."

"Yeah, it was nice talking to you too, Kate. Good-bye now."

He hung up, before I could hang up on him. I shook my head, and then drove home alone.

It wasn't until I saw my grandpa's note on the fridge that I remembered he'd wanted to talk about something. But that would have to wait. According to his quick, somewhat messy scrawl, one of his friends had called him at the last minute, wondering if he wanted to play some poker.

Your Grandma would never let me go, his note said in closing, *so I had to take the opportunity. We'll talk later. See you tonight.*

Love, Grandpa

P.S. Destroy this, please. Your Grandma would kill me for being a bad influence.

I smiled but did as he instructed. I tore it into a hundred tiny pieces, and then tossed them into the garbage, half wishing I'd burned the note instead as I watched the pieces flutter into the trash.

I wondered what to do with the house all to myself, and then realized I should probably pick a dress to wear for tomorrow.

I kept my formal dresses in a small closet in the entryway, under the stairs. I owned four dresses worthy of prom or other formal dances. I rifled through them, trying to decide. I finally narrowed it down to a deep maroon, floor length satin gown that bloomed out gently at the bottom and a light blue one with a poofy skirt that fell to mid-calf.

I eventually opted for the maroon one, thinking that the darker, deeper color better suited the occasion, and my mood. I took it out of it's protective plastic bag to let it air out a little, and then hung it on the door. I had some perfect black heels, and I thought that a low side ponytail full of curls would work great with the spaghetti-strap top. It would be a formal look, but it wouldn't take long. I hoped Aaron would approve, because this would be our last official date together, as far as I was concerned. I just prayed that I'd have the courage to go through with it. I'd never ended a relationship, and I was almost more scared of that conversation than I was of the Demons.

Once I had tomorrow night's wardrobe figured out, I went upstairs and drew the curtains closed. It was still bright, but I was so tired after everything that had happened this week. I fell asleep easily.

When I woke up, the sun was going down. I was still tired, and thought briefly about rolling over and falling back asleep. Then my stomach growled, and I headed downstairs. I heated up some leftover chicken pot pie my grandma had made last night and quickly ate the delicious square of homemade goodness. Then I cleaned my plate and listened to the silence in the house.

It was strange, for it to be this quiet. It was almost eight now, the sun almost fully set. The twins should have been home, but I couldn't hear them moving around upstairs. I wasn't exactly worried yet, but I decided to check on them anyway.

I moved up the stairs and stepped up to Jenna's bedroom. The door was closed, and I tried to turn the knob. It started to twist, and then stopped abruptly. It was locked. "Jenna?" I called out. I tapped on the door with my knuckles. "Are you in there?"

There was no answer.

My first feelings of fear began to prickle my scalp. I crossed the hall and tried Josie's door—again, it was locked. "Josie?" I knocked more firmly on her door. "Josie, come on."

I glanced between their closed doors and then started back for the kitchen—trying to keep my fear in check. I was being irrational. They were just mad at me still—maybe they'd convinced a friend to take them home with them. This didn't have to be about Demons. Some things were still normal in my life. They had to be.

I looked up the number in the phone book and quickly dialed.

Mrs. Collins answered on the fifth ring. "Hello?" she sounded slightly frazzled.

"Um, Mrs. Collins? This is Kate Bennett—Jenna and Josie's sister."

"Oh, hello—I was just getting ready to call you again. I hope you don't mind—the party's running a little longer than expected. They said it would be fine with you and your grandparents if they stayed for the movie. It'll be done just after ten, if that's all right. I'm really sorry if that's a problem. I could bring them home now if you'd rather?"

I was breathing easier now, and I forced a smile that luckily leaked into my voice. "No, of course not. They can stay. Should I come pick them up after the movie?"

"No need. I'm taking other girls home, so it shouldn't be a problem."

Someone in the background was screaming wildly for mom, and so I let her go and ended the call. I shook my head at myself and my overreaction, and then headed up to the bathroom. There I enjoyed a long, hot shower, and then meticulously blow-dried my hair, trying to make it appear as full as possible. That done, I went back to my room, and the next thing I saw was the inside of my eyelids.

I woke up briefly when I heard a car pull up to the house, and glancing at the clock I saw it was just after ten. Knowing the twins were back safely, I fell back asleep in the same second I'd surfaced. Only this time, I slept deeply.

thirty

I felt really good in the morning. Extremely rested. I felt like I was myself again, which was good. I needed to make it through the date with Aaron as smoothly as possible. I got dressed in a comfortable but nice-looking outfit, and then I headed downstairs. I glanced at the other doors in the hall, knowing the twins would probably sleep until noon. They didn't recover well after late-night parties, despite their youth.

I found Grandpa in the kitchen, just finishing his cup of coffee as he looked out the back window. He turned to smile at me and asked me about my night while I looked in the pantry for some cereal.

"Sorry I stood you up yesterday," he began.

"Don't apologize—you needed it. Grandma works you too hard in that yard."

"Yeah, well—it's looking good though, isn't it?"

I nodded and poured some milk into my full bowl.

He watched me eat for a moment. Then he set his mug in the sink. "Well, if you don't need your car this morning, I'm going to take it to the mechanic and get that oil changed."

"That should be fine. I'll be hanging out with Aaron pretty much all day, so I shouldn't need the car."

"Oh, the Fall Ball, that's right—Grandma mentioned that." He looked like he wanted to say more, but at the last second he changed his mind. "Well, I should be back soon. No more than an hour."

"Be safe," I told him.

"It's not my intention to drive like a maniac," he assured me.

I gave him a smile and then he was gone, already holding a spare set of keys to my car. I heard the front door open and close, and I was alone.

I finished my breakfast, then returned to my bedroom. I read for a while, but the silence in the house was driving me crazy. I finally decided that an angry pair of sisters was better than a sleeping pair, and I knocked on Jenna's door.

"Jenna? Wake up." I crossed the hall in two steps, and knocked on Josie's. "Come on, you guys, wake up. I'm bored."

There was no answer. From Josie, I could understand—she was a heavy sleeper. But Jenna usually woke at the slightest sound.

I moved back to Jenna's door, knocked once, harder than before. "Jenna?"

The momentary panic I'd felt last night was returning. "I'm going to get the key," I told her. There was a key for all our bedrooms, tucked away in the kitchen. By unspoken rule we weren't supposed to threaten each other with them. We were supposed to respect privacy, and all that. But I wasn't in the mood.

When Jenna didn't reply, I went downstairs, opened the right drawer, and snatched up the two keys I needed. I almost ran up the stairs this time, and it took a few tries for my suddenly unsteady hands to fit the key into the lock.

Finally it slid in, and I turned it quickly. I pushed the door, and it swung open.

My heart nearly stopped.

Jenna's room was empty. Her bed hadn't been slept in.

Almost in a daze, I moved for Josie's room. I unlocked it, twisted the knob, and found a similar sight. The only difference from Jenna's empty room was that Josie's was a complete mess.

I couldn't tell if she'd slept in her bed, because she never made it—it always looked slept in.

For a short moment, I didn't know what to do. And then I was running down the stairs, back to the kitchen, snatching up the phone and looking in the memory until I found it—*James Collins*.

It rang several times, and I found myself pacing, gnawing on my thumbnail.

Finally someone answered—a small voice. "Yeah?"

"Is your mom there?" I asked.

The small boy answered very slowly. "Nope, I think she's at the store."

I tried to think of something to say—what to ask.

"Who is this?" he asked.

"I'm Kate. Is Josie or Jenna there?"

"Um . . . they were last night. Their sister picked them up, though."

My knees went weak, and I had to clutch the edge of the counter to keep from falling to the hard floor. Suddenly everything fell into place. The car I'd heard—not the twins, but Grandpa. The twins had been picked up by a sister—definitely not me.

"Did you notice the kind of car they left in?" I asked, desperately hoping that he wasn't as young as he sounded. I needed him to confirm my suspicions, though it was the last thing I wanted to face.

"Um, yeah, it was silver, I think. Why?"

I know it wasn't a lot to go on, but somehow I knew. It didn't matter that the only witness I had was a seven-year-old boy—Selena Avalos had kidnapped my sisters.

I didn't answer his question. I thanked him thinly and then hung up. I held the phone for a long moment, just trying to breathe. How had I let this happen? I knew they were in danger. So what if Toni kept an eye on them at school? I should never have let them go to that party. And I never should have gone back to sleep without making sure it was really them.

I tossed the phone onto the counter and pulled out my cell from my pocket.

It rang twice—more like one and a half, really—and then I heard Patrick's voice, slightly tired. "Kate?"

I couldn't breathe. I was shaking. My head hurt. My heart was pounding. "She has them," I croaked.

His voice was more alert, more focused—more concerned. "Kate? What's wrong?"

"Selena Avalos. She has my sisters." Now that I'd told some-one—admitted my horrible mistakes aloud—I couldn't remain standing. My legs folded, and I sat heavily on the floor, my dizzy head pressed against the cupboards behind me.

The only control I had seemed to be in my arm—the one that held the phone almost painfully to my ear.

"Where are you?" Patrick asked quickly.

"My house," I whispered, tears stinging in my eyes. "Please hurry, Patrick."

The front door was unlocked, and Patrick walked in without knocking. He'd just hung up the phone when he pulled up to the house, and I was just closing mine when our eyes met. He was standing just inside the door, I was still sitting on the floor of the kitchen—only the long entryway separating us. His face was a perfect blend of pity, fear, and anger.

He didn't bother to close the door. He crossed the space between us in several long strides, and then in one swift motion he was crouching next to me, gathering me in his powerful arms.

I fell against him, aware that Toni would be coming in right behind him, but not caring.

"I should've done something," I groaned into his shoulder. "This is all my fault."

I'd told him everything I knew over the phone, during the few minutes it had taken him to drive here, and he was shaking his head—protesting my self-beatings just like he had in the car. "No, it's not. You couldn't have known. *I* should have seen it, though. I'm so sorry."

Patrick pulled me to my feet but continued to embrace me until my trembling subsided.

Once I stopped shaking he released all but one hand and we both turned to face Toni, who was hesitating in the open doorway.

"Come in," I told him, wiping quickly at my face, trying to dry the tears. I wasn't crying anymore—the shock and fear—and even a good portion of the guilt—were fleeing. Taking over my emotions now was anger. I wanted to rip Selena's eyes out. She would pay for messing with me and my sisters. They were all I had left.

"So," Toni said, closing the front door and walking slowly back to the kitchen. "What's the plan?"

Patrick's voice was very low, and there was a deep undercurrent of something dangerous. "She gave us her number—obviously for this purpose. They want Kate—it's going to be a trade."

"Then let's do it—call her."

Patrick shook his head at me. "We can't do that. It goes against what the Guardians stand for—"

"They're my sisters!" I exploded at him, yanking my hand out of his. I know he was stung, but in that second I didn't care. Let him hurt a little. This was as much his fault as it was mine, and I didn't want to feel all the responsibility. "I don't care about you Guardians—your laws, your rules. I couldn't care less if all of this just disappeared. They're two little girls, and they don't deserve this! They've been through enough pain. They've lost their parents—they don't need this!"

Patrick's eyes never left mine, though I could see the hurt in his tense face. "I'm sorry," he whispered. "Of course we'll get them back. I never meant that we wouldn't."

I continued to stare at him, already wishing I could take the words back—it was obvious that they'd cut him deeply. But instead of apologizing I tried to steady my breathing.

"Then you'll call her?" I asked at last.

He nodded. "If that's what you want." He looked up at Toni. "Call Jack Williams—we'll need all the help we can get."

"You got it, man." Toni pulled out his phone and wandered back into the family room, dialing quickly.

Patrick pulled out his own phone and flipped it open. He typed out her number from memory and then held the phone to his ear, still watching my face.

In the quiet room, I could just make out the muted sound of the ringing. After several tense seconds, someone answered. The words were quiet and distant for me, and I couldn't make sense of them.

Patrick's tight face never wavered as he spoke. "All right, you have my attention. Where are they?"

She said something briefly.

He didn't answer right away.

She repeated her words, more firmly this time.

Stiffly, he extended the phone to me. "She wants you," he said softly, eyes tight.

I took the phone quickly. My fear was gone. "If you've hurt them, I swear I'll drive a knife in your heart myself."

I heard the husky laugh of Selena Avalos, and it made me sick. "Now, now, remember what I said about getting uppity? Your sisters are fine—for now. They wouldn't stop talking at first, but once the drugs kicked in . . . they've been a lot more manageable."

"Where are you? What do you want?"

"I propose an exchange. Or rather, my boss does."

"Quin Romero."

"Not bad, for a watchdog. But still a little too high and mighty, for my taste. I'll call you back in fifteen minutes. Be on the road, and I'll tell you where to go. Go ahead—bring your Guardians. I'm sure they'll enjoy the ride."

"I want to talk to them," I said forcefully, but she'd already hung up. I let out a shaky breath, and then I snapped the phone shut and handed it back to him. My voice was wooden. "She'll call back in fifteen minutes with instructions. She wants us in the car."

Patrick slipped his phone into his pocket, nodding to show he understood.

The front door suddenly opened, and Grandpa caught sight of us from the entryway, though his eyes were squinting until almost closed. They had yet to adjust from the bright sunlight outside, so he walked quite slowly into the kitchen.

My mind scrambled for some excuse to have Patrick here—then I wondered if Patrick would have gone invisible. There was no way for me to tell, so I decided to force a smile and—for the moment—pretend like I was alone. Of course, I knew Grandpa would notice my tears. He was too observant to not notice, but maybe he would be blinded enough that I could escape before it could really register.

Grandpa stepped into the kitchen, still squinting. He took in my face, and then he glanced at Patrick.

My mind scrambled for a good lie to explain his presence.

And then my grandpa said something so unexpected, it took me almost a full minute to realize all the implications—and even then I didn't fully understand. "Kate," he asked me slowly, his brow furrowed tightly. "Would you mind telling me exactly what a Guardian is doing in our kitchen?"

thirty-one

Patrick recovered long before I did—all the dots connecting faster than mine were appearing. His eyes were wide, but his voice was composed at least. "You're a Seer," he stated, surprise almost making it sound like a question.

Grandpa Bennett nodded once, giving Patrick the once-over. "I don't think I ever met you. You have to understand, though, I left the life of a Seer years and years ago."

"Grandpa?" I finally choked. "You're a *Seer!?*"

He shrugged a single shoulder, his dirty suspenders almost creaking with the motion. "Since I was about twenty-five or so. Nearly died in the Vietnam war—you've heard the story before, I just left out the small detail of my newfound Sight. Of course, I stopped helping the Guardians several years after I married your Grandmother."

So many things suddenly made sense to me—it was more information than I could digest in a single second. "You can see my aura—that's how you read me so well. You can see my emotions. You cheated!"

Grandpa nodded calmly. "Yes. And when I visited you in the hospital and heard you talking about colors and auras, I knew exactly what was happening to you."

"But . . . then why didn't you say anything?" I tried to keep the accusing voice to a minimum.

"Before I had the chance, you were back to normal—or so you pretended. Very well, I might add. I thought your feelings of isolation came from your parents' death—not your secrets. Forgive an old man's inability to handle a situation. I just supposed that the Guardians had become super-efficient, and that they were able to deaden your Sight while you were still in the hospital. I guess I was so relieved that you weren't like me, I didn't bother to ask you much about it."

"What about Grandma?" I asked, wondering if my life could fall apart any more than it already had. "Does *she* know about all this?"

Grandpa snorted. "Do you think that woman could handle her world getting that shaken up? She's always liked things just so." He nodded toward me, a knowing look in his eye. "You'll find that the less you can tell the people you love, the better."

"I can't believe it," I whispered. "You're a Seer. All this time . . . you've known everything."

He sent a hard glance back toward Patrick. "Well, not quite everything. I had no idea you were involved in all of this. I just thought you suffered from severe boy problems."

Toni started speaking to us from the other room, heading quickly back to the kitchen. Grandpa jumped and twisted around in surprise, so we were all facing him when he would finally make his appearance at the door. "Well, Jack's definitely in. He'll bring Jason along too, and then we can . . ." Toni's voice trailed off as he caught sight of my grandfather. "Um. Hi." He smiled, though it was small and awkward. "I'm a friend of Kate's. We're just trying to plan a little get-together, you know, live it up like youngsters do . . ."

"Toni, relax," Patrick cut in quickly. "He's a Seer."

"What? You're kidding!" Toni shook his head in disbelief. "Wow, what a small world. It's like it runs in the family or something."

"If I may," Grandpa broke in loudly, overriding the next needless comment Toni might utter. "I think I have a right to know what you two have dragged my granddaughter into. What are you all doing here?"

My Guardians looked to me, and I tried to think of a gentle way to explain the situation. In the end, I just said the awful words. "Josie and Jenna are gone. A Demon has them. They want me, but I don't know why."

Grandpa stared at me. I watched his face and his aura, and they reacted the same. Shock. Disbelief. Fear. Anger. Determination. "Where are they?" he asked, suddenly sounding a lot younger than his almost seventy years. "Do we know?"

"We have a number," Patrick explained, when I didn't answer right away. "We called, but the Demon didn't tell us much. She'll be calling back in the next ten minutes or so, to give more instructions. We're supposed to be in the car."

"Jack said he could meet us anywhere," Toni offered.

Grandpa grunted. "Huh. One of *those* Demons, eh? The ones that like to play games. I prefer the more direct ones."

"You're not coming," I said, too shocked by the thought of my grandpa accompanying us on a dangerous mission to think about my words. "You could get hurt."

"These Demons made this personal, Kate. They messed with the wrong family." Grandpa turned back to Patrick. "You got an extra knife on you?"

"Are you sure you're up to this, sir?" Patrick asked.

"What you trying to say?" Grandpa grunted. "Out with it. I don't like people who can't be frank."

"I think he thinks you're old," Toni supplied.

Grandpa regarded Toni firmly. "I may appreciate frankness, young man, but tactfulness has its place too."

Patrick and I gave Toni matching looks, and he got defensive. "What? We were all thinking it!"

Grandpa wasn't through. "Look, I did this for years. I know how it works. Besides, I have a right to protect my family. And you need all the help you can get. How many Demons are we talking about, anyway?"

"That's uncertain," Patrick admitted. "We know the leader—Quin Romero—and we know he has plenty of help."

"Romero, you say?" Grandpa frowned. "That name's awful familiar."

I glanced back at the clock on the stove—it was nearing eleven. Almost time for Selena's call. "She wants us in the car," I reminded them. "Should we take yours or mine?"

Grandpa spoke to Patrick, the obvious leader. "These Demons aren't expecting me. I'll go in Kate's car, following at a discrete distance. Call me when you learn more. We can make up a plan as we go along."

"I love those kinds," Toni enthused, obviously trying to get on my grandpa's good side. "They're always somehow the most memorable, compared to plans that are, well, planned."

Patrick nodded to my grandfather. "It sounds like a plan, Mr. Bennett." He stuck out his hand. "Welcome to the team."

I almost thought I saw my grandpa smile despite the circumstances, and I could see from his very chaotic aura that he was more than a little happy to be back in the action. "Call me Henry," he told Patrick, taking his hand and shaking it once.

Patrick nodded and then looked to Toni. "Get him a knife—I'll meet you in the car."

"Yes sir." Toni mock saluted, and then pulled out one of his hidden blades. Grandpa gave me a quick hug, whispering that everything was going to be all right. And then he took the dagger Toni offered, and the two walked out of the house, Toni filling Grandpa in on everything we knew about Quin Romero.

I moved to follow them, but Patrick's soft voice made me turn back. "Kate—you need to drink something."

"I'm fine," I protested, but he wasn't interested in what I had to say. He tried opening a few cupboards, and soon found the cups. He took one out, filled it in the sink, then carefully brought it over to me.

I took it but didn't drink right away.

"Go on," he prompted. "It will help steady you. Trust me."

I sighed, and then took a few experimental sips. Then I realized how thirsty I was, and soon enough I'd drained the whole glass. Without a word he took the empty cup, refilled it, and handed it back to me. "Thank you," I whispered. I took a swallow and then waved toward the cupboard right behind him. "There's some Tylenol in there. Could you get me a couple?"

He did, and after I'd swallowed the medicine, I realized that he was watching me very closely. "Are you going to be okay?" he asked, noticing my stare.

I rubbed my fingers over the outside of the glass, unsure of how to respond. "Once my sisters are back," I finally said.

He seemed to understand that. "I'm sorry," he repeated again—so softly I barely heard him.

I walked to the sink, dumping the remaining water down the drain. Then I set my cup down, and at last I turned to face him. I looked into his eyes, my own feeling tight and burning slightly. "I'm sorry," I breathed. "I shouldn't have said those things to you."

"You were upset. It was understandable."

"But it wasn't right. I'm very grateful for everything you've done. Everything you're doing."

He didn't know how to react—what to say.

I embraced him gently, and his arms slowly wrapped around me. "Everything's going to be all right," he whispered. "I won't let it be any other way."

I swallowed hard but didn't reply. I didn't have to. He knew I trusted him.

It was really the only thing I could do at this point.

thirty-two

Patrick was driving and Toni was in the backseat, holding a phone against each ear. With his own he was connected to Jack, and with mine he was able to communicate with my grandpa, who was following us in my car.

I held Patrick's phone with anxious fingers, awaiting Selena's call. I'd switched off the stereo the moment we started driving, and so aside from the sounds of the engine and Toni's occasional words, the car was silent.

We'd just pulled out of the subdivision when Patrick's phone went off. I answered on the first ring, which made Selena laugh.

"Eager much?" she chuckled deeply.

"We're in the car," I told her. "Where are we going?"

"Katie dear, some patience, please. Are your Guardians with you?"

"Yes."

"Are they unhappy with me?" she couldn't help but ask, sounding very pleased with herself.

"Not as much as I am."

She laughed again, and then her voice grew slowly serious. "I want you to get on the highway—head east."

"Where are we going?"

"Buh-buh-buh," she reprimanded me gently. "I can't give you

an address, dear—it would ruin the fun. Now, I'll call you in about thirty minutes. Don't speed, though, or you won't be in the proper place. And you wouldn't want to miss a turn—your sisters are waiting for you."

She hung up.

I kept the phone at my ear longer than necessary before finally letting it fall to my lap. I snapped it closed, and then addressed the tense immortals in the car. "She wants us to get on the highway, and head east. She'll call us back in thirty minutes to give us more directions." As I spoke I glanced at the blue digital clock on the dash, making a note of when to expect her.

Toni repeated my words into the phones, and then he leaned forward to address Patrick. "Jack's headed toward us right now—if we can make a quick pit stop, he and Grandpa can travel together."

Patrick nodded, eyes on the road. "Just pick a place."

"There's a store up three blocks from here," I offered. "It's on the way, and we could leave a car unnoticed."

Toni relayed my words into both phones, and in minutes we were pulling into a crowded parking lot.

Jack was already there, slouching against the hood of a sleek black car. Jason—the short Seer with dark brown hair and glasses—was standing next to him, playing some sort of hand-held video game. I don't know why that annoyed me so much, but it did.

We pulled up next to them, and Grandpa stopped next to us.

Jack straightened and walked over to our car—moving for my window, which Patrick rolled down with the push of a button. Jason followed his Guardian slowly, eyes glued to the screen of his electronic device.

"G'day, mates," Jack drawled, leisurely stooping down to look in at us. "Sounds like you've got yourselves one corker of a party—thanks for thinking of us."

Patrick nodded once. "Thank you for responding so quickly."

"We were in the area—spent last night in a bodgy motel just south of here actually. Wouldn't recommend it to my worst enemy."

Before I could get frustrated with him, he was nodding toward Jason, still concentrating on his game. "Jason here's been ace. He's taken the skimpy bit of information that Demon's given us and started to look for some possible destinations."

Jason glanced up at us, nodding.

I felt incredibly guilty for judging him, but guilt was something I was getting used to.

"By what I've found," Jason told us, running his thumb quickly across the touch screen. "Given the thirty-minute drive down the highway, I'm betting we're headed for an industrial area. It looks like it's abandoned, so it would be a good place for a bunch of Demons to hide a couple kidnapped girls."

I heard Grandpa's car door open and close, and he started to wander over. Patrick rolled down his window, but before he could repeat what little we'd guessed, Grandpa was whistling loudly.

"Jack! Didn't realize they'd been talking about you!"

"Henry?" The Australian Guardian straightened, so he could look over the top of the car. He had a huge grin on his face but confusion in his eyes. "You crazy loon—how'd you get roped into all this?"

Grandpa pointed toward me. "That's my granddaughter. And don't be calling me a loon, you lousy oaf. Why didn't you tell me you were here helping my granddaughter?"

"I wasn't, originally. I've been tracking Far Darrig, just like I told you yesterday."

"Yesterday?" I wished I could see their faces. "You two know each other?"

"Know each other?" Grandpa chuckled. "We were unstoppable once. He was my Guardian, a long time ago."

"Yeah," Jack laughed. "He wasn't the best Seer I've ever had, but by-diggity he knew how to party."

"Well, I had better Guardians, so there."

Jack pushed his tongue out, and they laughed.

I was still feeling like my whole world made no sense, but I realized my grandpa had lied to me. "You weren't playing poker with friends yesterday—you were catching up with Jack."

Grandpa nodded. "Who knew the fool was in the area?"

"Who knew you were still alive and had your marbles intact," Jack said, laughing. "How old are you now? Ninety?"

Patrick cleared his throat loudly, and everyone glanced in his direction. "We really need to get going," he hinted.

Jack slapped the top of the car and leaned away. "He's right, enough earbashing for now. Who's driving? I vote *not* the senior citizen."

Grandpa frowned in his direction. "Just for that, I'm going to drive. But we'll take your car—I don't want anything happening to Kate's."

Jason looked up from his device, peering back into the car toward Toni. "I'll try to pinpoint our destination as we get more information. Hopefully we'll know where we're going before we get there, so we can make some sort of plan."

Toni nodded, but surprisingly didn't make a smart comment.

Jason walked back toward the black car, heading for the backseat. Grandpa and Jack followed, arguing lightly as they walked.

"There's no time to waste, Jack—these are my granddaughters we're talking about. Give me those keys."

"No way."

"What happened to 'no worries'?"

"It doesn't apply now."

"You said it applies everywhere."

"That was before we lived this moment." Jack got in the

driver's seat, and Grandpa reluctantly—but still quickly—moved for the other side.

I shook my head in disbelief, and Toni piped up from the back. "That wasn't weird or anything."

Patrick shifted out of park, and we were back on our way—Jack following close behind.

Selena called twice more, at shorter intervals each time. We were off the highway and in the outskirts of a dirty city. By now, Jason was quite certain that we were heading for the industrial district on his maps, and some tentative plans were beginning to be set when my phone rang.

It was lying on the backseat, discarded after my grandfather and Jack began to carpool. Toni scooped it up, and glanced at the caller ID.

"It's your boyfriend," he told me, before passing it forward.

I took the phone but didn't answer it right away. I looked at the dash—almost exactly 12:00 o'clock. I'd completely forgotten about our date.

I answered the phone at probably the last possible second, still unsure about what I would say.

"Kate, where are you?" Aaron asked, sounding upset. "I'm at your house and no one's here. We're going to be late."

My hand steadied my forehead. "Aaron, I'm sorry—I won't be able to do this today."

There was a brief silence, and then he spoke—his voice hard. "What do you mean you can't do this? It's been planned for a week. You can't just bail at the last second."

"I'm sorry—something came up."

"What? What could have possibly come up? Are you with Lee?"

"No. I'm with my grandpa."

I heard him take a deep, steadying breath—I knew him well enough to know that he was trying really hard to keep from getting any angrier. "Is something wrong? Are you okay?"

"I'm fine. Please, you just have to trust me."

"Well, you've made that kind of hard lately. I mean, what's going on with you? You're not even yourself anymore. You notice that, right? You can see that?"

My hand fell. "Aaron, I have to go."

"No. Kate, don't hang up. I need some answers. Just tell me where you are. Are you at least coming to the dance tonight?"

I closed my eyes tightly and pinched the bridge of my nose with two trembling fingers. "I don't know," I admitted. "I'll try. I promise."

There was a really long silence, and then he finally spoke. He tried to sound rough, but there was an undercurrent of pain in his words. "Kate, are you cheating on me? Are you with someone else? Is that why you've been so weird lately?"

"No," I choked, and I could see Patrick send me a worried glance at the strangled sound. "That's what you think? That I've been secretly dating someone else?"

"Well, you haven't left me a lot of other options. Is it Patrick?"

Just then Patrick's phone went off in my lap—Selena was calling back.

"Aaron, I have to go. I'll try to make it to the dance."

"Kate—"

I hung up on him, feeling awful for doing it, but knowing that I had no other choice. Besides, the more controlled part of my brain assured me that maybe somehow this would make our imminent breakup easier.

But I couldn't think about that now. I continued to hold my phone, and with my other hand I hurried to scoop up Patrick's.

"We just passed the gas station," I told her, skipping any greeting.

"Good, you're right on schedule. Turn left at the next street, and follow it until it ends. We'll be inside. Come on in—the door's open."

She hung up, and I relayed her words to the others.

While Toni talked to my grandfather, Patrick sent me a quick look. "Are you all right? Is Aaron okay?"

I spoke very quietly, staring at my phone. "I think he's given up on us."

Patrick didn't say anything for a short moment, and then his voice was so quiet, I almost wondered if I was hearing him correctly. "He hasn't. He couldn't. He would never let you go that easily. No one would."

I glanced toward him, but he was already looking back at the road, concentrating on turning up the appropriate street. I didn't know what to make of his words. I didn't understand what he meant by them. Was he just trying to make me feel better? Or was there something else? Something deeper?

I couldn't keep thinking about it. Toni leaned up between us, phone still at his ear, though he was speaking to us.

"Jack's going to pull behind one of these buildings, then they'll continue on foot. They'll plan on staying out of sight but nearby if needed."

Patrick nodded. "Good. Tell them to be careful."

Toni repeated that message, and then handed the phone to me. "Your Grandpa wants to talk to you," he explained.

I put the phone to my ear, and then I heard my grandpa's gentle voice. "I know you're scared, honey. But we're going to fix this. And we'll have you home in time for your ball, I promise."

I cracked a smile. "I just want them to be safe."

He knew I meant the twins. "I know—and they will be. So will you. Trust your Guardians, Kate—they know what they're doing, and they'll do whatever it takes. They always do."

"Thanks, Grandpa. Be safe."

"You too. And be brave, hon. Don't let those Demons intimidate you. I love you."

"I love you too."

We ended the call, and I glanced in my side mirror to see that we were already alone on the road.

"Looks just like home," Toni muttered, peering through the windshield at the looming warehouses.

The road was coming to an end. It had been paved once but was now more dirt and loose rock than anything else. It led right up to a large, abandoned building, which seemed the perfect end to this whole ominous trip. Patrick was slowing the car down and soon we were completely stopped. He shut off the car, and I broke the sudden silence.

"I think I like your warehouse better."

Toni nodded behind us, scanning the building with a critical and practiced eye. Still, despite his obvious concentration, his tone remained surprisingly light. "Yeah, I'd have to agree with Kate."

Patrick seemed to ignore us both. He reached up his sleeve without a word and pulled out a very small knife. It was sheathed in a leather holster and looked extremely deadly. I should have known it was coming, but I was still a bit surprised when he extended it toward me, his eyes tight. "I'd feel better if you have it," he said, the serious edge in his voice bordering on dangerous.

I hesitated for a split second, but then took it gingerly, holding on to the adjustable straps of the holster instead of the actual knife. I didn't argue though, mostly because I figured I wouldn't have it for long. In every movie like this I'd ever seen, the good guys were asked to discard all their weapons as soon as they entered the building. But I think my major reason for not resisting stemmed from Patrick's heavy but mostly silent insistence. If he thought I would be better off with the weapon, then I'd humor him. I was willing to trust whatever he did or instructed.

The click of Toni's seat belt releasing returned me to the present. "Let's do this," Toni muttered as he pushed open his door and stepped out.

Patrick unlatched his own seat belt just as Toni's door slammed shut. He glanced in my direction, as if sensing my sudden dilemma.

"Where should I put it?" I asked anyway. I now knew why Patrick always wore long sleeves—it was a convenient place to hide a blade.

"Put it around your leg," he suggested, one hand resting on the steering wheel, the other fisted on his knee. Though we'd been in such a rush to get to our destination, now that we were here, he seemed content to wait for me.

I took off my seat belt before bending over to pull up my left pant leg. Patrick watched as I set the holster against the outside of my calf, and then carefully cinched the straps. He didn't utter a word as I adjusted and finally velcroed the thing tightly into place. It felt bulky and uncomfortable, but as I pushed my pant leg back down, I saw that the slight flair hid the weapon well.

"Like that?" I asked, looking up for his approval.

He nodded, and then glanced out the window to where Toni was standing to admire the hulking building before us. Searching for possible escape routes? Trying to judge where the twins would be held? Looking for an alternate and better place of entry?

I couldn't quite focus on what he might be doing, because in the last minute the urge to say something to Patrick had become unbearably strong.

Patrick was reaching for his door when my hand suddenly flashed out and wrapped around his arm. "Wait," I begged softly, not exactly knowing what made me to stop him. I knew I didn't really want to say this to him. Especially not right now.

He looked over at me, though, his expression confused and his eyes questioning.

I swallowed hard, and my fingers briefly tightened their hold. "Patrick, in case something happens . . . If something goes wrong—"

He shifted more toward me, his eyes sinking into mine. His voice was smooth and hid his worry quite well. "Kate, nothing's going to go wrong. I promise, I'll get you out of there." He was pretty good at the whole Guardian thing. The sincerity in his words made my heart pound.

"I know, but . . ." I bit my lower lip, knowing that I shouldn't continue, knowing that I couldn't stop now. Because if I didn't make it out, I knew that he'd be there for my family. Grandpa would be able to comfort Grandma. But there was another person who would feel abandoned if something did go wrong, and even after everything that had been happening between us, I couldn't help but care for him. "Please," I asked, already internally wincing at how this would come off. "If things don't work out, could you help Aaron understand that . . . I'm sorry?"

A muscle in his jaw flexed, and some un-namable emotion clouded his eyes. And then he nodded once—more like ducked his head—and then replied softly. "I promise." His head lifted, and his eyes were tight. "But I will keep you safe, Kate."

He flashed me a pretty forced, very short smile, and I let my hand slip from his arm. He opened the door and pushed his way outside, slamming the door perhaps a bit too sharply behind him.

I took a deep and bracing breath, and then followed him out.

By the time I joined my two Guardians, standing near the hood of the car, Toni had already finished delivering his quick diagnosis of the building to his fellow Guardian.

Patrick was nodding, and then—after sending a glance in my direction—he asked Toni, "You ready?"

"And then some," was the short, oddly eager reply.

Patrick exhaled slowly. "Then let's go," he said, that dangerous edge back in his voice.

thirty-three

As we walked away from the car and toward the obvious front doors, Patrick took my hand. I don't know if he thought I needed the contact or if it was for his benefit. But I wasn't complaining. Even though—in retrospect—I probably shouldn't have brought up my boyfriend a minute ago, my pounding heart felt a little bit better about this terrifying situation. I knew Aaron didn't deserve what I'd been putting him through lately. And though Patrick really didn't deserve the potentially awkward situation I'd just landed him in, he was a Guardian. He was the best, as far as I was concerned. And if things went bad, I was relieved to know that he would be there to help Aaron.

Patrick's fingers flexed around mine, pulling me closer to his side as we approached the doors. Toni was at my other side, whispering little bits of advice that I was basically ignoring.

"Keep your fear in check. Let them know you're strong. If you have to, threaten them with the knife—it'll buy you some time. Follow our lead, but don't worry if they talk directly to you. Do whatever you have to to ensure your sisters' safety, but try to avoid getting in a car with them. High-speed chases aren't exactly Patrick's forte."

"You're bringing this up now?" Patrick asked, voice low and incredulous.

"It was an awful experience for me. I felt sick for a week. I was lucky to survive at all."

Patrick squeezed my fingers again, and I looked up at him. "It's going to be okay," he assured me once more.

Toni sighed loudly. "I wonder if Selena will remember me. I mean, I was able to avoid her at the school, but . . . Well, I suppose I'll find out soon enough."

We were to the doors. Toni opened one, and Patrick and I stepped in together.

Selena Avalos was standing in the center of the large room, her arms folded delicately across her chest. Her long manicured nails tapped an impatient rhythm against her arms, and her head was cocked to the side. Her hair was full and wavy, the dark chocolate locks spilling down her back. Her eyes were bright and focused solely on our slow approach. She was wearing a flattering pair of tight dark jeans and a low-cut red blouse. Her thin black aura was like the finishing touch to a dark but impressive masterpiece.

She looked stunning, in an evil sort of way.

"Welcome," she called to us in her deep, resonant voice. Her accent was thin and exotic. If I wasn't so mad at her, I probably would have felt that I'm-inferior-in-her-presence sensation that I'd experienced the first time I'd seen her. She was everything I wasn't, and she flaunted it extremely well.

She gave me a creepy smile, winked a luminous eye at Patrick, and then she saw Toni.

Her smile fell and then grew slowly back until almost all her teeth were showing. "Antonio Alvarez, back from the dead."

Toni's hands were in his pockets. Out of everyone in the room, he seemed the most relaxed. "Hello, Selena," he said casually, giving her a small smile and a nod. "I was wondering if you'd remember me."

Her full red lips twisted into a pout. "Is that how you think of me? After we shared so much together?"

He shrugged. "It was a long time ago."

"Yes, it was." She shook her head sadly, her eyes still dancing. "How time flies when you're dead."

Toni drew to a stop along with us, still several feet away from the Demon. "You look older," he commented smoothly.

Selena's smile widened. "Really? You look younger. Sometimes I forget how young you really were back then. I hope there are no hard feelings."

"No, of course not," Toni laughed quietly. "You only used me, betrayed me, and then practically organized my execution. Why would I hold a grudge over something as stupid as all that?"

"Good, I'm glad that's all right. I would hate to think there was anything . . . unsettled between us. And for the record, I was quite taken with you. Once."

"That's a coincidence. I was just about to say the same thing about you." His eyes ran quickly over her body. "Are your hips getting bigger? I thought it was impossible for immortals to gain weight? Or did that happen before you died, and now you're stuck with them forever?"

Her grin was set firmly in place. "You always were a charmer, Antonio. It's a pity you and I didn't get to play together for long, back when we were alive—I think I would have enjoyed that very much."

"Well, I'm just glad to see that you're doing great. I mean, Romero's underling forever, huh? How's that working out for you?"

Her eyes were like icy daggers. "I must admit I'm surprised to see you here, on *their* side."

"Not what you expected?" Toni asked, smile wide.

"Hmm, not exactly. I thought you had a bit more . . . Demon inside you."

"So how did you die, Selena? What was it? Or should I ask, *when* was it? Cuz personally I think you'd look a lot better if you'd died back when I did. It was a good year for you. A young look."

Watching her face, I knew that nothing bothered her more than these gentle jibes that Toni kept delivering. She only loved herself, that was abundantly clear. But despite her looks, she worried about them. She was sensitive to what others thought, and the things they said. Toni must have known this.

I think she realized what he was trying to do because her arms suddenly fell to her sides, ending the conversation. "I think that's enough chit chat, Antonio—we're boring your friends, I'm sure." She turned back to me, but then focused on Patrick. "We won't make this complicated. The twins are upstairs, waiting for two self-sacrificing guardian angels. You may each take one, and then you may leave. Your Seer stays here. If you don't leave with the sisters immediately, Romero's men will be forced to . . . make this difficult. But first things first. If you Guardians would be so kind as to drop your weapons."

Patrick released my hand slowly, and then he pulled his longest knife out of his belt.

Selena gestured flippantly for him to lie it on the floor, and he did so. I felt Toni doing the same thing beside me. But I didn't move. I guess being considered a dog had its benefits—she didn't think I had a weapon. Which, true, it's not like I knew how to use it, but still. Any surprise we could pull on them would be a plus.

Selena waited for them to take out their hidden blades as well, which were strapped to their legs. As they straightened, she spoke. "You can pick them up on your way back out, if that's not too much trouble." Then she walked toward us, focusing on me for the first time.

I tried not to flinch as she extended a hand toward me, but I felt Patrick and Toni stiffen, and I think some fear showed in my eyes.

Selena laughed at us. "Easy, I'm only waiting for her to touch me. After all, if she's going to be staying, we need to be able to touch."

Knowing it could be worse, I lifted my hand without further prompting. It hovered there in the air, and I waited for her to close the last of the distance.

It was a strange thing, her not being able to touch me. I held my hand stationary, and her open palm lowered until I could feel the heat of her skin, a breath from mine. But there was something in that thin breath of space that protected me from her touch. It wasn't a visible shield, or one that I could feel. It was more like I could sense it. It was the first time I was aware of the protective shield, because it was the first time I'd actually had the choice to break it. Not that I really had a choice, of course. Even now, in this brief hesitation, I could feel Selena's impatience.

I'd stopped breathing, I realized, so I hurriedly pulled in a breath. And then I lifted my hand just slightly, and the top of my hand brushed her skin.

With the barrier gone, Selena was free to grasp my hand. Her nails bit into my flesh in a horrible handshake, and I winced. "Thank you," she murmured gently, her tone as mocking as her words.

She released my hand and stepped back, before Patrick could intervene. She looked away from us, turning around and walking quickly away, further into the room.

We didn't follow immediately. Patrick reached silently for my hand, wanting to see the painful marks left by her nails, but I just shook my head, wiping my stinging hand against my leg. I'd shown enough weakness in Selena's presence.

"Are you coming?" Selena called, not bothering to turn around.

Toni moved to follow her first, but I was right behind him. Patrick took up the rear, staying very close behind me.

We followed her across the dirty floor, around the large piles of twisted metal and other pieces of junk that spotted the room. It took about a full minute to cross the huge factory floor, and then Selena was opening a single door, set against the back wall.

She stepped inside, and we filed in after her.

The room was an old office, with no furniture except an old chair and a few metal filing cabinets set against a wall. But the room wasn't empty.

I counted eight Demons, Selena making nine. They all looked dangerous and had impressive muscles. They were all Hispanic, and I imagined that they—like Selena—had been working for the same man for a very long time.

Romero was easy to pick out. He was dressed in an immaculate dark suit, and he was sitting comfortably on the only chair. He was against the back wall, but though there was quite a space between us, he was completely focused on Toni, Patrick, and me.

He looked like an accomplished gangster. He had gray streaks in his otherwise dark hair, and he had lines on his square face. I guessed his age to be fifty or so, though of course I knew appearances weren't everything. He had thick lips and a thin mustache. The effect made him look a little weird, but that didn't mean I wasn't afraid of him.

Once we'd taken a few steps into the room, Toni halted, and I took my place next to him. Patrick smoothly came up on my other side and we watched as Selena moved to stand in the back corner of the room—her part done for now.

Romero's eyes brightened when they landed on me, and he stood from his chair, fixing his suit jacket as he straightened. "Ah, Kate! It is wonderful to finally meet you. I have learned so much about you from my sources—I feel I already know you."

"That doesn't seem very fair," I said, sounding a lot braver than I felt. "I know hardly anything about you."

He smiled and wagged a dark finger in my direction. "I like you," he said happily. "You are not like other Seers I have met in the past. They are all like, 'please, please, don't hurt me,' and that gets old very fast, no?" His mimicking voice was sickening, but somehow I kept my face straight.

He began to walk slowly toward us, his gait easy and unhurried. He looked first at Patrick and then at Toni. His eyes narrowed, and his small brow furrowed as he tried to recognize the Guardian in front of him.

"Haven't I met you?" he asked at last, stopping two steps away from us.

Toni smiled thinly. "You killed me once."

Romero chuckled. "I'm afraid you will have to be a bit more specific, my friend. I have killed many people."

Selena spoke from her corner. "It is Antonio Alvarez. Surely you remember him?"

Romero turned back to Toni, sudden understanding in his eyes. "Ah! The little thief, yes. The one you favored, if I remember right?" he questioned, glancing back toward her.

Selena tilted her head, causing her already flirtatious eyes to become all-out smoldering. "You know I favor only you, my love."

Toni made a light gagging sound beside me, but Romero was grinning as he turned back to us—or rather, to me.

"Well, Kate, I don't mean to take all day. I'm sure your Guardians have other things to do."

"I want to see my sisters," I said.

Romero's head bobbed. "Yes, yes, all in good time. But first, would you do me the honor of shaking my hand? And all of my men, of course. Just a precaution, you understand. I don't foresee the need for any unpleasantness though, do you?"

He stuck out his hand, and I had little choice. I willingly touched him, and he shook my hand slowly, his skin pampered and soft.

He released my fingers after a moment that was just a little too long, and then he stepped aside, silently ordering his men to follow his lead.

One by one, each of the other Demons present waited for my touch. Usually it was a quick handshake, sometimes it wasn't even that much. Patrick seemed to stiffen at every new touch, and I worried that he was going to do something stupid. Luckily, Romero was talking the whole time, so Patrick had something else he could focus on. I know it helped me.

"It's truly amazing how long plans slowly come together. Imagine the beauty of placing my lovely Selena in your sisters' school, where she could watch them and find the perfect opportunity to use them. All my close watching and patient waiting has finally borne fruit. Here you are, ready and willing to do whatever I ask."

I finished tapping my fingers against the last Demon's fist, then I straightened and focused on Romero. "What do you want?"

"Ah, a tricky question, my dear." Romero turned away from us and began to pace the room slowly. "What I want and what I need are completely different things, unfortunately. My sources informed me that you are young to this life. Is this true?"

"Yes."

"But you have heard of the Demon Lord?"

Though I didn't know much about the evil Demon that had proclaimed himself king, I knew he couldn't be a nice guy. Patrick had mentioned him once but had made it sound like I'd never hear of him again.

I guess that was a false assumption.

"Yes," I told him, still sounding brave despite my hammering heart. "I know a little."

"Hmm, I sense your fear of him. That is good—it means you know enough." Romero looked toward Selena. "Since my death, in the year 1854—on my fiftieth birthday, no less—I have served the Demon Lord loyally. Selena, my love who preceded me in death, said many nice things about me to him. He gave me a noble position as soon as I returned as a Demon—a place near his right hand." He shrugged a little, turning back to face me. "But someone spoke lies of me. Lies the Demon Lord believed. Now, I am a hunted man. He will kill me unless I bring him some gift. And so

I waited—watched. And when I heard of Far Darrig's new hunt, I decided I would get there first. Beat the Demon Lord's most loyal servant. What better way to prove my loyalty?"

I could feel the hairs on my body rising, and I struggled to keep my face smooth. "Far Darrig? What does he have to do with me? What does any of this . . . ?" My words died as understanding flickered in the back of my mind.

Patrick spoke lowly, more anger and fear in his voice than I'd ever heard before, though he was still perfectly controlled. "Far Darrig is after Kate."

"Why?" Toni demanded. "What could the Demon Lord want with a new, inexperienced Seer?"

Selena answered before Romero could. "Not all the details are clear. But he wants her nonetheless. And the Demon Lord always gets what he wants."

Romero cleared his throat, pulling all eyes back to him, where he wanted them. "Perhaps Kate can ask these questions of the Demon Lord personally, when she meets him."

"You're taking me to him?" I asked, struggling with the thought that I was being kidnapped. "You don't even want me? You did all of this—spied on me, killed your spy—all to give me away?"

Selena nodded. "More or less."

Romero glanced at his gold watch, feigning surprise. "My, my, look at the time. We have a private plane waiting for us." He leveled a look at me that I assumed was supposed to look caring. "Besides, your sisters will be waking up soon, and it would be a shame for them to realize they've been kidnapped. What a horrible thing for a child to endure."

I swallowed hard, trying to focus on my anger and not my fear. "You'll let them go?" I asked.

The Demon smiled reassuringly. "Of course." He turned, waving abruptly for two Demons to step forward. "Bring them down. Quickly."

The two Demons left, and there was a short silence. I wondered how I was going to get through this. My hope that somehow Patrick and the others could save me after getting my sisters safely out was fading rapidly. A plane? How were they supposed to compete with that?

Toni spoke, breaking the tense air. "So, Selena, would you be offended if I asked how you died? Just for old time's sake, of course."

Selena smiled slowly, and then walked sinuously to Romero's side. She was almost a head taller than the short man, and the sight was almost comical. "If you must know, it was in a fire. Do you know what fire feels like, Antonio?"

"I enjoy a S'more now and then, but my experience with fire ends there."

She laughed, but without mirth. "It was very painful. But do you know what the worst part was? The pain of knowing that all of my beauty would be gone. So imagine my elation when I realized that life doesn't end at death. That I could live forever, my immortal beauty forever a part of me. Prison was miserable, but I never have to go back. I will live in this perfect body forever."

"You know, interesting fact about Heaven—I hear you get to be twenty-five forever. Doesn't that sound great? That's how old you were when we met, wasn't it?" He shrugged. "Oh well— thirty isn't a bad look for you, either. Better than forty, anyway."

Selena's smile was like ice.

Romero chuckled and took her smooth hand. "Now, my dear, let's not get angry. He's not worth it." He craned his head around us, and we naturally turned to follow his gaze. I nearly gasped in relief at the sight of Jenna and Josie, looking sound asleep and completely unharmed, each cradled in the arms of a Demon.

"Ah, bless them. They were a little annoying when conscious, but drugs are my business and I knew what to do."

I rushed back to the Demons, who were just stepping into the room, and I ran my hands over both my sisters—feeling their shoulders, touching their sleeping faces, rubbing their arms.

Romero continued to speak. "They'll probably wake up in the next hour or so. They won't remember a thing. Consider it my gift to you."

I could feel Patrick behind me, and I knew what had to happen next. I glanced up at him, trying to push back the tears in my eyes. "Please take them," I whispered, though I knew everyone would still hear my words. "Keep them safe."

He stared into my eyes and I could see he had a hundred things he wanted to say. Most would probably be excuses not to leave me, knowing him—but he didn't say anything. He only nodded and then looked over his shoulder. "Toni."

I heard Toni move toward us, and I mouthed a thank-you to Patrick.

His mouth drew into a tight line, and his eyes burned with some unfathomable emotion. And then he stepped past me and carefully shifted Jenna's sleeping body out of the Demon's arms and into his own.

Toni took Josie, grunting a little under her dead weight.

Patrick turned around to face Romero, holding Jenna tightly. "You will regret this, Romero. You have my personal word."

The Demon merely smiled.

I felt one of Romero's stooges come up behind me, and then I became a literal prisoner as two strong arms wrapped tightly around my shoulders, pinning my arms to my sides.

"I trust you can see yourselves out?" Romero asked kindly.

Patrick gave me a final look—one I couldn't read, so I hoped it didn't hide a message of some kind—and then he turned and started back across the factory floor with my sister tucked safely in his arms. Toni followed a step behind, and despite my own situation I could feel a huge weight leave my chest. They were safe. They would be okay. Patrick wouldn't let anything happen to them.

The nightmare was over for them.

thirty-four

Selena's voice grew clipped. "Come. We'll be late. That plane can't wait forever."

Romero nodded, and I was pulled toward a door on the other side of the office—one that would lead directly outside and in the opposite direction my Guardians were headed. We were soon walking down a very narrow alley, Demons taking up positions around us.

Selena was in the lead, Romero right behind her. They weren't talking to me, but I picked up the words easily.

"The Demon Lord will surely accept this gift," Romero was saying. "I'll get my position back, and you, my dear, will no longer be on the run."

Selena grunted, but even that sound coming from her was somehow delicate. "If we can make it to the plane. And are you sure he's staying in Las Vegas? He usually prefers the Bahamas this time of year."

"I have many sources, my dear. The Demon Lord is not as untouchable as he seems. Someday, he will learn that."

Selena sighed and glanced down at her fingernails, her steps slowing just a little. "I really wish you hadn't said that, my dear."

Romero laughed a little, thinking she was making some joke. "What do you mean?"

Selena tugged at the hem of her blouse, as if she were

straightening it, flattening it against her slim waist. "Because I'm the one who betrayed you to the Demon Lord. Even now, I do not work for you, but for him. He has promised me a . . . how did you put it? A noble position."

In the flash of an eye, she stopped walking and gracefully pulled something out from under the fold of her shirt. Romero turned to face her, shock on his face. He realized what she was holding the same second I did—a small dagger.

The blade flashed in the sunlight, and I watched in horror as Selena drove the knife right into Romero's heart. I was too surprised to do anything more than watch with an open mouth as Romero groaned and slowly fell to his knees.

He tried to form words, but nothing came out. In the end, he slumped limply to the ground, rolled onto his back, and died at her feet.

I waited for the other Demons to react—try to kill her or something. But they didn't. It took me a second too long to realize that they weren't surprised. This had all been part of a great plan. Romero had been the only one in the dark.

Selena clucked her tongue at his dead body and blew him a final kiss. "I'm sorry, my love. I only do as you have taught." She glanced back at me, caught sight of my surprised face, and smiled. "I disgust you? That will not hurt my feelings. I am used to the glares of jealous women."

"You're a monster," I told her evenly, hoping that the venom I felt would be heard in my voice.

She smiled. "I prefer Demon." And then she turned away from the man she'd just killed. We all started moving again, as if nothing had happened.

At the end of the alley, I could see the waiting car. It was a black Lincoln limousine with darkly tinted windows, idling and ready, parked only a few yards from the buildings. The back door was already open for us. I guess Toni was right when he said that these Demons lived an expensive lifestyle.

Selena had just disappeared into the car when it happened. The driver's door opened, and I expected a Demon chauffeur to step out. Instead, I found myself staring at Jack. He was even wearing the old chauffeur's hat. He winked at me and then spoke to the Demons who had yet to notice him.

"I don't think you blokes want to get in there—your driver's got himself a bit of a knot on the noggin, and I don't think he's up to safely dealing with the traffic."

For a moment, everyone just stared at him. And then Jack pulled out two knives, seemingly from thin air.

The sight of the weapons spurred the Demons into action. The two closest to him lunged, hoping to get him off-balance. But neither of them wanted to get too close to the swinging blades. I wondered if they were afraid to be facing an immortal, when they themselves did have a weak spot. But then I figured that was why they were trying to disarm him.

I looked around wildly as the Demon's grip on me tightened, hoping to catch sight of the others. For a moment my heart sank—Jack was hopelessly outnumbered—and then I saw Toni. He'd been hiding at the end of the alley behind a rusting dumpster and was now behind us. He slammed heavily into a stunned Demon's back, and they both hit the ground.

Still, there were five other Demons unoccupied—not counting Selena. And then Patrick darted into the fray, from the same direction Toni had come from. I watched him for a moment, almost awed by the sight of him in a fight. He looked so concentrated—so deadly. Knowing that he was here for me—to protect me—made my stomach flip. I saw the knife in his hand flash in the sunlight, but then the converging Demons interrupted my view of him, and all I could hear were grunts of pain and an occasional yell.

So much was happening so quickly, I hardly knew where to look or what to think.

The Demon holding me wasn't as distracted as I was. He shoved me toward the car, even as Selena started screaming for someone named Jose to get me inside.

I was hauled roughly forward, and though I fought to struggle and drag my feet, I was no match for Jose's size and strength. I stumbled reluctantly to the car and was forcefully flung inside. I crumpled to the floor at Selena's feet but didn't really have time to get my bearings before Jose was pushing in after me.

Selena barely waited for him to get his last leg inside before she slammed the door closed and locked it soundly. She raised her voice at Jose, worry cracking her words. "Go! Get to the front! Don't let anyone inside and get us out of here!"

Jose was already moving, long before she'd finished. Once he was past me, I was moving too. I scrambled across the floor, crawling desperately for the other door, which hadn't yet been locked. I heard Selena move to follow me, but I was able to grab the handle and push the door open before she could stop me.

I literally fell out of the car, my hands shooting out to catch me before my face hit the hard ground. The lower half of my body was still inside the limo, but I was working hard to fix that. I crawled quickly, but not quickly enough. Selena's fingernails dug into my swinging right leg, keeping me in place.

"You're not going anywhere!" she hissed, murderously angry. "Get back in the car!"

I tried kicking her, but her grip was too good. She was right—I wasn't going anywhere. And I was completely terrified. She pulled, and I started sliding back into the limo. My stomach was being crushed against the bottom rim of the open door by the time my groping fingers snagged the jagged edge of a nearby pothole.

The blood was rushing to my head, and my palms scraped painfully against the sharp rocks that littered the ground. Despite my fears, I continued to pull for all I was worth, hoping that gravity alone would be enough to help me break free from her horrible grip.

I heard her groan in anger and frustration. The engine thrummed suddenly to life, and I felt the car lurch forward as the rear tires kicked up dirt. I lost my hold on the crumbling pothole, but my hands continued to grope as the ground started rolling past, surely gaining speed—I was gasping and getting dangerously dizzy. I was leaning out of a moving car!

The sounds of the fighting faded from the other side of the vehicle as the rear tires struggled to find traction on the dusty asphalt, and I thought I could hear running. But who was giving up? The Guardians or the Demons?

Selena's nails were as sharp as daggers. I swore they were making holes through the denim, and I could feel pinpricks of sweat or blood coming to the surface of my skin. I continued to struggle, sure that getting out was still in my best interest—even if doing so was the most dangerous thing I'd even tried: falling out of a moving vehicle. Because the limo had found traction and was now really accelerating. I couldn't stay like this for much longer. And if I didn't get out now, I wouldn't survive the fall.

Selena seemed to follow my train of thought. She couldn't pull me back in, but she was also unwilling to let me continue on this way and end up dead. She needed me alive. Or rather, the Demon Lord wanted me alive. And so she gave up, mere seconds after the car had begun its desperate getaway.

I was gasping in pain, my trembling arms and hands too gashed up to remain groping at every rock and pot hole we moved past—we were going too fast. It was all I could do to keep my head from smashing into the ground that was flashing past.

"This isn't over," Selena barked, biting each word off like a curse.

And then the painful biting in my leg was gone—had it even been a full five seconds since the car had come to life? Selena released me, shoving my legs out the door even though I was already falling toward the passing ground. I was able to let out a strangled gasp of fear as the blurring road raced up to meet me, and then my shoulder bit harshly into the rocky ground, jarring my entire body. I crashed onto my side, the momentum from my fall combined with the acceleration of the limo and Selena's push causing me to bounce and roll across the broken and dusty asphalt, away from the narrow road and down a slight decline. I wanted to cry out, but my mouth was clamped shut—a protective instinct as the side of my face was ripped up against the dry rocks. After a painful eternity, my body came to a stop. I was curled on my side, every inch of me aching, an ugly desert brush I'd barely avoided obscuring my view of the limo that I could hear now speeding away.

I hurt—a lot. Memories of the painful car crash I'd barely survived resurfaced, and I started shaking. I tried to tell myself that the limo probably hadn't even gotten up to thirty, but obviously that didn't make me feel much better.

I was suddenly aware of shouting back by the warehouse, and I laboriously attempted to fall onto my back so I could look for my friends.

"The car!" a stressed voice yelled. Toni? He sounded so far away.

"Kate's in there!" my grandpa cried. "I saw them push her in!"

They must not have seen my less-than-graceful fall, and though I wanted to reassure them I couldn't make my voice work—the breath had been literally knocked from my lungs. I squinted through watering eyes, able to see a few bodies on the ground, maybe a hundred feet away—Demon bodies, I hoped. I assumed they were dead, because they had no aura.

It was strange. I didn't feel sickened at the sight. Maybe that was because I'd seen so many deaths lately. Or maybe it was due to the fact that I was hardly aware of anything but pain. I was heavily bruised and pretty cut up in places. But I was pretty sure that nothing was broken, which seemed amazing to me.

A few people were standing back where the limo had been. Though the dirt was still settling back against the road, I could make out Jack, supporting a limp Demon with one arm, his fist clutching a handful of material near the Demon's throat. He was pummeling the poor Hispanic.

There were other figures too. One had a colorful aura—Grandpa. Two others had thin silver threads outlining them. Jack was preoccupied, but the other three figures were staring after the limo, standing in the middle of the road.

Toni was the first to speak, breathing heavily. I couldn't hear the words, but he was obviously speaking encouragingly to the man next to him.

Patrick had both hands on his head, fingers digging into his hair. He didn't seem to be listening closely to his friend's words. I didn't need to see his aura to know that he was tired and frustrated. He spun around sharply, away from the sounds of the fleeing limo. He kicked at an offending rock, sending it skirting down the road. He turned back to say something to the others, but he suddenly stopped and jerked back around. Miraculously, he'd caught sight of me lying there, curled in a loose ball a short distance off the road. I don't know how he'd spotted me when the others hadn't, but I didn't care.

I couldn't hear him, but somehow I knew that he gasped my name. Fear and relief shone on his face even as the others fought to follow his gaze. He darted forward, sprinting down the driveway toward me, the others following more slowly—as if they hadn't quite caught sight of me yet. I don't think I'd realized how far I'd actually gotten in the limo until I saw him running toward me. He'd never get here fast enough, in my opinion.

He veered right when he got closer, jogging across the rocks and dry dirt until he was skidding and dropping to his knees beside me. One hand slid beneath my head, the other brushed the hair off the exposed side of my face. "Kate?" he asked desperately, leaning closer, swallowing with difficulty. His blue eyes darted over me, always lurching back to my face before they could wander far.

My eyes fluttered against the dust he'd kicked up, and I winced. "Ow."

"What hurts?" he asked quickly, breathing heavily. "Is anything broken?"

"Ow," I repeated, entirely unhelpful.

His blue shirt was dirty, and there was a long rip near his left shoulder. Blood surrounded the area, and though I was worried for him, I couldn't yet make myself form real words.

His light fingers touched at my stinging cheek, a deep grimace twisting his face as he gauged my pain. "Kate," he breathed, jaw clenching tightly in anger. His trembling fingers lifted from my skin and clenched into a tight fist.

By now Grandpa was laboriously crouching down on my other side, one hand resting on my uninjured shoulder. "Baby? Baby can you hear me?"

"What happened?" Toni asked with a puff, skidding to a halt near my feet. He remained standing, his brow furrowed in confusion. "They pushed her out of a moving car? How does that make sense?"

Again, Patrick lowered his hand onto my face, touching at a thin trail of blood. I groaned deeply, and I felt Patrick's fingers freeze against my face, worried his touch had hurt me. "I jumped, Toni," I croaked painfully.

Toni let out a short laugh. "And you still hurt yourself? You're a wimp," he told me, his tone making the insult affectionate.

"Where are the twins?" I asked, grimacing as I tried to sit up. Patrick's arms went around my back, gingerly supporting my weight. I leaned heavily against him, grateful in more ways than one for his presence.

Toni answered the question when it became obvious that Patrick's voice wasn't ready to cooperate yet. "Patrick and I carried them out to the car, where Jason was waiting. He took them home, and we joined Jack and your Grandpa—who can really kill a Demon, by the way—back here. Personally, I feel the plan deserves four stars."

"Maybe three, mate," Jack argued, coming up beside him and slapping his shoulder. "Guess we scared that Selena Avalos, eh? Enough that she'd leave you behind."

"I wasn't really making it easy for her to take me," I said, already feeling better now that I was safe in Patrick's arms.

Grandpa was shocked. "Avalos? That was Selena?"

Toni almost sounded offended. "Is there any immortal person you don't know?" he demanded.

And then I got to see something a girl doesn't get to see every day. My grandpa was blushing. "I may have, uh, run into her before. Once or twice. It's a shame I didn't get to really see her. It's been years."

Jack winked at him. "She still looks great."

Patrick was ignoring them, his eyes on only me. He carefully examined the side of my face, the one that was stinging like a mother. He flinched for my benefit. "That doesn't look good."

"It doesn't feel very good," I admitted.

"Does anything feel broken?"

I shook my head gently, one bleeding hand coming up to push back my hair. "No. I think I just got the wind knocked out of me. A little bruised—that's all."

Patrick shifted his weight, preparing to lift me. "Come on— let's get you home."

He helped pull me to my feet and then kept his arms wrapped firmly around me when I swayed. I glanced up at him, for the first time noticing blood on his forehead. There was no cut, but it was easy to see where there had been one. I grimaced, knowing that—even if it had been healed after just a second—it must have been painful.

"Are you okay?" I asked him.

He let out a shaky laugh. "You're asking an immortal, remember? I'm fine."

"But there's blood—"

"Kate, I'm fine," he repeated, more firmly, yet still gentle. "Now come on—we need to get you cleaned up." He started to slowly help me forward, and Jack ran ahead to bring his car closer so I wouldn't have to walk as far. Grandpa and Toni followed behind us.

I still hurt pretty bad, but I was beginning to feel better enough that feelings of embarrassment were surfacing, unable to be ignored. "Am I the only one who got hurt?" I asked at last.

Grandpa let out a hard laugh. "Annoying, isn't it? Probably the only downside of working with immortal people. Makes you feel like a wuss."

"Don't worry about it," Patrick whispered to me, holding me close. "Don't feel bad."

"I wasn't even in the fight," I complained.

"You took on Selena," Toni clarified from behind. "Something not many men are able to walk away from unscathed. Even immortal people."

"True enough," Grandpa sighed in agreement.

I couldn't see the look Toni gave my grandfather, but I could imagine it. "So seriously," Toni asked him. "Is there anyone else you know, that I should know about?"

I could hear the shrug in Grandpa's voice. "I don't know. You an Elvis fan?"

"Huh?" He was obviously surprised by the question. "Um, no. Not really. He was fine, but . . ."

"Hmm. You looked the type too. Anyhow, I knew him. He was the last Guardian I served with."

"You're kidding!" Toni cried, incredulous. "Elvis is a Guardian!?"

"I've got signed posters and records and everything. 'Course, he signed 'em all after he was dead, so I don't know how that affects the value. Always told me he chose to be a Guardian to be closer to his fans, you know? Watch over them and everything."

There were a million things I could have commented on. But I didn't. I just let my grandpa and Toni have their unbelievable conversation as I laid my head against Patrick's shoulder, loving the feel of his strong arm around my back.

thirty-five

Once we were in the car—me squished in the backseat between Patrick and Toni—Grandpa dug around in the glove box to find a first-aid kit. Finally he let out a grunt of satisfaction and quickly opened it to get a couple bandages for himself. Then he closed it and passed the box back to us. Patrick took it, searched inside, pulled out a couple alcohol wipes, and then reached silently for my hand. I sighed, knowing it was going to hurt but reluctant to fight him. He cradled my hand gently and began to clean the deep cuts and shallow scrapes alike. The alcohol stung, but it didn't hurt as much as I thought it would. Maybe your body can only register a certain amount of pain, and then it switches to just discomfort.

Once he was satisfied that all the dirt and infection had been removed—he even tended the little cuts on my arm—he reached for my other hand, intent on repeating the process. By now we were almost back to the highway and the ride was a lot smoother.

While he worked, I glanced forward, asking questions of anyone that knew the answer. "What about all those bodies? What will happen to them?"

Toni answered easily. "We'll call Terence. He has connections."

Patrick elaborated with a low, concentrated voice. "We'll

have to go back there later, but it's out of the way enough we can get you home first."

Grandpa piped up from the front seat. "We've got to get you ready for the dance—if you're up to it."

"Oh. Right." I'd almost forgotten. I dreaded facing Aaron tonight. I just didn't have the energy, and he was already so upset with me . . . I sighed, and Patrick continued to stroke the wipe over my palm.

He checked my other arm, but the scrapes were minimal, so he turned his attention to my face. He brushed the hair away from my cheek and gingerly began to clean the cuts there. I winced, and he murmured an apology. But he didn't stop.

We all ignored the one topic we didn't want to bring up—that this nightmare wasn't over. Grandpa and Jack didn't know about Far Darrig, and the fact that he was after me, and the three of us in the backseat didn't bother to enlighten them. There would be a time to worry about that, but it could wait. I needed it to wait.

By the time we pulled into the driveway next to the blue Altima, all my injuries had been carefully attended to. I still ached and stung, and I was covered in dirt, but after having my skin stroked by Patrick's gentle fingers, I was feeling much better.

Grandpa and Jack shared a quick good-bye, and Patrick helped me out of the car. He kept a hand wrapped around my elbow, though at this point I wasn't really unsteady—just sore. Grandpa's door was open, but he was still talking to Jack. I suddenly remembered I still had Patrick's knife.

I bent over, but Patrick must have thought I was falling, because he pulled me back up. "Kate?"

"Your knife," I told him, waving down to my leg. "I still have it."

Patrick's lips pulled into a very fast, tired smile. "Keep it. You might need it again."

"I didn't even use it," I admitted. "I kind of thought I would."

Toni snorted in the car, and I knew he'd overheard. "Trust me—you'd be in worse shape if you'd tried. We need to train you first."

I heard the front door of the house open, and Jason rounded the corner by the garage. He was pushing his glasses back against his nose, closer to his eyes. Surprising me, he came around the car to stand in front of me, and he addressed me for the first time.

"They're still sleeping. I laid them on a couch inside, if that's all right."

"That's great," I told him. "Thank you. So much."

He smiled just a little, his nerdy face stretching tightly. "I didn't mind. This was cooler than my calculus homework any day. College isn't nearly as fun as this Seer stuff."

Grandpa pulled himself out of the car, and Jason turned toward him. He slipped wordlessly into the passenger seat that Grandpa had just vacated. Toni was just climbing out through his door. I called out a quick thank-you to Jack.

"No worries, miss Kate," the Australian Guardian said happily. "This is what we do, in the land Down Under."

"You're in New Mexico," Grandpa reminded him loudly.

Jack cleared his throat loudly. "Enough earbashing! We're off!"

Patrick closed the door, and we stepped back as the black car slowly backed out of the drive and then disappeared down the street.

Toni whistled lowly. "That is one weird guy."

Grandpa reached for my hand, and I reluctantly pulled out from under Patrick's arm. Once at my grandpa's side, I turned to face Toni and Patrick, standing dirty and slightly bloody before us.

"Thank you," Grandpa told them. "I appreciate all you've done for my family."

"All part of the job," Toni assured us, winking at me

flirtatiously. "We can swing back by the store to get your car if you want."

I nodded my thanks for his thoughtfulness.

Patrick's hands were in his pockets, his crystal-blue eyes on me. "Call if you need anything."

I nodded once. "I will. See you Monday?"

His lips tugged into a thin smile. "Yeah. Monday."

And then he lowered his gaze and followed his partner to their car, where Toni was already shutting the driver's door.

In seconds, they were gone, and it was just me and my grandpa standing in the driveway. His old hand rubbed my shoulder, and his voice was smooth and comforting. "Let's get you ready for the ball, eh?"

The twins woke up just as I got out of the shower. They had no memory of their kidnapping, just as Romero had promised. Jenna was a little surprised that they'd managed to sleep until about three, but Josie was more confused as to how they'd ended up on the living room couch together, instead of in their beds.

"Actually," Josie said, glancing around with narrowed eyes. "I don't even remember getting into bed. Did we just crash here?"

Since it was the easiest answer, I told her they had.

They didn't doubt me, but maybe that was because they were interested to know what had happened to my face.

"You're ugly," Josie informed me. "Like a corpse from a cheap movie."

I told them I'd fallen at Lee's, but they didn't question me— mostly because Jenna had just remembered that they were supposed to be mad at me for lecturing them yesterday. And so I got the silent treatment, not that I minded. They were here and safe, and they were secure in their own world. No Demons haunted them, for which I was grateful.

Though there was plenty of time that I could have called Aaron and arranged to at least go to dinner, I ended up just asking him to come pick me up for the dance.

He sounded sullen and hurt—still upset too—but he agreed to get me around eight.

I worked hard at my makeup, trying to cover up the several long gashes on my face. In the end, I think I made it worse. So I removed it all and tried again, with slightly better success the second time around. It was still easily visible, but the edges didn't look so bad at least.

Grandpa cooked us some pancakes for an early dinner, but the twins refused to eat at the same table with me, so they took theirs into the family room. Grandpa and I ate together, and we talked quietly.

He told me a little about his life as a Seer and how easy it was for him to accept his new lifestyle. But in time, it grew hard. He returned from the war, got married, and continued to work for the Guardians. For many years the Guardians—someone like Terence, I imagined—gave him the money he needed to support his family. It was a few years after the birth of his son—my father—that he finally told the Guardians he was done.

I had a lot of questions I wanted to ask him, but it was easier to just listen to his stories. So that's what I did.

At seven I went back into the bathroom and tried to fix my hair. I decided to leave it down, in an attempt to better cover my facial cuts. I curled it, though my lightly bandaged hands were throbbing by the time I finished. It wasn't the best job I'd ever done, but it would have to do. I touched up my eye makeup, and then it was time for the dress.

I stood in my bedroom for a long time, just looking in the full-length mirror on my door. From the black heels that just peeked under the long skirt, up the silk maroon dress, to the silver necklace around my throat, I thought I looked pretty good. But it was the emotion in my eyes that kept me looking. Was it sadness? Regret? I wasn't sure. But I was captivated by that glimpse into my soul. The thoughts I'd never quite admitted to myself, the desires I'd never fully realized until this moment, all of them staring back at me.

There was a knock on my door, and I spoke without thinking. "Come in."

Grandpa poked his head in first and then stepped fully into the room. He was smiling at me, taking in my appearance with a loving eye.

"You look great, honey. Almost breathtaking."

"Thanks."

He tilted his head to the side, regarding me closely. "Hmm, except for that."

My fingertips brushed against the uneven skin of my left cheek. "I know. I did my best, but—"

"Not that," he broke in. "I meant your aura."

"What about it?" I asked, feeling defensive.

He shrugged. "It's fine, if you like brown, and gray . . . but personally I like to see you surrounded by clouds of yellow and lines of blue. That suits you much better."

"Grandpa, what do you mean?"

"I've seen you around Aaron. I know what your aura does. I also know what happens when I say one word—Patrick."

He watched me, and though I swear I kept my face straight, he slowly started to smile. But it was a kind of sad smile. "That's more like it. The yellow my granddaughter deserves."

"It's not that simple," I whispered. I looked down at my hands, where the left one was fingering the bandages on the right.

"Life isn't simple. You have to know that by now. But emotions . . . those are simple."

I glanced up at him, my eyes stinging. "I think I might be falling in love with him," I whispered, and though I'd never thought the words aloud before now, I knew they were true.

"He's not who I would have chosen for you," Grandpa admitted softly. "Aaron is much safer, but . . . You're not happy with him. And that's what matters to me most of all—your happiness. No matter where you can find it."

The doorbell rang downstairs. It would be Aaron, coming to pick me up. I turned to my bed, picked up the small black purse, and then looked back at my grandpa. "Just because you know something's right, doesn't mean it's easy."

"The right thing usually isn't," Grandpa assured me.

thirty-six

New Mexico, United States

I was in my room, lying on my bed. My eyes kept returning to the cheap clock on my desk, as if magnetized and unable to resist making contact. It was nearing nine o'clock. Kate was surely in Aaron's arms by now, moving slowly on a dimly lit dance floor to a song about perfect love.

There weren't words to describe how I felt about this. Throbbing heart? Absolutely. Twisting stomach? Every time I imagined his hand resting at the small of her back. Aching mind? Whenever I remembered her beautiful face, close to his in an intimate kiss.

In a word, I was miserable. Utterly, physically sick with misery.

Watching her go through today had been torture. Seeing her fear, watching her in the arms of a Demon, having to leave her there . . . it had been agony. Fighting to reach her—thinking I'd failed—and then catching sight of her, bleeding and still on the ground. All of that had been gut-wrenching. Thinking I'd completely failed her in her first real moment of need had left me feeling empty inside. Running that distance to try to reach her, to see if she was even breathing . . . And as I'd slipped my hand beneath her head, thinking that maybe she was gone—I'd almost died myself.

But all of that—it was nothing compared to what I felt now. Because even though it had been the longest day of my eternal life, at least I was with her. I was near—even if I wasn't at her side, touching her hand, feeling her body next to mine—I was close, and I knew that she wanted me there.

But now, lying alone in an abandoned warehouse, I didn't have that surety. She was in another man's arms, and that was what she wanted. That's what hurt me the most. To want someone so badly, and to know there was no way that person could return those feelings.

I knew I was being ridiculous. I was overreacting. Today had been proof to her that the life of a Seer was dangerous. Kate would never want to risk her life and her family again. Who would? As soon as she knew she was safe, she was going to ask me to leave. She wouldn't want to be a part of this.

I wouldn't blame her. I couldn't.

It might be days, or maybe even weeks, considering we had the Demon Fear Dearg to worry about. But eventually, she would ask me to go. And I would. I would have no other choice. But just because it was inevitable didn't make it any easier to digest this very acute pain. For the first time in two hundred and thirty years, I knew that I could have fallen in love. It would have been just like falling—so easy, and I admit unexpected—like a stumble in the dark. Guardians were generally alone. It was the simple truth. We had friendships, but we were forever alone at the same time. Not because we couldn't have relationships—some Guardians did—but . . . Heaven was for love and happiness. The life of a Guardian was generally sacrifice, and nothing more than that. It was Guardian 101.

I'd been stupid to think that—even for a moment—I could have anything more than that with Kate.

I'd been lying here since Toni and I got back from returning Kate's car. I'd parked it in the driveway, thought about going inside to check on her, and then simply joined Toni in the Altima. We were silent the whole drive back to the warehouse, and I'd been left with my thoughts— thoughts that mocked my highly potent and varied emotions. I kept remembering that moment—that brief, sweet moment—when Kate had put her hand on my arm, stopping me from getting out of the car. I had a thousand worries coursing through my mind: how to secure Jenna and Josie, how to stop Selena and Romero, how to keep Kate safe despite the odds . . . and then, idiot that I was, I thought she was going to say something completely different. Instead, Aaron's name filled every available space in the car, and I couldn't breathe.

Of course it made sense for her to bring him up. He was her boyfriend. She loved him. She was concerned about him. I'd been an utter fool to think that I meant more to her than someone as good as Aaron. For as much as I hated to admit it, he was good. More than good.

That didn't mean I wasn't stung by the rejection in her words, though. Regardless of the intimate moments we'd shared, she cared more for him than me. The kiss that had left me reeling was, for her, something else entirely.

I didn't blame her, though. How could I?

I wasn't aware that we were back at the warehouse until Toni was parked in the garage and had switched off the engine. Neither of us moved to get out, but I had no urge to speak. I was pitying myself too deeply to have a conversation right now.

"You're being an idiot, you know," Toni said suddenly.

I glanced over at him, unsure of his meaning.

He rolled his eyes at me. "You keep acting like you've got a choice. Love her, or don't. That's a really dumb way of looking at the situation. It's love, man. You don't get a choice."

I didn't respond.

I reached for the door, and he finished quickly. "You don't get a choice, but you do get a say in her life. And you know it." I tugged the handle and pushed the door open.

Toni's words came faster, and his voice grew louder in an attempt to follow me. "You're just afraid to come out and say what you want, because you think that by keeping yourself away from her, you're doing her a favor." I was out of the car, turning back to push the door closed. My friend shook his head at me, as if I were hopeless. "Dude, you're not doing anyone any favors."

I slammed the door, cutting off his words. I didn't want to hear them. I didn't want them to be true. I walked rapidly away, and I was out of the garage before he'd opened his door to follow.

I'd moved straight for my room, and Toni—mercifully—hadn't followed there. In fact, I'd only seen him once since we'd made it back. He'd come to tell me that he'd called Terence, and that he'd meet us at the bodies, so they could be disposed of.

My response had been less than verbose. I looked to him, the rest of my body unmoving on the bed, and he understood my silent words. For the first time, he didn't offer a sarcastic remark. He only nodded his dark head before closing the door again, leaving me alone with my thoughts. I heard him walk around the living area for a couple short minutes, and then he opened the outer door and was gone.

I silently thanked him for knowing what I needed, and then I closed my eyes tightly, trying to remember the last time I'd cried.

And now I was looking at the clock again—nine exactly. Toni had been gone for hours. He'd probably decided to go to a movie or something—any excuse to stay away from me and my depression. I couldn't blame him. I wasn't the best company right now.

I wondered how I was going to survive. Being around Kate at school, pretending that everything was fine. I thought often of the kiss we'd shared, that night at her house. Too often. It wasn't healing, because I kept digging at the scab. I never should have done it, but strangely, I didn't regret it. I'd apologized to her, but that had been a lie—the only lie I'd ever uttered to her. I wasn't sorry for kissing her. And though it was the most exquisite pain to remember it—to know that it would never happen again—I relived every second of that endless moment again and again. Alone on my bed, I imagined my arms around Kate. Her hands on my face, my mouth on her soft lips. It was beautiful, and heart-rending.

And then—drowning in my sorrow—I barely heard the soft knock on the door.

I waited tensely for him to respond, my heart pounding and nerves making my fingers keep touching my hair, pulling on my necklace.

The hall was dark, but I could see the light around the door, and I knew Toni had left the light on in their makeshift living room, just like he said he had. He hadn't seemed at all surprised by my phone call, and he was actually very helpful. Yes, Patrick was home. And no, Toni wouldn't be back for a long time. The way he'd said that made me blush a little, but before that could register in my voice, I'd said good-bye.

The door was still closed. I didn't hear any footsteps. Should I knock again? Try the door? Maybe he was in his room, and he couldn't hear me.

Then all at once I distantly heard a door open, somewhere in the rooms beyond. In the quiet warehouse, his footsteps seemed extremely loud. I pulled in a last steadying breath and self-consciously ran a bandaged hand over the satin material of my dress.

The door opened, and if it wasn't for his body shading my eyes, I would have blinked in the sudden flow of light. I wasn't smiling—I couldn't seem to make my face muscles work.

Patrick wasn't smiling either. He was just staring at me, and for one moment I wavered, wondering if I should have come. And then he whispered my name.

"Kate."

I smiled, though it was small. "Hello, Patrick." I swallowed, fighting the stupid urge to clear my throat. "Can I come in?"

His blue eyes were riveted on me, and he couldn't seem to form words. He merely stepped to the side, still holding the door for me. I slipped past him, my long skirt swishing smoothly, my heels tapping against the floor, just slightly louder than my heartbeat.

I stood in the center of the room, the single lamp in the

corner casting long shadows across the room. I turned back to face him, where he still stood next to the door, just barely letting it fall closed, almost like it was an afterthought. His stare had not yet wavered, and his forehead was slightly furrowed.

"What are you doing here?" he asked quietly, his gaze taking in the sight of me in a dress.

I hoped he approved, and when I caught sight of his wonder-filled face, I knew that he did. A slight blush crept under my cheeks, but it was pleasant—not embarrassing.

My smile was a little easier this time. "I'm sorry—it's pretty late. Toni said you'd be up, though."

"Kate." His eyebrows were drawn tightly together, but his voice remained quiet and even. "I don't understand."

I looked away from him, turning around to inspect the room. "I talked to Aaron tonight. I've been meaning to for a while now. Our relationship hasn't been the same since my parents died."

He didn't say anything. My back was to him, and I hesitated to turn around. For some reason, not looking at him made this easier. It helped keep my voice from wavering. I sounded sure, confident, and calm. So I talked to the sagging couch, one set of fingers picking at the bandage on the other hand. "I ended things with him tonight. I know it was rotten timing. We should have been enjoying our last date together, sharing one last dance."

His eyes were like magnets on my back, dragging, begging me to look at him. It was a pull I couldn't refuse, despite my good reasons to keep looking at the ragged couch—anything but him.

I caved, turning to meet his stare, and though there was half a room between us, I'd never felt so close to anyone. He was watching me closely—his face almost guarded, his eyes full of hope—a hope he was struggling desperately to hide. That more than anything made me walk toward him, my eyes tenderly trying to tell him that everything was going to be okay.

I stopped a step away from him, and I noticed he wasn't

breathing. My words came out in a whisper, my eyes firmly on his. "But I didn't want a last dance with Aaron. I couldn't stand one more night of pretending. I didn't want to spend the night with him. I didn't want to spend it with anyone. Except for you."

Patrick pulled in a shaky breath. His eyes traveled over my face—looking for any sign that this was a dream or some other form of a lie. And then he lifted a single hand, his fingers lighting so softly against my face—the side I'd tried to cover with makeup. He swallowed with difficulty, and I could feel his body trembling through his gentle fingertips. His large hand slowly moved to cup the side of my face, and I closed my eyes in pleasure, leaning into his touch. His thumb stroked the skin under my eye, and then I felt his other hand, softly pushing my hair over my shoulder, tucking the curls delicately behind my ear.

"Kate," he breathed. "I . . . I think . . ." and then he took the final step, and I felt his body against mine. He kissed me, and I kissed him. He touched me so gently—held me so lovingly—kissed me until I was dizzy.

He pulled back, only to lay his mouth against my forehead, his hands tenderly cradling my face. "I love you," he stated softly, lips brushing the lightly bruised area with a gentle kiss. "I think I have since the first moment I saw you."

I opened my eyes and smiled, loving the feel of his lips on my skin. "I'm sorry it took me so long to get here," I whispered.

I felt his head shake ever so slightly. "You're here. That's what matters. If this is what you want."

I slipped my bandaged hands over his shoulders, wrapping my arms around his neck. I pulled him closer, bringing his lips back to mine. I kissed him, and then spoke against his lips—knowing that I'd never answered a question this truthfully, this confidently. "Yes. You're exactly what I want."

And then he kissed me, stopping all other words in their tracks.

epilogue

Midnight
New Mexico, United States

I was sitting in the dark motel room. It was late—very late. But I wasn't tired. I rarely slept anymore. Not since my death.

My phone was in my hand, the focal point of my unyielding stare as I waited patiently for my master to call. I knew he would, because things hadn't gone as planned. That was the only time he contacted me during a mission.

Usually, there was never any reason for him to call.

The black phone vibrated suddenly, but I wasn't startled. I raised it smoothly to my ear, my voice deep.

"Master."

"Far Darrig."

"Is the situation under control?"

The Demon Lord sighed expansively. "Romero has been dealt with. Selena is . . . properly upset."

"What about the Seer?"

"There's been a slight change of plans concerning her. She is more strong-willed than I imagined a mere teenager to be."

"I'm not Romero. I can handle her."

"Of course you could. But I don't want you to. I have something else in mind. I will have her—but she will come to me."

"Very well. Shall I return?"

"No. Not yet. I have one more thing I need you to do for me. It concerns her Guardians."

I didn't hesitate. "Anything."

"Selena tells me that the Seer has a weak spot for her Guardians, one in particular. Patrick O'Donnell. He is your new target. Are we clear?"

My voice was neutral. "Yes."

We talked for a few more minutes, arranging the final details. A very small smile twisted my lips—an unfamiliar sensation.

When he ended the call, I closed my phone and stood. There was much to be done. But it was the work I enjoyed. What I did best.

about the author

Heather Frost was born in Sandy, Utah, and raised in a small northern Utah town. She is the second oldest of ten children, and she loves her family very much. She is especially grateful to her wonderful parents for their decision to homeschool their children. She graduated from Snow College with an associate of science and is currently pursuing a bachelor's degree in English.

Heather has always been an avid reader, and reading and writing are among her most favorite things to do. She also enjoys playing the flute, listening to all types of music, and watching a wide variety of movies. Ever since she wrote her first story—at the age of four—she has dreamed of one day becoming an author. *Seers* is her first published novel.

acknowledgments

Thanks to my parents: Mom, for being my first critic, and Dad, for being so supportive. I love you both! I also need to give a special thank you to my sister Kimberly—she's heard more about my imagination than any person should have to. While I'm at it, thanks to my entire family for keeping me around, despite my many peculiarities. You're the best friends a person could have. An extra special thanks to Jacob, who helped inspire this. I also need to express my appreciation to my Heavenly Father and Savior, Jesus Christ, for giving me all the opportunities that I enjoy.

Karen, thanks for reading. Annaka, you're awesome, and in all ways that count, my sister. Jill, thanks for the excitement you shared. Ashley, you could have been doing a million other things—thanks for doing this. Mr Walton, thanks for your name. Girls of the Townhouse: Ari, Erin, Lauren, Niki, Dixie and Courtney—"It was all in the past!" You're all amazing, and thanks so much for reading about the figments of my imagination. Emily and Landen, you are both special to me, and you will be forever. Emily, thanks for putting up with me, even when the needle was sitting on my lap the whole time. To my first unofficial fan club: Rex, sorry about taking you away from your homework—but not really. James, thanks for reading and appreciating my work—you still hold the record! Rich, thanks for asking to get in on the story—it really boosted my confidence. Also, a special thanks to the good people at Cedar Fort, who made all of this possible. Especially Shersta, Heidi, Laura, and Danie; you're all awesome—thanks for your time, talents, and energy.

Thanks to anyone else I may have missed, anyone who has supported me at any time in my life, and to anyone who has read this. Broad enough?

Special Sneak Peek

demons

by
heather frost

coming soon from
Sweetwater Books

prologue

May 10, 1797
Wexford County, Ireland

My lower back was beginning to ache. I'd *been hunched over for far too long, but I wasn't about to move. I was finally getting it right. The shading wasn't too dark around her eyes, and the gentle planes of her small face were sloped almost to perfection.*

This in itself would have been reason enough not to move. I was a painter—sketching had never come easily to me. When I worked with paints, it required no thought. The canvas called to me, guiding my strokes. But the art of drawing was an entirely different experience. I would agonize over every line, second-guess every mark I tried to make. Sometimes I enjoyed the challenge, while at other times I had to force myself through each second. Today was surely a mixture of both.

There was another reason I refused to acknowledge the muscles screaming in my body, the reason for my taking up the sketch at all, even though I would have rather spent the day working on a painting of my mother's garden that I'd started a few days ago. I'd recently finished a painting of my father's cherished church, where he was the local pastor, and my mother loved it so much that she insisted I immortalize her flowers. That is how I would have spent the day, had I not remembered the dream.

It was simple, as dreams go. Just a face. At first, I believed it to be pretty, but upon further staring I realized the deeper beauty. Small, delicate, and perhaps more rounded than most people would consider attractive. But there was something so warm, so real about that face. She had a small smile playing about her lips, and her hair was long—a combination of blonde and brown. It looked so soft, and I remember wanting to reach out and touch the subtly waving locks. But I couldn't. In my dream, I stood frozen. I simply watched her, and though she didn't seem to notice me, I had a feeling that she knew she was being watched. Her eyes were green at first glance, but a deeper appreciation revealed thin flecks of gold.

It felt like I stared at her all night. Her image was burned into my mind, and I was sure that it would be forever. Still, I was working feverishly to finish this unjust portrayal of her unique beauty. And though it did not capture her completely, my drawing was one of the best sketches I'd ever managed to create.

"My brother, the genius!" a boisterous voice called suddenly, breaking into my thoughts.

I glanced up quickly, my pencil pausing instinctively but still resting against the paper. I smiled as I watched my younger brother approach. He had just celebrated his sixteenth birthday two days ago. I would be eighteen soon, but I knew he would still take pleasure in the fact that he was "gaining" on me.

Sean strolled across the yard, stepping through the long green grass with full but leisurely strides. He looked a great deal like me, though many claimed he had inherited more of my mother's attractive looks. He was certainly the stronger personality between us. Where I was often seen as shy and studious, Sean was always smiling and thoroughly involved. He was the first to begin a dance and the last to leave any social event. His quick wit was praised by many, and he was acutely aware of this admiration.

Though I had plenty of reasons to be jealous, I was not. He was my brother, and I loved him. As he loved me.

"Your dedication amazes me," Sean continued, his hands deep in his pockets. It was the characteristic pose the men of our family took, but he always made it seem so natural instead of nervous. "I've never finished a thing in my life," he said with an oddly satisfied grin, jumping easily over the small stream that trickled through our back pasture.

Our modest home of gray stone and brown wood dominated my view, a dirt lane and rolling hills the only other things in sight. It was a backdrop I loved, and one I often called upon to help fuel my creativity. The old stump I sat on was at the back edge of our land, though it wasn't close enough to the rudimentary fence for me to recline. But sitting here afforded me the most inspirational view, so I suffered through the slight discomfort.

I watched Sean close the remainder of the distance between us, and I finally spoke. "You've never regretted that before."

"Ah, but I don't regret it now. I merely state fact." He stooped before me, and I quickly lifted my pencil as he snatched my unfinished drawing away. He brought it closer to his face, so he could inspect it critically.

While he did, I stretched my knotted back muscles and flexed my stiff fingers. I didn't rush him to speak—I knew he would give his opinion with minimal urging.

I expected a jibe of some kind, but instead his voice was mildly surprised. "This is good, Patrick." He paused, then added playfully, "What is it supposed to be?"

I frowned at him, and he laughed as he caught sight of my face. "Merely teasing you, big brother. Really, it's quite good. Who is she?"

He held out the thin book that contained my drawings, and I took it back quickly, running my eyes over the sketch. "I don't know. While I dreamed, I saw her face."

"She's pretty."

"Yes," I whispered, gazing into her eyes. "She is."

He cocked his head, coming around me to look at the sketch over my shoulder. "You know, she's almost familiar."

I glanced over at him, very interested. "Are you sure?"

His brow furrowed, eyes drawn to her face. "Yes. But I can't imagine where I might have seen her. Surely not your dreams, though."

We shared a quick laugh at that absurd thought, and then Sean slapped a hand against my shoulder, pulling me out of my thoughts before I could become submerged.

He knew me well.

"Mother wishes you to come inside." His blue eyes—an almost exact repetition of mine—grew knowing. "Sarah McKenna came to call on her, and we're to entertain her until mother can finish listening to father's preparatory sermon."

I hesitated, my eyes darting back to the page before me. "I'm nearly done."

Sean sighed loudly. "Patrick, you are the epitome of hopeless. Surely you are aware that Mother arranged this for your benefit."

My brow furrowed in confusion. "But Sarah called on mother."

"Diabolical, isn't she?"

"Which one? Mother or Sarah?"

Sean shrugged. "Both?"

I chuckled with him, scooping up my work under one arm so we could walk together back to the house.

Sarah McKenna waited in the parlor. She was wearing a nice dress of pleasant blue, and her red curling hair caught my artistic eye as it always did. The color was just so bright, so vivid. It was piled carefully on her head, in a way only a woman could accomplish. She sat near the window, thumbing through one of father's philosophy books. As we entered, she looked up and a smile spread across her face.

She was my same age, our birthdays mere weeks apart. We had played together as children, and she had teased me through adolescence. Now as we approached adulthood, it seemed she always found an excuse to visit my parents. Her eyes were a beautiful blue, and her skin was pale and lightly freckled. Her face was very feminine, and somehow managed to be smoothly angular.

She was perhaps the most beautiful woman in the province. And she knew this, sometimes to her detriment. But though her quick tongue could often get her into trouble, her dazzling eyes seemed to always repair any damage.

She laid the book aside and stood. "The O'Donnell brothers. It's a pleasure."

"The pleasure is strictly ours," Sean said, offering a quick bow.

I added my own nod, and a not-so-graceful "Good day, Miss McKenna."

She smiled at me, and then noticed the brown leather book under my arm. "Your drawings. Have I interrupted the master at work?"

"You flatter me," I said honestly, following her glance to my book.

"May I see your newest masterpiece?"

"If you wish."

She nodded. "I do."

I shifted the book to her hands, and she opened it to the last drawing in the otherwise blank book—it was almost in the exact middle. I watched her face as she studied my drawing, and I felt my stomach tighten when she frowned.

Sean stood next to me, silently watching this exchange. I was grateful that he didn't leave because I knew I'd soon run out of things to say to her; his wit would come into play beautifully, as it always did.

Finally, Sarah looked up at me, her eyes impressed. "You've improved. The last sketch of yours I saw was . . ."

"Horrible beyond comprehension?" Sean supplied, his tone exceedingly helpful.

I sent a warning glance toward him, but Sarah was laughing lightly.

"It wasn't like your paintings," she admitted. "But this . . . you have captured emotion. But it is almost a nameless one. Who is she? And what is she thinking that creates that smile, and so captures your attention?" She shook her head lightly. "Whatever it is, I would certainly like to learn it."

I nearly blushed, but somehow managed to keep calm. "I don't know who she is. Nor what she is thinking . . ." I shrugged slowly. "Perhaps I'll never know."

Sarah smiled at me. "Why, Patrick, you speak so mysteriously."

"I don't mean to."

Sean grunted. "But of course he does. Miss Sarah, he is just so above us, isn't he?"

"Yes. I would have to agree." And watching the way her eyes drifted back toward me—so slowly, so easily—I suddenly realized a startling truth. Sarah McKenna was genuinely taken with me.

Perhaps even more startling, I realized in that moment that I might genuinely be taken with her.

Present Day—Midnight
New Mexico, United States

I waited. There had been so much waiting the *past few weeks. But it was nearly over now.*

I stood in a small city park, just beside the pool of yellow light cast by the lone street lamp. It was a quiet night—no cars could be seen, and even the sounds from the highway were distant, as if muffled by the dark night. Humans were asleep in their homes, unsuspecting of the evil that lurked in their midst. Unaware of me.

All at once I heard a car approaching down the otherwise quiet street. I straightened, angling my body toward the sound. In seconds a pair of headlights flashed across me as the car pulled out of a side street and moved toward the park, coming to rest against the curb. The headlights switched off. The car continued to run. I heard the power locks disengage, and I stepped up to the passenger door in front of me. I pulled it open before ducking smoothly inside.

There was no illumination in the car, but from the glowing light outside, I could see the scarred face of the driver. A man I'd seen many times, but never really spoken to. Takao Kiyota was his name.

He was reaching into his jacket, pulling out a thin spray bottle. It looked like a small bottle of innocent perfume, but I knew differently.

He handed it to me, skipping a greeting and moving on to the warning. "There isn't much. Only one dose. You cannot fail."

I stuffed the bottle into my own pocket without bothering to study it. "I never do," I said.

Kiyota's head bobbed once, allowing that, before he continued. "The Demon Lord assures me that your target will be susceptible. Romero reported as much when his Seer saw him at the club last week."

"I'm sorry I missed him. I was in the area."

The Demon Lord's personal Seer smiled, but it was completely chilling. It was a smile I knew well, for it was identical to mine. "Yes, that was a pity, wasn't it?"

I glanced out the windshield, my words firm. "I will be doing this differently than originally discussed."

"How differently?"

"I'm unwilling to approach O'Donnell so directly. This situation requires a bit more finesse."

"Are you sure that's wise?"

My non-answer was answer enough.

The Seer nodded slowly. "Very well. But you must not forget the stakes. There is more than the Demon Lord's fury at risk."

"I'm perfectly aware of the risks. That's the reason I'm here. I would not entrust this Seer to anyone else. Kate Bennett is mine."

He nodded, more confidently this time. When he spoke, his voice was very low. "You're sure she's the one?"

"I'm positive."

His lips compressed into a thin line. "If you're right, she's worth more than the Demon Lord first imagined."

Again, I didn't bother to comment. Instead I got right to the point. "I could use your talents, if you can spare a couple of days."

Kiyota's answer was immediate. "My orders were to see that you have everything you need."

I smiled darkly, fingering the bottle in my pocket. "Excellent."